Dedications

I dedicate this book to my sons, Ross Romero and Brendan Totten, whose continued support and love encouraged me to keep writing; to Jeffery Daniels, my creative writing teacher and mentor who encouraged me to turn a characterization and short story into a play or novel, and continues to give me the courage to keep writing; to author Del James, whose book The Language Of Fear was my go to book if I needed to get into a particular frame of mind when writing certain sections of For Jarmila. Your writing inspired me to be myself and write whatever came to mind, even if that took me to some very dark places. I hope someday to meet you outside Twitter land; and to the City of Chicago, especially the Humboldt Park neighborhood, who wrapped its arms around me and made me a part of the family. I'll always be West Side Represent.

March 09, 2019

      William "Jolly" Rogers didn't get his nickname because he was nice; quite the opposite. He was nicknamed Jolly because he had a reputation for scaring his crew. His raised voice was said to raise the hairs on the back of people's necks. 56, 5-11, medium build, long red hair, serious blue eyes. What he lacked in presence he made up for in a domineering, commanding personality. A tour manager for the past 15 years, and many years on the rock and roll tour circuit before that, he clawed his way to the place where he wanted to be.

      Now after all those years on the road, the years of stress, lack of sleep, grueling demanding schedules, incompetent crew and staff and super egotistical band members who were convinced they were rock stars, Jolly decided an early retirement was not only in order, but desperately needed. He said goodbye to his last tour three months previous and entered a life of mowing grass, remodeling his kitchen, and hitting the casino poker rooms.

      He was bored. Completely and irrevocably bored. A workaholic by nature, he used to pick up tours between tours to stay as busy as humanly possible. This drive led to three divorces. The road took its toll on relationships. Now at 56 he didn't see the need for a lasting relationship. A girl here and there on the road satisfied anything he needed physically. Emotionally, his motto was "Who gives a fuck?". He didn't need the baggage. He was going to fire up his bar b que, kick up his feet on the lawn chair, pop a bottle and soak in relaxation.

      And then the phone rang. His immediate thought was his sister or brother in Southern California, where he was born and raised. He moved to Chicago 10 years previous, to be more centrally located to music tours. His family wanted him to move back. He was very close to his brother and sister, adored his nieces and nephews. But after his parents died, he didn't want to go back to SoCal. He had been very close to his parents. They had encouraged his career path and did all they could to support him along the way. A lot of parents may have discouraged their kids from entering into the music business. His parents believed following your passion was what would make you successful. They were correct. He had one of the best reputations for tour manager in the business, and was sought after by many bands, managements and record labels. He was proud of all he had accomplished.

      He couldn't ignore the phone. Picking it up, on the other end he heard a familiar voice. His long-time friend Scot Lev. Scot was band manager out on tour with a difficult band that got lots of media attention because of their constant juvenile antics. Lenehan, named after an obscure character in a James Joyce novel, were four twenty-somethings that made life a living hell for anyone in a management position. 5 months into their last tour, promoting their second platinum album, they had already fired two tour managers. The firing of the first one, Dan, came about when Lenehan lead singer, Jack, threw a microphone at him from the stage and screamed "You're fired, Daaaaaaaaaan!". The microphone hit Dan in the center of his forehead. The YouTube views reached nearly a million; the incident became a popular social media meme. Seven stiches, an out of court settlement, and an apology from Jack, the incident was filed under "Stupid Things This Band Does".

The next tour manager fared little better. Jack had fired him only two weeks previous to Scot's phone call. Scot needed a tour manager. He had road manager Everett and himself doing the best they could, but this tour was a shit show even without the band antics. Financially they were doing well. Sold out shows, added dates. But a management company that did the minimum for the band and the tour meant he and Everett were way past their eyeballs in shit. They couldn't manage the band and corral the boys and put up with lack of proper equipment and constant mix-ups in the itinerary. They needed someone with real bravado to whip this tour into shape. Scot asked if Jolly could find some room in his Grinch sized heart to join the tour for the last four weeks.

"It's only four weeks, Jolly. What's four weeks to you? Piece of cake."

"When?" asked Jolly.

"Wednesday. Little Rock. Two-day run."

"*This* Wednesday?"

"I know it's short notice. But it means a lot to me."

Jolly had to think a minute. Back on tour. Only four weeks. With a band that was heinously uncontrollable, sold-out shows, but a host of technical problems. Did he want to take that on? Or did he want to wait until his lawn grew so he could mow it again. Early retirement wasn't all it claimed to be.

"I'll be there. I'll fly a red eye in for the 13th."

"Thank you. I don't know what else to say. You're a good friend, Jolly."

"Yes I am." he said, hanging up the phone.

Packing his bags, he took time to look over all Scot sent him by email and special courier. Other info he knew from media. The band's second album was #2 on the charts. They had singles from the second album at #2 and #3. They were a band that was going places, if they didn't destroy themselves before they got there. Promo photos showed the emaciated drummer, Benny Mann, about 5'7", black spiked hair, black eyes, heroin addict. Clearly someone would have to teach him to cover up the needle marks on his arms. Obviously that responsibility would fall to Jolly. Next was mercurial, perpetually late lead singer Jack Connelly, standing six feet on a slim frame. Long blonde hair. Green eyes the fans claimed looked like emeralds. Infamous volatile personality. Mt. Vesuvius. Ready to erupt. Standing next to him in the photo was punctilious guitarist Chandler Riley, also six feet tall with long blonde hair, but with blue eyes said to melt hearts. People mistook he and Jack for brothers. Although not DNA related, they claimed each other as brothers. This despite the notorious infighting between them that fueled band fandom fodder. Jack's lateness clashed with Chandler's precise timing and this led to doors being slammed and objects thrown. Last in the promo shot was bassist Johnny Dunne. Long brown hair, brown eyes, 5'11'. Had a reputation for being a quiet mama's boy. Didn't engage in after show parties. Spent down time practicing his bass guitar. The easy one, road crew called him.

Then there was a mysterious girl that was always with the band. She wasn't in the promo pictures. Scot had sent a letter with the promo pack explaining the situation. Her name was Jarmila Malone. She was short, skinny and pale with dull blonde hair. You couldn't miss her. She was always around. She had been friends with the band since childhood. Some traumatic childhood experience led the band into taking her under their wing, long before they were a band. She had been their first and most loyal fan. She never missed a rehearsal, gig or tour. They were very protective of her. She had all the privileges and access the band had. And she was annoying AF. Scot's advice was to avoid her as much as possible.

Great, thought Jolly, one of those band add-ons he'd have to deal with no matter how he'd try to avoid her.

Week One, Little Rock-Memphis-Nashville

Jolly took a red eye from Chicago to Little Rock for a two-day show. Sold out, both days. He liked and disliked that. He liked bands who were successful. It meant a big fat paycheck for him. But the added work and stress made a migraine inevitable. Especially with a tour with this many problems and a band that was out of control. But he admitted he thrived off of hard work. It gave him a great sense of purpose in life.

He arrived at the hotel early in the morning. Stopping by the vending machines to grab a juice, he noticed a laundry room off to the side. A skinny girl in a red tank top and a short black skirt, skin so pale almost translucent, sat atop a table next to a washing machine. She had on gold glitter spiked heels. Her legs were bare. She was reading a book while sucking on a Dum Dum lollipop.

"Hello," said Jolly, extending his hand, "I'm Jolly Rogers, the new tour manager. You must be Jarmila Malone."

She barely looked up, but he could see her eyes were the color of cornflowers.

"What are you reading?" asked Jolly

She held up the book and returned to reading.

"*The Language of Fear*. Del James. Excellent read." said Jolly

A barely perceptible head nod.

"Well, I'll see you later." said Jolly, turning to leave.

She took the Dum Dum out of her mouth and raised it in a goodbye salute.

The tour/band management office was large considering what was normal for tour offices. Usually, they were little bigger than a utility closet. This one had a long white table that went the length of it, with plenty room for chairs. Jolly sat at the very end away from the door. Scot sat beside him.

"Hard copy." said Scot, pointing to the portable printer.

"Hell yeah", responded Jolly, "Everything gets hard copied. Fuck digital. Emails get lost, entire itineraries go somewhere in the twilight zone. Once all the financials completely disappeared. Gotttta have a back-up."

Jolly set up his laptop and tablet, put his cell phone and blue tooth on the table. Scot handed him a two-way radio.

"Really?" inquired Jolly.

"Most definitely." answered Scot. "I know your loud ass voice carries, but 'Get your ass over here *now*' sounds much better on a two-way."

"I met that girl, Jarmila." said Jolly.

"She's annoying AF. What did she have to say?"

"Uncommunicative. Doing laundry. Absorbed in *The Language Of Fear* and a Dum Dum."

"Strange. She's usually on speaking speed dial. Girl never shuts up. Annoying AF. But she's got good tastes in books. Really into Joyce, Poe, George R.R. Martin, Del James, Charlaine Harris."

"I read she's been with the band a long time."

"Since they were kids. They met when she was 8 and they were 10. Her father and grandmother died when she was 12, within a short time of each other. She had no one to take care of her. Her dad's relatives rejected her because her mom was half Latina. And she was an out of wedlock baby. Her grandmother raised her. When her grandmother and father died, she didn't want to go into the system. The band took her in. Every night she'd sneak into one of their parents' houses to stay off the street. Weird thing was, when they got their own places, she continued the rotation. Still does, even on tour."

"The band doesn't mind sharing?"

"Apparently not. Except for Johnny, the bass player. Real mama's boy. Saving himself for marriage. She'll stay in Johnny's room, but no sex."

"I've seen some wacky shit on the road, but this is a first for me."

"It was for me also when I first became their manager" Scot said, "Where are your assistants?"

"Two of them had a flight delayed and the other one is flying in tomorrow. Where's yours?"

"Shera is at the box office straightening out a comp ticket issue and Camille is getting Benny a wrist brace."

"He hurt his wrist?"

"Unfortunately, he sprained it punching a wall."

Jolly shook his head. What did he get himself in to.

The hospitality room for the crew was surprising empty. Jolly was going to take his contractually agreed upon dinner hour. This was not the normal pace of things on tour, but Scot didn't have a lot of room to deny requests, he was desperate for a tour manager. Jolly had a freeway on this tour.

Usually, if the option was available, he took his dinner in the dressing room with the band. But now he wanted the silence of being unplugged. Two of his assistants, Keith and Kirk, had arrived and could handle any problems that might crop up in the next hour. An hour of complete and total nothingness. This helped him gear up for the craziness he was sure would follow. Then the air changed in the room. It became almost electrified. He looked up from his plate of food. Sitting down next to him was that band girl. Jarmila. She munched on a snack size bag of Flamin' Hot Cheetos, Cheetos dust all over her fingers. She wore a black Lenehan t-shirt with the logo of their first album on the front. A short purple lame skirt barely covered her thighs. She was wearing vintage black shoes, open toed with clunky heels. 1970's. Jolly loved a woman in vintage high heels. Made his head spin.

"Hiya." she said.

"Hello." he answered.

"What's that you're eating?" she asked, pointing to what he held in chopsticks.

"Kimchi."

"What's that?"

"Spicy fermented cabbage."

Jolly thought, the girl had never heard of kimchi.

"What does it taste like?"

"You want some?" he held some to her lips.

"Ugh, smells nasty!" she exclaimed, pushing it away, "Have you been to Japan?"

"Yes." he smiled. Kimchi was a Korean dish. But he supposed this wasn't a good time for a geography lesson.

"Is that where you learned to use chopsticks?"

"I learned to use chopsticks in Manhattan."

"Manhattan's in New York, right?"

"Yes." Jolly answered, feeling like he was talking to a child.

"We're going to New York. It's going to be the same day as Jack's birthday."

"I know."

"Are you from Chicago?"

He grinned at the way she pronounced Chicago. Shee-cah-go. This girl, born and bred Chicago.

"No. I'm from California. Southern California."

"Do you have brothers and sisters?" she asked, putting the empty Cheetos bag on the table.

"Yes. I have one brother and one sister."

"Do they live in Chicago?".

"No. They live in Southern California."

"Do you visit them a lot?"

Scot was right. She was one Energizer Battery. Going and going and going.

"Not as much as I'd like to."

"Do your parents still live there?"

"My parents are deceased."

"I'm sorry. Mine are too. Were you close to your parents?"

"Very. What about you, Miss Malone. Were you close to your parents?"

"I was raised by my grandmother."

"Paternal or maternal?"

"Paternal. But she passed on when I was 12 years old. Right after my dad passed on." she sighed.

"I'm sorry to hear that. And your mom? Were you close to her?"

"She was murdered when she was 15. I didn't know her. She dropped me off at my grandmother's house the day after I was born."

This poor girl, thought Jolly, had nobody but four buck wild boys to take care of her.

"After my grandmother and dad passed," Jarmila continued, "I had nowhere to go. I didn't know my mother's family, and my dad's family didn't want to have anything to do with me. They said I was bad luck because I was born out of the marriage bed. I packed some things and I asked Jack if I could stay the night so I wouldn't have to sleep on the streets. And he called the other guys and they figured they could take me in one night each. They were living at their parents' places then. During the day I rode the city buses and trains or stayed at the library. If it was nice out, I'd go to the city parks and people watch. Sometimes at certain parks I'd swim because it was free. And there were showers so I could shower and change clothes. Chandler's washer and dryer were in his parent's garage so I could wash my clothes there. He has three brothers and two sisters. His one sister is always buying vintage clothing and she only wears it once or twice. Then it goes in the box in the garage for Goodwill. Chandler says I can have anything I want out of there."

"Hence the glitter gold shoes I saw you were wearing when I first met you. Very late 70's. Disco."

"These are vintage too," she said, putting a leg up on Jolly's thigh, "70's disco for sure."

Jolly removed her leg from his thigh. This girl was flirting, whether she knew it or not.

"Can you teach me to use chopsticks?" she asked.

"Now?"

"Yeah. If you have time. I'm not supposed to bother you or interfere with your work."

"Says who?"

"Scot. He's the band manager."

"I know who he is and what he does. But I'm the tour manager. My tour, my rules."

"That means I can talk to you?"

"As long as you're not interfering with my work. And I'd let you know if you were. I have some time left," he said as he stood, "what do you like to eat? Don't say Flamin' Hot Cheetos. You're so thin, you should eat something healthy. Processed foods are not good for you."

"I like hot corn chips too. Especially the Vitners brand."

"I'm going to pretend you didn't say that. What about…steak. Or are you a vegan?"

"I'm not a vegan. Or a vegetarian. I like steak but only off the grill."

"I do too. One of my favorites. I grill at home all the time. How about chicken? Vegetables?'

"I like steamed broccoli."

"Steamed broccoli it is!" he said as he put some broccoli on a plate and grabbed a pair of chopsticks.

Putting the plate before her, he unwrapped the chopsticks from the paper band. Leaning behind her he put the chopsticks in her hand. He held her hand but realized it would be better to sit next to her and give her a visual demonstration. He sat down and picked up his own chopsticks.

"Watch." he said as he picked up a piece of chicken.

She fumbled with her own pair of chopsticks. Jolly put his down and put his hand on her hand, picked up a piece of broccoli, and slowly guided the chopsticks to her mouth. The click of a pop can made him look up. Jack was standing in front of the table, cold stare, Cherry Coke can in his hand.

"Do you need something?" Jolly asked.

"There's no Cherry Coke in da dressing room." answered Jack, no inflection in his voice.

"I'll have some sent right up." said Jolly, getting out his cell phone from his pocket and texting.

Jack moved toward Jarmila, cold stare never wavering.

"C'mon, you're going back to da dressing room." he said as he grabbed her forearm tightly.

"But I'm not done eating," she said in a quiet voice, deflated, "Jolly is teaching me to use chopsticks."

"*You're going back to da dressing room now.*" said Jack, sternly, "*You can fuckin' eat there.*"

Jack pushed her in front of him and left the room. Jolly had always tried to keep band personal business from professional business. He set boundaries that he made an effort not to cross. Inevitably there was always something personal that would cross the line. It couldn't be helped with a tour full of real, live people. But this incident made him wonder if he himself had crossed a line with Jarmila.

The first night of the Little Rock shows was uneventful. As uneventful as a production like that can be. Chandler was still having trouble with a monitor, and Benny had a problem with a snare. But these things can be worked out. Better equipment would be a good start. The band had the budget. Jolly talked to Scot and it was decided next tour there'd be brand new equipment. Jolly might even catch a show or two on the next tour. Jack had a voice he hadn't heard in quite a while. And he could work a crowd until they were mesmerized No wonder shows were being sold out at a rate that dates had to be added. Jolly predicted it wouldn't be long before their ballad "The Only Cost" would be number #1 on the charts. Ballads as first-time hits made him nervous. But right behind was a powerhouse of a rocker, "Scandalous", an infectious tune that put Lenehan crowds into a wild frenzy.

Sitting in the empty dressing room, band securely sent to the hotel in a limo surrounded by a variety of hangers-on, groupies, and fanatics, he was sure they'd be entertained until the early morning hours. He didn't care what they did after the show, as long as they made soundcheck at 5:00pm the next afternoon. He despised lateness. Late soundchecks led to late start times, and he detested late start times. Late should be stricken from the vocabulary. When the dressing room door opened, he expected a cleaning crew. Instead, it was Jarmila. Miss Malone. He noticed she had changed into a gray dress. He was surprised she hadn't gone with the band.

"Hello Miss Malone. You didn't go with the band?" he asked.

"Too many people. I don't like all that crowd and noise." she answered.

"Oh, you're a quiet one." he continued, "aren't you bunking with one of the band tonight?"

"I'm with Jack tonight."

She didn't seem to thrilled at that plan.

"Can I hang with you for a little while?" she asked.

"Of course. But I can't say I'm very entertaining. Milwaukee has no caterer."

"How'd that happen?"

"Previously poor management. Unless I get a caterer for Milwaukee, it will be Filet O' Fish all around."

"I like Filet O' Fish."

"It's bad for you, Jar. You need to eat better. No more Flamin' Hot Cheetos and Dum Dums. You need to tell me what you like so I can put it in the rider."

"Scot says I can't have anything put in the rider for myself because I'm not in the band and I don't work for them."

"Fuck Scot. My tour, my rules. You want something, let me know. If you say Flamin' Hot Cheetos, hot corn chips or Dum Dums, you and I will have a conversation."

She kissed him on the cheek.

"That was unexpected." he said.

"You're very nice. Everyone says you're mean, but you're very nice."

"Keep saying that and I'll hire you as my publicist." he teased.

"Well, I got to go. Les the security dude is headed back to the hotel, and if I'm not back soon Jack won't be happy. Goodbye my nice friend."

"Goodbye Miss Malone. See you tomorrow."

And with that he watched her skip like a child out the door.

Jack paced his hotel room. Jarmila should have been back an hour ago. When she refused to get in the overcrowded limo, she promised she'd get a lift with Les. Her and Les should have been right behind him.

When the hotel room door opened, he flew across the room and smacked her hard in the face, hitting her in her right eye and knocking her to the ground. This had never happened before, and she cried out in pain and shock. She lay on the floor on her stomach, asking Jack why he did that.

"You're fuckin' *late*!" he screamed, "Where da fuck were you? Fuckin' Jolly, right? Suckin' his cock, right? I called Les and he said you were still in da dressing room with Jolly. Were you alone with him? Were you suckin' his cock? I know you want to! You don't even know him!"

"I was just talking to him." she said on her place on the floor, too afraid to stand, "He was telling me about how there's no caterer lined up for Milwaukee. And how if I want something it can be put in the rider, no matter what Scot said. He was being very nice to me."

"I bet he was!"

Jack took off his belt and put his right foot on the small of her back. He pulled up her gray dress. He started striking the belt repeatedly on her bottom, over and over, drawing blood as the belt lashed against her bare skin. She whimpered, but he told her if she made a sound, he'd make it hurt worse. He'd spanked her before. The band had rules for her to keep her safe after she turned 18 and had adult freedoms. They wanted to make sure no one took advantage of her, and she was so naïve they had to keep her on the right track. Breaking the rules had consequences, but Jack always reminded her that he did it out of love and care. She wasn't like other women her age. She had been sheltered by them to protect her so she wouldn't become another statistic. Jack was the only one who meted out the discipline. But never this harshly.

She tried to move away from the stinging blows but his foot was firmly planted on the small of her back. She buried her head in her arms and silently cried. It seemed to go on forever. Then Jack pulled her up by her hair and threw her on the bed, face down. He took off his pants and got on top of her. Holding her wrists tightly, he viciously sodomized her, whispering in her ear that he was only doing this because he cared for her, and didn't want her to be harmed by any stranger. They didn't know Jolly. He was new. She shouldn't get friendly with him. Tears fell down her face. Jack had also done this to her before, but never like this, where he hurt her until it was unbearable. Jack never took her vaginally. He said he wanted to minimize the chances of pregnancy. She was too uneducated to understand.

Pulling her off the bed, he then handed her the over the shoulder purse she was carrying when she walked in the door. He demanded she return the spare key card and told her to get the fuck out of the room. She couldn't go to the other guys' rooms. She was too beat up and had a black eye. Getting a spanking from Jack for rule breaking was one thing; being beat up was another. She didn't want to cause any trouble within the band. She decided to go to the bus and lay down. But she knew it was locked and needed someone to open it.

Jolly sat at the hotel room table with his assistant Keith beside him, a laptop each in front of them. Jolly was screen sharing on the hotel room tv.

"Item 11?" asked Keith.

"Hmmm, let's run it by Scot. Sounds more like an internal band issue. I'm a tour manager, not Judge Judy."

A soft knock on the door. Jolly went to answer it. But when he opened the door, there was no one there. He stepped out into the hallway. Jarmila, her back to him, was limping away.

"Jarmila?" he inquired.

She turned around. One side of her hair was covering one side of her face.

"Do you need something?" he asked.

"No." she answered.

"I heard a knock on my door and…"

"I wanted access to the bus because I wanted to lay down."

Jolly moved closer to her. She flinched as he moved her hair away from her face. Her right eye was starting to bruise and swell shut.

"Sure, I can get you on the bus. But first why don't you come to my room and I'll put ice on that eye, so it doesn't swell shut."

He put his right arm around her shoulder and steadied her with his left hand. Slowly they inched towards his room. She winced with every step.

"Do you want to sit down?" he asked, once in the room.

She shook her head no. Jolly dismissed Keith who gathered up his laptop and said he'd see him later on.

"Do you want to lay down? You can lay down on this bed, I'll move all my equipment." he said as he took away a laptop bag, his briefcase and a suitcase from the spare bed.

Jarmila laid down slowly, on her stomach. Jolly noticed blood on the back of her dress.

"Um…" stammered Jolly, "there's blood on your dress. Would you like one of my t-shirts to wear instead? I can send the dress out to be laundered."

She nodded her head yes. Jolly went to one of his suitcases and took out the softest t-shirt he had.

"Here," he said, handing it to her, "let me get ice for your eye."

He went to the bathroom and retrieved a clean washcloth. Then went to the ice bucket and wrapped ice in the towel. Gently he handed it to her. He noticed she hadn't changed into the t-shirt.

"Do you need some help with that?" he indicated to the shirt.

She nodded yes. Gently he helped her lift her dress. She had a red lace bra on underneath and nothing else. He gently took off her shoes. When he went to help her put on the t-shirt, he noticed her entire bottom was covered in bruises and lash marks. Some of her skin had been torn. He quickly pulled the shirt down. She was shivering, so he pulled up the cover on her and went to the clothing rack to fetch another blanket. Gently he placed it on her.

"Warmer now?" he asked.

She nodded her head yes. Jolly didn't like the feeling of indecision. He could always solve issues and problems. He was proud of his confidence in making things right. But this was above his paygrade.

"Jar, listen." he said gently, grabbing a chair and putting it near the bed, "I'm going to ask you some questions. You don't have to answer them. If it makes you uncomfortable, tell me and I'll stop."

She nodded her head yes.

"Did a stranger do this to you?" he asked.

She shook her head no.

"Did someone on the crew do this to you?"

She shook her head no.

"That's good. Because if it was one of the crew, I'd have to fuck somebody up and fire them. Did someone in the band do this?"

It was the question he didn't want to ask. Jarmila shook her head yes.

Shit, thought Jolly.

"Okay…okay…" he paused, "was it Johnny?"

She shook her head no. Of course, it wasn't Johnny, Jolly thought. Johnny considered her his little sister.

"Was it Benny?" he continued.

She shook her head no.

"Was it Jack?"

A tear rolled down her cheek as she shivered underneath the blankets. Great, thought Jolly sarcastically. I've got a psycho sadist on my hands.

"Has this happened before?" he asked.

"Not this." Jarmila barely croaked out a whisper.

"Not this…bad?"

She shook her head no.

"It's never been this bad. Did you want it? Was it some adult game you were playing that went too far?"

Another tear rolled down her cheek as she shrugged her shoulders. Jolly didn't know what to make of that. Either she wanted it or was being forced. Either way, he had to protect the band. Ethically and morally, it hit him hard. But if this went public, it could be the end of this band's career.

"Do you want to still go to the bus?" he asked, "You can stay here as long as you like. And Jar, I want you to know that whatever you tell me stays with me unless you want me to tell someone or do something. I'm very loyal and you can trust me, okay?"

She nodded her head yes. Jolly took his tablet to the other bed and arranged the pillows so he could sit up and work. At 7:00am he suddenly woke, and looking over to the other bed, he saw Jarmila had left.

Scot loved a good swim in the morning. It energized him for a hectic, busy day. Although second days of two gig runs weren't quite as hectic as the first. But he could never guess what kind of mood the band members were going to be in. Sometimes it was like dealing with a herd of angry buffaloes. And sometimes, it was a nice solitude. Most of the time, it was somewhere in between.

Sitting opposite Jolly in a diner across the street from the hotel, a good hearty breakfast in front of him, he knew there was something heavy on Jolly's mind. Jolly was a hotel buffet breakfast man. He didn't like to waste time ordering and waiting for food. He was a man all about accurate timing, and not wasting any precious minutes that could be utilized in some useful way. His invitation to Scot for a diner breakfast had to be about serious content.

"Your boy Jack is a psycho." Jolly said, cutting into a stack of pancakes, "I know you understand what I'm saying."

"I suspected Jack's a rough one. I've seen the bruises on Jarmila's wrists after she has spent the night with him. This morning I passed her in the hallway and noticed she had a black eye. But hey, consenting adults, they do what they want."

"Until it's no longer consensual."

Scot put his coffee cup down.

"Are you saying she's not consenting?" Scot asked.

"I don't think she understands what consent means. I think she's possibly…how can I say this…slow."

"She quit going to school when she was 12, after her grandmother and father passed away. I don't think she attended much school when they were alive. She was one of those children who gets lost in the system. She's not quite as bright as someone her age should be. She's more like 13 than 22. Arrested development. I think that's why the band is so protective of her."

"So protective she gets beaten to hell. You should have seen her ass. Covered in bruises and marks. Like belt marks. Broke her skin in places."

"When did she show you this?"

"Last night. Jack kicked her out after he brutalized her. She wanted to go to the bus and lay down, so she came to me."

"Makes sense. She had no place else to go. Chandler and Benny had guests, and I know she wouldn't want Johnny to see her injured in anyway. It would cause problems with Jack and Johnny. Johnny loves her like a sister. He'd kick ass if someone hurt her. She's always tried to keep peace within the band, not cause any trouble. The band is everything to her."

"She told me this has happened before. But not this bad. How often does this happen?" asked Jolly.

"Brutalized like you described, I can't think of any time in the two years I've been with them that it's happened like that. They have some rules she has to obey, they say, to keep her safe. She's naïve and there's a lot of craziness on the road, crazy people who would do anything to get to the band. She breaks a rule, she gets a spanking from Jack. He's the disciplinarian."

"What the fuck have you gotten me into?"

"Oh, it's not so bad. Band has their private business. Jarmila, she's like a kid. They don't want her wondering off somewhere and ending up in a ditch dead. She has no ability to keep right. She doesn't know how to really take care of herself. She had very little parental guidance growing up. They're just trying to keep her safe in the only way that works."

"If this went public, it could be the end of the band. I'd go back to retirement and watch the paint dry in my front room. But a whole lot of people would be without jobs. People who rely on this tour to feed their families and keep a roof over their heads. For some, they could pick up another tour easily. But for most of them, they could be out of a job for months All because of your psycho lead singer."

"I'll talk to him," Scot sighed, "I'll tell him to keep her in his room if he's going to get rough with her."

"Maybe you could tell him not to get rough with her."

"Consenting adults."

Jolly put money over the check and stood up.

"Until it's not consensual."

Jolly stood next to the couch Chandler was seated on in the dressing room.

"I'm telling you", he said to Chandler, "you can't continue with that monitor. We're getting you a new one."

"But I've had that one for years! It's my lucky monitor! You can't just toss it out like trash!" exclaimed Chandler.

"You can take it home and make a shrine out of it for all I fuckin' care." responded Jolly, "But it's being replaced, going bye bye, it's going to where all deceased nevermore monitors go. You're not a fuckin' garage band anymore, Chandler. You're a platinum artist. Act like one. In-ear monitors, Chandler. Next tour, in-ear monitors. Modern technology, a wonderful thing."

"I have *two* platinum albums." emphasized Chandler.

"And soon, Gods of Thunder be willing, you'll have *two* multi-platinum albums." said Jolly.

"Two?" asked Benny.

"Yes." responded Jolly, "Don't you ever look at the charts and read the industry papers?"

"No." he said.

But, thought Jolly, I bet Benny knew where the best heroin dealers were.

Jolly was looking toward the top of the stage. He felt a nudge on his arm, but he didn't look down.

"What do you think?" asked Jarmila, pushing a catalogue into Jolly's arm.

"I think if that falls on me, I'm going to die." said Jolly, not looking down.

"No, what do you think of this?" said Jarmila as she shoved the catalogue into Jolly's arm again.

Jolly looked down at the catalogue as Jarmila pointed to a picture.

"I think it's a very nice microphone." he responded.

"But do you think if a person received it as a gift, they'd like it?"

Everett, the road manager, walked up and looked at the top of the stage.

"I think whoever received that as a gift would be very happy." said Jolly, looking back up.

"We could rebuild it," said Everett, "half way up".

"But how much is that going to delay us?" asked Jolly

"I want to get Jack this for his birthday. I want to give him a special gift." said Jarmila.

God bless her great big heart, thought Jolly. Jack practically breaks her in half and she wants to get him a birthday present. If he'd been Jarmila, he'd order the microphone just to beat Jack with it.

"We could just reinforce it and deal with it permanently when we tear down." said Everett.

"Would it take less time?" asked Jolly

"Considerably." answered Everett.

"Then do that."

Jarmila fell in step with Jolly.

"So do you think it's a really nice microphone?" she asked Jolly.

"I think it's a very nice microphone. And I think you have a good heart."

Back in the dressing room Jolly was going over the itinerary. Or at least he was making an attempt to an uninterested band. They went where they were taken. Where they went was the same old same old to them, just a different name for a different city. Jack was the only one interested in band issues. He tended to be the band businessman.

"If Memphis is so close, why do we have to leave tonight after the show?" asked Benny.

"If you paid attention to what I'm saying, or if you read your itinerary, you'd know you have a radio interview at 7:00am and another one at 10:00am. And two meet and greets with radio winners. Then you have the rest of the day to do whatever it is you do on a day off. Please stay out of jail. Just make sure you're at the venue in time for soundcheck at 5:00pm the next day." answered Jolly.

"I hate meet and greets." said Jack.

"But I bet you like the money you get when fans purchase your albums and concert tickets." responded Jolly.

"Whatever." sneered Jack.

In the tour office, everyone on staff was there except Scot. Jolly sat on the side of the table. Keith was at the head of the table, next to Jolly. Scot's assistants Shera and Camille sat next to each other, and Jolly's other two assistants, Kirk and Chandra, sat across from them.

"Fuck, marry, kill, who's on your list today Jolly?" laughed Scot as he entered the room.

"Kill. I'll start with the company you ordered those panels for Jack."

"I ordered them three weeks ago. They're still not here?" asked Scot.

"Oh, they're here. And they're aqua, not blue. They're in the hallway, go look." said Jolly.

Scot went into the hallway and returned quickly.

"Jack is going to lose his shit." he said, "We should rename this tour the "Jack Is Going To Lose His Shit" tour."

"No way you can convince him aqua is just as good as blue?" asked Jolly.

"This is Jack. Jack always gets what he wants, and Jack wants blue." said Scot.

"Keith, get this company on the phone and have them send the correct color panels. Blue, not aqua. And send them out *today*." Jolly said.

Keith dialed the company and was placed on hold for a representative. Chandler appeared in the doorway with a tall, thin, beautiful brunette.

"This is my friend Helga. I was wondering if I could get her a ticket and a pass for tonight." he said.

"I've already sent passes and comps to the box office," said Scot, "but I can send Shera up to get them."

"I've got some," said Jolly, "Kirk, take a pass and a comp out of my briefcase."

Kirk opened Jolly's briefcase and took out a large tan manila envelope.

"All access?" asked Kirk.

"V.I.P." answered Jolly.

Kirk handed Helga the backstage pass and comp ticket. After Helga and Chandler said thank you, they left hand in hand.

"Does Chandler realize Helga probably has a penis?" asked Jolly.

"I'm sure he does." answered Scot, "Chandler has no preference. He's up for anything. Women, men, women who used to be men, men who used to be women, or anything in between or a combination thereof. Chandler fucks everything."

"Isn't he the married one?" asked Jolly.

"Yes" answered Scot, "To a woman assigned female at birth, in case you were wondering."

"No judgements here," said Jolly, "to each his own."

Keith was now arguing with the representative of the panel company.

"Hand me that phone." said Jolly.

Keith handed Jolly the cell phone, putting it on speaker.

"With whom am I speaking?" asked Jolly, "Great, Tammy. Now listen closely, Tammy. Three weeks ago, we ordered panels in the color blue. But today the panels arrived in the color aqua. Aqua is not blue, Tammy. Aqua is blue and green. It is *not blue*. Blue is blue." He listened while Tammy went on and on about how aqua is the same as blue. "No, Tammy," continued Jolly, "aqua is not the same as blue. Aqua is a variation of blue and green. That is not what we ordered. We ordered blue. And you're going to send us blue. So, Tammy, with your minimum wage job and your three-dollar headset and your one-hundred-dollar refurbished computer from Craig's List, fuckin' click on the picture of the *blue* panels and click on our account and send them to us *today*! Have a nice day, *Tammy*."

The silence in the room was thick. Keith started laughing and everyone but Jolly joined in.

"Now that's the Jolly I know!" laughed Scot.

Little Rock's second night was better than the first. The crowd went into a frenzy at every song. "The Only Cost" got the whole house singing along to the chorus. Jack would put the mic in the direction of the audience, and bring it right back to sing along with them on the last words. He was the commander of all his performances. Combined with his voice, and a stunning line-up of talented musicians, there was no way but up for these guys. If Benny didn't die from an overdose, or Jack be committed to a state mental facility.

After the show, Jolly could hear Jack ranting all the way from the venue to the tour bus. On his left he passed by Benny, who had one arm around a black-haired girl and the other hand around a bottle of Don Julio tequila.

"Who's your friend, Benny?" asked Jolly.

"This is Alice." slurred Benny.

"Pleased to meet you, Alice." responded Jolly.

To Jolly's right side, Chandler, one arm around Helga and one around a man, said "Aren't you going to ask who my friends are?"

"Pick one, Chandler." said Jolly.

"Gotta love 'em all!" quipped Chandler.

At the bus, Jack was screaming. Shirtless. Too dangerous for a singer's voice to be screaming, and too dangerous to be shirtless when still sweaty from the show.

"What da fuck! I'm told to go directly to da bus from da dressing room after da show and da bus is fuckin' locked! How da fuck can I get in a locked bus? Where da fuck is Scottie?"

Jolly opened the bus. Jack entered first and continued screaming. Benny and Alice followed, then Chandler and his two companions, and then Johnny who had been standing quietly by the bus, next to Jarmila. She stood by the door as Jolly leaned in.

"You're not the only one with a digestive system, Jack." said Jolly.

Jack came flying halfway down the bus stairs.

"I don't pay him to take a shit!" he screamed, "I pay him to manage my band!" And then he went back into the bus, still complaining.

"I wouldn't take it personally." said Jarmila, "Jack doesn't like touring. He likes the studio better, where he has more control."

"I never take anything personally." said Jolly, motioning for Jarmila to get on the bus.

"Time to say goodbye to all your friends." said Scot as he entered the bus, "We're leaving for Memphis."

Jack was already in a bunk, headphones on, reading a music magazine. Jarmila put her hand through the curtain. Jack pulled the curtain aside.

"Can I talk to you?" she asked.

Jack sat up and took off his headphones.

"I mean, in private." she whispered.

The only place for privacy in a tour bus was in the back. Jack put his magazine in the bunk and stood up, taking Jarmila's hand as they went to the back. The back of the bus was a nice lounge area. It was great for peace and quiet, listening to music, having sex, or sleeping. It was a multi-purpose area. Jack sat down and looked at Jarmila, who sat next to him, on the edge of the seat.

"I have to tell you something, and I think you're going to get mad at me." she said.

Jack stared silently.

"After you beat me and threw me out, I needed to lay down. But Benny and Chandler had company and I didn't want Johnny to see me like this. It would start a fight with you. I went to Jolly's so he could let me on the bus. But he convinced me to go to his room to get ice for my eye. I was really sore and I knew I couldn't walk to the bus. He offered to let me stay on the second bed. He saw blood on my dress so he helped me into one of his t-shirts instead. That's when he saw all the belt marks and blood. He started to list people to see who did it because I wouldn't tell him. I nodded no, until he got to your name and I didn't nod I just started crying. That's when he knew it was you. I never told him."

"This is serious shit you did Jarmila. Serious shit. Telling someone you don't know da band secrets. I thought you love and care for me and da guys."

"I do!"

He grabbed her hand and started twisting it.

"But then you do some serious, dumb shit that could end our careers. Fucked up part is, we're really taking off. We're at da top of da charts, ready to go double platinum on both albums. Getting ready to play bigger venues da next tour. If there is a next tour, cause you did some serious shit that could shut it all down." Jack said, as he let go of her hand.

"I'm sorry. I'll make it up to you." she said, tears running down her face.

"You *will* make it up to me. But this is serious."

"I'll talk to Jolly and tell him how important it is to keep it quiet."

"No. You won't talk to him about this again. Let it be. But this is really, really serious. I'm going to have to punish you for this. This is seriously breaking an important rule."

"But Jack, please don't! I haven't healed yet. Please!"

"I'm not going to punish you now. I'll wait until you heal up. And I promise you I won't ever take a belt to you again. I did that out of anger and I'm sorry. I overreacted that you were flirting with Jolly."

"I wasn't flirting!"

"You were letting him feed you."

"I asked him to teach me to use chopsticks, that's all."

"Regardless, it was wrong. You don't know him and it could have led to dangerous things. I'm only trying to protect you. I punish you to keep you safe. It's purely out of my love and care for you. Haven't I always kept you safe and taken care of you?"

"Yes."

"Don't you know I have your best interest and safety at heart? Even though sometimes I have to punish you, I am doing it out of love for your well-being. It doesn't make me feel good at all. It breaks my heart to hurt you. But then I know when it's done, you'll understand what's right from wrong and safe from unsafe." he rubbed his finger along her forearm, "Next time I'm using a paddle on you. Da seriousness of this calls for more than just a regular spanking. It's going to hurt you, a lot, but I'm not sorry for that. You could have put da band in serious jeopardy, and you really need to learn a lesson about how serious this is. You know why you get punished, right?"

"Because I don't know about the dangerous shit in life."

"You're 22 but your decision making is still like a kid's. You never had anyone to guide you until you started staying with us. Since you were a minor, we really couldn't do anything physically with you. Da threat of social services was enough. We had to wait until you were 18. And you went crazy, remember? Gone for days, high as hell, drunk off your ass. That's why we stepped in and made rules for you to follow. So we wouldn't have to bury our friend. We all love you, Jarmila. You're a special kind of girl."

"But I'm scared." she said as tears flowed.

"I'm da one who should be scared and crying. I could be losing my career. Then what, I play in some lounge band for da rest of my fuckin' life?"

"I'm scared because you've never used a paddle on me. Except for the belt that one time, you've always used your hand. You don't have to do it anymore. I understand when I do something wrong and I'll say I'm sorry I promise."

"We tried that, Jarmila. It did not work. Remember? You promised you wouldn't drink or get high anymore and I found you in a club drinking and snorting coke. You know how it is in your family. Addiction runs deep. Your father died from alcoholism. I'd rather you be mad at me for whipping your ass black and blue then see you in a coffin."

"Okay, I understand." she said as she looked down.

"You still have to make this up to me." Jack said as he stood up, locked the door, and pulled his pants down. Sitting down again, he met her gaze. "You're going to give me head, da whole way to Memphis."

"But that's two hours from now!" she protested.

"Maybe I'll have time to fuck you up da ass, too. You like that, don't you?"

She nodded her head yes, but wanted to shake it no.

Memphis, Tennessee was a town with a lot of history and a lot of Lenehan fans. First there was a 7:00am radio show, where the band ruled the air. Promoting the show was one thing; getting fans excited, especially future fans, was always the band's motive. They played a couple songs and the radio phones lit up. Social media was flaming. They were trending on Twitter. They loved their fans, and their fans loved them. 10:00am, another radio station, another interview, a couple more songs. For a band whose members disliked morning events, and grumbled to Scot on their way to any, once arriving they put everything into anything they did for the band. An 11:30am meet and greet had the band smiling and taking pictures. Jack especially had an aura where he could make any fan feel like they were his favorite. On to another meet and greet at 1:30 pm, and the band had the rest of the day off. The show wouldn't be until the next day.

Benny wanted to tour graveyards. It was decided head of security, Les, would go with him. Johnny was interested in touring old mansions. Band security Arnold was put on that detail. The band could not go without security. They were too famous in Memphis to go off alone. Chandler and Jack went to visit a medical museum. Both were avid fans of anything unusual. Band security Floyd got that detail, although he was no fan of dissected body parts and deformed babies in glass jars. But a job was a job, and for the most part, he liked his.

Jarmila sat in the lobby eating Flamin' Hot Cheetos with a Diet Coke. Jolly almost walked past her without noticing her. He turned and sat next to her.

"I'm surprised you're not enjoying a day to explore Memphis." he said.

"The only thing I'm interested in is graveyards. But I don't want to go with Benny. He's got bad juju. Death is always following him around."

"Because of his heroin use?"

"Yeah, and he drinks a lot, and does a lot of hallucinogens, and pills. You can feel death following him."

"Did you try to talk to him about your concerns? Or has the band?"

"He won't listen to me. Says it's his own business. And the band don't do interventions. You live, you die, that's life. They can't legitimately say shit anyway, because they all drink and do drugs too. It would be hypocritical to call Benny out on his drug use."

"But they're not as bad off as Benny."

"No. Jack snorts coke, and he always has his bottle of Don Julio tequila. Chandler likes Mollies. Benny does too. And heroin. And Xanax. And they all smoke weed and drink."

"And Johnny?"

"He might have a drink to celebrate a birthday or something with the band, like going platinum. Mostly he stays away from that shit. He stays away from a lot of tour shit. He avoids the girls after him by making me pretend I'm his girlfriend. Sometimes guys go after him too, but he still pretends I'm his girlfriend."

"Guys are Chandler's thing."

"And girls, and transgendered, and anything in between or a combination of. If It's human and is of legal age and has holes, Chandler will either fuck or get fucked. He loves sex. He'd have it 24/7 if he could."

"Does his wife know?"

"Oh yeah, as long as he keeps it on the road. She packs his suitcase with condoms. One time she caught me in bed with him and she took me to get Plan B. Made me promise not to disrespect her by having sex with her husband in their marriage bed. When we're back home in Chicago, we do it in the garage."

"I'm not supposed to be asking you things about the band. But it sure helps in the short time I have to get to know them. Which helps me do a more efficient job."

"Why can't you ask me about the band?"

"Because it's band business. If I have questions, protocol is to ask Scot or the band. I'm stepping over boundaries here. But you're easy to talk to. And very honest. I love honesty. Not a lot of it in show business." said Jolly.

"I don't lie." she said, "I like you. You're very nice. Everyone said you're mean, but I think you yell because it's part of your job. I don't think you yell out of meanness. You're just doing your job."

"I still want to hire you as my publicist. You can tell everyone I'm not mean. I'm just doing my job." he laughed, "Have you eaten today?"

She held up the chips and pop.

"Miss Malone," said Jolly sternly, "that is not a meal. You and I are going to have a serious conversation about healthy food groups. I'm going to get lunch and then go check out the venue. Want to join me?"

She clapped her hands like a little girl being told she was getting a new present.

"Yes! I won't be in the way, will I?"

"No. If you were, I'd tell you. Now what would you like for lunch? Memphis has some excellent bar-b-que. Would you like to try some?"

"Yes!"

"Then off we go in search of excellent bar-b-que. Let's ask the front desk. They usually have good suggestions."

After getting a few suggestions from the front desk, Jolly and Jarmila headed down a block to a restaurant known for its famous pulled pork.

"Do you like pulled pork sandwiches?" he asked her.

"I've never had one."

"Please don't tell me you solely exist on chips and pop."

"No. I like steamed broccoli, and lobster, and steak. I really like steak but only if it's grilled."

"I remember you telling me that. That's how I like it too. Slow grilled, maximum bar-b-que sauce."

"Yes! Sweet Baby Rays!"

Their food arrived, pulled pork sandwiches, greens, mac and cheese, coleslaw. Heaven on a plate.

"What's that?" asked Jarmila, pointing to the greens.

"Collard greens. You've never seen collard greens?"

"No."

"Try them, you'll like them."

"Yuk!" she said spitting the mouthful of greens back on the plate.

"Okay, but I promise everything else on the plate you'll like."

"I don't really eat much. I'm picky."

"Jarmila."

"Yes?"

"It's a very pretty name."

"I was named after my great-grandma, Jarmila Bisnik. She emigrated to Chicago with her parents from Bohemia when she was 8 years old, back in the early 1900's. It was her eighth birthday the day she saw the Statue of Liberty. I have the same birth date she had. She never liked it here. They settled in Polish Triangle. Do you know where that's at?"

"By the Jewel food store on Paulina?"

"Yeah, near there, on Ashland. I don't think the Jewel was there back then. She didn't like it there because kids made fun of her accent. Her parents wanted her to assimilate to fully American, so they only spoke English to her. She wanted to move to the Pilsen neighborhood. Lots of people from Bohemia settled there. She had relatives there. She married her dad's first cousin. He was like in his 40's and she was 14. But he lived in Pilsen, so she got what she wanted. They went on to have a bunch of kids."

"You don't keep in touch with any of your relatives?"

"No, they don't want to have anything to do with me. They called my momma a Humboldt Park whore."

"I don't think I'd have anything to do with them either. But you got the band as family. Sometimes family is more than the blood that runs through your veins. Jarmila sounds like an old Eastern European name. But Malone sounds Irish."

"My grandmother married a guy named Padraig Malone, an immigrant straight out of Dublin, Ireland. She got in the family way, that's what they called pregnancy then. She had to marry him. That's the way they did it back then. It was a scandal if you had baby out of marriage. I heard he was a mean drunk. I never met him, he died before I was born."

"Well Miss Malone, time to head to the venue,"

"But isn't this your day off?"

"I don't have a day off. But you're more than invited to tag-a-long to this next great adventure. Who knows what wonderful shit is in store for us tomorrow."

"But can we ride in a private car and not a van? Vans are so tacky."

"You're hanging out with too many rock stars, Jar." laughed Jolly, "Yes we're taking a private car."

The venue was empty save for the venue staff and some vendors. The stage was empty. No equipment cases lined the walls behind the stage.

"Where is everybody? Did the show get canceled?" asked Jarmila.

"The show isn't until tomorrow. I gave the crew the day off. They'll load in tomorrow morning. Don't you have an itinerary? Doesn't anybody on this tour have an *itinerary*?" asked Jolly

"I don't have one. I just go wherever the band goes."

'I'm going to give you an itinerary. And you're going to fuckin' read it."

"Now you're being mean."

"Thanks for reminding me. I almost forgot my reputation for meanness."

"Now what are we going to do?"

"Are you getting bored, Jar? Because I can send your ass back to the hotel."

"Somebody needs a nap."

"You know if you weren't so traumatized by what Jack did to you, I'd turn you over my own knee. Keep being a brat, Jar. Watch what happens."

"I'm sorry. I was just curious as to what you are going to do next."

"I'm going to check in with house production, then check out the dressing room and managers' office, then hope to God the opening band is not somebody's nephew's band who's taking guitar lessons from some old lady from Dubuque with three fingers missing. I dislike this pick a local opening band deal on this tour. Next tour they'll have a permanent opening band."

"Being a tour manager isn't any fun, is it?"

"It's a lot of work, and I like to work. Even if I'm complaining about it. Walk with me, Jar. I could use the company."

They went to the production office where Jolly had a brief conversation about the next day's show. Then he went to check out the dressing room, which met his approval. Most of the items on the rider were being loaded in. He liked the band to have everything there when they showed up, not have it being loaded in while they were already in the room. Next, he called the catering company while checking out the managers' office. On some tours, managers associated with the band were separated in different offices. He didn't like that. He felt it was more efficient and time-saving to have all the managers and assistants in the same room. Some rooms were crowded shoulder to shoulder. This office was quite a decent size. He didn't know how the previous part of the tour had been, but he sure got lucky with the offices he'd gotten so far.

"Sit with me Jar," said Jolly, "I need to do a little work and then I'd like to talk to you, if you don't mind."

"Sure."

He spent about fifteen minutes making sure hotel rooms were secure and travel plans for Nashville were in place. Nashville was the day after Memphis. Then it was a travel day to

Indianapolis, and a day off before the show. Jolly's opinion was that this band got too many days off. Those days could be filled with more shows, which meant more exposure for the band and more tour revenue. But Jack was Mt. Vesuvius, ready to erupt. He put so much into his shows, added with his volatile personality, meant taking a few days off here and again. Jolly had many years in this business, and took advantage of those days off to schedule radio interviews, tv interviews, meet and greets, etc. Then he'd let the band loose in whatever city they were in.

He closed his laptop and put it in the leather case.

"Now, Miss Malone, I'd like to have a conversation with you about something serious."

Her face dropped. She had a way of smiling and then suddenly becoming sad. Then she'd stop talking and nod or shake her head. A thought crossed Jolly's mind that Jack must beat her into submission. She looked to the ground.

"Jar, look up at me. Look at my face. I want to make sure you are understanding what I am asking you. And get that fuckin' lollipop out of your mouth. I can't believe you share them. Every time I see you share them among yourselves, my skin crawls. Haven't none of you heard about communicable diseases? I swear I'm going to strike Dum Dums from the rider."

"Benny would be upset. He needs the sugar."

"Benny needs rehab. Maybe if we put a trail of Dum Dums to the door of a rehab he'd go." Jolly said sarcastically.

Jarmila laughed. Jolly loved to hear her laugh. It was innocent and musical. But then her face fell again.

"You wouldn't really hit me, would you?" she said tearfully.

"Jar, sugar, I would *never* hit you! It's not right. It was totally out of line for me to say that and I'm sorry. Please forgive me. Sometimes I speak out of line. I want to talk to you about something. But if I'm getting too personal, let me know. I was advised to stay out of your navigational pull, but I'm glad I didn't take that advice. I really like you. You're becoming a good friend. You seem to put me in a better mood because you have some type of innocent joy that surrounds you. I can't explain it. But it's good to be around you. As long as you're not slamming me with conspiracy theories on Tab soft drink and aliens at area 51 and Mary Jo Kopechne and Marilyn Monroe and how rich people get away with murder in a socially acceptable way. Seriously, no disrespect to you, but I tune you out when you start on conspiracies."

"That's okay. I think everyone else does too. Especially when I start to talk about my great-grandma Jarmila, the one I was named after."

Jolly took her right hand in his left.

"I would love to hear about your great-grandma." he said, "I'm going to make time in the next few days so you can tell me all about her. Right now, though, while I have a few minutes, I want to talk to you about something personal. I don't like to get into a band's private affairs. It's complicated and I don't like complicated. Look at me, Jar. Look at my face."

She raised her face to his.

"Do you understand what consent is?" he asked her, "Do you understand what consensual means?"

"Yeah, it means a person can do what they want to another person if they are both of legal age."

"No, sugar, that is not what it means. It means if someone suggests something to you like...sexual...and you want to really do that, and I mean *really* do that, and that person wants to really do that, then it's okay. Nobody can do something to you that you don't want them to. No matter what they say to you, okay?"

If he had a pre-teen daughter, this is the talk he'd be having with her. Jarmila was like a pre-teen. He didn't think she was developmentally delayed. He was sure she was just undereducated and isolated too much by the band.

"But on my 18th birthday Jack said since I was of legal age, he could do anything to me."

"Well Jack is a grown man who knows that's wrong. You need to tell him no if you don't want him to do something to you. He's old enough to understand the word no. I'm going to ask you a very personal question. It's really just out of curiosity, so you don't have to answer. You never have to answer any question I ask you if it makes you uncomfortable. Do you understand? I'm just trying to be a better friend to you." He put his hand under her chin and lifted her face.

She nodded yes.

"I'm curious about this rule thing the band has for you. It's my job to keep everyone on tour safe, and that includes you. If something is happening and you aren't in agreement with it, tell the guys you don't agree with what they are doing to you, okay? If you're too frightened to do that, I can help you. I can help explain what you want to say. Because I don't think you really want Jack punishing you for breaking some rule the band made up just to keep you under control. You're 22-years-old, you don't need to be treated like that."

"I don't want you to talk to them. It's okay."

"You're okay with that then?"

"When I turned 18, I went wild. I did a lot of drugs and drank and disappeared for days. I'd only show up in the studio where they were recording their first album and then I'd be gone until the next day. I never missed a recording session, but I'd only stay for a minute and then off I'd go away again until the next day. I didn't do that before then because I was afraid the police would pick me up and turn me over to Social Services. But when I turned 18, I knew I was out of their hands and could do what I wanted to do. I went insane. The guys were really worried because I didn't have any street smarts, they'd always watched out for me. We'd known each other for years and they didn't want to hear I overdosed or got murdered like my momma. They sat me down and made rules for me. They said they loved me and I was all they had to keep their hearts together. They were already finishing up their first album. They told me I was their backbone, their first and most loyal fan, and if something happened to me it would crush them. They couldn't imagine being without me. They set down some rules. No smoking, no weed, no drugs, no alcohol. No going off with anyone not associated with the band unless they knew them and I had permission. No talking to strangers unless it was hi and bye. Band secrets were kept within the band, no telling anyone else. Everybody agreed on the rules. I agreed on the rules, because I never really had rules before. My grandmother and father mostly ignored me. Except when my grandmother got in one of her moods and she'd hit me in the face and pinch my arm. She demanded I clean the house so I missed a lot of school, because she didn't think I was cleaning right and made me do it over and over again. I didn't know about rules, or rule breaking. Sometimes I'd take coins out of the grocery money or out of my poppa's coat pocket and I'd ride the buses and trains and stop at parks and libraries. I didn't think it was stealing when I took the coins. I didn't understand what right from wrong meant. The guys just wanted to keep me safe. We agreed on the rules. Then there were the consequences for breaking the rules. The guys discussed some and gave me a choice: If I break a rule I either get banned for five days from seeing the band play or record or perform, or I get a bare bottomed spanking with a bare hand. I chose the spanking. I'd only been spanked once before, when Jack gave me a birthday spanking on my 18th birthday. The pain doesn't last long. I couldn't stand the thought of not being there when the band was performing. The pain of a spanking would go away quicker than the emotional pain of not being there with the guys. I love them so much. And I know they are only doing that because they care for me and want to keep me safe. Jack was picked to do the punishing. It's okay, it doesn't hurt that much."

"Except the other night when he beat the hell out of you."

"He said he was sorry and he'd never do that again. He's never done it before. He said he did it out of anger, and he'd never use a belt on me again. He felt really bad."

"Scot saw your black eye. He saw the bruises on your wrists too. He assumed it was consensual, some adult game you and Jack are into."

"I don't like it. But I don't want to cause problems in the band. I want them to be successful rock stars like they want to be. I don't want to do anything that would make them upset. That's why I go along with it. I don't want them to stop being my friends. They're the only friends I have."

"I don't think they'd stop being your friends. But if you don't like something they are doing to you, tell them no. Tell them you don't like it and want them to stop."

She nodded her head yes.

"This is one of the strangest situations I've come across. But if this is what you agree on, no judgements here. To each his own. But I want you to understand that if someone does something to you and you don't want it, you can always confide in me. Whatever you tell me will not go beyond me. I've told you that before and I will always abide by it. Sometimes just talking to a friend helps. It's much better than keeping it inside and letting all those emotions build up with no place to go."

"I'm glad you're my friend." she said, and kissed him on the cheek.

"That was unexpected. Do you want to go explore the city? I'm going back to the hotel and get some more work done."

"You should take a day off."

"If I did Benny would overdose, Chandler would be arrested for having sex in a public place, Jack would haul off and punch someone because his coffee wasn't hot enough, Johnny would spend the day calling his mom and then spend the rest of the day crying because he misses her, the equipment would get lost somewhere in between Indianapolis and Lansing, and then I'd find the nearest roof to jump from."

"I'd miss you if you did something like that."

"I know you would. You have a good heart. But I'm only kidding about jumping off a roof. The longer we are friends, the more you will get used to my sarcasm. Now where would you like to go, Miss Malone?"

"Back to the hotel. I've got *Fahrenheit 451* to read. I've never read it before. Jack has a whole library in his house and he lets me take any book I want, so I pack a whole bunch for the tour. I like to read. I'll sit in the lobby until the guys come back."

"I can put you in one of their rooms. There's no need to sit in the lobby."

"I don't like to be alone. I get kinda scared."

"Well, you can hang in my room until they return. But I have a lot of work to do, so I need you to find something quiet to do."

"I'll read a book. I won't bother you. I promise."

"Okay then, back to the hotel we go."

"Can we take a private car?"

"I should put you on public transportation for asking me that question. Of course, we're taking a private car."

Show day. Jarmila was walking around with a catalogue, trying to find Jolly.

"Where's you assistant?" Jarmila asked Jolly, who was standing behind the stage. It was few hours to showtime, and already problems were cropping up.

"Which one?" he asked.

"The one that can order this microphone." She pushed the catalogue toward him, "Scot said I should tell your assistant to order it. The mic I'm getting Jack for his birthday."

How nice of Scot, thought Jolly, to push this off on him. Like he didn't have enough on his plate already. Whoever advanced this show got the stage dimensions incorrect. Who can't measure shit? Now he was going to have to do some re-figuring, with only a few hours until showtime. His cell phone beeped.

"Keith." he said to Jarmila as he looked at his phone, "He's in the tour office. Tell him I said to order that item. I gotta meeting. I'll see you later, okay?"

"Thank you." she said, and kissed him on the cheek.

Memphis, like Little Rock, went wild. If the logistics worked out, they could have easily added another show. Sold out. Another sold out show. This whole tour had been one sold out show after another. Jack's esoteric way on stage had audiences captivated. He was like a mermaid, singing songs that drew you in and never let go.

And something happened during that day, before they ever took the stage. Scot heard about it first, then relayed it to Jolly. They decided not to tell the band until after the show. Swollen egos in this band could have a positive or negative effect. You just never knew. Instead, they waited until the band took the stage. Then they ordered champagne and caviar, and the green and white balloons Jack liked so much. Jarmila, the staff and what crew could be spared were gathered in the dressing room. After the show, when the boys walked in, puzzled looks crossed their faces.

"Who died?" asked Jack.

"Your status as an unknown band." said Scot, handing Jack an industry paper, "You're officially a multi-platinum band. *Both* albums went double platinum at the same time. And "The Only Cost" moved up to #1 on the charts, and "Scandalous" moved up to #2. It was like a tsunami of chart topping."

Lots of cheering and whoops and hollers, kissing and hugging, and Jack grabbing Jarmila tight to him and whispering in her ear, "We couldn't have done this without you, babe."

"But look here," said Jolly, "Penny" is in the top ten. At #9."

That was a surprise to everyone except the band, who always believed every one of their songs could be on the top of the charts. "Penny" was a trippy ride into some part of Benny's heroin addled mind. He wrote the lyrics and Chandler wrote the music. The name of the song sounded like a ballad, but it was a powerful sojourn into some unknown, Alice-In-Wonderland on LSD excursion. The management and record label thought it was too long for air play. But the band insisted it be released as a single. Probably the music powers-that-be thought Led Zeppelin's "Stairway to Heaven" and Guns N' Roses "November Rain" were too long for air play. But look where that got both bands. Sometimes bands just knew what would work no matter if they were being told the opposite.

Lenehan were officially rock stars now.

Jolly sat in his usual seat in the bus, in the first seat on the lounge, facing the opposite table, his laptop in front of him and his phone within reach. Scot always sat on the opposite side, his back to the front of the bus. It gave them both a good view of any arguments or fights that could happen within this band. From where they sat, they could easily get up and intervene. Fights happened. Jack and Chandler had volatile personalities, but Jack was usually the instigator in any argument. Arguments ranged from Jack being late for soundcheck to Chandler eating the last mango. It was the first of the famous infighting Jolly got to see up close and personal. Before, he had only heard of it from industry gossip, fan sites, and incidents taped by staff, crew or fans and uploaded onto social media.

"You don't even like mangoes." said Chandler, earlier in the dressing room. The band had just made double platinum on both their albums, and they were arguing about mangoes.

"It doesn't fuckin' matter if I like them. You think you're da shit and can eat da last mango. Maybe somebody else wanted a mango. Now because you're an entitled piece of shit somebody won't get da mango they've been waiting for all day." responded Jack.

"Does anyone here want a mango?" asked Chandler to the room. Silence. "See nobody wants mangoes. If you're so fuckin' concerned about the lack of mangoes, why don't you take your 1970's blue suede pants and you're 1980 polyester shirt and walk down to the 24 hour market and buy your stupid ass some!"

"This fuckin' shirt is silk!" screamed Jack, and threw an orange at Chandler.

Chandler responded by picking up several oranges and throwing them at Jack. Jack then took a swing at Chandler, which thankfully missed. Chandler drove himself into Jack and pushed him into a wall, and the fight was now officially on. Pummeling, kicking and screaming at each other, fists flying everywhere, band security Les and Arnold each grabbed one of the boys. Les held Jack in a bear hug, Arnold held Chandler's arms.

"This is what I'll do," said Jolly, "I'll put you in separate buses for the trip to Nashville."

"That's what I fuckin' need," yelled Jack, "my own fuckin' tour bus. W. Axl Rose has his own tour bus. Why can't I?"

"Because you're not W. Axl Rose and you'll never be that talented." ridiculed Chandler.

"I'm going to fuck you up!" screamed Jack, trying to get away from Les. But Les had a tight grip on Jack. He knew the boy well enough to not let go.

"Okay, children," said Scot, "unless we resolve this, one of you is riding in the crew bus."

"Like fuckin' hell!" shouted Jack, "I'm a fuckin rock star with double platinum albums and three fuckin' top ten singles. I'm not riding in no fuckin' crew bus!"

"You think you got those on your own?" asked Chandler, sarcastically.

"It's my voice and my personality that keeps this band going. Read da fuckin' media reviews." snapped Jack.

Jolly's patience had left him somewhere between the last mango and flying oranges.

"Maybe we should give you a choice, just like you gave Jar." he said sarcastically, "maybe then you'd remember not to fight about mindless shit that has nothing to do with this band's path of success."

"Stay out of our fuckin' private band business, Jolly." sneered Jack. He looked at Jarmila with a stare like laser beams. She started crying. "Stop fuckin' crying! What are you fuckin' crying about?"

"Lay off her Jack," said Johnny, "she gets upset when there's any discord between the band."

"Can we all just go to the bus and pretend we like each other, so we can get on the road?" asked Benny.

"Excellent idea, Benny." said Scot, "Why don't I accompany Jack, to the bus, and then Jolly can accompany Chandler? Then Jack can stay in the back of the bus all night if he wants, okay?"

Jolly thought, these boys had some serious growing up to do.

Now on the bus, a sense of calm finally achieved, Jolly and Scot worked. Benny sat with Alice next to him. Alice had become a figure in the band's entourage. Management only allowed people working for the band and members of the band to ride in the bus. And occasionally wives and family. Insurance and all that complicated crap. Alice, with the black hair and the stunning blue eyes, had some type of positive effect on Benny. He wasn't shooting as much heroin, and he'd cut down on the drinking and the pills. Love, it can do all kinds of miraculous things to people.

"There's nothing better than a clean butthole", said Chandler, who was sitting next to Benny, across from Jolly, "Nothing better than licking a clean butthole. I always keep mine clean for that purpose."

"Disgusting." said Benny.

"TMI," said Jolly, "TMI."

"See," continued Chandler, "that's the problem with y'all. Y'all got to let your freak flag unfurl. You're all too tight about shit. You'd feel a lot more liberated if you'd try things you've never tried before. Y'all too inhibited."

"I'm not licking a man's butthole. I have nothing against anyone doing that, but I like women only." said Benny.

"Then lick a woman's butthole. It's amazing. Will send you where you never thought you'd be."

"Once again Chandler," said Jolly, "TMI. I have nothing against your freaky shit. But I don't want to hear a play by play."

"I'm only trying to get y'all to be less inhibited."

"I've done a lot things on the road," replied Jolly, "and I've never licked a butthole, woman or man, and I have no desire to ever do that. But no judgements here. To each his own. I'm 56 years old, and I have no intent on changing things."

Jolly looked at Alice and said "What do you think of all this craziness, Alice?"

"I think it's funny. All of you seem to make life entertaining. Although I guess it can be difficult when you're all together for months at a time. You don't get to see your families a lot. That would be a downer."

"I want to apologize for the fight earlier," said Scot, "Jack is a master instigator. What makes him magnetic on stage, makes him a pain in the ass offstage."

"It's okay. Benny says it happens. He says he and Jack rarely get into fights, and Johnny is shy and quiet. Benny told me it always seems to be between Jack and Chandler." said Alice.

"I want to apologize also." said Chandler, "Jack gets to me sometimes and I forget my manners."

"It's okay." replied Alice.

What a nice girl, thought Jolly. Usually, these road hoes just want the action around the band, or the money. But this girl seemed very sweet. She seemed to really care for Benny. Benny and she started kissing, and Benny led her to the back.

"I wouldn't try and oust Jack from there." said Scot, "he's there with Jarmila and I don't think he's happy."

"It's because of what I said." stated Jolly.

"It needed to be said. At least you had the balls to say it. I tried talking to him, but anything about Jarmila and he shuts me down." said Scot.

"I'll just go to my bunk." said Benny.

Tour bus bunk sex. Not the most comfortable, but it'll do if there's no other choice.

If Memphis seemed completely Lenehan crazy, Nashville outdid that. A 2:00pm outdoor public meet and greet held by a local radio station had people lined up as early as 6:00am, to make sure they could meet the band. It also gave time for the band to settle into their hotel rooms, relax a little, get some sleep in an actual bed and not a bus bunk. Jolly made sure everyone was in the lobby at 1pm. But of course, Jack was late.

"He's probably with Jarmila. Those two are attached at the hip lately." said Scot.

'That's because Jack says Jarmila is his only now, for the rest of the tour." said Benny, "He says we can have her during the day, but at night she's his. I don't care, I have my Alice." he pulled Alice closer to him and kissed her lightly.

Benny's calling her "my Alice", thought Jolly, we're making progress here. Maybe she can get him off the heroin.

"I think it's bullshit", Johnny said, anger in his voice, "she's like a little sister to me, I like to spend time with her when we have down time. We watch movies and talk about things. She makes life on the road easier. I miss my ma, but I got a sister to talk to. Now Jack has decided things have to be his way, and I don't want a fight. Fights upset Jarmila". He didn't like her upset.

"I had a dream that Jack realized the world doesn't revolve around him. Then I woke up with Jack screaming about a particular pair of leopard print pants he can't find, and I realized I'm still in hell." Jolly quipped.

"It doesn't bother me too much," said Chandler, "I only need her when I can't find someone else to fuck."

"You're a beacon of sunshine, Chandler." said Jolly, "It must make Jar feel really good about herself that's she's just some convenient hole for you."

"You don't understand our relationship," Chandler said, "I love her. Sex is just an added bonus. She came to me for it, I never went to her that first time she said she wanted it from me. Besides, Jack and Benny already had their turn with her before I had her. When she wants sex, I'm not turning her down."

Though not in his job description, he realized he'd have to have another talk with Jarmila about how sex, friendship and love were different things. This band had completely brainwashed her into thinking things they wanted her to believe, to their own advantage.

Jack arrived at 1:15 pm with Jarmila. Her sad face was on and she looked at the ground. Something not good had happened, thought Jolly.

'Great for you to show up, Jack. You're late." said Jolly.

"I'll show up when I want to fuckin' show up. I'm not your trick pony, doing whatever you want. *You* work for *me*." Jack emphasized, "And where da hell is Scottie?"

"Scot decided to go on to the venue. He knows a lot of people there. Has some good friends he hadn't seen in a while. He's taking some of my usual duties and I get the wonderful job of escorting you to this meet and greet."

"I hate meet and greets." grumbled Jack.

"You've said. But you sure like more fans, because more fans mean more ticket and record sales, and that's more money for you." said Jolly, sarcastically.

"Fuck you, talkin' to me like I don't know shit." yelled Jack, "I ran this band long before we got stuck with incompetent mouthy tour managers."

Les walked into the lobby.

"We should get going soon." he said, "The crowd is pretty large and it's going to get difficult getting the band in and out."

The meet and greet took a little longer than Jolly was comfortable with. But fans were of the upmost importance, and making them happy was always the goal. After the meet and greet it was decided to head straight to the venue. With the band settled in the dressing room and 45 minutes before soundcheck, Jolly decided it was dinner hour. Well, a 45 minute dinner hour. Once again, he found the crew hospitality room almost empty. That was a good sign. It meant people were working. Of course, people had to eat. But they better eat when they're on a break. God forbid they leave something unfinished to go eat. "Starve, motherfuckers," Jolly would yell, "I've got a show to run."

Jarmila bounded in just as he was filling up a plate.

"What's on today's menu, Jolly?"

"All kinds of good healthy stuff. But why don't you eat with the band in the dressing room?"

"Why don't you?"

"Because I like the absence of chaos." he answered, "If I'm in the dressing room I get interrupted from my meal to handle a thousand and one things the band is requesting. Contractual dinner hour be damned."

"I like the quiet too. If I eat there, Jack yells at me about getting fat, and Chandler wants me to suck him off, because it gives him an appetite. He's a monster if he hasn't had a hardy meal before a show."

"I find that interesting. I know a lot of musicians who will only have a light snack before a show, because they feel weighted down otherwise. Like, sluggish."

"Not Chandler. He eats as much as he fucks."

"And he never gains weight. Ahh, the metabolism of the young."

He took a bite of a burger. "Now. Miss Malone, what's wrong?"

"Nothing" she looked away.

"How long have I known you now? A week? I don't make friends easily. I'm aloof and have unresolved trust issues. It takes me time to get to be friends with people. But you, Miss Malone, I don't know what it is. I've never felt a friendship happen so quickly. You're easy to talk to and your smile makes my day so much better. But today I saw your face, and I know you get sad when something is bothering you. Is something bothering you? Do you want to talk about it? You say you don't lie, but I think you're lying to me now. That hurts my feelings."

He stood up and got a clean plate. He got a burger and filled it with all the trimmings. Then he piled on some coleslaw and put it before Jarmila.

"Eat." He said in his commanding, tour manager voice.

"I'm not very hungry." she responded.

"Miss Malone, you're going to eat. You don't have to eat all of it, but I expect you to take a few bites."

She took a bite of the burger. "I love burgers with everything like this."

"I'm glad. I make excellent burgers on the grill. When you come over to my house for steak, I'll make burgers, too. I make then by hand, none of this pre-made shit. I chop up some onions and put them *inside* the burgers before I grill them. Fuckin' delicious!"

"Are you inviting me to your house?'

"Of course. I want my new friend to give me a review of my food."

"I'd like to visit your house. Do you live in Humboldt Park? All the band lives in Humboldt Park, except Benny. He moved to Smith Park. Lives across from it. They all grew up in Humboldt Park, even Benny. Chandler bought the house he grew up in when his parents moved to the suburbs. Jack inherited a huge three-story house from his great aunt when he was 18. And a lot of money to take care of it. It's old, like from 1890. It's got a two-story coach house in back. It's directly in front of Humboldt Park. It's got beautiful views of the park. Johnny bought a house and rehabbed it and moved his momma in. She's a real nice lady. Was a cleaning woman. She came from Poland. Worked three jobs so Johnny could take music lessons. His dad died shoveling snow, when Johnny was young. You'll meet his momma at the Milwaukee shows. She's coming up with Jack's momma and grandfather."

"I live in Noble Square. On a quiet street. As quiet as a city street can be. By the way, I do not like family shows," said Jolly, "too complicated and too much extra work. I know it's important for the band. They all miss their families. Life on the road gets lonely. Now that you've eaten something you're going to tell me what's wrong, Miss Malone."

"I still have your confidence, right?"

"For life."

"I got caught smoking a cigarette. Worse, it was Jack's last cigarette in the pack, I didn't know it, he usually keeps a couple packs around. When he woke up and went for his cigarette pack, there wasn't any left. He was very mad. Super mad, because he always needs his wake up cigarette. I don't like to see him angry. I admitted I had smoked the cigarette, but I didn't know it was his last. I told him I was sure he had another pack. He had me call Benny to bring him another pack. He was still super mad even after he got cigarettes. But since he promised me that he'd never hit me in anger again, I had to wait for him to calm down. I broke a rule. No smoking. That's why we were late coming down to the lobby today."

"That's why you had a sad face. And you were walking very slowly. It pisses me off that they treat you like a petulant two-year-old. But I work for this band, and sometimes I have to put aside my anger, even when it hurts me to see my friend being treated wrongly. Maybe you should weigh the positives and negatives of smoking when you know it's a rule breaker. Smoking isn't good for you. For you, it's twice as bad."

"It's my last bare bottom over the knee spanking." Jarmila said quietly.

"Well, that's good."

"Next time it will be a paddle."

"Well, that's not good."

"Do you smoke?" Jarmila asked.

"Occasionally, if I'm immensely stressed. I used to smoke a pack and a half a day. My mom died from lung cancer, so I cut down on smoking,"

"Did your dad die from lung cancer too?"

"No, he died from complications of the flu. He got very sick and my sister took him to the hospital. His organs shut down and he died."

"Did you get to see him before he died?'

"I was on a tour in Texas and I flew right out, but by the time I got to LA he was in a coma. I like to believe he heard me tell him I love him and goodbye."

"I'm sure he did. I read a couple books that say even when people die, they can still hear things for a few moments."

"You have such a good soul, Jar. You're always trying to make people feel better."

Music started from above the hospitality room.

"That sounds like church music." said Jarmila.

"It is. It's "How Great Thou Art." answered Jolly.

"You go to church?"

"Not since I was a kid."

"Catholic?"

"Episcopalian. You?"

"I never belonged to any church. I rarely go. I went to Chandler's wedding. He and his wife are Catholic. But he's not a practicing Catholic, except when his family wants him to go. Like if the band is not playing on Christmas or Easter. Johnny goes to Mass as often as he can. He says he's going to marry a nice Polish Catholic or Irish Catholic girl. He's waiting on the right girl, one who's a virgin. He prays every day that God finds him a nice girl who's a virgin. And that he plays good bass guitar. He always prays that before he goes onstage.'

"At least God is answering one of his prayers. It's difficult to find a virgin in the 21st century."

"I think he'll find one. I was a virgin until I was 18."

"That's because the band was waiting for you to become legal."

"I initiated it. Except for Jack. But he didn't really take my virginity. On my 18th birthday he told me he had a present for me, and after he gave me a birthday spanking, he put his penis up my butt. He said I couldn't get pregnant that way. He's always done it that way. It hurts really bad, but not so bad if he's in a good mood. I've never had vaginal sex with him like I do with Benny and Chandler."

Jolly was starting to regret the promise he made Jarmila that she could tell him anything. His heart did go out to her, because he was sure she had no one else to talk to about this. The band liked to keep their secrets.

"Listen to me Jar. Are you paying attention to what I'm going to say to you? It's rare, but a woman can get pregnant even if she's having anal sex. It's very rare, but it can happen. Plus, if Jack isn't using protection, you can get all kinds of scary and deadly diseases. And I know you're not the only woman Jack is with. He gets his fair share on the road. I've been here a week and have seen him with other women."

"I know. He takes them to the back of the bus. Usually before showtime. He says it helps him relax."

Jolly would have never guessed that when he signed up for this tour, he'd be a combination of Dr. Phil and Maury. He should have asked for a bigger salary.

"Well, sugar, I need to go back to work. Although I could sit with you here all night and be most contented. But unfortunately, I don't get paid to be content. I'm going up to the balcony and see how the sound is. Walk with me?"

"Yes!" she exclaimed, once again clapping her hands like a little girl, "I never get to go out front."

"Well first I need to stop by the office and pick up a two-way radio, because Scot seems to think we're on a 1980 Def Leppard tour."

After stopping by the tour office, they started making their way out front of the stage area.

"Not even when the band plays?" asked Jolly.

"Not since their club days."

"Why?"

"The managers they've had since their club days say I have to stay in the dressing room or on the side of the stage. Because I don't work for the band. I'm just a guest."

Jolly stopped on the stairway to the balcony and turned to Jarmila. He lifted up her laminate pass that hung around her neck.

"What does this say, Jar?"

"It says All Access All Areas Band."

"Do you know what that means, Jar?"

"It means I can stay backstage and go on the bus."

This poor child, thought Jolly, they keep her so clueless.

"It means, sugar, that you can go anywhere you want in any venue the band is playing in. You can go tap dance on the roof if you please, though I wouldn't recommend it. But you could if you wanted to. That pass gives you access to everything it gives the band access to. Don't listen to anyone who tells you differently. If any of my crew or staff or security tell you that you can't be out front, let me know and I'll fire their ass. If *anyone* who works in a venue tells you that you have to go backstage, that you are not allowed out front, let me know. And Heaven help Scot if he tells you that you can't go out front. We've been friends for years but if he says anything to you about staying backstage, he's going to hear my mouth."

"Why are you so nice to me?"

"Because you're a very nice person. Nice people should not be treated the way you are being treated. Was the other tour like this, the one for the first album?"

"Pretty much so. I stayed by the side of the stage so I wouldn't miss a performance."

They reached the first row of the balcony and sat down.

"Now tell me something, Miss Malone." Jolly said, "If this band insists on doing their own soundchecks, then why are they wasting half of it playing cover tunes?"

"It's a tradition. It helps them warm up so they can soundcheck individually. It's really Chandler who insists on soundchecks. He's real picky about the way he sounds. I've heard of bands that let the roadies do soundchecks. Listen, they're playing the Robert Johnson version of "Sweet Home Chicago". I love this version. Chandler says Robert Johnson made a deal with the devil at a crossroads so he would become famous, and the devil kinda went back on the deal because Johnson died before he became famous. He didn't become famous until long after he was dead."

And there was that accent again. Shee-cah-go.

"I know the story and the legend." said Jolly.

"Well Chandler says he wants to go to hell so he can spend eternity with Robert Johnson and jam with him all the time."

"I don't think Chandler will have any difficulty getting into hell. Satan probably already has a bondage room set up just for Chandler. He'll be happy for eternity."

"He does like stuff like that. He doesn't try it on me, but he does on other people who like that kind of stuff."

"I know he is into that. I've been in his hotel room when he was organizing his adult toys by type and size. Is there anything he doesn't like?"

"Kissing women. He'll only kiss his wife. And me. She's pretty straightlaced about shit. I mean, she has to give in to his craziness on the tour if she wants to stay married to him. She loves him. She's a totally Catholic-married-for-life kind of girl. But at home, he's all Ozzie and Harriet."

"Except when he's in the garage fucking you."

"Okay, but he was fucking me before he started dating her, so I came along with the package."

"I can picture his marriage proposal: Will you marry me? Oh, and this is the girl I'm fucking, and will continue to fuck while we're married. And by the way, did I mention I also like to suck cock and take it up the ass. So, is it a yes?"

"I think you probably got that marriage proposal pretty accurate. But she did say 'yes'." Jarmila laughed, "What do you think of this tour so far?"

"You're all a bunch of stark raving mad lunatics. Except for you. You're a good heart. A brat sometimes, but good at heart." Jolly sat up straight, "Oh hell no. They are *not* playing "Stairway to Heaven". We have a soundcheck to get through. We don't have time for this." He got on the two-way radio, "Everett, tell the band to cut the fuckin' Zeppelin tune and *start an actual soundcheck*."

The band responded by playing Willie Nelson's version of "Always on My Mind."

"This is why I recently upgraded to Extra Strength Tylenol." quipped Jolly.

Week Two, Indianapolis-Lansing-Detroit

Nashville was a roaring hit and the next stop was Indianapolis. Once in Indy, the band had an extra day off. The first day, their arrival day, Jolly decided to just let them recharge. The shows had been intense. The fans had been intense. It wouldn't hurt to let them have a couple days off. Except of course, on the second day, Jolly had scheduled a podcast interview at 10:00am, and a radio contest winner meet and greet at 1:00pm. Then a band meeting at 3:00pm in the hotel conference room, in which Jolly insisted Jarmila be included. She was as much a part of the band as any of them, and she deserved to be included.

"A committeeman is coming to this show with his two daughters," said Jolly, 'Try not to do anything too crazy on stage. I don't want to spend the night filling out forms to bail your asses out of jail."

"This isn't a fuckin g-rated show!" shouted Jack, "We do what we want! If they want something to take their kids to, try Disney On Ice."

"People of all ages like your songs, Jack." Jolly said.

"Well, I don't write Teletubbies songs." sneered Jack.

"I could wear a g-string on stage and claim I thought that's what a g-rated show was." Chandler grinned.

"No Chandler," said Jolly, "no g-strings on stage. No getting butt fucked or butt fucking or giving head or any of those things you like to do between drum and bass solos."

"But," protested Chandler, "I was on all fours and on the side of the stage. I'm pretty sure none of the fans saw me. It was well worth it, too. That dude was super-hot and knew how to make a man come. I hope we play Memphis again soon. I'm ready for round two of that sweet thang."

"TMI, Chandler," said Jolly, "TMI."

"Oh, but y'all don't say shit about Benny when he ran around that hotel parking lot in Tulsa, stark naked except for his cowboy boots, screaming that his clothes were full of lice." Chandler complained.

"That was before my time as your tour manager. I'm sure the entire incident was captivating. You are not, and hear me clearly, going to do any random sex acts on the stage tomorrow night. Am I clear enough?"

"Sometimes I sit at the drum set naked." added Benny.

"Not tomorrow night Benny," said Jolly, "tomorrow wear clothes. At least shorts."

"Tomorrow is a very important gig. It sold out in 15 minutes. It's going to be insane and you all have to be on top of your game." said Scot, "The guest list is quite large. Not as large as Milwaukee's will be, but there's a lot of people you all are going have to meet after the show. Then we're headed for Lansing. No guests on the bus. Well, Alice of course. We've cleared permission for her to join the rest of the tour. But nobody else."

"No fair!" yelled Chandler, "What if I have somebody I want to be with? My needs are just as important as Benny's!"

"Maybe you'll run into Helga," said Jack, "and find her penis."

Chandler flew across the table and took a swing at Jack. Jack, nimble and quick as lead singers get, leaned back in time to avoid the punch. Scot and Jolly quickly put an end to the fight.

"Can we all act like adults and stop talking about butt sex, naked drumming and chicks with dicks and get back to talking about important things, like, tour itineraries?" Jolly said. "Has anybody here read the tour itinerary I gave you?"

"I did." said Jarmila.

"Who fuckin' cares if you read it, Jarmila." Jack sneered, "You just fuckin' go where we fuckin' take you."

"You don't have to be so mean." said Jarmila.

"And you don't have to be a mouthy stupid bitch." Jack responded.

"Scot," said Jolly, "I think the next radio contest should be how many times Jack can use the word "fuckin'" in a five minute conversation."

"Excellent idea!" laughed Scot.

"Why don't you two just shut da fuck up." Jack snapped.

"I love these productive band meetings." Jolly said sarcastically.

The band went back to Jack's room, Jarmila with them. The first thing Jack said was for Johnny to turn around.

"Lift your skirt and pull down your panties." Jack commanded Jarmila.

She did as she was told. Johnny turned away from her because he'd never seen her naked. She was his sister. Nobody could tell him otherwise.

"She looks healed up to me," Jack said, "what do you all think?"

"That those scars aren't going to go away. Does it still hurt?" Chandler asked.

"No." she replied.

"Get dressed." Jack commanded her, "You can turn around now Johnny."

On the suite side of the room, Johnny sat in a chair and the rest of the guys took the couch. Jarmila sat on the coffee table, facing the guys.

"We need to discuss what happened and what is going to happen. We need to discuss it as a band because it could affect da whole band. Da issue is still out there because we don't really know Jolly and we don't know him enough to trust him. He could sell a story and we'd all be fucked. Goodbye careers and platinum albums and packed houses."

"Did you really hit her in the eye?" asked Johnny.

"It was an accident." replied Jack.

"Should have seen her ass after he whooped her." added Benny, "When she came to my room that morning, I was like damn girl, what did you do to piss Jack off that much?"

"I don't think I want to know." Johnny said quietly.

"She was fuckin' flirting with Jolly. She was letting him feed her. This was on da first day he was here with us!" Jack raised his voice, "I know I got out of hand, I was angry! I said I was sorry and promised I'd never hit her out of anger again. I think she's suckin' his dick! Or fuckin' him."

"I'm not doing either!" Jarmila emphasized, "We just talk."

"Really, Jack," said Johnny, "he's like over 30 years older than her. She's not doing anything with him. You let your jealousy get in the way of your common sense."

"I am not jealous. I am worried he's trying to take advantage of her. I'm just protecting you, Jarmila." Jack said, "Now let's get back to this business. You betrayed da band, Jarmila. You betrayed each of us. You know one of da rules is no telling private band business. And you go and tell someone you just fuckin' met!"

"I didn't tell him anything! He asked me a bunch of questions and I nodded my head yes or no. But when he got to your name I started to cry. That's how he figured out it was you who beat me." Jarmila started to cry.

"Save your fuckin' crying," Jack sneered, "Trust me, you'll need those tears later."

She looked at him like a deer in the headlights.

"We need to agree as a band what to do." Jack said, "This is more serious than a couple slaps across her bare ass. This could ruin everything for us, and we need to make sure she doesn't do stupid shit like this again."

"But I said I was sorry!" Jarmila cried.

"What's your ideas?" asked Chandler.

"After she told me what she did I told her I was going to use a paddle on her this next time, after she healed up from when I beat her. I figure this may be painful enough to remind her that she needs to keep her stupid mouth shut." Jack explained, "I think we all need to be there for it. Because she betrayed us as a band."

"That was a pretty stupid thing to do." Benny said, "You could have just gone to Johnny's room or any of us."

"But I didn't want Johnny to get mad at Jack about my black eye or you guys to get mad at the belt marks. You and Chandler had company. I don't want any problems in the band."

"Now you've caused a real big potential problem with the band." said Benny. "I'm in."

"Maybe we could go talk to Jolly, as a band and explain the situation." suggested Johnny.

"Yeah, let's go give him more shit to sell to magazines." Jack said.

"I'm sorry Johnny. I love you like a brother. I didn't mean to make you distrust me. You don't want them to punish me, do you? Not like that, right?" begged Jarmila.

"I love you like a sister, but you betrayed me, and I feel broken into a hundred pieces inside. I know nothing has happened yet, but it's tough to think of my music when I'm thinking at any time someone could make public info that should stay within the band. It would kill us as a band." Johnny continued, "I don't want to ever see you get hurt, but I'm siding with whatever the band's decision is. You need to learn Jarmila. You're an adult and I hate treating you like a child. But this seems the only way to get through to you. It's the only way to keep us all safe."

"Chandler?" asked Jack.

"I'm in. I'm not going to have some stupid bitch be the cause of my band falling apart because she can't keep her mouth shut. I got a nice paddle too. Has holes in it. Hurts like a bitch. Bet you won't forget this, Jarmila." Chandler seemed almost too excited about it.

Jack took out the itinerary and said "Everyone is on board?" nods all around, except Jarmila, "Our next day off is da day after Detroit. We'll plan it for that day."

"Nobody gives a shit what *I* think." cried Jarmila, "I could just leave and never come back!"

"Exactly," said Jack, "nobody gives a shit about what you think. You betrayed our trust and now you'll suffer da consequences. Go ahead and leave. Where ya gonna go? You only have us."

Jarmila knew Jack was right. She had no place else to go. She stood up and ran into the bedroom and slammed the door.

An hour and a half before doors opened at the Indianapolis venue the lines were so long extra security had to be called in. The anticipation in the air was reaching a fever pitch. This venue had general admission in front of the stage. This show was going to be one wild ride. The band fed off of audience reactions, but Jack was the one who really brought the house down. His interactions with audiences were legendary.

"The lines are blocks long," said Jolly as he entered the dressing room, "and doors don't open for another hour and a half."

"This is going to be in-fuckin-sane." Chandler said.

"We really need to be da best out there." Jack said, "I know we're always da best, but tonight we really can't let anything go wrong."

"Johnny," said Chandler, "go pray to your God of equipment that the monitors don't quit tonight and my guitars sound right."

"Yeah," added Benny, "and ask that God of yours to make sure that snare drum doesn't fuck up again."

"Y'all could pray yourselves, you know," said Johnny, "God listens to everyone."

"The management company needs to stop holding on to your budget like the last life jacket on the Titanic and buy you new equipment." said Jolly, "Instead of this excuse they keep giving that it's only a few more weeks left on this tour, and you will all get new equipment next tour. Bullshit, it's all bullshit. They see the numbers. They know where you're at."

"I'm contacting the record label tomorrow and telling them unless they at least replace the malfunctioning and broken equipment, the band will cancel the rest of the tour." said Scot.

"But what if they say okay, cancel the tour and we'll drop Lenehan from the label?" Johnny said, concerned.

"Lenehan has two double platinum albums, sold out shows, three singles and an album at the top of the charts. You're making them lots of money with the potential to make lots more." said Jolly, "If they were stupid enough to drop you, there'd be a dozen more record labels beating a path to your door to sign you on. You don't have anything to worry about. Go out there tonight and kill it like you always do."

Lenehan took the stage with a tune they thought would be a good fit for Indianapolis. It was a song called "Face of Today", a tribute to the legacy of the band Blind Melon's lead singer Shannon Hoon, who died of a drug overdose in 1995. Hoon wasn't born in Indianapolis, but he was born and bred in Indiana and was an Indiana boy through and through. Hoon was a very talented musician, and Lenehan was often quoted in the media that it was Blind Melon's song "Change" that encouraged them to become a band. "Face of Today" was a shout out to a part of a lyric from "Change" that was put on Hoon's gravestone.

The crowd became a delirious, screaming mass. The reaction was so positive, Lenehan could have sung that one song and gone home with rave reviews. The band all smiled at each other. Good choices were made when a band agreed on something, no infighting, no punches being thrown. Just a nice civilized talk about what would be best to start this show. It worked.

"Fuckin' what up Indianapolis!" Jack screamed, "Ready for some rock-n-roll?"

The crowd went wild. Lenehan went into their first set list, songs from the new album mixed in with songs from the first album. In between Jack kept the crowd included in everything to ensure them they were a part of the show. During the middle of the second set, Jack included the audience on the chorus of "The Only Cost" by directing his microphone to the audience and then back to join in on the last words. But the audience sang the whole song the entire time it was played. A first for the band.

Back in the dressing room, the band was exhausted. Jack leaned back in a chair with his feet up on a table, shirtless with a towel around his neck. Jarmila was behind him massaging his shoulders. Benny had Alice on his lap as she massaged his arms. Chandler was taking a short nap, and Johnny was playing his bass guitar unplugged.

"Okay Gentlemen, meet and greet, let's go." Jolly said as he entered the dressing room.

"I hate meet and greets." Jack said.

"I understand because you always remind me how much you hate them," said Jolly, "but it's necessary."

The meet and greet was large. Tons of people to say hi to and take pictures. In addition, there were more fans waiting outside in back. Regardless if Jack hated meet and greets, he made every fan feel special. Benny ate up the attention, Johnny was his polite self, and Chandler was checking out who his next conquest would be.

When the meet and greet was over, Chandler went up to Scot.

"I found a real nice man. Beautiful." he told Scot.

"Great. You've got an hour. Jolly is settling the show, and then we're off to Lansing." Scot responded.

"Can you open the bus?"

"Driver's in there already. We leave in an hour. Got that?"

"Yup." said Chandler, and went, hand in hand with his new friend, out the doors to the bus. A few hellos to the packed crowd outside and he was off to satisfy whatever need he needed.

"You got us four fuckin' gigs in a row." complained Jack, crashed out on one of the bus lounge seats. He was laying down with is legs on Jarmila's lap. Jolly was sitting in his usual seat, Jarmila next to him. The bus had just started its journey to Lansing.

"It's not like you've never had four gigs in a row, Jack." Scot answered, "Besides, it's the booking agent who books your gigs. Go complain to them."

"That's what I pay *you* to do. These gigs are super intense. It's never been like this before."

"It's only going to get more intense as you go up. Get used to it. My suggestion would be to stop drinking so much and stop the cocaine. Don't run your body down. You'll be dead before you're 30." Scot suggested.

Benny went up to where Jack was laying down. Jack sat up and Benny sat next to him.

"Go fuckin' sit somewhere else Jarmila," snapped Jack, "there's no room for you here."

She stood up and went across to the other lounge seat and sat next to Alice.

"Where's Johnny? Is he in the back?" asked Jarmila.

"No," answered Jolly, "he's got a headache and went to lay down in his bunk."

Benny took out a small mirror and a small bag of coke. He put the coke on the mirror and took out a credit card to cut it into four lines. He rolled up a hundred-dollar bill. He offered it to Jack first, who snorted a line non-stop.

"Oh shit, that's some killer shit." he said, "You've got to put that dealer on your Christmas card list."

"I got it here." Benny responded, snorting a line, "Gonna put Indianapolis on my favorite city list."

Benny offered some to Jolly but he declined. He then offered some to Scot.

"No thank you, I'm working." responded Scot.

"A hundred-dollar bill!" exclaimed Chandler, walking from the back of the bus, "We have arrived bitches, we have arrived!" Jack offered him the mirror and he snorted a line. He offered it to Alice.

"No thank you, I don't do anything heavier than weed. I only smoke it once in a while." she said, "But maybe Jarmila would like some?"

Jack glared at Jarmila, who caught his eyes and looked down.

"No thank you," she said quietly, "I don't do drugs."

Lansing was a bit of a disappointment for a band who was used to larger venues and sold-out shows. The venue was a small old theater with theater seating all the way to the front. But Lenehan could play in a closet and still give 100%. Jolly was standing in the front row, leaning on a theater seat. No general admission in this venue. His legs out before him, crossed. Arms crossed, he held in his left hand a stack of stapled papers. Jarmila skipped up next to him.

"Watcha thinking?" she asked Jolly.

"Lots of things." he answered.

"Like what?" she said as he sat down and she sat next to him.

"Hmmm..." he said, "I'm going to tell you something, but for now, you have to promise me it's between us only, okay?"

"Confidence works both ways."

"Good. The band has asked me to sign on with their next tour."

"Oh my God!" exclaimed Jarmila, "This is excellent!"

"Well don't get ahead of yourself. I haven't made up my mind yet. Or signed anything."

"I'm surprised because I didn't think Jack liked you, and he usually has the last word in everything for the band."

"He doesn't like me personally. But I'm not here to win a Ms. Congeniality contest. I'm here to run this tour. He sees what an excellent job I've done getting things back on track."

"Things have improved a lot. The guys say that makes them perform better onstage, when they don't have shit to worry about, because you take care of all that."

"I try my best. This tour was a disaster. But it's looking good now, don't you think?"

"Yeah. The guys say you're the best tour manager they have ever had. They say other bands are jealous because Lenehan got you and you're the best in the business."

"I think jealousy is why Jack doesn't like me personally. I suspect he doesn't like us being friends, or you making new friends."

"Oh well," she sighed, "maybe it's time he accepted me making new friends."

"That makes me happy to hear you say that, Jar. You're finally getting the courage to leap into independence. A little late, but late is better than never."

"What's that you got in your hand?" she asked.

"The catering rider for Milwaukee."

"No Filet O' Fish?"

"No Filet O' Fish." Jolly laughed, "What's in your hand?"

"Kale juice blend."

"Very healthy. I'm proud it's not Flamin' Hot Cheetos and Dum Dums."

"But it smells funny. Here, smell it." she said as she opened the bottle and put it towards his nose.

"It does smell off. Here, let me see the expiration date." he said as he took the bottle from her, "Date says good until April 2019, so I think you're okay to continue on your healthy route."

He returned the bottle to her.

"I'm glad, because it tastes pretty good."

"Do you want me to put it on the rider?" Jolly asked her.

"No, I'd rather have cherry juice. The Juicy Juice brand if that's okay."

"Anything except the junk food you eat is okay with me. Consider it done. Cherry juice. Juicy Juice brand."

She kissed him on the cheek.

"You've got to stop doing that, Jar. People are getting the wrong impression. If you were just some chick hanging out, I wouldn't mind. But you are deeply involved with the band. Boundaries, Jar. Remember we talked about boundaries and not crossing them."

"But I just want to show you my appreciation for everything you do for me."

"A simple thank you would do."

"You don't like me to kiss you?"

"Honey, I love you kissing me. I'm not trying to be crude, but nature takes over when you kiss me. You're a very attractive woman. But I have to follow these boundaries or I'll be out of a good reputation, that I'd like to keep even though I'm technically retired."

"But if you sign on to the next tour, you won't be retired anymore!"

"Good point! More of a reason I have to keep a good reputation."

Lenehan took the stage for soundcheck. First song up, Guns N' Roses "November Rain".

"Big Guns fans, huh?" Jolly asked.

"Yeah, mostly Jack. He likes the piano parts. Are you going up to the balcony?"

"No, I'm going up to mezzanine. Walk with me, Jar."

As they settled into mezzanine, Chandra walked up with a clipboard and pen in her hand. A large tan manila envelope was under her arm. She handed the clipboard to Jolly.

"Everybody's list or just ours?" he asked, going through the papers on the clipboard.

"Everyone's, even the crew. It's a small list." answered Chandra.

"It's a small venue." Jolly said sarcastically, putting his signature on the last page.

Chandra walked off to the box office.

"Why do you insist the guest list be in so early? Scot never sent it up until right before doors opened. Until you came on tour."

"Scot knows that's bullshit. Getting the list to the box office early means less mistakes."

"But what if someone decides like at the last minute, they want to see their boyfriend or girlfriend or spouse working?"

"Who fuckin' says at the last minute, 'I want to go see my boyfriend or girlfriend work'? They're shit out of luck. My tour, my rules."

Jolly typed something into his phone.

"Now they're playing BB King's "I Been Downhearted"." Jarmila said.

"They have quite a repertoire. If they would only play their own songs and they could do an actual soundcheck, that would give me a massive hard-on."

"Like I do?" smiled Jarmila.

Jolly looked her straight into the eyes and said, "No comment, Miss Malone."

After the show, Jarmila was on one end of a couch in the dressing room reading *Vogue Magazine*, Dum Dum in her mouth and Chandler was at the other end reading a guitar magazine. Jack was sitting in a chair that was parallel with his bare feet in their usual spot resting on a coffee table. Dum Dum in his mouth. Across from the couch Benny was curled up asleep in an armchair. After the amount of energy Lenehan put into their shows, resting and recharging was necessary, before doing any necessary band related after-show happenings.

Johnny walked in and went toward the couch. He tried to get Jack to move his legs and let him by, finally giving up and stepping over Jack's legs. He sat between Chandler and Jarmila. He gave Jarmila a kiss on the cheek.

"What's up little sister?" he asked her.

"Ooooo Johnny shave that stubble off your face." she responded, pushing him away.

"You complain when I practice my bass, saying I'm being anti-social. Now I'm being social and you're complaining about stubble." he said, playfully rubbing his face against hers.

"Johnny, stop it!" she said, pushing him away again, "You're giving me hives! My whole face is going to be red!"

"What flavor is that?" Johnny asked.

"Cotton Candy." she answered, putting the lollipop in his mouth.

"Hey, Johnny," said Chandler, "look at this."

"Whoa!" Johnny exclaimed, leaning over toward Chandler to look at the magazine, "I'd like to own that. It would become my new favorite bass guitar."

"Ask 'em to buy it for you. They're getting us all new equipment for the next tour. We can have anything we want." Chandler replied, "But I'm never getting rid of Lucille."

"You make it sound like Lucille is your wife." remarked Jarmila.

"Doncha know," said Johnny, leaning toward Jarmila, "all married guitarists are bigamists. Their guitars are their first spouses. Then there's the other spouse, the one usually at home."

Johnny put the lollipop back into Jarmila's mouth as he rubbed his face against hers again.

"*Seriously*!" exclaimed Jarmila, pushing him away again, "Go shave."

"Yeah Johnny," said Chandler, reaching under the collar of Johnny's t-shirt and grabbing chest hair, "you need manscape lessons."

"Get off me." Johnny said, slapping Chandler's arm.

"I'm tellin' ya, I keep it smooth down there." said Chandler, "On your wedding night, Johnny, you're gonna drop your pants and your virgin bride is going to run screaming from the room cause that big brown bush gonna pop out and she's gonna think she married Bigfoot."

"If she calls me "Bigfoot"," replied Johnny, "It won't be because of my pubic hair."

"John Michael Dunne!" exclaimed Jarmila, shocked because Johnny didn't make salacious comments.

"Did he just say that?" asked Chandler, astounded also to hear a comment like that from good Catholic boy Johnny.

"I think another bass player walked in here." Jack laughed, pretending to look around the room.

"Massage my temples, little sis?" Johnny asked Jarmila, putting his head in her lap.

"Sure big bro." she said, putting the magazine on an end table.

"Get your fuckin' dirty ass shoes away from me!" yelled Chandler, scooting closer to the arm of the couch.

"Smell them. I stepped in dog shit earlier." replied Johnny, putting one of his shoes in Chandler's face.

"Dude has double platinum albums and he's wearing 10-year-old, $1.99 shoes from the bargain bin at Target." scoffed Chandler.

"These cost $19.99 and they're from Walmart!" exclaimed Johnny.

"His momma bought them for him." said Jarmila, staring at Chandler, "They are very nice shoes."

Chandler rolled his eyes. Jolly entered the room.

"Good evening, Gentlemen," he said, taking a seat in an armchair on the opposite side of the coffee table, "great fuckin' show."

"I'm so glad you enjoyed it." said Jack, "Lenehan lives to make sure you enjoy our shows."

"I wonder why people call you an asshole." Jolly said, reaching over to take the lollipop out of Jarmila's mouth and toss it in the nearest trash can.

"I am who I am. Fuck anybody don't like it." Jack said.

"Is he okay?" asked Jolly, cocking his head toward Benny, "Does he need Narcan?"

"Nah," said Johnny, sitting up and putting his head on Jarmila's shoulder, "he's just sleeping."

"He kind of looks like a puppy dog all curled up in a chair." said Jarmila.

"Especially from this angle." Johnny said, sitting upright and moving Jarmila's head to his shoulder.

"Most definitely." agreed Jarmila, sitting upright again.

"Would anyone like to address anything from the show? Any insights? Issues? Happy thoughts?" asked Jolly.

"This venue was too fuckin' small. I don't like small fuckin' venues." complained Jack.

"The rest of the venues on this tour are bigger. I don't know how this one happened." Jolly said, "Anything else?"

"We pretty much discuss shit as we go along." said Johnny.

"Okay then," said Jolly, "meet and greet. Very few people in there. Won't take much time. Then on to Detroit tomorrow morning. 9:00am. No lateness."

Chandler, Johnny and Jack went to the door. Jolly woke up Benny who followed his bandmates as Les led them out to the meet and greet.

At the hotel, Jarmila went with Chandler. Jack had company that reminded Jolly of those Troll dolls with all the hair. Scot had picked up a girl he was previously acquainted with. Jolly had never seen Scot with anything but a full workload in front of him. It was good to see his friend enjoy himself. Jolly made sure everyone was able to access their hotel rooms, then he went to his own. He didn't need a suite like the band members. He just wanted a simple room, two beds, one for himself and one for all his equipment and work. On this night he had planned to sit back and listen to music, and maybe watch a movie or two. Detroit was pretty much taken care of, except for minor things that could be taken care of later on at the venue. He could relax, for once. Unless, of course, something went wrong. On any tour, something inevitably went wrong.

Sitting there listening to Zappa's *200 Motels*, he couldn't stop thinking of Jarmila. He hadn't known her long, but he never felt this way about a woman. She touched his heart in a way it had never been touched before. He needed to put thoughts of her out of his mind, but he couldn't. Her innocence, her boundless joy, her musical laugh. He never felt this way about any of his wives. He was not a man to jump into relationships. An early life on the road had taught him to be extremely cautious. Three divorces enhanced his mistrust. It wasn't that he was in love with Jarmila. No fuckin' way. There was no such thing as love at first sight. And Jesus, he was a 56-year-old man and she was a 22-year-old woman who sometimes acted like she was 13. He decided he was going through a mid-life crisis. Then again, it was perfectly normal for a heterosexual man in his 50's to get stiff for an attractive 22-year-old woman.

Chandler was sitting up against the headboard of the bed, naked. Jarmila was giving him head. He pulled her up by the shoulders and sat her facing him. She put a condom on his penis and guided him into her. Rolling her hips back and forth until he groaned with rapture, she then rolled off him and reached over to light a cigarette, handing it to him.

"You're the fuckin' best, Jarmila." he said.

"I'm sure you say that to every single person you're with." she answered.

"Yeah, but I only mean it when I say it to you."

"Be glad Jack is preoccupied. Or he wouldn't let me be here."

"He's such an ass lately. Or more of an asshole then is normal for him."

"It's because he doesn't like my friendship with Jolly. He acts jealous."

"But he suggested we bring him on for the next tour in August."

"Because Jolly's really good at what he does." Jarmila said.

"I'll agree with that. Damn girl, you wear me out."

"Get some sleep. Early departure tomorrow. Can I sleep next to you?"

"Positively." he said, putting out the cigarette and scooting down in the bed, holding her in his arms.

9:00am departure for Detroit meant getting everyone on the bus by 9:00am. Jolly compared it to parting the Red Sea. Or striking water from a rock. Or any of those things Biblical Moses had to put a lot of effort into doing. Maybe Moses had Extra Strength Tylenol, too.

But surprisingly, everyone, even perpetually late Jack, was on the bus at 9:00am. Jolly thought he must have fallen into a Twilight Zone episode. At any moment Rod Serling would wake him and tell him that it's past 9:00am and Benny has nodded off on heroin, Chandler is completely out of the only shampoo he will use, Jack is having a meltdown over what color Converse All Stars to wear and holding Jarmila hostage until she helps him make a decision, and Johnny would be in the back of the bus crying about missing his mom. It didn't happen that way. For once, everyone was on the bus, tired, hungry, but ready to go.

"I need something to eat, Scot." Chandler whined.

"Food is on the way." Scot answered.

"We got two dates in Detroit. Sold the fuck out," stated Jolly, "You guys are amazing. I haven't been with a band with these advantages in a long time. You are positively killing it. "Penny" went to #6, and everything else is staying the same."

"What's on the schedule for Detroit when we get there?" asked Benny.

"The first day nothing, really. A meet and greet after the show." Jolly answered, "I'll get you settled into your rooms and you can do whatever, as long as you're at soundcheck by 5:00pm. You're getting a hell of a lot of air play. Like, every other song is one of yours. And you're murdering social media. Blowing it the fuck up. The second day I've scheduled a couple radio interviews for you all, a podcast, and a meet and greet but it's another after show one. I know it's been a busy week, but you'll get a day off after the second Detroit show."

"A whole day off in Detroit!" said Jack, derisively, looking at Jarmila, "I wonder what we'll do with our day off? Hmmm…Jarmila? What do you think we'll be doing?"

Jarmila started crying and ran to the back of the bus.

"Wonder what's up with her?" Jolly asked, as he took the food from the delivery guy.

"If I knew the answer to that," said Scot, "I would write a best seller on psychology and fucking retire with my royalties."

"She's not that bad, Scot. She's a good kid." said Jolly, handing out the food.

"She's your little creamette. Follows you everywhere." joked Scot. "Where's Alice?"

"She had to go back to Milwaukee. Her uncle died." Benny answered.

"I'm sorry to hear that." Scot said.

The same sentiments were given all around.

"Is she coming back out after the funeral?" asked Chandler.

"No," answered Benny, "she's going to wait until we get to Milwaukee."

"Well, it's not far away from that gig," comforted Scot, "it's only another week."

"Yeah. But I miss her." Benny said, taking a bite into a breakfast burrito.

Jolly had a feeling Benny would spiral down while Alice was away.

"She's a very nice young lady." stated Jolly.

"I think I want to marry her." he said.

"Marriage is fun!" Chandler exclaimed, "I'd be glad to give you any advice."

"I don't think Alice would be the kind of wife who would pack a suitcase for Benny filled with condoms and dildoes for tour." Jolly laughed.

"I swear I'm on a tour with a bunch of nuns!" Chandler laughed.

"You didn't order yourself anything to eat?" Scot asked Jolly.

"I got up early and ate at the hotel breakfast buffet. Omelettes to order. Fuckin' amazing. I'm going to go see what's up with Jar. I'll take her the food she ordered."

Jolly went to the back lounge and found Jarmila in a fetal position, sobbing. He gathered her up in his arms.

"Miss Malone, what is wrong?" he asked.

"I can't talk about it." she sobbed.

"You can talk about it with me. It might help to talk."

"I can't."

"I brought you the food you ordered. Turkey club, extra bacon."

"I'm not hungry."

"Miss Malone, you are going to eat, even if it's only a couple bites. There's thick cut fries in there. You said turkey clubs with extra bacon and thick cut fries were your favorite sandwich. You can't let me down and not eat. You wanna see me cry?"

She looked up at him and gave a small smile.

"You wouldn't really cry, would you?" she asked.

"No, but I got a little smile out of you. Now here. You need to eat."

He opened the container of food. She sat up and put ketchup on the fries and ate one.

"There now," said Jolly, rubbing her shoulders, "get some food in you and you'll feel better. Did you sleep well last night?"

"Yeah. I got to stay with Chandler because Jack had a girl with him. I like sleeping next to Chandler. He always holds me in his arms. And he smells like vanilla so it puts me right to sleep." she answered.

"It's nice to have a friend who makes you feel good."

"Like you." Jarmila smiled.

"Same. I love to see you smile. Brightens my whole day. If there's anything you want to talk about, I'm here, always, okay?"

"Is it going to be a busy day for you?"

"Not too busy. It's a two-day show, so that can be a pain in the ass. But the crew left last night so they could load in early, and things seem to be running along. Now if I get there and there's an ass load of problems, my mood will probably change. But that doesn't change the fact that I am always here for you if you need me."

She put her head against his chest and said "Thank you. Can I kiss you?"

"Since we're not in a public place, yes."

He thought she'd kiss him on the cheek like she had before. Instead, she kissed him on the lips.

In the dressing room in Detroit, a half hour before soundcheck, Chandler was having a conversation about penis.

"Jarmila," he said, standing near the band's food buffet, "don't I have the biggest dick in the band?"

"Yes, Chandler," she responded, "you have the biggest dick in the band."

"No, Chandler," said Jack, "she misunderstood you. She thought you asked *who* is da biggest dick in da band. Which, of course, is you."

"Fuck you, Jack." exclaimed Chandler, "I had her last night and she sucked my cock so hard I thought my brain was going to explode. She squeezes a man when he's inside her pussy. Which you wouldn't know since the only place you'll put your dick is in her asshole."

"Fuck you and stay outta my private business. You ain't got no room to say fuck all about anal sex since you've had at least one dick up your ass in every state we've been in."

"Do you all realize you talk about Jarmila like she's not in the room?" asked Scot, "How do you feel about that Jarmila?"

"I guess I'm used to it after all these years." she responded.

"Oh shit," noted Jack, "Scottie gives a shit about Jarmila. It's da fuckin' apocalypse."

"You are such an asshole, Jack." said Scot.

Jolly walked into the dressing room. "Soundcheck time, folks."

"Jolly," said Jack, "did you know Scottie gives a shit about Jarmila?"

"No, I did not." scoffed Jolly, "But I'll make sure to note that in my big book entitled "Trivial Shit I Don't Care What Jack Connelly Says.""

"Fuck you." responded Jack.

"You have such an expanded vocabulary. It truly blows my mind." Jolly said caustically.

"I'd fire your stupid ass if I could." Jack sneered.

"But you can't. Because I made sure to put in the contract that Jack Connelly cannot fire me."

As the band went out to soundcheck, Jolly sat down next to Jarmila. He handed her a comp ticket.

"What's this for?" she asked.

"It's your own ticket so you don't have to worry you're taking up somebody else's seat. And it's in a V.I.P. box. Best seat in the house."

"You're the best, Jolly!" she said, kissing him on the cheek.

Scot watched the entire incident and shook his head.

"Going out front with me, Miss Malone, for soundcheck?" Jolly asked.

"Yes!" she cried out in excitement.

Just like a little girl, thought Jolly.

"Where are we going to sit today?" she asked Jolly.

"Well, it's a big place, I think the balcony would be good. Gives a sense of what people up there are hearing. I want everyone to be able to experience the best concert ever."

Kirk arrived with the guest lists, and the comp tickets and backstage passes envelopes. Jolly looked over the guest list, signed the last page, and sent Kirk on his way.

"Where's Chandra? Doesn't she always do box office?"

"Chandra is helping in wardrobe where a tempestuous Jack is upset because he can't find his rattlesnake skin belt. He says he's going on stage naked if he doesn't get to wear his rattlesnake skin belt. Personally, I don't care if he goes on stage naked. Would solve a lot of wardrobe issues with him. But the label would be on my ass about all the fines they would have to pay."

"A fan in Texas gave him that belt. It's very special to him."

"There has to be something Freudian in giving someone dead rattle snake skin as a gift. 'Hi, I love your music, here's some dead rattlesnake skin.'." said Jolly.

"Better than a live rattlesnake."

"True."

"Do you think they'll find the belt?"

"That's why I sent Chandra. She's already convinced him they'll find it by showtime. I swear he goes through wardrobe just to find something to complain about. I'm surprised Bella hasn't quit because of his tirades."

Bella was in charge of wardrobe. A tall African-American lady, large of size and large of voice, she did not take shit from anyone. But Jack could be quite a specimen to handle. The band took the stage for soundcheck.

"They're playing Blind Melon's "Change"!" squealed Jarmila, "That's the song that convinced them to become a band."

"How old were they then?"

"15. They're all the same age. Well, Jack will turn 24 first, his birthday is the day they play New York. Then Chandler and Benny were born in late April, just hours apart. Johnny was born the next day. But their parents didn't know each other until they all started taking them to toddler class. That's how their parents met. The guys have been friends ever since."

"Then you met them."

"I met them when I was 8 and they were 10. I met them behind Roberto Clemente High School. Kids set up temporary ramps in the courtyard and I saw them doing bike tricks. Benny offered me his bike to ride, but I didn't know how because I never owned a bike. I tried to see them whenever I could. Whenever I could get the change together to take the bus to Humboldt Park or Logan Square. There's a bike and skate park in Logan Square. They were nice to me. They are my first and only friends. Well, and now you." She put her head on his shoulder.

Keith walked up with a clipboard of papers and his cell phone out. Jolly looked through the papers and signed the last one.

"Caterer is ready for Milwaukee. I forwarded you the email." said Keith, "Scot *is not* happy about that situation."

"Fuck Scot," shouted Jolly, "I'm a week away from those shows and the guest lists already have more characters than *Gone with the Wind*. Chandler's got so many relatives I think Ireland is empty. And you know at the last minute, Jack is going to tell me to add to the guest list his cousin's best friend's ex-wife's great aunt's ex-husband's fourth wife. I need two extra hospitality rooms, and I'm not leaving crowds of people with nothing to eat and drink. Get me a coffee. Large. Jar, do you want a coffee?"

"Yes please. Small, one cream, no sugar. Thank you." she replied, "Chandler has a huge family and they love going to his shows when the shows are near or in Chicago. Benny's cousins are driving up from San Antonio, Texas to see him play. He doesn't have a lot of family in Chicago. Since his momma died, he really only has a few relatives in Chicago, and they're elderly so they don't attend his shows. He's happy his cousins are driving up. He hasn't seen them in a while. San Antonio wasn't on this tour."

"Which is exactly why I'm telling Scot we need two extra hospitality rooms. One for family and family friends, and one for the radio winners and contest winners and all the hoes that follow this band around."

"Oh! They're playing "Estranged"! This is my favorite song!" Jarmila exclaimed.

"Are you a big Guns N' Roses fan?"

"I *love* that band. But I've never seen them live. The guys don't let me go to any concerts but their own."

"I was on tour with them."

"You were their tour manager?"

"No, I was just a roadie for load in and load out."

"Was it fun? Did you meet Axl? Is he an asshole like they say he is?"

"Not really fun. Busy. I did encounter Axl on several occasions, and he is a very nice person." Jolly smiled.

"I wish I could meet him."

"The way this band is going, I wouldn't be surprised if they became the opening band for a Guns N' Roses stadium tour."

"You don't think Lenehan will be headlining stadiums next year?"

"Not next year. Maybe in a couple years. But who knows? As fast as their career is rising, I'm beginning to think they signed a deal with the Devil at a crossroads."

Keith returned with the coffees. Jarmila said thank you, but Jolly did not.

"Go to production and tell them to open the doors at the exact time the tickets say the doors will be opened." he said to Keith, "There's going to be a big crowd and I don't want to get fines because people are lined up for blocks leaving trash everywhere. Go to the stage and tell the double platinum artists to stop playing fuckin' cover tunes and do an actual soundcheck. I have a sold-out rock show to run, not a fuckin' Sweet Sixteen party."

"You're not very nice to Keith." stated Jarmila as Keith left, "You didn't even thank him for bringing you coffee."

"He's my employee. I don't have to thank him for anything. He gets a big enough salary. If he wants a thank you for coffee, he can go work at Starbucks. He can quit if he wants. What the fuck do I care? I'll hire another assistant. Besides, I don't think he'll quit. He's got the hots for Chandler."

"You're being mean. Now I see why people say you're mean."

"That hurts, Jar. I thought you believed I am a nice person."

"You are to me. But you're hell to other people. No wonder you got that reputation for scaring people."

"Are you hungry?" he asked.

"Yes."

"Let's go have dinner."

This time the crew hospitality room was crowded. Jolly got himself a plate and one for Jarmila. He still didn't trust she'd get herself anything healthy. Or that she would try and survive solely on steamed broccoli. He wanted her to expand her food horizons.

"Am I keeping you from working?" she asked Jolly.

"No. Why would you think that?"

"I feel bad about always following you around and sitting with you talking about stuff when you probably should be working."

"I'm working when I'm talking to you. I'm a great multi tasker. That's why I always have my phone, laptop or tablet with me. Sometimes all three. Sometimes I also have a two-way radio because Scot thinks we're on a 1984 Iron Maiden tour. Sometimes I'll use my blue tooth, depending on where I'm at. You should get one. Better than being wired up to that phone when you're listening to music. When we are talking, I'm doing other stuff at the same time. Except when you start with these conspiracy theories. I tune you out when you start those. Tab soft drink *was not* invented by aliens at Area 51 to control the minds of housewives in 1963. It was invented by the Coca-Cola Company as its first diet drink."

"Okay, you keep believing that. But someday the government will have to tell the truth."

"I truly love you, Jar, as a good friend." he said, shaking his head.

"I love you."

Lenehan took the stage with a song from their first album called "Suffer The Children" that started off on piano and exploded into a rowdy tune about abused children who turned the tables on their abusers. The song never made the charts, but it was a crowd pleaser at the live shows.

"Hello De-fuckin-troit! Are you ready to tear da roof offa this motherfucker?" screamed Jack.

The crowd went into a hysteria. This was going to be one of those nights where Lenehan held the crowd captive from first note until the last encore. After a full show and three encores, the band was camped out in the dressing room like they had just run a marathon. Johnny, who usually always had a bass guitar in his hands, was laying on a couch, his head and shoulders in Jarmila's lap. She was massaging his temples.

"Headache again?" Jolly asked Johnny.

"Yeah. But I think I just need to eat something." he answered.

"If it gets worse, or doesn't go away, we're going to have to get you to a doctor." Jolly said.

"Yeah. I'll let you know." responded Johnny.

"I think you should skip the meet and greet." advised Jolly.

"No," responded Johnny, "I can't let my fans down."

Chandler was sitting at the end of the same couch Johnny and Jarmila were on. Benny was crashed out on the floor, fresh needle mark in his arm. Jack was shirtless, leaning back in an arm chair, one foot up on the table in front of him, towel over his face.

Scot was sitting on another couch next to Jolly. He handed Jack a newspaper.

"They're saying you're a young W. Axl Rose." said Scot to Jack.

Jack removed the towel from his face and grabbed the newspaper from Scot.

"Fuck that shit!" he exclaimed, "I'm *nothing* like Axl. I'll *never* be that talented. That voice, those fuckin' lyrics, da poetry. Their music goes to your soul. I'll never be that talented."

"It's not such a bad person to be compared to." Jolly said, "They could have said you were like Vanilla Ice."

"There's nothing wrong with Vanilla Ice," said Johnny, "he's very talented too."

"I swear if someone compares me to Vanilla Ice, I'm quitting da fuckin' business!" yelled Jack, "I'm Jack Connelly and I'm going to be known as Jack Connelly and known by *my* talents, not compared to someone else."

"Well," said Chandler, "I'm Chandler Riley and very confident in my talents. And I'm also super fucking gorgeous. People love me and I reciprocate their love. Everyone wants to be at the center spin of my tornado."

"Oh, you're a tornado all right," said Jack, "you're a fuckin' disaster."

After the meet and greet, Chandler had hooked up with a very gorgeous guy, beautiful black skin, gorgeous brown eyes; Jack wanted to get some rest; Benny had to be helped by band security to the limo; and Jarmila asked Jack if she could stay the night with Johnny to make sure he was okay. Jack agreed she could.

"But remember, after tomorrow, what's going to happen." he sneered.

"I haven't forgotten. I was just hoping maybe you'd forgive me and change your mind." she replied.

"No." he whispered in her ear.

In the limo, Chandler handed Jolly a box of Narcan.

"You should always carry Narcan with you as long as Benny is around." he told Jolly.

"Thanks." responded Jolly, "Have you ever had to use it on him?"

"Yeah," answered Chandler, "once or twice this tour. Not since Alice came on board. Benny needs his Alice or his heroin. He can't be without at least one of those."

Back at the hotel, Jarmila sat up at the head of the bed and Johnny laid with his head and shoulders in her lap. She massaged his temples.

"Everett game me some prescription strength Ibuprofen. Do you want a couple?"

"Yeah." Johnny responded.

Jarmila reached for her purse on the side table and took out a bottle. She took out two large white pills. Grabbing the Pepsi can from the same table, she handed it to Johnny. He sat up on his elbows and took the pills, washing them down with the Pepsi. He handed the Pepsi back to Jarmila.

"Thank you." he said.

"You're welcome."

"I can tell something is on your mind." he said.

"Just worried about the day off coming up. Jack said it's still on."

"Yup."

"You can't talk him out of it?"

"Have you ever tried to talk Jack out of something he's determined to do?"

"Yeah, I guess you're right."

Johnny turned slightly to Jarmila so he could face her.

"If it was the wrong thing to do," he started, "I'd definitely step in and put my foot down. Don't know if it would help, but I'd definitely would at least try. But Jack's right. For years now we've had these rules for you. They're not tough rules to follow. Don't drink, don't do drugs, don't smoke, don't run off with strangers. For years now Jack has been smackin' your bare butt every time you break a rule, and it's not doing any good. You're still drinking and smoking and snorting coke behind our backs, and you think we don't know it. We're moving up, Jarmila. Jack doesn't have time to smack your butt several times a month because you want to act like a child. You're an adult, you know those things are dangerous."

"But they do all kinds of dangerous shit."

"I'm not talking about them. I'm talking about *you*. You betrayed the band. After all these years we've been like family, and you go and betray us. You sat at every holiday dinner me and my ma had since you were 12. And you still betrayed us, like Judas! I don't know what to think of that. I love you like a sister, and you reward me by possibly ruining everything I have dreamed of, everything I've worked so hard for. The situation is not resolved. We don't know if Jolly is going to tell the fucking media what we're doing to you. People are not going to understand we're trying our best to keep you safe. They'll see it as abuse and you know those abuse organizations will rain down hell on us. That would be the end of the band."

"But Lenehan signed him on for the next tour!"

"Who told you that?"

"I just heard it."

"He's fucking good. His reputation as best tour manager out there is right. But if he goes to the media, he's fired and we're fucked."

"I don't think he'll go to the media. He's very loyal. He told me he'd keep it between us. He's really nice and I like him a lot."

"Jarmila, Jack would lose his shit if he heard you say that. There are some lines you cannot cross. He's our employee. You can't run off and have a romantic relationship with him. It just can't happen. You spend too much time with him is the problem."

"He's interested in what I'm saying. Y'all too busy for me now."

"I'm sorry if this tour has been so crazy. It's because we've got almost an entire tour of sold-out shows. We've never had that before. And with our music going up the charts, we don't have as much free time as we did before. But that didn't mean I wasn't here for you if you needed me. You didn't have to go off and tell a stranger everything."

"I didn't want you to see my black eye. I thought you'd go after Jack and that would cause problems in the band."

"I would have confronted Jack. But you have to stop blaming yourself for fights that happen in this band. That would have been between me and Jack. It wouldn't have been your fault."

He positioned his head back in her lap and took her right hand in his left.

"I know you're sorry for what you did," he said, "but you're old enough to make better decisions. This was a bad decision. I know it's going to hurt you, bad. I hate to see you hurting. But I'm with the band on this. I think after this you won't break rules anymore. I think this will teach you a permanent lesson. I'm sorry but I can't think of any other way. My loyalty to the band is always first. I have to protect the band. We all do."

She took her hand out of his and massaged his temples until he fell asleep.

On the second day of the Detroit shows, Jolly was backstage by stacks of equipment cases. Chandra was following him, one stack of green sticky notes and one stack of blue sticky notes the size of notecards in her left hand. Keith was next to Jolly with a clipboard and a list. Everett and two roadies were standing by. Jarmila walked up, snack size bag of Flamin' Hot Cheetos in her hand.

"Whatcha doing?" she asked Jolly.

"Making load out more efficient." answered Jolly.

He would say blue, and Chandra would put a blue sticker on the case and the roadies would pull the case out to the center. This was repeated several times, blue, blue, green, blue, green, green.

"Can I watch?" Jarmila asked.

"As long as you stay out of the way." responded Jolly.

She hopped up on one of the cases that had been pulled to the center.

"Blue." continued Jolly, "Why isn't this one labeled? *Everything has to be fuckin' labeled!*"

He stopped a minute to rest his arm on a stack of cases.

"We could move those cases into the empty spaces and move these across the room with the other ones." suggested Everett.

Jolly was looking at Jarmila, her fingers covered in Cheetos dust.

"You get that shit on the equipment, and you and I are going to have a conversation." Jolly said to Jarmila.

She stared into his eyes and rubbed her fingers on her skirt.

"Okay," sternly said Jolly, "you're done." He motioned with his hand for her to hand over the Cheetos bag. She handed it over and he gave it to one of the roadies, telling him to throw it out.

"Let's go see what's on the other side." he told Everett.

"Can I go with?" Jarmila asked.

"If you stay out of the way." Jolly answered.

The second show in Detroit was much like the first. Packed house, crazy fans. Lenehan had changed the set list around because certain songs were getting more airplay than others. Music from their first album was getting heavy airplay as well. They opened the show with a medium rhythm song called "Countess", from their first album. From there they took off like a bullet train. When, in the second set, they got to "The Only Cost", this audience also sang the entire song.

""The Only Cost" is one motherfuckin' trip to the bank." Jolly said in the dressing room after the show.

"It's going to send this band into triple platinum status. People are going to want the albums to see what the other music is like." said Scot.

The band was thoroughly drained. The next day was their day off, and they were all looking forward to getting some decent rest. They were going to take care of the Jarmila situation during the day. They kept it between themselves, leaving Scot and Jolly out of it. This was between the four of them and Jarmila only. At night they planned on going to see a local band. The drummer was said to be the reincarnation of Keith Moon. He was that good. The singer was said to sound somewhere between Jim Morrison and David Bowie. If they were good enough, Lenehan would start pitching them to the label to add that band as a permanent opening band for the next tour.

Scot's friend in Lansing knew of an excellent club in Detroit that had V.I.P. rooms, frequent famous guests, and a reputation for privacy. Scot, Jolly and Everett decided that is where they would go on their night off. Nights off for managers weren't a frequent occurrence. The three of them were going to make the most of it.

When Jack and Jarmila entered his hotel room, he saw the armless wooden chair he ordered from concierge was where he told them to put it, right in the middle of the living room part of the suite. That was a perk of being a rock star; you could order anything and nobody asked questions.

"Take your clothes off and sit in that chair." Jack commanded Jarmila.

"Are you going to punish me now?" she asked.

"No, I'm going to make you sit in that chair until I wake up and me and da guys are ready to punish you."

"You're making me sit in a chair for the rest of the night and most of tomorrow?"

"That's what I said."

"Do I have to take off all my clothes? Can I leave my socks on? My feet get cold."

He agreed she could leave her socks on. She took off her dark green dress, took off her dark green bra, and slid off her black lace panties. She took off her heels, but left her pink fuzzy socks on.

"Sit in da chair." Jack commanded her.

She sat in the chair. He went to a side table and picked up a paddle. He put it in her lap. It was 14 inches long, oblong, with tiny holes drilled into it. She started to cry.

"Stop fuckin' crying. You're going to sit here and think about what you did. I'm going to bed." said Jack.

He turned off the lights and walked towards the bedroom side of the suite.

"You're going to leave me in the dark? You know I don't like the dark or to be left alone!" she cried.

"Should have fuckin' thought of that before you opened your stupid mouth." Jack snapped, turning around, "Now I'm going to get a good night's sleep."

He walked into the bedroom and slammed the door.

Jarmila cried most of the night off and on. Sometimes she'd fall into a quick sleep, then startle awake again to find she was still sitting naked, holding a paddle in her lap. She started crying again, scared of the pain she was anticipating experiencing. Maybe the guys were only trying to scare her. Scare her enough she'd never break a rule again. Johnny was right. The band was going places. They didn't have time for her anymore.

She fell back asleep, and was startled awake by Jack roughly grabbing her forearm. She could see from the small ray of light coming through the curtains that it was daylight. But she had no sense of what time it was. The whole band was standing around her.

"Jesus, Jack," exclaimed Johnny, "at least put some clothes on her!" Johnny had never seen her naked.

"You're going to see her naked ass anyway." responded Jack, "Go to fuckin' confession later if you need to clear your conscious."

Jack let go of her forearm while Benny took off his shirt and put it on Jarmila. She was shaking. Jack grabbed her forearm again, so tightly she yelped. He took the paddle out of her lap and pushed her toward the bedroom. In the bedroom, Chandler moved the table away from the window to the middle of the room. The table was square, which pleased Jack, or he'd have had to contact concierge to send one. A square table was much better than a round table, in case he had to tie Jarmila's legs to the table legs. He wanted her to stay still while he punished her.

"Can I say something?" Jarmila asked, while she and Jack were standing in front of the table.

"No matter what you say," answered Jack, "this is still going to happen."

"I just want to know how many times you're going to hit me." she said.

"20. Chandler talked me down from 25. If it had been solely up to me, I'd of gone for 50. Because I'm sick of your stupid shit. You need to permanently shut down your stupid shit." Jack answered, "Bend over da table."

She obeyed, tears already falling from her eyes. Johnny held her arms down.

"I'm sorry." he said.

"I understand." she whimpered.

Jack put the paddle against her bare bottom.

"This is how it's going to happen from now on. No more of this bullshit bare hand on bare ass shit. It's been years now and it's never worked. You're still breaking da rules. Now da punishments are going to get harder, until you stop doing stupid shit for good. I don't have time for your stupid shit anymore. You're a fuckin' adult. Stop acting like a kid. I know I said I'd never hit you again out of anger, but you have me fuckin' super angry. My whole career could be gone because you can't follow a simple fuckin' rule. I'm angry and you're going to feel how angry I am."

Jarmila started begging and pleading, saying over and over again how sorry she was, and she promised she'd never do anything like that again, and please don't punish her like this. Tears rolled down her cheeks. Jack pushed up the shirt Benny had given her to wear.

Benny stepped forward. "This might sound weird. But shouldn't we gag her to stop her from screaming? If she screams a lot, somebody is going to call the police. This would be hard to explain."

"I've got gags in my room," Chandler said, "but, Jack, don't you have a bandana?"

"They're in my tour bag on the luggage rack." Jack answered.

Chandler went to the luggage rack and took out a black bandana from the tour bag. He twisted it and tried to put it in Jarmila's mouth, but she refused to open her mouth. Jack raised the paddle and came down on Jarmila's bottom, with a hard thwacking sound. When she cried out, Chandler put the bandana in her mouth and tied it to the back of her head.

"Swift." said Benny.

"Practice." responded Chandler.

Jack hit her four more times. Her muffled cries could be heard through the gag. Benny stepped forward towards Jack and put his hand out.

"This involves the whole band." he said, "The burden shouldn't only be on you."

Jack handed Benny the paddle. Being a drummer, Benny had a lot of strength in his arms. He beat Jarmila with five resounding smacks. She raised her legs up and down and twisted the middle part of her body. Benny handed the paddle to Chandler, and Jack pushed her down to the table, pressing on the middle of her back with his hands to keep her from moving. This would go a lot faster, he thought, if she wasn't moving.

"If you move your legs again," Jack threatened, "I'll tie them to da table."

Johnny, with tears in his eyes, told her to cooperate so this would go faster and be over with. She shook her head back and forth in a no, and pleaded as best she could under the gag. Chandler had a lot of experience with various spanking implements. And he had plenty of experience being spanked. He knew exactly what hurt the most from any implement. He was as angry at Jarmila as Jack was. He had trusted this girl all these years and she betrayed them in the worst possible way. He took his time smacking her bottom, making sure each of the five smacks were as hard as he could make them be. Her muffled cries became more frequent and she tried to twist away from Johnny's grip on her arms.

Benny, Chandler and Jack looked at Johnny. Johnny considered Jarmila his sister. Where would his loyalty take him? To his sister's side, or to the band's? He nodded to Chandler, who gave him the paddle, and Chandler took over his place holding down her arms. She had cried so much the tears had soaked the bandana in her mouth and formed a pool of water on the table underneath her chin.

"I'm sorry I have to do this," Johnny said to Jarmila as he stood behind her, paddle raised, "but you betrayed me. I'm disowning you as my sister."

Jarmila began sobbing. The physical pain would never be as bad as the emotional pain of losing any of the only friends she had ever known. But losing Johnny as a brother broke her heart. She loved him most of all of anyone in the band. Johnny hit her hard. Of all the guys, he hit her the hardest. All five swats make an echoing sound in the room. She had hurt him the most. He wanted her to feel the pain he was feeling.

When they were done, Jack untied the gag from Jarmila and told her to stay bent over the table. The band went to the living room part of the suite and made plans as to when to meet up to go see the local band. Chandler said the band had invited them to a pre-show dinner, and then an afterparty.

"We're fuckin' rock stars, being treated like fuckin' rock stars." said Chandler.

Johnny didn't like the fact they were all acting like this was a normal day. They just beat their best friend, and he disowned her as a sister. But what the hell, all the guys could talk about was being treated like rock stars. His soul was torn. He had to go with them because they were going as a band.

Benny, Chandler and Johnny left after deciding they would meet up in an hour in the lobby. Jack returned to the bedroom.

"Can I get up now?" Jarmila asked in a whimper.

"No. I'm not done with you yet." answered Jack.

He unzipped his pants and put the tip of his penis to her anus.

"Please no, Jack, please no!" she pleaded, "I hurt so much now. Please, no more pain!"

"You know this is a part of your punishment."

He sodomized her brutally. He held on to the back of her neck and said if she made a sound, he'd hurt her even more. After he came inside her, he took a good look at her bottom.

"Nice and dark red, getting purple." he sneered, "Your ass looks good in those colors."

He took a shower and got dressed for the evening. As he left, he told Jarmila she better still be over that table when he got back.

Scot was already on a couch in a V.I.P. room at the club his Lansing friend had recommended. He had his arm around a well-built blonde woman. Next to her was Everett, lips locked to a woman with skin the color of obsidian and long curly hair, the curls in long loose definition. Next to Everett were two other women. One was big hipped and thin waisted, breasts pressing against a simple strapless black mid-length dress. Her skin was the color of a mocha candy bar and her straight brunette hair fell below her shoulders. The woman next to her was a small, thin, pale skinned redhead wearing a pale green dress, and dark green thigh high fishnet stockings. These girls were dressed to party.

On the table in front of them was an unopened bottle of El Jolgorio Mezcal Tobaziche, two bottles of Moet & Chandon MCIII, one opened and one unopened, and lots of various glassware. This club was a private club, known to celebrities as a place you could do most anything. You had to know somebody who knew somebody who knew somebody to get in. Jolly walked in and sat between the brunette and the redhead.

"Jolly, this is Katie," Scot said, pointing to the blonde next to him, "and that's Damini," he said, pointing to the girl Everett was with, "and that's Abelia," he said, pointing to the mocha candy girl on Jolly's left, "and that's Bernice." he said, pointing to the woman on Jolly's right side.

"Bernice. That's an old-fashioned name. Are you an old-fashioned girl?" asked Jolly.

The woman laughed and took a sip of champagne. These girls were young, thought Jolly, but legally old enough to drink. That was old enough for him. Everett put a foil packet on the table and opened it. Several pills were in the foil. Jolly took one and placed it on his tongue and transferred it to Bernice's tongue. He then took another pill, put it on his tongue and transferred it to Abelia's tongue. Scot took out a medium size plastic baggie full of cocaine. Everett put some on a small handheld mirror and cut several lines. Scot did a couple lines, offered some to Katie. Katie did a line, and handed the mirror to Everett. Everett returned the mirror to the table and Damini did a line. Everett took a long drink of champagne and did a line. He then put more cocaine on the mirror and cut more lines. He pushed the mirror closer to Jolly's side of the table. Jolly offered Bernice a line, and Abelia followed. Then Jolly did a couple lines himself.

"Isn't anybody gonna open that Mezcal?" he asked.

He filled up Bernice and Abelia's glasses with more champagne, and opened the bottle of El Jolgorio. Pouring himself a tumbler, he took a long sip. The three managers needed this night, and they were already loosening up. But never could music business people be in the same room and not gossip about something related to the industry.

"Dude, I am telling you, that band Snake uses auto-tune." said Jolly.

"Who names their band Snake?" asked Everett quizzically.

"A band who thinks they're better than Lenehan." Jolly responded, "Dude, they fuckin' auto-tune their live fuckin' shows."

"No fuckin' way!" exclaimed Everett.

"I'm fuckin' *serious*. Gable used to be their sound engineer until he signed on with Lenehan. He told me they use auto-tune for everything because that fuckin' asshole lead singer *can't fuckin' sing*." emphasized Jolly.

Abelia was rubbing Jolly's thigh, reaching higher and higher. He kissed her, then poured himself more El Jolgorio.

"Their manager called me wanting to pitch Snake as an opener for the next tour." Scot said.

"You should tell them we already have a Partridge Family cover band booked." laughed Everett, taking out a small plastic baggie of marijuana and rolling several joints. He put the joints on the table.

"Don't give Scot ideas," said Jolly, picking up a joint, "he will seriously go and fuckin' tell them that."

Bernice was kissing Jolly's neck as he lit the joint. He took a long drag of the joint and shotgunned it into Abelia's mouth.

"You like that Abelia?" he asked. She nodded yes. "What other things do you like?" he asked her. She whispered in his ear. "Ah nice," he said, "very nice."

He had a sudden thought of Jarmila, that she was too young for him. These girls were about the same age. But hell, even at 56, he deserved to have fun. No reason to sit around watching reruns of Jerry Springer, waiting for the nursing home to have an open room. Damn, he thought, here he was in a V.I.P. room with two beautiful girls, expensive drugs, expensive liquors, with two of his very good friends, on a rare night off, and all he could think of was Jarmila. He hadn't seen her since the concert the night before. Jack probably had her tied up in a closet.

"Who is going to be the opening band for the next tour?" asked Jolly, "Please don't tell me local bands from whatever city we're in."

"We're looking at some bands. The boys are out tonight checking on a local band that's supposed to be extraordinary. Rumors are drummer sounds like the reincarnation of Keith Moon." said Scot, "And hey, what is this 'whatever city *we're* in' shit. Is this a hint you've made your decision about joining the next tour?"

Jolly did another line of cocaine. "Well, I haven't signed any contracts yet."

"You should think of signing as soon as they come through. Otherwise, management may pick someone else." stated Scot.

"This band's getting a whole new management team, that I know *for sure*." Jolly responded. "And fuck me, they'll sign me on at the last day if I hold out. I'm just that fuckin' good."

"Okay," said Scot, "now you sound like Chandler."

"That boy." Jolly shook his head, "But there's nothing wrong with confidence in oneself. Even if he's talking about his butthole."

"Which is the cleanest butthole." laughed Scot.

"Goddamn if I ever get interviewed about being Lenehan's tour manager, I'll be sure to mention I signed on to this tour because I heard the guitarist has the cleanest butthole."

"Ah damn," laughed Scot, "We're all going to hell!"

"I'm going to lose my job." Everett said.

"No. Pretty much everyone on tour now will stay the same. It's the higher ups behind the desks that are going to be new. This management company does not release the budget correctly. The band has this big budget and shitty equipment. The label is not going to have much choice: new management team or the band will shop different labels." said Scot.

"Hardcore!" exclaimed Everett.

Everett did another line of cocaine, put a pill on his tongue, and stood up, holding Damini's hand.

"I'm off to one of those infamous private rooms this club has." he said, and he and Damini walked out of the room.

Abelia was hands up on Jolly. Bernice was putting her tongue in his ear.

"Well," Jolly said to Scot, "time for me and my company to head to the hotel."

He high fived Scot's hand and left the club with Abelia and Bernice.

Week Three, Fargo-St. Paul-Milwaukee

Fargo, North Dakota was over 13 hours from Detroit. This required an early travel day, as the next two days after that were sold-out shows in Fargo. The band had never played Fargo. Jack, with an ice pack on his head, leaning against the back of the lounge seat on the bus, started complaining.

"I hate these fuckin' insanely long bus trips. Why can't we get a private jet?" he asked Jolly, who was seated next to him, in his usual seat.

"Did you morph into Jay-Z?" Jolly asked sarcastically. "When you give me an album that sells 10 million copies, then you can have your own plane."

"Fuck me, why are you so happy in da morning?" Jack asked Jolly.

"Tequila Sunrise. Hair Of The Dog always works. Did you have a rough night, Jack?"

"I had a fangirl night." he smiled.

"Personally," said Scot, "I like Bloody Mary's for Hair Of The Dog. It's got V-8 in it so you know it's a healthy hangover drink."

"By any chance do you know where Jarmila is? And Benny, and Chandler?" Jolly asked Jack. He knew where Johnny was, because Johnny was sitting next to Scot.

"She was in my room but I sent her off with Benny when I got back to da hotel last night." said Jack, "They should be here on da bus. Jarmila said she was tired and was going to lay down in a bunk, and Benny's in a bunk riding da heroin highway to hell. Chandler is on his way. He had to blow dry his hair first."

Chandler stepped up into the bus right as Jack finished his sentence.

"Aw shit!" he exclaimed as he pointed to Jolly, "There's the lover boy now. Old boy got himself up to some sumthin' sumthin' last night. Was in the parking lot early this morning kissing a brunette and a redhead good bye."

"Doesn't anyone on this tour have any privacy?" asked Jolly.

"Not when you're kissing two girls in a parking lot." laughed Jack, "Which one did you kiss goodbye first? Da brunette or da redhead?"

"The brunette." answered Jolly.

"Awwwww!" exclaimed Jack and Chandler simultaneously as they threw their hands in the air.

"Doncha know ya gotta kiss goodbye da redhead first?" Jack asked, "Otherwise you get bad luck."

"What if there's no redhead to kiss goodbye?" asked Jolly.

"Then you shit outta luck!" laughed Jack.

Jolly shook his head and sighed as the bus took off.

"How come you don't have a hangover?" Jack asked Chandler.

"Cause I'm still *fucked up*." he answered.

"Jolly and Scot say they drink alcohol in da morning to stop a hangover." stated Jack.

"Fuck me!" exclaimed Chandler, "Jolly been too busy being all up in some girl's sumthin' sumthin to even notice he has a hangover."

"You all just need to leave me alone." joked Jolly, smiling.

"Don't worry Jolly", said Jack, looking concerned at Jolly, "for your next birthday we'll get you Viagra!" He started laughing.

"You're so not funny." responded Jolly, "How was that band you saw last night?"

"Fuckin' a-maz-ing!" declared Chandler, sitting down next to Johnny.

"The drummer is like God of Thunder. Seriously dude, fucking astounding. They're really a good band. I'd like them to be our permanent opener for the next tour." said Johnny.

"I second that." stated Chandler.

"I'm on board, and I know Benny is too. If he wasn't faithful to Alice, I swear he woulda fucked that drummer last night. He woulda totally turned bi. It was a complete drummer lovefest." Jack said, "Scottie, you gotta get this band on tour with us."

"I'll talk to their manager. But first I need to see them play and someone from the label needs to see them play." responded Scot.

"You will fall in love." said Chandler, "Well, not as much as you love us, but close."

"I'll never love anyone as much as you, Chandler." quipped Scot.

"I know," said Chandler, "because I'm so fuckin' talented. Every time you go to that good ole ATM and put money in, you're like 'Damn, that Chandler is talented.' They should put my face on the hundred-dollar bill."

"Chandler," said Jolly, "do you ever come down from the clouds?"

"Why should I?" answered Chandler, "I'm too fuckin' gorgeous to hang around with mere mortals."

"I'm taking Xanax and getting sleep." said Jack.

"How much Xanax you got?" asked Johnny.

"Enough to share if you want some." answered Jack.

"You got one of those headaches again, Johnny?" Jolly asked.

"Yeah." Johnny answered.

"You want some Extra Strength Tylenol? Might be better for a headache than Xanax."

"Yeah sure, thanks." Johnny responded.

"I'll take some Xanax." said Chandler, "I need seriously uninterrupted sleep."

Jack gave Chandler 2 two milligram Xanax and Jolly gave Johnny an Extra Strength Tylenol.

"Johnny, we have a two-day run in Fargo. If your headache doesn't get better, I'm taking you to a doctor there."

All three band members went to the bunks to get some sleep.

"I'm going to the back of the bus." said Jolly to Scot, "I have to make some phone calls and I don't want to disturb anyone's sleep."

"Cool. I think I'm going to try and catch a nap." Scot said.

Jolly made himself comfortable in the back of the bus. He made a few phone calls, then tried to get some sleep. He had to admit he wasn't 20 anymore, and having two girls in one night wore him out. But damn, he thought, it was fun. Jarmila woke him up, sneezing. She was wearing a flouncy blue plaid skirt that looked like a schoolgirl uniform, a tan men's button-down shirt, and black La Perla heels. That girl, thought Jolly, must have a suitcase full of nothing but sexy heels.

"You coming down with a cold, Miss Malone?"

"No. Allergies." she answered, "I always get allergies at this time. Did I wake you up? I'm sorry, I'll go back to my bunk. I was just looking for Kleenex."

"No, it's okay. I need to wake up anyway. I was just taking an old man nap." he smiled.

"You are not an old man." Jarmila said, sneezing again.

"There's Kleenex by the shelf by the TV. By the way, where were you yesterday? I missed having you as my not-exactly-an-assistant assistant."

Jarmila was too short to reach the Kleenex box without standing on tiptoe. When she stood up on tiptoe to reach the Kleenex, her skirt went up. Underneath the skirt she had on a sheer pair of pink panties, and underneath that were deep red, purple and blue bruises.

"Jar, come here." said Jolly.

She moved toward him.

"Turn around." he commanded as he pulled up her skirt and pulled down her panties.

She reached around with her free hand.

"Hey!" she exclaimed, "Boundaries, remember?"

"Do you want to talk about that?" he said as he pulled her panties up and her skirt down.

"I do but I don't want to get in any more trouble."

"What exactly did you do this time for Jack to beat you hard? *Again*."

"Do I still have your confidence?"

"Miss Malone, I have told you that you will *always* have my confidence, and I do not go back on my word."

"Okay, but I think you're going to get mad."

"I may get mad but it won't be at you, and I promise you nothing will happen if I get angry."

"It wasn't just Jack. It was the whole band. Even Johnny. They all took turns at me with a paddle that had holes in it. It felt like bee stings. Johnny says he's disowned me as a sister."

"People say all kinds of things when they're upset. I wouldn't get too worried about that. Johnny will probably get over it in a few days and you'll be back to being his little sis again. But it does blow my mind that he'd *ever* take a hand to you. Do you feel comfortable enough to tell me what happened?"

"This is the part I think you're going to get mad at me about."

"Come here." he said to her as he pulled her closer to him. She was standing between his legs. He took her hands in his, "Look at me, Jar. Look at my face so I know you understand what I'm going to say. No matter what you did, even if I got angry with you, it wouldn't last long.

In these past couple weeks, you've driven me over the hedge a few times. Like when you smeared Cheetos dust on your clothes while looking *directly* into my eyes. You can be such a brat. But I never stay mad at you for long. Please, if you want to tell me something, tell me. It will make you feel better to talk about it. Don't I always say that to you?"

"Yes."

"Do you believe me when I say it?"

"Yes."

"Okay. I'm here for you. Everyone is asleep. We have some privacy now to talk about anything you want to talk about."

"Okay. I want to talk to you about what happened."

"I suppose you can't sit down?"

"No."

"I'll get you some ice from the mini fridge. Lay down."

Jolly went to the mini fridge and took out the small ice tray from the freezer. He searched the cabinets for a large sandwich bag. Upon finding one, he filled it with ice. He sat next to Jarmila and put the ice bag over her skirt.

"I don't really feel any relief." she said, "can you put it under my skirt?"

"That won't be too cold for you?"

"My ass is on fire. I won't mind the cold."

"When I write my memoirs, I am definitely including how part of my tour manager duties was putting ice on a pretty girl's ass."

"You make me laugh."

"Good."

"Here's what happened. Remember the first night I came to your room? And you asked me all those questions and you figured out it was Jack who beat me? Even though I didn't tell you? Well, the band says they don't trust you and you could sell the story to magazines and go public with what happened. Then that would be the end of the band. They all had a meeting with me and said Jack wasn't going to spank me with his hand anymore for breaking rules. Instead from now on they're going to beat my butt really hard with a paddle until I learn to follow rules and shut the fuck up. They said they are too busy now to constantly keep me in line. They said I'm an adult and they aren't going to waste time on something that doesn't work. From now on it'll be 20 swats of the paddle if I break a rule. But I don't think I'll break any more of the rules. This hurt really bad. Worse pain ever. And it was humiliating. Johnny had never seen me naked. It was embarrassing for me."

"I'm so sorry this happened to you, Jar. I had no idea this was going on. I knew some things, but not everything. Like I have said before, I try to stay out of a band's private business. I'm having trouble making sense that they trust me enough to want me to tour with them again, but they don't trust me with you. I would *never* sell a scandal to a magazine or go public with something that is a band's private business. It would be the end of my career. I know you agree to the things the band tells you to do, but I don't think you actually want them to do those things to you. What they are doing to you is not right. You're an adult. Shit, if you were their kid, Social Services would have taken you out of the home. Do you feel trapped, Jar? Like if you don't stay with the band, you have no place to go?"

"I don't have any place to go. I don't have my own place to stay. I take turns staying with the guys. I don't even have my own money unless one of the guys gives me money. I mean, all I have to do is ask, but I don't have a job or anything like that. I don't earn the money they give me."

Jolly moved to the floor by Jarmila's head.

"Listen to me, Jar. Look me in the face so I know you understand, okay? I have a three bedroom house. I'm rarely home so I hired a housekeeper to come in and dust and make the place look like someone is there, so I don't get robbed while I'm gone. If you want the abuse to stop, because that's what they're doing to you, abusing you, then I'll give you keys to my house and I'll make sure you get there safely. You can stay as long as you like. You can fuckin' move in if you want. I will never ask for anything in return. I want you to be safe. You are not safe staying with these guys, although I know you consider them life-long friends."

"They'd seriously fire you and not ask you out on the next tour if you helped me leave this tour and let me stay at your house."

"I don't give a shit! I've got a fat retirement account just sitting in the bank waiting for me. I was thinking of saying yes to the next tour because it's hard to get the road out of your system. But I'd be perfectly happy staying at home and making grilled steak and hamburgers and taking you to the casinos. Have you ever been to a casino, Jar?"

"No."

"These guys keep you way too isolated. I know they mean well. There's some crazy danger out there for young people. But these things they do to you, the rules, the punishments, it's not right, Jar." he stood up and took the ice pack from her bottom, "This is melting. Do you want me to see if there's more ice? There's probably some in the fridge in the front of the bus."

"No, I think I'm okay. The pain isn't so bad. I think I can sit up if I sit on the edge of the seat."

Jolly put the ice pack on the table and helped her sit up. He sat next to her.

"You let me know, Jar. Whatever you want to do, I've got you. Don't think you're trapped here. There are options. I'm very fond of you, Miss Malone. You are melting my infamous ice-cold heart."

"I like you a lot too." she said, kissing him on the lips. She moved to sit on his lap, "I had a dream about you, and a fantasy."

"Oh yeah," he said, "are you going to tell me about them?"

"Well, the dream I will. Dreams aren't ever what they are about, it's always something else and the dream is just a representation. I don't mind telling you."

He put his arms around her waist.

"Ok, so this was the dream. I feel kind of stupid telling you." she said.

"Why?" he asked.

"It was a stupid dream. Anyway, we were laying on some grass, and it was sunshiny, and I was wearing one of your shirts because my belly had gotten too big from our babies I was carrying. Twins. A girl and a boy. Jarmila and William. And I was wearing blue jeans shorts but had to unbutton the top button because of my big belly. You lifted my shirt and ran your hand down my belly and the babies kicked and we were happy and then I woke up because I was sneezing."

"Damn allergies." Jolly smiled, "Now tell me about this fantasy. You know fantasies are usually what you really want to do with a person."

"Too embarrassing."

"There is nothing you should be embarrassed about that you want to tell me."

"I'll tell you, but you have to let me kiss you first."

"Okay. *One* kiss."

She kissed him on the lips, long and slow. Then kissed him again. And again.

"Miss Malone, that was three kisses."

"I swear it was one long kiss divided up into three sections."

"You owe me two extra fantasies. Now tell me about this one. I'm intrigued."

"I feel super embarrassed."

"Don't. There's not a lot you can tell me I haven't already seen or heard about before. Unless it's about Chandler. That boy is a whole new category of super freak."

"Ok. But you won't laugh?"

"No."

"Ok. I was over your knees, and you had my skirt pulled up and my panties down. You were massaging my butt and telling me I would never get hit again. The you put your hand in front and me made me have an orgasm. I've never had one of those before, so I'm not sure the fantasy is right about what they're like in real life."

"You've *never* had an orgasm?"

"Never. But I don't really like sex. It's not very much fun."

"That's because you've never had sex with someone you deeply care about, or who deeply cares about you. It would not only be fun for you it would be an experience like you've never had before. It can get even better if you're with the right person." Jolly started massaging her left butt cheek over her panties.

He moved to kiss her, long and deep. He pulled the legs of her panties to the middle, and massaged both butt cheeks. She made little whimpering sounds and squirmed on his lap.

"I'm sorry, does it still hurt you?" he asked.

"A little, but it's okay. I feel funny. Like an electric charge going up my belly."

Jolly put his other hand in front, and went under her panties to rub her clit. Gently at first, and as she moved, he went faster, until she put her head on his chest and made little gasps, and then sat still.

"Wow. Wow. I don't know what to say. It was…indescribable. Like my whole insides were electrified, but in a good way. I know you might have crossed a boundary, but I won't tell anyone.

"Jar, I have crossed several boundaries and am now miles away."

Eight hours into the trip and they stopped at a truck stop. Jolly explained to Jarmila they were switching drivers, because the company only allowed a driver to drive so long before taking a break. She said she knew about that from the previous tour. He'd be back, Jolly told her, on the departure from Fargo to St. Paul. She was happy. The driver was very nice to her and often brought her a coffee when he got one for himself.

There was a diner at the truck stop, and Jolly suggested everyone get something to eat. Johnny said he didn't feel like going into a diner, his head hurt him too much. Jarmila asked what he wanted and offered to bring it to him. She then sat next to Jolly with Scot on the other side of the table. Scot's opinion was that she was way to glued to Jolly's side.

"Don't you want to go sit with the band?" he asked her.

"No. It's quieter over here." she answered.

"I think it would be better if you sat with the band. They're you're friends." said Scot.

Jolly looked up from the menu at Scot.

"I'm not hungry," said Jarmila, "I'm going back to the bus. When you're done, bring Johnny a corned beef on rye. He don't want no chips or fries, just the sandwich and a grape pop."

She got up and left the diner, heading to the far side of the outside of the bus so she could smoke a cigarette without getting caught. No cigarettes for her were a band rule.

Back in the diner, Jolly and Scot gave their food orders to the waitress.

"Why do you have to be like that with her? She wasn't doing anything wrong. You are rude to her for no reason. What the fuck did she do to you? Sacrifice your first born to Satan?" asked Jolly to Scot.

"She's annoying, and the band could concentrate more on their music if they didn't have so much invested in her."

"They seem to be doing fine."

"*You've* got too much invested in that girl."

"Are you saying I'm not putting 100% into my job? This tour was shit when I joined. I turned that round. See how well they're doing now? Or, did you suddenly get early onset dementia?"

"Jolly, she's nothing but trouble. I've known her two years and she's nothing but a trainwreck. I warned you not to get caught up in her shit."

"I'm perfectly capable of handling my own personal shit. I don't need your help Scot." he motioned for the waitress, "Can you make mine a to go order? And also add to the bill a corned beef on rye, no fries, and a grape pop. Thank you."

"You don't have to be like this Jolly. I'm just looking out for a friend."

"And so am I." Jolly moved to the counter to wait on his food. When it arrived, he returned to the bus.

Chandler had gone looking for a cigarette. He didn't want to have to go back on the bus and come back out again in the cold. He saw smoke coming from the other side of the bus and thought Johnny must be up smoking a cig. He'd get one from him. Instead, he found Jarmila.

"Ummmhummmm." he said, holding his fingers out for the cigarette, "You know you're not supposed to be smoking. Sometimes I think you like to get your ass beat. Maybe you like the attention."

"Fuck you." she said, handing him the remains of the cigarette.

"You know what this means. I have the option to be the one punishing you."

"Have you seen my ass Chandler? It's still black and blue from the last beating. Just fuck it and get it over with."

"There's other options. You could go back to Chicago."

"And stay where? Jack, Benny and Johnny won't have me in their houses now. Am I supposed to live in your garage?"

"Better than living on the street."

"Just get it over with already. I'm sick of it all."

"Then stop acting like a child." stated Chandler.

"Just tell me when and where and I'll be there to 'get what I deserve'."

"There's another option." said Chandler.

"What, I size code your dildoes?"

"You're so mouthy lately. You used to be so compliant and non-complaining. I think Jolly has fucked you up."

"Yeah, blame the new guy. Don't blame it all on how y'all treat me like I'm a convenient blow-up doll when you can't find someone else to fuck. We used to have conversations and laugh and make fun of other bands. We used to argue old school politics and Chicago corruption. We used to go to the zoos and museums and the lake and the parks. We used to *have fun.*"

"Jarmila, I'm sorry we don't have as much time anymore. This tour is crazy insane. I'm lucky to get a couple hours sleep."

"Maybe *you* should think of priorities, what outside the band is most important to *you*. 24 Hour Party People are going to be in Fargo. They're planning to party in Jack's room."

"Oh shit, "said Chandler, "I didn't know that. I've been off social media all day so I could catch up on sleep. It's weird they're coming to Fargo. It's our first time playing there."

24 Hour Party People was an unofficial Lenehan fan club named in honor of the movie of the same name that honors Tony Wilson who founded the Factory Records label and The Hacienda Club. He brought punk music to the forefront and changed the music scene forever.

The group, consisting of 10 to 30 handpicked hardcore partiers, were known for their non-stop partying, imbibing of club drugs like mollies and mescaline, cocaine, heroin, marijuana, lots of liquor, and sex orgies that would make a Roman at a Bacchanalia blush.

Jarmila did not like to be around them. Under the watchful eye of the band, she was unable to imbibe on anything, so what was the point of being there.

"What's this fuckin' alternative you keep talking about so I can get it over with and go back to being nothing to you."

"You're everything to me! You're my special girl! Here's what I'll do. When we get to the hotel in Fargo, you give me head. I'll invite Jack too. You let us do what we want to you, and you'll be free from a paddling. Okay? Agreed?"

"Only if I can go back to Jolly when you're done with me."

"Yes, you can go back to your boyfriend."

"He's not my boyfriend."

"Seems like he is. He's always looking at you like a hungry jackal waiting for the lions to finish eating their kill so he can have the bones."

"He was just in Detroit with two girls in case you forgot. What with you spying in the parking lot."

"I wasn't spying. Dude was in plain sight in the daylight!"

"He's not my boyfriend. Now can we go back on the bus, it's cold out here."

"Yes, but do you agree to my terms."

"Yes, but will Jack agree to them?"

"Yeah, he'll be in a partying mood."

The bus arrived in Fargo, North Dakota at 9:15pm and by 10:30pm, twenty-eight members of the 24 Hour Party People unofficial Lenehan fan club were in Jack's suite doing what they do best: partying. In Chandler's suite, Chandler was completely naked, sitting on the sofa, Jarmila between his legs giving him head. He loved the way she gave head. Like it was the only thing in the world that she had as her responsibility. She was totally into it, and that got him hard. A knock on the door interrupted the sex act.

"It's Jack." said Chandler, "Let him in."

Jarmila stood up. She was wearing a red spandex dress with spaghettis straps. Underneath she had on a matching red silk bra and red silk panties. She wore a red garter belt with red garters to hold up her sheer red stockings. On her feet were her favorite pair of red Louboutins.

"I want your love, I don't wanna be friends" he sang the Lady GaGa "Bad Romance" lyrics to Jarmila as he walked by her, "What da fuck, Jarmila. You auditioning for da Handmaid's Tale? All dressed in red." he laughed as he sat in a chair next to the couch.

He was wearing no shirt and tight blue denims that hugged his long skinny legs. He was carrying a small zip lock baggie of cocaine. He put all of it on the table top and cut two big lines. He snorted one line. Chandler did the other.

"Ah shit," said Jack, "not as good as Indy."

"Who brought it?" asked Chandler.

"Da fat girl that organizes these 24 Hour Party People trips."

"Ah I'd fuck that bitch all down the highway. Ain't nothing like a thick girl make a man go boom, baby, boom!" laughed Chandler.

"She wouldn't fuck you. She's all up on Benny's jock."

"Why Fargo? Why not Milwaukee or Chicago? They should have come out to the St. Louis show early in the tour."

"Or da Cali shows. I think Scot told them Chicago and Milwaukee are not good places for them to party cause of all our families out for da shows."

"Gotta be choir boys with the families around."

"All I know is, Fargo gonna be on *fire*. Bitches brought peyote and salvia."

"Isn't salvia just a sage plant?" asked Jarmila.

"Shut da fuck up, nobody asked you. What da fuck you standing there for? Get on all four on da couch."

Chandler moved to lay down on the couch and Jarmila got on all fours facing him. She started to give him head again.

"Whoa, whoa," he said, lifting her face, "Jack you gotta use lube. I don't want my dick bitten off."

"Where da fuck is it?" Jack asked.

"In the bathroom." Chandler answered.

He went to the bathroom and returned with it, pulled down Jarmila's panties, pushed up her dress, and applied it to her. She flinched when his finger went in her anus. He unzipped his pants and pushed himself inside her and she cried out. Then Chandler guided her mouth to his penis. After a little while Jack said, "Switch with me Chandler."

Chandler got off the couch and switched with Jack. Jack positioned Jarmila so her breasts would rub against his penis. After they both came, they let Jarmila sit up. Jack returned to the chair, his penis still hanging out of his pants. Chandler picked up various clothing items and started to dress.

"You're not going to wear a shirt?" Chandler asked Jack.

"I lost my shirt somewhere between Glenda and Gabriela." he laughed as he lit a cigarette, "I figure I'll be butt naked in an hour, so what's da point of putting on another shirt?"

"Any pretty boys over there?"

"I think you're shit outta luck dude. These dudes seem to be boyfriends of some of da girls that came up for da show. But hell, I've been around you so long my gaydar is offline."

"Maybe one of them will be curious."

"I've seen you in action. You're like fuckin' Eros. People want to fuck you, Chandler. Jarmila, why da fuck are you still here?" he sneered at Jarmila.

She pulled up her panties and pulled down her dress.

"I just wanted to get my purse. It's under the table by the chair you're in."

"Well then fuckin' get it and get da fuck outta here. Isn't your little friend waiting for you?"

She moved to grab her purse. Jack viciously grabbed her arm and pulled her over his lap. He pulled down her panties and pushed up her dress.

"Jack, Chandler said I could go as soon as you did what you wanted to me. He said you were in on the deal." she cried.

"Well fuck me, Jarmila, maybe he betrayed you." said Jack, as he and Chandler started laughing, "How does that feel, bitch?"

"Let me go, Jack, I did what you wanted!"

"Did you make a deal with her, Chandler?"

"I don't recall", said Chandler, "I think I said after we did what we wanted to her, we wouldn't paddle her."

"But shit," said Jack, "We could cane her, strap her, fuck do all kinds of things to her. And fuck her up da ass again."

"Sounds like a plan to me. That's some tight ass right there." said Chandler.

"Are you seriously telling me, Chandler, that until today you've never been up her ass?" Jack laughed.

"Let me go!" yelled Jarmila.

Jack took the lit cigarette and put it close to the bare skin of her bottom. She could feel the intense heat and her skin was starting to get very hot. She didn't want to move for fear the cigarette would touch her.

"Hey, ya know we have a rule in this band for you, about not smoking?" asked Jack.

"Yes." replied Jarmila.

"But Chandler says he caught you smoking out by da bus. Maybe I need to put this cigarette out on your ass to remind you you're not allowed to smoke." He moved the cigarette closer. Her skin was getting redder.

She cried. Tears came down her face and dripped onto Jack's jeans. He put the cigarette in an empty beer bottle on the table. He put a hand on her bare bottom.

"You can go to your little friend," he said to her, "but just remember who you belong to."

He pushed her off of him. She straightened her clothes and grabbed her purse, running from the suite.

Jarmila stood outside Jolly's hotel room and texted him. She knew his phone was on. As a tour manager, he had to be available for emergencies 24/7. Jolly opened the door. He was wearing a brown sleep shirt, brown sleep pants and a tan robe.

"I woke you up, didn't I?" asked Jarmila.

"I don't mind, baby. What's up?"

"Can I stay with you tonight? Jack has the 24 Hour Party People in his room. Chandler and Benny are with him. Johnny fell asleep again with one of his migraines."

"Always consider this your room, too. You can be my roomie. Did I give you the spare key card?"

"No."

"Remind me to give it to you."

"Okay, I'll "remind" you to "give it to me." she laughed.

"I'm going to "remind" you that I can still stand you in a corner for being a brat."

Jolly took off his robe and returned to his bed.

"Can I take a shower here?" she asked.

"Absolutely."

"Fuck I forgot my bags in Chandler's room!" she exclaimed as she took off her dress. Standing only in bra, garter belt, panties, stockings and heels, Jolly instantly got hard.

"Do you want me to get them for you?" asked Jolly.

Jolly had spare key cards to all the band's rooms, in case of emergencies, and to wake people up for departures, soundchecks, interviews, etc. The job should have fallen to Scot, because Scot's the band's manager. But Jolly didn't mind.

"Can I use one of your shirts? I'll wash it tomorrow and give it back to you before the show."

"Don't worry about that." he said, dismissing the idea with his hand, "My shirts are in the big brown suitcase. Pick any you want. There's some sleep shorts in there too, but I think they'll be too big for you, even with a drawstring."

"That's okay. I'll just wear the shirt. Can I use your shampoo and body wash? I don't like the hotel bath stuff."

"Absolutely."

She took off the rest of her clothes and put them in a neat pile on the spare bed. She put her heels by the night table.

"Are you having laundry sent out tomorrow?" she asked.

"Yes."

"Can I include my dress and stuff?"

"Absolutely."

"You're a man of few words tonight. Did I say or do something wrong?"

"No, sugar. I have a pretty girl standing before me completely naked. I have more thoughts than words." he smiled.

"I'm sorry," she said, realizing Jolly wasn't used to seeing her like that, "I'm used to Jack, Chandler and Benny. They don't even notice anymore. I'm going to go take a shower now."

Jolly watched her cute little perky bottom bounce to the bathroom. He thought, God, she has such a nice little ass. She was so skinny, but had a perfectly round ass. But she still had bruises, and that made him feel like he had a knife in the gut.

She came out of the bathroom 25 minutes later, hair wrapped in one towel, body in another. She took off the towel around her hair and rubbed her hair vigorously. Then she took off her body towel and bent over to rummage through one of Jolly's suitcases for a shirt. Jolly looked on.

"Why are you looking at me like that?" she asked him, standing up.

"Because I'm a healthy heterosexual man who's getting a nice view of a beautiful woman's body."

She quickly slipped on a shirt. She was so skinny the shirt almost reached her knees.

"You know that's my favorite Anthrax shirt?" he asked her.

"Do you want me to take it off and get a different one?"

"No. I would have to take a very cold shower if you did."

"I'm keeping you up."

"You most *certainly* are."

"I meant I'm keeping you *awake*."

"I know what you meant. I was being my usual sarcastic self." he smiled.

"Oh shit, my brush is at Chandler's too."

"I have a brush and a comb in a small leather case by the coffeemaker. You can borrow them. Bring them over here. Sit by me. Have you ever had your hair braided?"

"No." she said.

Jolly sat up in bed as she brought the comb and brush to him. He patted the space between his legs. She sat down and leaned a bit forward so he could brush the back of her hair first.

"You know how to braid hair?" she asked.

"Yes." he said as he finished brushing the back and brushed the rest of her hair.

"Who taught you? Willie Nelson?"

"No." he smiled.

"Snoop Dogg?"

"No." he chuckled.

"Stevie Nicks?"

"I don't know Stevie Nicks!" he laughed, "But if I did and she wanted to teach me to braid hair, I wouldn't turn her down!"

"I wouldn't either."

"I though you weren't into women?" Jolly inquired.

"Yeah, but Stevie Nicks…who'd turn her down?"

"My sister taught me to braid hair. She was a time saver, like me. Big multi-tasker. I'd braid her hair while she put on her make-up."

"Is she younger or older?"

"Younger. So is my brother."

"Are they in the music business?"

"No. My sister used to be an RN, but she quit after having her first baby. Her husband owns this huge consulting firm, so she's a happy homemaker. She still volunteers at a free clinic three days a week for the poor, underinsured, uninsured, homeless, undocumented, etc."

"How many kids does she have?"

"She has three. Two girls and a boy. Girls are 12 and 14, boy is 15. My brother has two boys, twins, 18, start college in the fall."

"What does he do for a living?"

"He's a corporate lawyer. For a multi-million-dollar corporation." he said, putting the brush on the side table and grabbing the comb, "Now what kind of braids do you want? Two on the side or two on the side and a long braid in back?"

"I want two braids on the side. But can you put them under my ears and attach them to the back of my hair?"

"Absolutely. Very early Queen Victoria."

"You know about Queen Victoria?"

"Yes."

"I wish I could have lived in her time."

"Why?" Jolly asked, combing sections in her hair.

"Life seemed less complicated. Women had roles they understood and knew. I feel like the wind just takes me where ever. I never get to land and *be* somebody. Like, today Chandler caught me smoking out by the bus. He said he had the option to paddle me for breaking the rules. But he gave me some alternatives. I could go back to Chicago, or I could do whatever he and Jack wanted and then I could go to your room."

Jolly turned her face toward him.

"The band is giving you an option to leave the tour. This is a good thing, Jar."

"I'd have to stay in Chandler's garage because nobody else in the band will let me stay with them. They say they can't trust me anymore. And I think it would cause too many problems if I stayed with you."

Jolly put her face forward and starting braiding one side of her hair.

"Jar, go get the hair ties. They're in the same case as the comb and brush were in. And see if there's a barrette in there or bobby pins."

"You use barrettes?"

"They're extras for Chandler. It's kind of like when people have kids and they have to carry all this extra shit, just in case shit. I have to carry all this just in case extra shit."

She got the hair ties and two barrettes, then returned to sitting between Jolly's legs. Jolly finished braiding her hair and putting the two braids where she requested them. He fastened each braid to the back of her hair with the barrettes.

"Now, go put all this stuff back, and grab a handheld mirror from that case. You can look at the back of your hair in the dressing mirror." Jolly said.

She hopped out of the bed like a kid hearing the ice cream truck coming down the street. She was such a child at heart, Jolly thought. Jarmila looked at her braids then turned around and positioned the handheld mirror so she could see the back. She put the mirror on the dressing table and jumped back into bed next to him, giving him a quick kiss on the lips.

"I love it!" she exclaimed, "There's cocaine residue on the mirror."

"Yes."

"Why does everybody get to do cocaine but me? I get caught doing cocaine, I'm in trouble."

"Addiction runs deep in your family, Jar. The band is only trying to protect you. People with addictions that run in the family can get addicted to shit faster and then not know when to stop. They're more likely to overdose. Does addiction run in Benny's family?"

"Not that I know of. His momma would have a beer after work. Just one. Said it helped her sleep. I don't think he knew his dad. He never talks about him. I know his momma was from

San Antonio, Texas and moved to Chicago when she was pregnant with Benny. Of everyone in the band, Benny is the most reclusive, and the most private about his family."

"Interesting. Jar, do you do cocaine? Since I've been here, have you done any? There's a lot of coke floating around this band. Some drug dealer must be sending his kids to Stanford on the coke revenue from this tour."

She looked at him with a sad face.

"I know that face, Jar. I'll know if you're lying to me."

"I don't want to be punished by the band. They didn't catch me doing cocaine these last few times. I think tonight I should have taken the paddling for smoking a cigarette, because what they did hurt way more." she said, "Yeah, I've been doing cocaine once in a while. And I've been doing some since you got here. I try to sneak around by waiting while the band is onstage. Then I go to the ladies' room. The band is always too into themselves after a show to notice my eyes. Or that I'm high. Chandler says I'm naturally kin…kin…"

"Kinetic."

"Ki-neh…eh…"

"Jar, look at me. Look at my face. Kinetic. Ki-net-ic. Kinetic."

"Ki…net…ic. Kinetic!"

"There you go! "

"Chandler says I'm naturally kinetic. I'm full of energy. That's why I think they don't notice the coke has got me going fast."

"How often are you doing it?"

"I've only done it twice since you've been here. About six times this tour. Please don't tell the band!"

Jolly looked at her sternly.

"Of course, I'm not going to tell the band." he said, "But you have to promise me you won't do any more cocaine. And I want you to give me any that you have left."

"You're mad at me."

"I'm not as angry as I am disappointed and concerned. I don't want anything unpleasant to happen to you. I don't want to lose a good friend to drugs. I've lost quite a few."

"You promised you'd never hit me."

"I always keep my promises. To the best of my ability. That doesn't mean that I don't have thoughts of giving you a sound spanking if I thought it would work. But I think positive reinforcement is better than negative for you. Otherwise, the first time Jack whipped your ass you would have never broken a rule again. Maybe I'll get some Flamin' Hot Cheetos and for every day you stay away from drugs I'll give you a bag. Or some Vitner's Hot Corn Chips."

She playfully slapped him on his shoulder.

"Are you doing any other illegal drugs, Jar?" he said as he grabbed her hands.

"No. I don't really like marijuana. Though people tell me edibles are cool. I don't like the way it makes me feel. Like in slow motion. I don't trust shit like heroin. And I'm not sure what those opioid pills do to people. I *never* want to do anything that would make me hallucinate. I saw this old video from like the 70's where this girl takes LSD and she puts her baby in the oven and forgets about it. Another girl took LSD and went through the glass doors of her balcony and jumped off because she thought she could fly."

"Those are from old high school films they used to show in Health Class to scare people from doing drugs. They had some for alcohol, too. Those are called "Exploitation Films". Have you ever seen the movie "Reefer Madness"?"

"No."

"I'll find it and download it to your phone. It is so fuckin' hilarious. It wasn't meant to be when it was released 1936. But it's funny now. It's a cult classic."

"Like the silent 1922 version of "Nosferatu"?"

"I freakin' *love* that movie!" exclaimed Jolly.

"It's my favorite. The cinematography is amazing."

"You and I should watch it together when you come over for bar-b-que." Jolly said as he pulled her body close to his, "Though it is a really sexual film, without any sex in it. Bram Stoker's book "Dracula" was like that. It's full of sex masked in a horror novel. Those Victorians were so sexually repressed they had to get it out in the most creative ways."

He was sitting with one knee up and the other down. Jarmila put her head on his shoulder, and started massaging his crotch over his sleep pants. He pulled her hand away.

"We need to talk about what happened on the bus on the way here." he said.

"Okay," responded Jarmila, "But let me give you head first. Why waste a hard-on? Besides, I want to see if I do it with you, I'll like it. Because I like you, and you said if I like someone, that might make me like sex better."

"Jar, no. I want to be with you *so* bad I can't even put it into words. It's not only my body responding to a hot 22-year-old. It's deeper. It's weird! It's weird for me to feel this way. I didn't feel this way about my ex-wives, and two of them I dated for months before I married them. I've never felt this way. I haven't known you but for a short time but I feel like I've known you my entire life. I know that sounds cliché, and a line, but it's the honest truth, Miss Malone. You make me feel 26 instead of 56."

"Then what's the problem?"

"You're the band's girl. In *any* situation I would not cross the line of messing with a band's girl. Even if she was just a guest. It's an unspoken rule on the road; you don't mess with a band's girl."

"But you gave me my first orgasm."

"That doesn't mean we can be in a serious relationship. Sex, friendship and love are three different things that don't have to rely on each other. Shit, I disliked my 2nd wife, biggest cunt ever. But I loved having sex with her. Damn, it was good. But I wasn't in love with her. By the end of our marriage, I hated the bitch so much I'd only talk to her through my lawyer."

"You didn't like touching me?"

"Jar, I fuckin' loved touching you. I was so fuckin' hard I wanted to lay you down and fuck you until you were happy. I wanted to let you know how it felt when someone who likes you has sex with you. Someone who doesn't just think of themselves but wants to make you happy, too. But I can't be with you, sugar. With your relationship with the band, it's complicated, and I don't like complicated."

Jarmila sat straight up. Moved slightly away from Jolly.

"You don't want to be with me because of what Jack and Chandler did to me tonight."

He pulled her close to him. Stroked the outside of her arm.

"That's not true, baby. They raped you. That's not punishment. That's fuckin' *sick*. They have this complete control over you. Mostly Jack. And I think you're used to it, and you're such a lonely person, you let them do that. You're afraid to lose them as friends. But Jar, there are other people out there who would love to be friends with someone as sweet and honest as you. For example, Everett thinks you're very nice. He doesn't interact with you much because employees on a Lenehan tour can be fired for socializing with you. The band keeps you from the experience of making new friends, all under the excuse of protecting you. I understand why they feel the need to protect you. You can be naïve. That can be dangerous, especially on the road. But the way they handle it, it's not right. True friends don't abuse friends. True friends don't rape friends."

She started crying, great sobs that shook her skinny frame.

"Oh sugar," said Jolly, holding her tighter, "I know this is confusing for you. I wish I could wave a magic wand and make it all go away. Lay in the grass with you and sunshine on us. But It's never going to happen."

"Because I won't stop being friends with the band?"

"Jar, I'd *never* make a person decide between me and someone else. I'm not like that. They've been your friends for years. You've only known me for a short time! But I'd worry about how Jack would react if we started a serious relationship."

"You're worried he'd fire you."

"Fuck that! I don't give a shit! He can't fire me anyway, it's in my contract. He could put pressure on the label to get them to put pressure on me to resign. But I don't give a fuck! I'd leave the tour right now if I thought you'd be safe. I'm afraid Jack with have a meltdown and hurt you. It breaks my heart to see you hurt."

"You're worried about your reputation. You've said that before."

"I've thought about what I said to you before. I am not worried about my reputation. If I was "encouraged" to resign, the band won't say why. Because they know I'll tell the fuckin' world everything they did to you. It's not about that. It's that you're the band's girl. Would you leave them all for me? Because I couldn't have a serious relationship with anyone who was having a serious relationship with anyone else. I wouldn't care if you stayed friends with them. But could you do that without any sexual contact with them? I'm not by nature a jealous person. But I can't be thinking every night 'Is my woman having sex with the drummer or the guitarist tonight?' I couldn't deal with that. I want you to myself. I want every inch of you to myself."

Jolly kissed her, deeply, lasting.

"I love you." whispered Jarmila.

"I...I really like you. I wish I could say 'love'. I don't know what this feeling is. I'm too damn old and jaded to not understand what is going on with my emotions. But I feel like my heart gets bigger every time I think of you."

"You should get some sleep." she said, kissing him.

"You are always looking out for everybody else's well-being. You have a beautiful soul, Miss Malone."

She laid on her side facing toward the other bed, and he spooned her. His hand fell on her hip. She moved it to her bottom. He cupped it gently. He buried his face in her neck. Her hair smelled like his shampoo, instead of its usual blackberry lemonade scent. Her skin smelled like his body wash, instead of its usual scent of bergamot and cloves. He went hard again, and she backed her body up so his erection was against her back.

"Is that the TV remote or are you happy to see me?"

"Keep being bratty, Miss Malone. That corner over there has your name on it."

"Would you put me in it naked? And stand behind me, naked?"

"Is this fantasy #2 you owe me?"

"Tomorrow. I'm too sleepy now." she adjusted her body so it pressed harder against his erection.

Jolly reached over and turned off the bedside table lamp, then positioned himself against her again.

"Jolly?" she asked, quietly.

"Yes, sugar?"

"I'm scared of the dark. Can you open the curtains and let the moonlight in?"

"Of course, darlin'."

He got out of bed on his side and opened the curtains to the North Dakota moonlight. Then he returned to bed and his position against Jarmila's back.

"Thank you."

"Welcome."

"Jolly?"

"Yes, honey?"

"Do you think you could get me a bottle of water? I'm thirsty."

"Sure thing."

Jolly got out of bed and went to the mini-fridge and retrieved a bottle of water. He handed it to Jarmila.

"Is there anything else you'd like before I get into bed again? Iron your dress? Paint your toenails? Write to a long-lost cousin?"

"While you're on a roll you could solve global warming."

"Miss Malone, sometimes I think you are trying to take away my Crown of Sarcasm." Jolly grinned as he returned to bed, and his position again against Jarmila's back.

Jolly kissed her goodnight and once again buried his face in her neck. What was happening could either turn out to be really, really, really bad, or really, really, really good. But he had to make a decision. There was no leaving it up in the air.

He fell asleep to the rhythm of Jarmila's breathing.

Sometime while the North Dakota moonlight was shining through the windows, he woke up thinking he was having a pleasant dream about getting head. When he was a little more awake, he realized he *was* getting head, from Jarmila. She had pulled his sleep pants down a bit, and was sucking his balls very gently.

"Oh, okay, Jar," he said, "this…this cannot be happening. I have a good memory. I know we talked about this."

She popped her head up.

"Don't you like it?" she said.

"Yes, very much! But it can't…"

Jolly couldn't finish his sentence because Jarmila shoved his entire cock down her throat. She was sucking and licking at the same time. He thought, how does she do that? And then he thought, this is all a dream. I'm going to wake up alone, Jarmila will come to him later with tears in her eyes and fresh bruises on her ass, Jack will continue to be an asshole, and he will count down the days left until the tour is over and he can go back to retirement and mowing his lawn and losing money in the poker rooms at the casino and watching paint dry.

But it wasn't a dream. He felt Jarmila, soft and wet and tight, felt deep inside her, saw that she had moved on top of him. She was riding him up and down. The feeling was like nothing he had ever experienced. Even his second wife was not this good. Not even those two girls he had in Detroit. And they were about the same age as Jarmila.

She took off the Anthrax shirt she had borrowed from Jolly and he put his hands on her small, soft breasts. He liked breasts like this. Natural. He was not a man into surgically enhanced anything on a woman. He liked women natural. But for pubic hair. He didn't give a damn either way. Jarmila was completely bare. A fleeting thought that maybe he should look her ID up in the band's files crossed his mind. But she was of age. She was just so skinny she didn't look 22, and so naïve she didn't act like a 22-year-old. He had thought that since the first time he met her.

She leaned over him and whispered in his ear, "Fantasy #2 was that as I was standing naked in the corner, you were naked behind me and rubbed my butt until I came."

He wanted to explode right there in her. It was getting painful to try and stop it. He slowed down her rhythm and placed his hands on her bottom. He massaged it hard, not thinking at first that she was still bruised there. But she didn't flinch or cry in pain or move away, so he continued. He wanted her to come at the same time he did. This was his one solid thought. He wanted her, for once, to know the pleasure of sex with someone who wanted her to be satisfied too.

And when it happened, he felt the room shatter into multiple colors, and heard an animalistic cry coming from Jarmila. She slowly slid off of him and back to her side of the bed. He quickly turned to his side and cuddled against her.

"I love you." she said as they both fell asleep.

They woke at the same time. It was still dark out, but you could see dawn on its way.

"Is that Jack singing?" asked Jarmila.

"Yes. In the hallway. "Bad Romance". Lady Gaga."

She started to get out of bed at the same time he did.

"No, sugar. It's my job to corral the wild mustangs." he kissed her, "You go back to sleep."

He put on his robe and his Nike shoes and went to the door. In the hallway he found Jack, Chandler, three women, one a big blonde, one a skinny redhead and one of medium height and medium build with neon pink hair, and a tall, well-built muscular black man. Only the big blonde woman and the black man had clothes on. The blonde woman was wearing blue jean shorts and an orange bikini top, and the black man had on a leopard print speedo. The entire entourage was doing some dance that looked like they were trying to imitate Lady Gaga for a TikTok video.

"I'm a free bitch, baby!" yelled Chandler, swinging his hips.

Jack sang:

"I want your love, and I want your revenge

I want your love, I don't wanna to friends

J'veux ton amour, et je veux ta revanche

J'veux ton amour, et je veux ta revanche

I don't wanna be friends

I don't wanna be friends!"

He started his weird TikTok Lady Gaga bad imitation dance, and his entourage joined in. Jolly had a thought that either he had taken a time machine back to Studio 54 in 1977, or Andy Warhol was still alive and making a film in the hallway about Lenehan, or he had accidentally taken some terribly bad acid.

"You speak beautiful French, Jack." said Jolly, "But do you know it's after 5:30 in the morning? Some people want to sleep. They don't want to hear someone covering Lady Gaga songs at 5:30 in the morning. Especially from a group of naked people high on illegal substances. Take your party back to your room."

"You should hear my fuckin' Spanish!" Jack slurred.

"This is my friend Paulo." said Chandler, putting his arm around the tall black man, "He's from Brazil. He's going to teach me Portuguese."

"Absolutely thrilling!" exclaimed Jolly, "You'll be a multi-lingual band. But right now, you need to go back to your room. Or rooms. Or wherever the spaceship dropped you off. But you cannot stay in this hallway naked."

"But I got a nice cock." declared Chandler.

"I'm sure it's a very nice cock." said Jolly, "But I am not going to go looking at your cock to have a discourse on its merits. This is a hotel filled with families who do not want to see your cock, whether it is a nice cock or not. *Now go back to your rooms!*"

Scot popped his head out his hotel room door.

"Oh shit." he said, and went to retrieve his phone to call band security.

Les showed up within minutes of Scot's phone call. With him were three other band security guards who escorted the entourage back to Jack's room.

"Why was there not security where this party is at?" asked Jolly, "exactly how many rooms are they partying in?"

"One. Jack's." answered Les, "I am not sure where my guys are. I had Fred watching Benny and had Alejandro on the door, and Trent was running for things like pop and mixers, more liquor, etc. No one, guests or band in that room should have been able to leave unless they were leaving for good. I'll find out and let you know ASAP."

"Let Scot know. I'm going back to sleep for a couple more hours." said Jolly, angrily.

Jolly returned to his room to find Jarmila softly breathing, sleeping soundly. He slowly crawled in next to her, falling asleep to the rhythm of her breaths.

At 7:30am, fully dressed, he kissed her gently. She woke slightly, sleep in her voice.

"Where are you going?" she asked when she noticed he was dressed and gathering his things.

"I'm going to the venue." he answered.

"This early?"

"Yes, sugar. I have to make sure load in and set up is going well, and I have some business to take care of. And I want to grab a to-go breakfast sandwich and a coffee so I won't be so cranky."

"I'll get dressed and come with."

"No, honey. You stay here and get some sleep. Let's plan a late lunch. In our usual spot in a hospitality room. Does that sound okay?"

"2 o'clock won't be too late? I don't want to ruin your dinner hour."

"2 is fine darlin'. I'll be hungry again by dinner time, don't worry about that." he kissed her deeply, "You are amazing Miss Malone."

"Jolly, can you do something before you leave?"

"Absolutely."

"Can you bring my bags from Chandler's so I don't have to go knocking on his door?"

"Already done. They're by the luggage rack."

"Thank you. I love you." she said, falling right back to sleep.

"I love you too, Jarmila Malone."

But she was sound asleep and did not hear him.

By 2:00pm Jolly and Everett were working on an amp onstage. Scot stood by, sipping on a coffee. Jarmila walked on the stage.

"Oh shit," said Jolly, "I'm supposed to have lunch with you."

"It's okay if you're busy. I understand. I'll go get something to eat from the dressing room."

"Thanks." responded Jolly.

Everett popped up from behind the amp.

"Shit, Everett, you scared me," said Jarmila, "I didn't know you were behind there! Whatcha doing?"

Everett was in his late 40's, tall and lanky with straight blonde hair that stopped at the base of his neck.

"I'm working. You know, what people do, to earn money. Instead of waiting around for people to give it to them." He turned to Jolly and Scot, "I don't know. I don't think it can be fixed. We can just move another one here. Chandler won't be happy, but not a lot of options."

"Chandler is going to lose his shit." said Scot.

"I have a question." said Jarmila.

"The anticipation." sneered Scot.

"I was wondering if it was right for a man to put his mouth on a woman's vagina." Jarmila stated.

Scot choked on his coffee, Jolly put his hands over his eyes and Everett laughed.

"Well," said Everett, "I've been married 20 years so I must be doing it right. But Jolly here, he's been divorced 3 times so I don't think he's doing it right at all. Scot's only been married and divorced once. Maybe he has time to get it right."

"That's not what I meant!" yelled Jarmila, "I meant is it *okay* for a guy to do that."

"Jarmila," said Scot, "don't you have anything else do to? Lick some Dum Dums, or lick the band's balls."

"Fuck you Scot, and fuck you Jolly and fuck you Everett!" she screamed.

"I didn't say anything to get an outburst like that." Everett stated.

"Jar, apologize to Everett." Jolly demanded.

"No! Fuck him and fuck you!"

"Okay Jar, you can go to the dressing room." said Jolly, "And when you get there, you can stand in a corner. If anyone asks you why you are standing in the corner, you can tell them I said because you're a mouthy little brat who acts like a child, and will be treated like a child. Bye!"

Jarmila stomped off to the dressing room.

When she got there, Benny was sitting on the floor puking into a plastic trash can. Johnny was on the far side of the room, playing his bass guitar with his headphones on. Jack was sitting on one side of the couch, feet up on a coffee table in front of him. Chandler was seated on the other end of the couch, reading a graphic comic book. Jarmila bounced into the room. She first went to Johnny to ask him how his headaches were. He responded that Scot was taking him to a doctor the next morning, and he was going to have some tests run. She gave him a hug and told him everything would be all right.

"Will you pray for me?" he asked her.

"Of course, I will." she assured, and gave him a hug.

"Come over here, Jarmila." demanded Jack. He put his feet on the floor as she came over to him.

"Yes?" she asked.

"Sit in my lap." he said, taking a long hit from a purple marijuana pipe.

"You know they're going to say you can't smoke that in here." she told him as she sat on his lap.

"It's medical marijuana. I need it for my anxiety. I have a medical marijuana card. I mean, it's not technically mine but I am in possession of one."

"You're so crazy Jack Connelly."

"You love me anyway, right?" he said, leaning down to kiss her.

"I'll always love you. What happened this morning? I heard you singing in the hallway and rumor has it you were naked, dancing and singing to "Bad Romance" with your naked friends."

"That's what I've been told. But I'm a little hazy with da memories."

"It's those 24 Hour Party People. They keep you up in all sorts of drugs. How long are they staying?"

"Through St. Paul. Scot says no way does he wants them at any of our shows where we have family. I get it. With family we have to be on our best behavior. But it sucks. But they'll be in New York for my birthday. Why don't you join us tonight?"

"No way! I don't like all that chaos."

"Chandler," said Jarmila, "Do you have any Dum Dums?"

Chandler handed her an unopened one. She threw the paper on the floor and put it in her mouth. Jolly walked into the dressing room.

"Did I tell you to stand in the corner?" he addressed Jarmila.

"Go stand in da corner." commanded Jack.

"He can suck my dick." answered Jarmila.

"Did he tell you to stand in da corner?" Jack asked Jarmila.

"Yes." she said quietly.

"Then go stand in da fuckin' corner!"

She offered Jack the lollipop.

"What kind is it?" he asked, putting it in his mouth.

"Butterscotch." Jarmila said, as she stomped off to a corner of the dressing room, "Y'all treat me like a 9-year-old."

"You're acting like a 9-year-old." Jolly stated, cringing at the sight of Jarmila sharing a lollipop with Jack.

He explained to Chandler about the amp. Ever the perfectionist, Chandler had to go see for himself

Jolly gave Jack a shot of vodka.

"Hair Of The Dog." he said, "What's wrong with Benny?"

"Hmm." Jack pondered, "Could be the mescaline, or the salvia, or the peyote, or the PCP, or a combination, mixed in with lots of premium alcohol. It's not heroin. He did his last hit of that at midnight. I think."

"Maybe he needs heroin." said Jolly, "Maybe his body is going through withdrawals. Keith, I'm texting you a number right now. Woman's name is Constance. Works for a production company here in Fargo. I met her a long time ago on a Whitesnake tour. Lovely woman. Would have married her if she hadn't already been married. Great pussy though. Anyway, tell her who you are and that I'm requesting some way to get methadone in the next hour. Her brother is a nurse and might have some resources. If we can't get any, we might have to resort to heroin, and thinking about that gives me a headache."

Jolly got an alert on his phone. He went to the corner and grabbed Jarmila by the hand.

"I thought I had to stay in the corner?" she smirked.

"I don't trust any of these fools to keep you there. You're coming to the office with me and you can stand in the corner there."

"Whatever."

"Keep up that attitude, Miss Malone." Jolly said, "Watch what I do."

"I don't know what I did to deserve being treated like this!"

"You fuckin' ripped on Everett for no reason and you refuse to apologize."

"You're not treating me like an adult."

"You're not acting like an adult."

They entered the tour office. Scot was there with his assistant Shera, a lawyer from the record label, a paralegal from the record label, a representative from Lenehan's management team, Les, Les' brother-in-law who owned the security company, and the security company's lawyer.

Jolly sat next to Scot and leaned in, voice low.

"You give me total horse shit about having an extra hospitality room for family coming to the Milwaukee shows, but you give about three dozen drugged out people their own hospitality room."

"They're 24 Hour Party People." Scot said, "They're an exclusive, unofficial Lenehan fan club. They're very important because over half of them are social media influencers. Besides, they buy their own food, drugs and liquor."

"They're entirely drugged out of their skulls. And they are not the greatest influencers on our boys. Benny is *bad off*. Lenehan has never played this city before. They need to be on top of their game."

"They're young, they'll be fine. Besides, you know once they hit that stage, it's like they have a transformation. What's the annoying AF doing here, and why is she standing in the corner?"

"She's learning to be an adult. And I don't trust anyone else to follow through on that."

Jack and Chandler entered the room and sat down.

"Why do we gotta be here? Why not da rest of da band? We're *a band*. Band business involves da whole band." complained Jack.

"Three of Les' security guards had to go to the emergency room last night because of Ketamine poisoning. Someone put ketamine in their drinks, enough to have them lose conscious." said Scot, "Would any of you two like to own up to this?"

"Shit," said Jack, "there were like over 30 people in that room. Could have been anyone."

"Really?" asked Scot, "Okay Jack, you want to play it that way. But I see it as a person who did not want to be restricted to the room. A person who wanted to get a group of people to run the halls naked and sing Lady Gaga songs. A person who should have his name legally changed to Mayhem. Now, the label is going to take care of all their expenses. It's going to be discussed how pricey this latest escapade of yours is going to cost. Guess who will eventually pay that back? You and Chandler!"

"Why me?" yelled Chandler, "I didn't do anything. And you can't prove Jack did either!"

"Bullshit." said Scot, turning his tablet toward Chandler and Jack and clicking a link. There on Instagram was Jack, talking right into the phone camera about putting ketamine in the security guards' drinks, enough to "knock them out" so "we could go rule da world!" And there was Chandler putting ketamine in a juice drink and handing it to Fred, Benny's handler, "If Benny had died because no one was keeping a watch on him, how would you feel, Chandler?"

No answer from Chandler. Lots of figures were written on paper, one was agreed upon, all medical fees would be paid, there'd be nice compensation, and their jobs were still here if they wanted them. An apology from Jack and Chandler to the label, Les and his employees, Les' brother-in-law's security company, and Lenehan's management company, and people seemed satisfied, if still not angry at the incident. It was the latest escapade among the many Lenehan escapades that cost the label, and eventually the band, money.

Jolly grabbed Jarmila's hand and exited the tour office.

"Let's go eat." he said.

"Oh, so I'm outta the corner now?" she said sarcastically.

Jolly stopped and turned to face her.

"Seriously Jar, I'm having a super stressful day, and I don't need your attitude to compound it. Let's just have a nice meal together, okay?"

The crew hospitality room was slightly crowded. This venue was bigger, had a bigger crew and staff. Jolly was able to find a table in the back that was empty.

"Are you trying to hide me?" asked Jarmila.

"Why would I do that?" asked Jolly.

"Because Chandler calls me your girlfriend and Jack calls me your little friend."

"Since when?"

"Since before I stayed last night with you. Right after they took turns sticking their penises up my butt."

"I think they like to be mean to you, to hurt you. To keep you in line, because you are doing something without their permission. You have made a new friend. Truth be told, after this morning's incident, Jack needs his ass whooped."

"I'd pay to see that!" Jarmila exclaimed.

"Honey, I'd give you the paddle." They both laughed.

"Sugar," said Jolly, "I went back here so we could have some privacy. I want to talk to you about a few things on my mind, and I don't want to wait until after the show."

"Must be serious. I can sleep in Johnny's room tonight. Don't worry, I understand. I'm used to being fucked and kicked out."

"Miss Malone, I would never kick you out. I'm not that type of person. I want to talk about sex."

"Yes!" exclaimed Jarmila, "Especially about those nice balls of yours. I could suck those all day."

"Wonderful. Get me hard and go on with your day while I have a whole night of running a show with a case of blue balls."

"Well, you said you wanted to talk about sex."

"I'm serious, Jar."

"I'm listening."

"We did an incredibly reckless thing last night. Aside from the complications I have just entangled myself in. We had sex and we didn't use protection. I gave you a lecture about condoms, then went against my own advice. I want to apologize. Unprotected sex is very dangerous."

"It's okay, you don't have to worry. Chandler always wears a condom. Well, except when he was butt fucking me but that was the first time he ever did that. Jack never wears a condom with me, he might with other girls though. Benny wears one if he remembers to get some. It's 50/50 with him. But he's all Alice's now. He won't cheat on her. Well, I heard last night some of those 24 Hour Party People were on him."

She took a bite of some ribs Jolly had put on her plate.

"Jolly?" she asked.

"Yes, sugar."

"Why you asking all these questions? Do you think I gave you something?"

"No no no!" he exclaimed, "I just want you to be safe. I have a decision to make. It's going to affect my life in a big way. I have to look at all the components first."

The sad face came on her.

"Jar, my love, don't be sad. It will probably be a happy decision."

"I'm not hungry. I'm going back to the dressing room."

"Jar, don't do that to me. I honestly ran out of patience during Jack's failed attempt at a naked TikTok Lady Gaga imitation dance. You're seeing Mean Jolly now. Forgive me and come over here and kiss me."

"In public?"

"On the lips."

"What if someone sees us? What will people say?" she asked.

"Fuck them. None of their business. I'm kissing the lady I love." Jolly kissed her long and hard.

"You said you loved me."

"I did. I said it this morning to you but you had fallen back asleep."

"This changes a lot."

"For both of us. And we have a *lot* to talk about on how we'll handle this on tour. But one idea I have, and I don't have much time to discuss a bunch of ideas. But check this out. You know how they are complaining they're too busy to keep you in line and make sure you follow rules and all that shit?"

"Yeah. Made me feel like I'm a dog they didn't have time for anymore because their lives have gotten busier. I've been there for them. Always supported the band. I'm always there. I feel like now they're famous, they don't need me anymore. I'm kicked off to the side somewhere."

"I'm sorry you feel that way. I'm sorry they are treating you that way. I know it hurts because you've been friends for so long. But I think I have an idea where you wouldn't have to break up the friendships you have with them."

"I'm listening."

"They transfer you to me. It frees them up from worrying about shit outside, of focusing on how their career is going and where it's headed. I'll pitch it to them like that. I'll add "Jarmila duties" to my roster. Then nobody has to have a meltdown because you're talking to me, or have a coronary because I was teaching you to use chopsticks. You're my responsibility. I'll be your manager. What do you think of that idea?"

"But what if they want to have sex with me or me give them head?"

"Do you want to?"

"No. It isn't nice like it is with you. And Jack hurts me."

"Then if they ask you, or pressure you, let me handle that."

"Do you think you can?"

"They are feral, but I know I can. Might be some melt downs, threats, but I don't care. If it gets too serious and it's affecting them musically or onstage, I'll leave the tour and take you with me. If you'd go."

"I think I'd go. But it would hurt if they weren't my friends anymore."

"I'd help you with your hurt. I'd hold you until the hurt goes away." he said, "Now listen, my love, I have a ton of work to do. Can we have a serious discussion later at the hotel? Right now, sugar, I have to get tonight up and running. With people who are still high and drunk from last night, and a puking drummer."

"Go do your job. I've got *The Grapes Of Wrath* to read."

Jarmila sat on the drum riser reading, Dum Dum lollipop in her mouth. Her legs were dangling over the edge, wearing Sketchers instead of heels, Capri blue jeans, a black Anvil t-shirt that belonged to Benny. Soundcheck was over an hour away, she figured she had time to read a few chapters. She liked sitting on the riser. Her favorite song, Guns N' Roses "Estranged", was playing on the sound system.

Jack moved behind her, sat down, his long denim clad legs going past hers, his bare feet playfully hitting the bottom of her shoes. She gave him the Dum Dum and put the book down. He put the Dum Dum back in her mouth and hugged her to him. He put his mouth close up to her ear, and sang along with these "Estranged" lyrics:

"When I find out all the reasons

Maybe I'll find another way

Find another day

With all the changing seasons of my life

Maybe I'll get it right next time

And now that you've been broken down

Got your head out of the clouds

You're back down on the ground

And you don't talk so loud

And you don't walk so proud

Any more, and what for."

Then he said something to her and she picked up the book, stood up, took his hand and left the stage. From his position in mezzanine, Jolly witnessed the entire event.

15 minutes before showtime, security and Scot were attempting to take a can of Raid away from Benny who was spraying it randomly behind the stage.

"But don't you see the spiders? The fuckin' spiders! I've got to kill the spiders!" he screamed.

"I'm living in hell, right Scot?" Jolly asked.

"There wasn't any methadone to be had, and we checked everywhere. Unless he was a client at a clinic, he couldn't get any. We can get basically any illegal drug we want, but when we want a legal drug, we can't get it. How fucked up is that?"

"So…." inquired Jolly.

"One of the 24 Hour Party People gave him some MDMA."

"Brilliant! They're not even in the same drug class. Now less than 15 minutes before showtime, I've got a drummer who is over the fence, a lead singer who has gone completely psycho because they gave him Clase Azul instead of Don Julio, a bassist with a splitting migraine, and a guitarist who wants to know if he can suck off his new boyfriend during drum and bass solos. I've got equipment that doesn't work and a crew that's ready to quit because of all these problems. The best part is, this is the first time Lenehan has played Fargo. I'm counting the days, Scot, just counting the days and I'm a free man."

"You're a free bitch, baby!" Scot joked, referencing the band incident early that morning.

"Not in the slightest bit funny." Jolly said, grabbing the Raid can away from Benny, "The spiders are all dead now, Benny. You can go onstage safely."

Fargo was pretty much like every other venue: crazed fans, with the addition of the 24 Hour Party People like a pep squad at a high school sports rally. Jack being Jack, effervescent, vivacious. Even Benny and his imaginary spiders were killing it. Scot was right, thought Jolly, once onstage, Lenehan transformed.

There were several limos returning to the hotel. Scot had suggested the 24 Hour Party People be put in a party bus back to the hotel. Jack wouldn't hear of it. These were Lenehan's biggest fans and they were going to ride in limos just like he did.

Everyone was in limos going to the hotel except Jolly, who was settling the show, and the people riding with him: Jarmila, Johnny, Chandler and his new "fuck of the week" Paulo. Those four sat in the dressing room, waiting for Jolly. With them were two security guards. Andrew, who was second in authority to Les, and Nash, a new guy temporarily replacing one of the three security guards that were poisoned with ketamine.

Johnny was eating at a round wooden table. Chandler walked up to the opposite side of the table and looked at him.

"Hey, Johnny, I fucked your sister up the ass and it was so tight I'm going to fuck her again. Now that you've disowned her as your sister, you can have a go at her too."

Johnny threw the plate at Chandler just as Jolly was entering the room. He quickly grabbed Johnny's arm, while Nash held on to Johnny, and Andrew held on to Chandler.

"I'm gonna fuck you up so bad you fuckin' piece of shit!" screamed Johnny.

"Come at me fucker!" responded Chandler.

"Johnny, you're riding with me, Nash and Jar." said Jolly, "I'm calling for a private car. Chandler, you, your guest and Andrew are riding in the limo."

"What was that about?" Jolly asked Jarmila in their hotel room.

Jarmila told him the incident. Jolly undressed to take a shower.

"What would get in a person's head to be so cruel? Especially to someone who's their childhood friend." asked Jolly.

"Who knows. They've been like this for years. But it's gotten worse since there's more drugs and liquor around."

"Too much of that shit can fuck you up. Want to take a shower with me?"

"I've never showered with a man before."

"This can be your first time. I'm honored."

"But I am going to say no. I'm not ready for that yet."

"Too fast?"

"There's things I want to experience with you, but only a little at a time."

He kissed her and went to the shower. She phoned Johnny and talked to him about his appointment. Scot was taking him to a doctor and he would have some tests run to find out why he's having all these headaches and migraines. She assured him she'd pray for him, but not to get too worried. These were probably just stress headaches.

"Where are you now?" he asked, meaning what band member's room was she in.

"I'm at Jolly's. The 24 Hour Party People are still at Jack's. I ain't going near that shit." she answered.

"Me neither. I know Jack is always quoting "you only live once", but I want to live once a long time."

They both laughed.

"It's good to hear you laugh again." said Jarmila.

"Can you come over? I would like to say something to you."

"Jolly's in the shower. When he gets out, I'll tell him. But I don't think I'll spend the night with you. Unless you really need me, then you know, you're my priority."

"You've been spending a lot of time with Jolly. Something you're not telling me? You don't have to spent the night. Can you bring some of that Ibuprofen? It puts me to sleep, helps a lot with these headaches."

"It wasn't mine. It was Everett's. But I can stop by his room on the way over and get some for you."

"You're a doll."

"Too bad I'm not still your sister." she said, sadly.

"I want to talk about that. Is that okay with you?"

"Yes. Jolly is out of the shower. I'll be there in a minute."

Jolly took off his towel and put on green silk sleep pants and a black Van Halen shirt.

"Nice vintage Van Halen." said Jarmila.

"I love a woman who can spot good vintage." said Jolly as he put his arms around her waist.

"I need to go get Johnny some Ibuprofen from Everett. And Johnny wants to talk to me about something. What room is Everett in?"

Jolly buried his head in her neck. He kissed her gently, all the way to her ear and back down again.

"Ummmmm...302. I want to talk to you too. I'll wait until you get back." said Jolly.

Jarmila, in her black Anvil t-shirt and her Sketchers and her jean capris, did her usual bounce out the door.

Everett, dressed in Scooby Doo pajamas, answered the door. He motioned for Jarmila to enter.

"What's up?" he asked.

"Did I wake you?"

"No. I was up sorta watching the news and looking through some equipment websites."

"Johnny asked me to bring by a couple Ibuprofen. His doctor's appointment is in the morning at 9:00am."

"Sure, no problem." Everett went to a small red suitcase, looked at several prescription bottles, and took out one. He took out four white, oblong pills, "Tell him to take two at a time instead of one. Six hours apart."

"Okay, thank you. Everett, I am sorry for going off on you. Scot gets me mad, and Jolly doesn't stick up for me. I go off and everyone is a target."

"I forgive you. I know you didn't mean it. I've known you awhile now, and it takes a lot for you to get really mad."

"Hey Everett."

"Yes."

"Do you think Johnny has a brain bleed or brain cancer?"

"No. Probably stress headaches. That's why I take prescription Ibuprofen."

She gave him a quick hug and went to Johnny's.

Johnny's room was just a few doors away. He answered quickly. He was wearing only boxers. He motioned Jarmila into the suite.

"You guys get the nice suites and everybody else gets the janky rooms." she said, putting her purse down on the couch.

"We're the ones raking in the money, so we get the nice things first." he laughed, putting his head in her lap when she sat down on the couch.

"I know you're worried about tomorrow," she said, "but I want you to know everything is going to be all right. I want you to not worry."

"You're so good to me."

"Here's four Ibuprofen." said Jarmila, giving Johnny the tablets, "Everett says take two now and two six hours from now."

"Thanks." he said, putting the tablets on the coffee table in front of the couch, "I want to talk to you about what happened the other day."

"Yeah?"

"I am sorry for what I said. I was just angry and hurt. Mostly hurt. You'll always be my sister. I'm sorry I had to beat you like that. I was so conflicted, even up until the time the guys looked at me. I still wanted to walk out of that room. But I was so hurt that you would betray the band. I wasn't thinking clearly. All I could see was red. Please forgive me, Jarmila. I'll never do that again. Please accept me as your big brother again."

"I forgive you. But there's nothing really to forgive. I went willingly, and you were acting on your convictions. That's important, to stand by your integrity. Real talk, it hurt like hell. But I deserved it. I shouldn't have gone to Jolly's. I should have gone to one of you guys."

"It makes me feel better you've forgiven me. I don't know what's going to happen tomorrow. I'm scared."

"Don't be. They are going to have you see a doctor and probably run blood tests and an MRI or CT scan. You'll be *okay* and home by noon!"

"But what if they admit me to the hospital?"

"Then you tell them fuck off, you have a show to do."

"Can we move to the bedroom? I'm getting sleepy."

"I can go so you can sleep. But first let me get you a bottle of water to take these pills."

She moved his head from her lap and went to the mini-fridge to take out a bottle of water. As Johnny sat up, she gave him two pills and the bottle of water.

"I don't want you to leave yet." he said, "I was asking if you could massage my temples while I got to sleep."

"Of course!" she exclaimed.

They moved into the bedroom. Jarmila sat against the headboard and Johnny positioned his back between her legs, his head on her chest. She massaged his temples until she heard the sounds of his even toned sleep breathing. She slowly moved his head and put a pillow underneath it. On a notepad on the bedside table, she wrote "I love you, big brother. You have the courage of your convictions and the heart of a lion. Please call me as soon as you get back from the doc. Love, your little sister."

Back in Jolly's room, Jarmila took her shoes and pants off and got into bed. Jolly was at the table, working, laptop and tablet and phone with him.

"Whatcha doing?" Jarmila asked him.

"Working. Scot and I are in a discussion as if we should leave here tomorrow after the show- St. Paul isn't too much of a stretch-and get everyone settled in their rooms and let them sleep a little, or leave tomorrow morning, get them in the hotel, then make it to a radio interview at 1:00pm. What do you think?"

"I have no input as I don't work for the band."

Jolly gave her a stern look, "I was asking because I trust you know the band's sleep schedules better than Scot. Who can go back to sleep for a few hours after being woken up to get in the room, who can't, etc."

"I can't give you any solid info. The 24 Hour Party People are still here with us, through St. Paul. I don't think there is any word like sleep in that schedule."

"Those people give me a headache. But at least I get to keep you in my room while they're putting the band in a chemically induced coma. Speaking of headaches, how's Johnny?"

"I stopped by Everett's and got Ibuprofen for him. He says it helps him sleep. He took two and I massaged his temples until he went to sleep. Do you think he's going to be okay? Honestly? Do you think it's serious? Everett said it's probably stress headaches. That's what he takes the prescription Ibuprofen for. But what if it's cancer, or an aneurysm?"

Jolly put away his laptop and put the phone on the bedside table.

"My love," he said to Jarmila, hugging her in his arms, "I'm sure it's nothing but stress headaches and migraines. He's never been under pressure like this before. People think being a rock star is easy. But It's actually a hell of a lot more stress than a garage band. Plus, he's really missing his mom. She doesn't do FaceTime or video calls. She doesn't email or text. She doesn't have a cell phone. She's got an old school desk top phone. They write letters back and forth and call each other every day."

"He's a momma's boy, for real."

"Also, he is stressed about you."

"How do you know?"

"He told me. He wanted advice from someone who seemed they liked you. Not Scot. He wanted an unbiased, unhateful answer."

"What did he say exactly?"

"That he felt bad disowning you. I told you he'd come around once he cooled off. He said he was very sorry for what happened, and he talked to a priest who told him that was not the right thing to do, and he needed to ask forgiveness."

"What did you tell him?"

"I told him he should open up a dialogue with you."

"I love you, Jolly."

"I love you."

"I'm going to take a shower."

"Can I join you?" asked Jolly.

"You think in the hour I was gone I'd change my mind?"

"Horny man, tries his best."

She laughed and took a small suitcase into the bathroom with her. When she returned to the room, she was wearing a beige bustier with shiny silver embellishments that had matching garters attached, and matching panties.

"What do you think?" she asked, "I bought this outfit and haven't worn it yet."

"I think you're making me completely forget what I had to talk to you about."

"Well, I have to tell you something."

"You've run out of Flamin' Hot Cheetos and have decided to start to eat healthier foods?"

"No, asshole, I'm running away with Elton John." she said snidely.

"Tell him I said 'hi'."

"I just wanted to tell you I think you're incredibly sexy."

She got in bed next to Jolly.

"Well, tell me what you're going to tell me." she said.

"Scot and the band and I are going to have a meeting, about you, tomorrow at 2:00pm. In the hotel conference room. You are going to stay in the room until I get back."

"But what if I get hungry?'

"I'll make sure you eat before I leave."

"But what if it is a sunny day and I want to sit outside and read a book and I accidentally walk by the conference room, and my ear accidentally goes to the door?"

"It's cold outside, Jar. After you're done eavesdropping and reading a book outside in this cold ass weather, I'm going to warm your cold ass up for you."

"You're so mean."

He looked her in the eyes. She smiled.

"Okay," she said, "I can never stay mad at you for long."

"That's one of the things we have in common. Now, serious talk. I've already talked to Scot. He'll be at the meeting since he manages the band. I'm asking to take over the rules they have for you, which frees them up to concentrate more on their music."

"So, I am in their way."

"No, you are not. I'm just using this as an excuse, so we can be together all the time. Somebody wants sex from you, they'll have to talk to me first. My tour, my rules, my Jarmila.

"I hope this works."

"It will. I'm an expert at getting my way. Now, let's talk sex."

"Yes! Can we talk about your balls? You have really nice balls."

"Thank you. I actually want to talk about a question you asked me, Everett and Scot before the show. You asked a question if men like putting their mouths on women's vaginas."

"Yes. Because I've never had it done. But I used to eavesdrop on my grandma and her sisters when they had their afternoon coffee. They say they only got it on their birthdays because men don't like it. The guys have never done it to me. I was just wondering if it's like most men don't like it? Do women really like it?"

"I cannot speak for everyone. But I like it. Turns me on. I know yours especially would."

"Why?"

"Because I'm in love with every inch of you."

She turned over onto her stomach. He started to play with the garters.

"I have this weird fantasy. I think it's bad for me to have it considering what I have been through with the band sexually. It bothers me to have good feelings about something I don't like the band doing to me."

"What they did to you and your fantasies are two separate things. Even if your fantasy is a version of what they did to you. You might like some of the things they did to you if you liked doing that. But they force themselves on you. Just because you initiated sex the first time with Chandler does not mean he can have you to do anything he wants. Same with Jack. Just because of the fact you once turned 18 doesn't give him the right to act like he owns you. And I'm not sure what to say about Benny. You don't seem to complain about him much."

"He's gentle to me. Except when he paddled me. He's got strength in those arms of his."

"He's a drummer, that's why. Now tell me about this fantasy. Don't forget you still owe me a 3rd one."

"Don't you have work to do?"

"All done." Jolly smiled.

"Ummmmhmmmm. You are always working."

"It's a two-day run. Second dates are always less hectic. Or perhaps I should knock on wood. You know, you're going to have to tell me your fantasy soon."

"I have a question."

"I may have an answer. And before you ask, no I do not think the government is spraying paraquat on dispensary distributed marijuana to make people sick, so they can convince the public that marijuana is bad for you and make it illegal again."

"I wasn't going to ask you that. I was going to ask you if you have ever had anal sex with a woman? Because I know you only like women."

Jolly stared at her, "Some things are no comment."

"Which is you saying you did without saying it." she said.

"Do you want a list of all my sexual exploits since I turned 14?"

"Yeah. In detail, on a spreadsheet."

"I'm going to spread you in a minute." he said as he kissed her cheek.

"You are distracting me about my very important questions on oral and anal sex."

"You can't generalize it, Jar. People like all sorts of things and dislike all sorts of things. Before I forget," continued Jolly, "bring me your purse."

"Why, is there a certain shade of lipstick you're looking for to go with your barrettes?"

"Go stand in the corner. Go. Get your bratty ass up and go stand in that corner over there." he said as he pointed to the corner by the front door.

She obeyed. Jolly got up from the bed, retrieved her purse from the other bed, and went back to his own bed.

"What are you doing with my purse!" she exclaimed.

"Why so agitated? Got something to hide? I didn't say you could turn around. Put your face back in the corner."

"I've got tampons in there. I always carry them in there."

"I wasn't looking for a tampon. But today Everett said I was on the rag, so I might get one later."

Jolly emptied the contents onto the bed covers. Kleenex-Jarmila had seasonal allergies-lipsticks, chap stick, various items of makeup, a compact mirror, lotions, tampons, a couple different perfumes, hand sanitizer, a money clip with several hundred-dollar bills, and her band laminate. And what appeared to be cocaine.

"That's from the other day, when we talked, remember? You forgot to remind me to get rid of it." she quivered.

"Okay, I believe you." he said as he took her hand and led her to the bathroom, "Now you're going to open up the package and dump it down the toilet."

"But…but…I could give it to Jack or Chandler or even Benny. You do coke, you can keep it for yourself."

"No."

"But…but…"

"*NO*. Get rid of it *now*."

She opened the packet, pushed out all the contents, put the empty packet in the toilet and flushed it.

"You're mean." she pouted.

"No more cocaine, Jar. No drugs. That's *my* rule. But even after this meeting tomorrow, you are going to have to abide by those rules they set out. I'm only offering to manage you. You can't think 'Hey I'm free' and go insane. I don't think we should slam them with news of our relationship yet."

"Me neither! What if Jack gets upset and he leaves the tour completely? Or if he says to you 'Well, you broke your contract with us to watch over her safety, so now we're taking her back'. He'd probably beat me harder than ever."

"I love how we think along the same lines."

"Our business is our private business. But when the 24 Hour Party People leave, Jack will want me to go back to his room. He's not going to share me with the others, he said I was his until the end of tour. The night he and Chandler took turns going up my butt, when it was over, Jack put me across his lap and told me to remember who I belonged to. He called you my little friend. Chandler calls you my boyfriend. Johnny wanted to know what's up with us and why I spend so much time with you. I said I didn't want to be in all that chaos in Jack's room. But I think they suspect something."

"I don't think they do. I think Chandler and Jack are being derogatory and Johnny has been out of the loop with this health situation. He just wants the low down on what he's been missing. But I got it all covered. I know what I'm going to offer. There's always the option of us leaving. I can get out of my contract anytime."

"What if Jack or the rest of the guys start shit?"

"They have nothing legally binding on you. It's illegal to own a person or keep them as some type of sexual hostage. If they didn't let you go or tried to hold you with threats, I'll call the motherfuckin' cops! But I think they'll agree. Then I can watch out for your safety *and* fuck your brains out. Now. Come close to me in bed. Let's talk about oral and anal sex like you wanted to."

"It's okay." she said, cuddling closer to him in bed, "I know you want sex, so let's just do that."

"Jar, sugar, I'm going too fast, aren't I? You see, normally, a 22-year-old would be all over that shit non-stop. And I'd be trying to catch up. I need to slow down and let you guide me to what is comfortable for you."

"I'm glad you understand. I hope you're willing to wait for me and answer my stupid questions along the way."

"You're my new best friend, Jarmila Malone. That will always be first. Your questions are not stupid. Except when you're asking if the Big Bang Theory is a lie and we are all just Pod People being grown by aliens from a distant undiscovered galaxy."

"Someday the government is going to tell the truth!" she exclaimed and laughed.

He laughed with her, and drew her body closer to his.

"The sex with you is spectacular. Remember I told you about my 2nd wife?"

"The one you disliked so much."

"Yeah, that one. Incredible sex. But you are 100 times better."

"Maybe that's why you like me so much." she said as her sad face took over.

"Jar," he cupped her chin in his hand, "from the first moment I saw you I knew there was something different about you. I wanted that. It was a weird feeling! I had never felt that way before. I thought well shit, I'm having a mid-life crisis. It was something beyond the sexual feelings I get with other women."

"Like the two girls you fucked in Detroit?"

"You like that corner, don't you sugar?"

"You fucked two girls in Detroit! I heard Chandler giving you shit about it."

"I don't like this jealous vibe I'm getting from you. They were just two girls I picked up at a club. Things happen. I once fell in love with a stripper from East St. Louis and after her shift we flew to Vegas and got married."

"Was that your 2nd wife?"

"That was my 3rd. Got me for fifty grand. But that good ole prenuptial saved my ass from losing more. I lost everything with my 1st wife. I basically left that marriage with my integrity and a clean pair of underwear."

She laughed and turned over. He loved her musical laugh. He loved her big heart and her selfless attitude and her boundless energy. He loved her clueless naivete. And yes, he had to admit to himself he loved her constant questions and her conspiracy theories. But this new feeling. The one that had to be love, because what else could it be? It scared him and exhilarated him and exhausted him. He did not like the complex, tangled web he knew he threw himself in to. This was complicated, and Jolly Rogers did not like complicated.

"Is something wrong?" she asked.

"No, I was lost in my thoughts."

"Whatcha thinkin' about?"

"Your breasts, the second show, your bare pussy, the far left monitor that keeps going out, your lips, the guest list for Milwaukee that looks like the cast of "The Ten Commandments" decided to have a rave with the cast of "War and Peace". That damn guest list won't be final until the day of the show. Then I think of your bare pussy, and I calm down again. Or your perky little ass. I love your perky little ass. If you ever told me to kiss your ass, I'd get down on my knees and actually kiss your ass."

"Don't let me distract you from your work. *Ever.*"

"I wouldn't do that baby. You know my work is important to me. Important to do the best I can."

"I feel like I'm keeping you from your work."

"It's 4:00am Jar. I have to stop working eventually. Besides, Scot and I are on call 24/7 for the band and our staff. Everett is the same for the crew. I'd rather stay up talking to you all night. And look at this outfit, ummmhmmmm."

"Victoria's Secret."

"But where are the stockings and the heels. You know I love a woman in a good pair of heels!"

Jarmila got out of bed and went to her suitcase. She sat on the spare bed and put each red fishnet stocking on slowly, attaching them to the gaters, giving seductive glances to Jolly. The she took out a pair of Dolce & Gabbana satin sandals in black with red roses going down the back. She slowly put those on, leaned back, and spread her legs.

"How about these stockings and heels?" she said, suggestively.

"I think you need to come over here right now." he said, as Jarmila slipped into the covers, "No, first just stand there." he got up and moved his hands up and down her calves, "This turns me on. When a woman wears heels, her calves curve a little, and that makes me so hot."

Jolly returned under the covers. Jarmila took off her heels and joined him.

"We were going to talk about oral and anal sex when you hijacked my questions."

"Sorry, what are your questions."

"Can a woman enjoy anal sex?"

"Absolutely. If that's what she and her partner want. I hear it hurts a little going inside. But once there it is very pleasurable. For people who want it. You should go get a tutorial from Chandler. I'm not into men so I can't really say how it feels for the recipient. And I'm fairly sure there's no one on this tour who would talk about it with you either, since talking to you can cause an employee to be fired. Yes. I've given women anal and they seemed to really like it. I know you don't like it. But it was forced upon you. Of course, it's perfectly okay not to like it."

"Do you think I'd like it?"

"I don't know, Jar. You've been through lot of trauma. It could trigger something terrible. But I'll never do that to you unless you want it."

"Can we really talk about anything we want, even sexual stuff?"

"Of course. But know that I have to leave here at 8:30am for the venue. Scot is taking Johnny to the doc and I'm taking on some of Scot's stuff, so I need to be there early."

"Better than the 6:00am and 7:30am you usually leave." she kissed him softly. "You should get some sleep."

"I'll get an old man nap in later."

"You are not old!" she laughed, kissing him again. She started to play with his thighs, "Why you always wear clothes in bed?"

"I don't, if I'm making love. You surprised me last night."

"Did you like it?"

"I loved it."

"I loved it too and I love you."

Jolly started kissing her. He gently got on top of her and took off his sleep pants. He unfastened the garters and pulled her panties down until they were off her completely. He put his fingers into her vagina until she made little gasping sounds, then he slowly eased himself into her.

"Nobody ever did it to me in this position. It's really nice. I like having you on top." she whispered in his ear, "Jolly?"

"Yes sugar?" he said, looking at her face.

"Have you fallen in love with me?"

"Yes."

"Do you regret it?"

"No."

But he didn't have the heart to tell her that he may deeply regret what will happen when the truth became known about their relationship.

The conference room was filled with three very hungover rock stars and one with a bad headache. Scot and Jolly sat next to each other. The band sat at various places at the table.

"Just us?" asked Jack, "No assistants from da management telling us to calm down, no record label bigwig telling us we need to act civilized in public?"

"Nope." answered Scot, "Just us."

"Johnny's got cancer." stated Jack briefly.

"Nope." said Scot.

"Johnny's got a blood clot." stated Jack.

"Nope." answered Scot.

"Then why da fuckin' band meeting? Ya know I got three girls in my bed want to make me see da rings of Saturn." complained Jack.

"This is about Jarmila." said Scot.

"But *what da fuck is wrong with Johnny*?" Jack yelled.

"I'm ok, Jack," answered Johnny, "the docs didn't find anything concerning. They diagnosed me with stress headaches and gave me Klonopin and some over the counter pain reliever."

"*Klonopin*!" Chandler exclaimed, "That's some shit right there!"

"Which you will get none of," said Scot, "because it's for Johnny only."

"Can we get on why we are here. There's no meeting on da itinerary at this time." said Jack.

"You've read the itinerary!" Jolly exclaimed, "Look at you, all grown up."

"Fuck you, Jolly." Jack responded.

"Jarmila's dying?" Johnny asked in a whisper.

"No. Why would you think that?" asked Jolly.

"She hardly ever eats and she's getting thinner. I worry about her. She is my only sis."

"Oh, ok," sneered Chandler, "now that she's back to being your sister, you can't fuck her up the ass. It's okay. I'll get an extra one in there for you."

Chandler and Jack fist pumped as Johnny threw the chair next to him.

"What da hell!" yelled Jack, "You almost fuckin' hit me."

Scot grabbed Johnny. "Hey, let me call Shera and she can take you back to your room. You need to rest up before the show. I'll fill you in later."

Five minutes later Shera was escorting Johnny from the conference room.

"This isn't a band meeting if *all* da band isn't here. Fuck this, I'm going back to my room to see Saturn." sneered Jack.

"You're staying right where you are, Jack." said Scot.

"Gentlemen, Scot and I have a proposal for you." said Jolly.

"Aww, I'm sorry Jolly but Chandler already got a wife in Chicago. And a boyfriend down da hall!" laughed Jack, which got the three remaining band members howling with laughter.

"OMG Jack, Paulo has an x-large dick. Fits right down my throat. Slides like butter." Chandler described.

"Did anyone need to hear that, Chandler?" asked Jolly.

"Everyone," he answered, "cause I'm *fuckin' gorgeous*!"

"Ok…" started Scot, "now listen, "Jolly and I have been discussing Jarmila. We know things are much better for you now, but also a lot more hectic. Johnny is super stressed and you all have been acting like wild beasts roaming the earth in 10,000 BC. How about if Jolly takes over the Jarmila duties. He would be responsible for making sure she doesn't break the rules, and following through on any consequences you have for such infractions. He'll keep her safe. It would take a weight off and give you more time to concentrate on your music, or have more free time."

"He can't fuck her!" yelled Jack, "And she can't suck his dick! She's still *mine!*"

"That's perfectly acceptable Jack. I'm not taking your favorite toy away. Now this is a simple contract, between the six of us, briefly explaining what is going on. It's very important we keep this in-house." said Scot.

The three remaining band members signed, followed by Scot and Jolly. Scot assured the band that he would get Johnny to sign it later. Johnny would be the easiest one.

Back in his hotel room, the first thing Jolly saw was Jarmila curled up in a chair, pouting. He pulled up a chair next to her.

"I don't like time wasted. You could have been reading a book or watching tv or doing something besides sitting there and pouting." he said.

"What happened?"

"I am in charge of you now. You're officially a "Tour Manager Duty." I'm your manager now. Well, at least among us, the band, and Scot. We want to keep this in-house."

"I love you Jolly!" she exclaimed, hugging him, "I've never had a manager!"

He moved his chair in front of hers.

"This does not change the fact the band has rules for you, and they expect me to follow through with consequences if you break them."

"I don't like the sound of that."

"I know, sugar, but that's the way it's going to be to keep this whole situation from boiling over. You trust me, right?"

"Wholly."

"I've been really thinking about this. I wanted a way out if we needed one where we could go together and have the least negative impact for the band. And us."

"I love you." she said, standing, kissing him on the forehead.

"What, I don't get a kiss on the lips?"

She kissed his lips.

"I'm off to the venue." he said, "Coming with me or going with the band?"

"I have to get dressed. All I have on is this t-shirt. But I did already take a shower."

Jolly pulled her closer and put his hand between her legs.

"Maybe I'll be a little late to the venue." he said, pulling her onto his lap.

"No," she said, standing, "you will not be late. Work comes first!"

"You're a tough boss to have!"

"Give me 15 minutes and I'll be ready. Already did hair and make-up, got to decide on what to wear. What would you wear in Fargo, North Dakota at the end of March?"

"A parka. It's still chilly. I wouldn't want you to get a cold ass. Although I wouldn't mind warming it up." he said, pulling her closer to him.

"Wait until Scot finds out you missed the whole show because you were fucking me every which way til Sunday. That would *not* go over well. Although…if you warmed my butt up kissing it, I wouldn't mind that."

He playfully grabbed her bottom. "Is this fantasy #3 you owe me? Go get dressed. What are you wearing?"

"Well," she started, "I thought of this Veronica Beard Luvie Leopard dress. But do you think it looks too 60's?"

"I think you have excellent taste in designer clothes, but you're too skinny for that dress. You need to pick a dress that shows off that skinny waist and round ass of yours."

"Okay." she said, as she pulled out a bright flame colored dress with back straps, "It's a Bec & Bridge. I could pair it with some white Safety Pin Nappa leather sandals by Versace and an orange teddy underneath."

"How about a simple pair of panties underneath, because I need to get to the venue."

"Go. I'll meet you later."

"No. We'll go in one car. It's my first day as your manager, and I don't want the band to think I'm shirking my duties."

"You're so funny." she said sarcastically, dressing quickly.

The Fargo audience were like Lenehan addicts. The city had not been on any previous Lenehan tour schedule, and the crowd showed their appreciation. Jack's vivacity fueled the crowd's excitement. By the second set, Jack was on fire. A person could imagine flames shooting out from him.

"I have a grandfather," started Jack, "anybody here have a grandfather?" The crowd went feral. "I was named after my grandfather. Jack. He's 97 years old. Jogs every day. I swear it, he jogs every day. Could run my ass round da block a few times." the crowd exploded into laughter and shouts, "He used to be a jazz musician on da local Chicago circuit. Pretty famous in Chicago. He used to tell me stories of da days playing da jazz clubs. He was only 13 when he started playing piano in da clubs. Told me he didn't know how to play piano, but he pretended enough to get hired. Had to bring in money cause his mom and dad had a large family to feed. Told me stories about da behaviors da musicians and female dancers in da clubs got up to. And it was SCANADALOUS!!!!!!!!!!"

Jack then went into Lenehan's hit song, "Scandalous." The audience crazed reactions made the band exuberant. By the time three encores were finished, the band felt they had proved themselves the best live band on the circuit.

In the dressing room, Jack sat with a blue-haired girl on his lap. She was sucking on one of his fingers. Johnny was crashed out on a couch, the Klonopin making him sleepy. Chandler was standing against a wall kissing Paulo. Benny was in a chair completely nodded off. Scot walked in the room.

"Okay, only band, crew and staff in the dressing room. Everybody else *out*." he emphasized.

Andrew, the band security closest to the door, escorted the girl and Paulo to the 24 Hour Party People hospitality room.

"Why was it okay for Alice to stay in the dressing room with Benny when she's here but not my friends?" asked Chandler.

"Because," said Scot, "Alice is a part of the Lenehan entourage, cleared by management to do things like hang in the dressing room and ride on the bus."

"Why why why!" exclaimed Jack, "You sound like a fuckin' two-year-old Chandler. Everything to you is 'why' and 'not fair'."

"Fuck off, Jack." said Chandler, "Don't you give a damn about the girl you were with?"

"I don't even remember her name. She'll be in St. Paul. So will a hundred other girls who want to fuck me. I won't remember any of their names either."

"Well, I want to marry Paulo." declared Chandler.

"And fuckin' next week it will be some guy named Steve, then some dude named Bryce, then some transgender named Micha, then you'll see your wife and be like, 'oh shit, I'm already married!'" exclaimed Jack.

"We're leaving as soon as Jolly settles the show." said Scot, "Be ready in an hour. That way I may be able to get your asses on the bus in two hours. St. Paul. Not too long a ride. 9:00am radio interview, 12:30pm radio interview and meet and greet radio winners combined. Then you are free for the day."

"*24 Hour Party People all day what what*!" yelled Chandler.

"I hate these early fuckin' radio shows!" exclaimed Jack.

"And you hate meet and greets," said Jolly as he joined those in the dressing room, "because you tell us every time Lenehan has one."

Jarmila was right behind Jolly.

"Oh," sneered Jack, "now ya got your little creamette helping you settle da shows. How fuckin' convenient. Maybe she can get promoted from "Dick Sucker" to "Assistant Tour Manager"."

"She can put on her resume in the section about previous experience "Likes to Get Butt Fucked A Lot." added Chandler.

"I wasn't with Jolly when he was settling the show!" Jarmila cried, "I was talking to Everett while the crew was loading out!" she ran from the room.

"I don't know why you all have to talk to her like that." Jolly said, "You're supposedly friends."

"Mind ya own business motherfucker!" yelled Jack.

"Jolly, why can't we ride in the 24 Hour Party People bus?" asked Chandler.

"Because they have their own bus which they paid for, and you have your own bus which you paid for." Scot answered.

"I could use the sleep. I'm perfectly happy sleeping in our bus, alone, listening to something by Lil Peep." said Jack.

"You, not get laid?" Scot said sarcastically, "Are you coming down with the flu or something?"

"No. I don't have a perpetually needy dick like Chandler does." Jack answered, pointing to Chandler.

In the bus, Jack was already raging when Jolly told him he could not sleep in the back of the bus lounge, because he and Jarmila were having a meeting there about band rules, consequences and his expectations for her to follow.

"Oh, hell to da fuck no!" Jack screamed. "I'm not sleeping in a bunk!"

"But you sleep in a bunk most of the time." Jolly denoted.

"You just want Jarmila to suck your cock." Jack insinuated.

"She could do that in a bunk." Jolly responded.

Jack got right into Jolly's face.

"I'm going to fuck you up, motherfucker!" he screamed.

Les got in between them.

"You don't want to threaten me, Jack. You really don't." said Jolly, as he turned to Scot. "I'm going to the back to talk to Jar."

"Yeah, go let your little creamette suck you off!" exclaimed Jack.

Jolly turned around, but Scot shook his head no, and Jolly continued to the back of the bus.

Jarmila was reading *Gone With The Wind*. Jolly sat down next to her.

"You read fast." he said.

"I like to read. My goal is to read a book completely every two days. I have a lot of downtime. Especially on this tour, with all the added shows and radio interviews and meet and greets."

"You get lonely a lot out here?"

"Before I met you, yes. Especially since nobody but the band could talk to me, because of the fact crew and staff could get fired for fraternizing with me. Which I think means they can't talk to me or hang out with me." Jamila smiled at Jolly.

"Basically, yes. That's what that means."

"I'm surprised you're not upfront working."

"Jack is having a meltdown I need to be away from, because I lost my patience somewhere between Lady Gaga naked cover song TikTok dancing and Benny's snare drum that had its last rites."

"It's unable to be used?"

"Completely fucked up. Ordered a new one, will hopefully be in St. Paul before showtime Friday."

"I'm sorry you're having a shitty day. Jack is like this on tour. He hates touring. He doesn't have as much control like he does in the studio. He takes his frustrations out on *everybody*."

"He needs to grow up."

"You have to work to do. I'll leave you alone."

"Not too alone. I can work while you get closer to me."

She put the book down, curled up next to him, fell asleep.

In St. Paul, Minnesota, interviews and meet and greets done, Johnny was practicing his bass guitar in his room, the rest of the band were off with the 24 Hour Party People, who seemed to keep their reputation in tact by not sleeping. Everett, Scot and Jolly grabbed a quick lunch and headed to the venue. No day off for them. Johnny asked if he could go along, and they were glad he felt well enough to join them. However, once at the venue, Johnny realized he forgot his Klonopin, which he had to take at 4:00pm. He told Scot, who offered to go back to the hotel and get it for him. He said there was no need. Jarmila texted him and told him she was on her way, so he asked her to pick up his medicine in his room and bring it to the venue. He called front desk, explained the situation to the supervisor, who opened Johnny's room for Jarmila. She grabbed the medicine, put it in her tour bag, and thanked the hotel supervisor.

Once at the venue, Jarmila put her tour bag in the dressing room. She passed Johnny in the hallway and told him where she put his medicine, in the front pocket of her tour bag. He hugged and kissed her.

"You're the best sis ever!" he claimed

The venue looked good. Everett, Scot and Jolly stood in front of the stage. Jarmila bounced up next to them.

"You did the stacks differently." she noticed.

"Bigger venue, more space to fill." said Everett.

"Think of the even bigger venues on the next tour." she said.

"Oh I am. All new equipment. Gonna be like Christmas in August." Everett stated.

"Jarmila, if you were regular fan, and this was the first time you saw a stage like this, what would you say?" asked Scot.

"I'd say, 'When is the band going to play?'" she answered.

"Good answer, Jarmila, good answer." said Everett.

"I'm going to pick up Benny's snare. What are you going to do today, Jolly?" asked Scot.

"Milwaukee."

"That'll take you most of the day." laughed Scot.

Jolly did a brief run-down of the venue. He would make a longer run-down the next day. He went to the tour office. He had given his three assistants the day off. He was all in his precious alone time when Johnny appeared in the tour office and closed the door. Most of his life he'd been in the behind the scene music business. Band members closing doors was never a good thing.

"Got a minute?" Johnny asked Jolly.

"For you I have as much time as you need." he said, motioning for Johnny to sit down.

Johnny handed Jolly a tall tan medicine bottle, filled with pills at the bottom, and a white small ball wrapped in what looked like plastic.

"I found this in Jarmila's tour bag in the dressing room. I had forgot the Klonopin at the hotel so she brought it to me. This was next to it in the front pocket of her tour bag. I thought you should know, now that you're her manager."

"Thanks Johnny." said Jolly.

"Jack's going to lose his shit."

"Let's not tell Jack or the rest of the band. Not right away. I'll handle this. Is that okay with you?"

"Yes. I don't want Jarmila hurt the way she was."

"I don't either. Don't worry, I'll take care of it."

The next night, Lenehan took the staged like they owed it. Jack acted possessed by the St. Paul crowd and the crowd loved it. They could have added a show, but the band's answer was no. They loved to perform, but they were not robots. They needed some down time. Jolly didn't have a lot of problems to deal with. He should have been super happy. But what Johnny gave him earlier made his mood fall. Jarmila said she never lies, and yet she'd lied to him several times on this tour.

In the bus on the way to Jolly's dreaded two date Milwaukee shows, he was preoccupied in his usual spot. Jarmila was next to him.

"Are the two dates pretty much the same so you don't have a double workload?" she asked Jolly.

"Unfortunately, no. These are family shows, most of the band's family will show up, and I have to put away Mean Jolly and put on Nice Jolly. There's a ton of equipment problems, but most of them will be handled by show time. The guest list keeps growing and growing and growing." He emailed Keith, cc'd Kirk and Chandra, messaged Chandra that the guest list would be huge, and if she needed help in making sure this was problem free, he would pull someone from merchandise. The Milwaukee gigs, of all gigs, had to be perfect. They were like a practice run for the upcoming last shows on the tour: Chicago. The legendary Vic Theater. 2-day run. It would be the first time Lenehan was headlining shows at The Vic.

After pulling into Milwaukee, Jolly and Scot got everyone settled in their rooms. No scheduled interviews, but Jolly was on the fence. Family was important. But exposure was, too. He weighed the good and bad and decide since both shows were sold out, a little less exposure wouldn't hurt the band.

He and Jarmila settled into Jolly's room. Jarmila said she was going to take a shower. Jolly sat at the table with his laptop in front of him. He had a couple hours to get some business done before heading to the venue. Jarmila came out of the shower wrapped in towels. She started to dress by putting on a pale satin green bra with white lace trim and matching satin panties.

"Jar, get the brush by the coffee machine."

"Shouldn't you be getting some sleep? Big day."

"I slept a couple hours on the bus. I'll be fine. My adrenaline is overflowing. Bring me the brush."

She went to the shelf the coffee maker was on. She came back to Jolly with the pill bottle in her hand.

"You went through my tour bag?" she asked Jolly, standing in front of him.

"Johnny found that when he was getting his medicine you brought him."

"Jack will lose his shit."

"I think I convinced Johnny not to tell the band yet. Band loyalty is tough to crack, but he says he doesn't want to see you hurt again. I don't think he'll tell them. Yet. I told him let me handle it first."

She went back to the shelf and picked up the brush. She started to lay across Jolly's lap.

"Whoa baby, what are you doing?" he said as he pulled her up into a standing position.

"You want me over the table? Or the bed?"

"Do you think I'm going to hit you?"

"You're in charge of me now, you're supposed to follow through on the responsibilities."

"I am *not* going to hit you."

"But what if they want proof?"

"Not in the contract we signed. They can ask, but I'm not obligated to show them." said Jolly.

"I love you, Jolly."

"Don't get too happy. I'm still going to punish you. Especially for lying to me. And you know how I don't want you doing drugs. Since when do you take pills?"

"This girl from the 24 Hour Party People said the pills would make me seem less high after I did coke, so nobody would notice."

"I'm happy they are gone."

"Until NYC. For Jack's party."

"I've already got indigestion from the anticipation. Sit on my lap. I want to brush your hair. It'll give me a few moments of peace before this crazy day explodes."

He brushed her hair and bent down to kiss her shoulder.

"I'm going to be super busy today. Do you want to get some sleep and come to the venue later?" he asked her.

"Yes."

"I'm still going to punish you, Jar. I haven't thought of how yet, but it's going to happen."

"At least it won't hurt."

"Not physically." he assured her, "But you won't like it. Now I've got a few more things to do and I'm headed to the venue. I love you." he kissed her and she went to bed.

Milwaukee, Wisconsin. Somebody built it too damn close to Chicago, thought Jolly. Close enough for family to drive up if they wanted to drive, or a quick plane ride if they were so inclined. He was not an enthusiast of shows where a ton of family were going to be. He understood the importance of family, but the extra workload drove him over the hedge. Even the crew's list was large, and it still was not in yet. He would give them until 5:30pm. Then they were shit out of luck. The band was different. Jack was well known to send Chandra running to the box office at the last minute to add a guest.

But, so far, so good. Benny got a new snare drum, and the band seemed very excited about being with family. Some, like Benny's cousins from Texas, were already there. Benny took them out to eat and see a few sights around Milwaukee. Some of Chandler's family had arrived as well. Jack's mom and grandfather weren't scheduled to be there until around 5:00pm. Johnny's mom was traveling with them.

By 3:00pm, Jarmila had woken, dressed and was at the venue. She saw Jolly in the hallway walking with all three of his assistants and some venue staff she only identified by their laminate passes. The words "Venue Staff" could be clearly seen. She stopped by Jolly and tried to kiss him. He pulled away.

"I'm super busy, Jar." he snapped.

She turned and walked away, slowly, shoulders down, pouting. Jolly turned around.

"Walk with me, Jar. I need your help with something." he said.

She took in step with him. He gave orders to his assistants and the venue staff who scattered in different directions. He and Jarmila went into the tour office. Jolly stood in front of his laptop. On the side was a clipboard full of papers.

"Help me out here, sugar." he said, pulling up pictures on the laptop

"Do I get paid for this?" she asked sarcastically.

"I'll kiss your ass later."

"Like for real, or are you just being ignorant?" she asked.

"Guess you'll find out. Now stop distracting me. I can't concentrate when I'm thinking of your beautiful ass. Look, we have ID's for everyone who works for the band or is in some way involved in the band. But we don't do that for family. I don't want to look like a fool and not know who the hell I'm speaking with. I had Kirk going through social media sites saving and downloading pictures. Help me with these pictures so I can identify them. You know the band's family pretty much, right?"

"Yup."

"Okay," he started, clicking on a picture to make it larger, "who's this?"

"That's Matilda Gernuy. She's one of Chandler's cousins."

Jolly went through the list.

"I don't see her on here."

"She's right there." Jarmila pointed out, "She spells her name G-e-r-n-u-y, not G-u-r-n-e-y."

"I guess it got spelled phonetically."

"No, the pronunciation is correct. It's just the way it's spelled."

Jolly wrote a note down by the name on the list, and checked the name.

"And this?" he said as he clicked on another picture.

"That's Matilda Howard, another one of Chandler's cousins. She's married, has some kids."

"She's a +5, so she must be bringing her whole family." he check marked her name.

Clicking on another picture, he asked "Who's this?"

"That's Jack's momma and grandfather. It was Jack's birthday. I know because it was nice enough to have a backyard bar-b-que and there's Jack's favorite green and white balloons in the background. That's his Auntie Stella next to him. She died a few days after the party. That's how I remember it was Jack's birthday.

Nice enough for a back yard bar-b-que in April in Chicago meant it must have been at least 35 degrees outside. Cold weather did not stop a Chicagoan.

"He looks young." said Jolly.

"Yeah, it was his 18th birthday."

He clicked on another picture.

"That's Johnny's momma." said Jarmila. "She's standing next to Ms. Pickford. That was at Benny's momma's funeral. They both got pink ribbons pinned to their dresses for breast cancer awareness. Benny's momma died last year of breast cancer. Ms. Pickford is a neighbor of Johnny and his momma. She won't be here. She thinks rock and roll is the Devil's music."

"And these people?" said Jolly as he clicked on another picture, this one with a large group of people that appeared to be outside in a park.

"Those are Benny's cousins, the ones coming from San Antonio, Texas. The first one in back, that's Mateo Gutierrez, the one next to him is his sister Juana Gutierrez. Next to Juana is Ximena Elizondo. And in front, the first one in the first row, that's Ximena's sister Petunia Elizondo. They're the only cousins that are coming up. In fact, I heard they're already here."

Jolly check marked those names, except Petunia.

"Petunia? Who names their kid Petunia?" ask Jolly, "I don't see her on the list."

"Her real first name is Eulalia."

"Oh. I think I'd rather be called Petunia." Jolly laughed as he found her name and check marked it, "Now on to Chandler's family. Or at least the major players in Chandler's family. If I went through all of them on this list, I'd be here past midnight."

He clicked on a picture, another large group of people standing in front of a house.

"That's Chandler's momma, and his daddy. Next to his daddy is Chandler."

"I know what Chandler looks like." Jolly grinned.

"Next to Chandler is his sister Jean Bellem. She got two kids, a boy and a girl, young, I'm not sure how old but they're under 6 years old. She's bringing them?"

"Yes."

"Next to Jean is her husband, Neil. Next to Neil is Chandler's brother Eoghan. It's pronounced Owen."

Jolly made a notation next to the name on the list. Jarmila finished identifying people in that picture and ran through the rest of the pictures with Jolly. She identified Chandler's siblings and aunts and uncles and cousins, all the ones on the guest list that a picture could be matched to. Still for many other names, pictures couldn't be found, because of privacy status or the person wasn't on social media.

"I spent too much time here. But at least I have some advantage when meeting them. It's easier to match a face with a name."

Chandra came into the tour office. Jolly handed her the clipboard that had all the papers on it.

"Take this, make sure everything is entered correctly. Add my notations. Print 5 copies out so I can get one to Scot and Everett as well. Don't take it to the box office yet. The crew list isn't complete and those assholes have until 5:30 to get it to me. If this gets fucked up, someone is getting fired."

"Mean Jolly is appearing tonight." laughed Jarmila.

"Yes. Don't fuck with me tonight, Jar."

"Can we fuck later?"

"Only if you wear those heels while I'm fucking you." he grinned, looking at the Jimmy Choo black stiletto open toed sandals.

"OMG I've fallen in love with a shoe man." she said as she kissed his lips softly.

He brought her face closer to his and kissed her intensely. He put his hand up her lavender Lucy In The Sky Starstruck mini dress.

"You're not wearing panties." he said.

"I'm surprised you noticed considering your fascination with my shoes."

"Don't test me tonight, Jar. You won't like Mean Jolly if he turns on you. Now, go put on some panties. We've got the band's family here. They don't need to see the world." Jolly said as he motioned his hands to below her waist.

Jarmila went to the dressing room to put on panties and Jolly went out front. Soundcheck was in less than 15 minutes and he hadn't seen any of Lenehan. Jarmila joined him. He pushed her into a dark corner by the floor level of the stage and stuck his hand up her dress.

"You don't trust me?" Jarmila asked.

"I trust you'll try to get away with as much as you can." Jolly said, looking sternly at her. He looked up at a stage light, turned to a roadie, "This is the third *motherfuckin'* time I've come by here and ordered to fix that *goddamned* light and it's still fucked up. Replace the damn thing! Jesus Christ on a cracker, my grandmother could have fixed that light by now, and she's been dead 20 years! The next time I come by here and it's not fixed or replaced, *you're fuckin' fired*! Walk with me, Jar."

Mean Jolly had come out to play. The one with the reputation of putting up with no shit, not suffering a fool, scaring his crew and staff by his screaming and yelling, and firing people who pissed him off and didn't do their jobs correctly. He walked up to the stage, put on Chandler's favorite guitar, and started playing.

"It's not the fuckin' monitor, *motherfuckers*. Jar, can you hear the guitar coming through the monitor?"

"Yes, Jolly I can. But he's been having problems with the monitors since the beginning of the tour."

"I didn't ask you for a history of Lenehan tours. I asked you if you can hear *the fuckin' monitor*!"

"You don't have to yell at me! Bitch don't sign my paychecks."

Jolly gave her a severe look.

"Come over here, Jar." he said as he sat on an amp, "What do you feel?"

"A humming, vibration! Is that bad?"

"No, that's good, that usually means it is working."

He played a few more notes on the guitar, used the pedals once or twice.

"It's the fuckin' guitar." he growled. He handed it to a guitar roadie, "Fuckin' fix it."

"That's Chandler's favorite guitar. It's a 1995 Gibson BB King Lucille ES."

"I know what it is. And I also know there's something wrong with it. Someone phone the local Catholic archdiocese and see if we can get a priest here to perform an exorcism on Chandler's favorite guitar."

"He's going to shit if he can't have Lucille up onstage tonight. His family is here and he wants to impress them. Do you think it can be fixed?"

"I don't know, sugar. I'm not an expert on fixing guitars. Walk with me." he said as he headed down the stage stairs. Halfway down the stairs he took the Dum Dum out of her mouth and gave it to a roadie to throw away.

"Hey, I just opened that one!"

"And I just threw it away!"

"You're so mean." she pouted.

He stopped at the bottom of the stairs and put his hand under her chin.

"Sugar, I'm going to yell tonight. But I'm not yelling at you. Know this. I'm loud and obnoxious and will probably fire at least half a dozen people tonight. This is not reflecting on you at any level. I am not yelling at you. I'm just yelling. At everyone. Except you. You I love. Walk with me, Jar."

They went to the sound board. Jolly moved the microphone towards him.

"It's 5:00pm kids and do you know where your guest list is? Neither do I. But if it's not in by 5:30 pm, ain't none y'all gonna have guests tonight." said Jolly.

"You said that in a perfect Chicago South Side accent. You could be a native Chicagoan." laughed Jarmila to Jolly.

"Where the fuck is Everett?" Jolly asked Keith as he walked by.

"I don't know. I'll find him." responded Keith.

"Also go order a cake from somewhere and have them put "Happy Birthday Mom" on it. Tomorrow is Jack's mom's birthday."

"Already done." answered Keith, as he left to find Everett.

Jarmila then followed Jolly to the light board.

"You see that light that is flashing on and off for no apparent reason?" Jolly asked Claude the lead lighting tech, "I've asked several times that it get fixed or replaced. And guess what? Neither has been done. Get the problem solved or *you're fuckin' fired*!"

They went to the balcony. Jarmila sat in a seat closest to the aisle. Jolly sat next to her.

"Why is Benny playing "I Dreamed A Dream" from "Les Miserables" on violin? And why is Johnny on piano and Chandler on acoustic? And why does Jack look like he's fallen asleep at the mic?" Jolly asked.

"They're practicing "I Dreamed A Dream" because it's Jack's momma's favorite song and he wants to sing it to her tomorrow at soundcheck."

"Jack's got a great voice. But shades of Satan I can't *wait* to see him pull this one off."

Jack started singing. Crew, and staff stopped working to watch. When he got to these lyrics, everyone was looking at him.

"I dreamed a dream in times gone by

 When hope was high and life worth living

 I dreamed that love would never die"

Jolly's jaw could have hit the floor.

"Holy shit. I knew that boy could sing, but damn. That boy can *sing*." said Jolly.

"He's had voice lessons since he was little. But he does have a naturally good voice." answered Jarmila.

"Walk with me, Jar." Jolly said as he stood up.

She followed him down the stairs.

"You know why I don't like shows where lots of family show up? It's not so much the uh…extra security, extra rooms, extra staff, extra food and drink, extra work…nah, I don't mind that at all. I love to work. I'm a fuckin' workaholic. It's the part where I have to be nice to the family. 'Nice to meet you Ms. Connelly, did you know your son is a sadistic psycho who's one step away from 'Put the lotion in the basket?' and 'Hello Ms. Riley, do you know your son likes to suck cock and you probably think he's going to hell because of it. But that's okay because he wants to go to hell and play guitar with Robert Johnson for all eternity.' Fake. I don't like being all fake and nice and shit."

"When you said 'suck cock' I couldn't help thinking of that line from "The Exorcist": 'Your mother sucks cocks in hell!'" said Jarmila.

"Terrifying movie."

Jack continued singing:

"And there are storms we cannot weather".

"Damn," Jolly said, "that boy can sing."

When they were passing the sound board, Everett handed Jolly the crew guest list.

"Oh, is this the crew guest list?" Jolly asked sarcastically, "With 2.4 seconds to go before you and your crew would *have no guest list.* How nice of you to get it to me with such accurate timing! Where were you? I don't give two fucks where you tell me you were as long as it is not 'I was getting head'."

"I was dealing with the stairs leading up to the baby grand. Jack wants it, but I don't think I can make it stable enough to be safe. I had a two-way with me." said Everett.

"I'd be glad you had a two-way radio *if we were on a 1983 Motorhead tour.*" responded Jolly.

"But Scot said everybody has to have one." said Everett.

"Did Scot die and reincarnate as me? I'm the one who makes decisions on this tour. That's why I have the title of Tour Manager. Because I take care of the tour. Scot has the title Band Manager because he makes decisions for the band. I don't give a shit if you have to have a crew member lift Jack up on top of the baby grand. *Fix the problem.* I keep telling him he's going to damage that baby grand if he keeps insisting getting on top of it. But hell, his money, he can burn it anyway he wants. Walk with me, Jar. We're going to the best seats in the house, V.I.P. box."

Jarmila followed Jolly through the venue and up a small set of stairs off to the right side. Then they turned left and came to a set of stairs that was roped off with a red velvet rope.

Jolly unclipped one side of the rope and let Jarmila through, went through himself, then re-clipped the rope. They went up a flight of stairs, sat down in the seats by the railing.

"Do you know why these are the best seats in the house, Jar?" asked Jolly.

"Because I get to sit here with you?"

"Aww, my sunshine." he said, and kissed her deeply. "I needed that. I need my sugar every day. These are the best seats in the house because you can see everything. Some people think right up in front is the best place. But I don't think so, unless a person likes it when a musician sweats and spits on them. Unfortunately, I don't have enough box seats to accommodate the entire families. I think Chandler went on Ancestory.com and invited anyone even remotely related to him. I'm doing this by rank. Mothers, fathers, grandparents, siblings, grandkids, aunts, uncles, cousins. Except Benny's cousins. They're on high priority status because they drove in from Texas, and he doesn't have a lot of family nearby. Walk with me, Jar."

"Where will everybody else sit?" asked Jarmila.

"I've got nice seats for them, just not as nice as V.I.P. box. Another pain in my ass when there's lots of family is complimentary tickets. Comp tickets are my nemesis. We only get so many comp tickets per show. Unless a person is working the show, every butt in here needs a ticket. Even General Admission. The fire marshals have a real beef up their asses about capacity limits. Could be because people die in fires in places that are over-capacity. That is why I need to make sure all the guests have comp tickets. But then Chandler invites the Irish Diaspora and I've got to pull comp tickets out of my ass. Plus, a lot of the crew are from the Chicago area and their families are coming up here too. And the show is sold out so it's not like we could go buy some tickets. Tomorrow is sold out too."

"What are you going to do if you don't have enough tickets?"

"Work a miracle like I always do."

They walked past the front of the stage. Chandra was walking in Jolly's direction. He handed her the crew guest list.

"Type this up and get all guest lists to the box office *now*. Check to make sure there's enough comps and passes. There's probably not going to be enough comps. Tell Ryan if he gives me his extra comps, I'll name my first fictitious grandchild after him." Jolly said. Ryan Walters was the Senior Talent Buyer for the production company that put on the shows at this venue. He and Jolly went way back as friends.

Jolly was in front of the stage, in the middle, looking up. When he saw Les, he called him over.

"Why are there no security at the V.I.P. box entrance on that side." he said, pointing to the side he and Jarmila had walked from, "I bet there's no security on the *other side* either. Fuck me, I should quit this job and become a psychic."

"It's an hour before doors open. I don't put security there this early." answered Les.

"Now you do! I have band families already backstage and I want to get them to their seats, preferably before doors open, so they can get comfortable before seeing their certifiably deranged spawn work magic on stage. Walk with me, Jar." said Jolly.

Lenehan was playing "Ass Like That" by Eminem. Jarmila started twerking and dancing. Jolly made a signal with his hands for the band to stop playing.

"Really, Jack." Jolly said, "Really? There are little kids backstage who can hear you sing that."

"Then they'll learn all da words." sneered Jack, and Lenehan started playing where they had left off.

"Stop dancing like that!" Jolly yelled at Jarmila, "You're not at a fuckin' strip club!"

"Because if I was, you'd marry me." responded Jarmila.

"Okay Miss Malone," said Jolly, "you can go to the dressing room and stay there until I send for you. Who knows, I might need more sarcasm."

"I don't want to go to the dressing room. I don't like all that family that will be in there."

"The family has their own hospitality room. No one is in the dressing room except a few people doing whatever their job descriptions say they are supposed to do. And stay away from wardrobe. Bella is in kamikaze mode."

"Jack again?"

"Jack always. Now, to the dressing room, Miss Malone. You are officially in time out."

She started towards the backstage when Jolly suddenly grabbed her and pulled her into a room in a side hallway. It looked like an office supply closet, with shelves of office supplies and chairs and desks, a couple computers.

Jolly closed and locked the door and pushed Jarmila against the door. He turned her around so her face was against the door. He pulled down her panties and cupped his hand between her legs.

"You gonna dance like that for me later, Miss Malone?" he asked, putting a finger in her vagina.

"If you want me to."

"Wearing nothing but those heels?" he asked, putting another finger in her vagina and pushing the two fingers up and down.

She turned around and kissed him.

"Do you want to make love?" she asked.

He removed his fingers and pulled up her panties, straightened out her dress.

"I do, but I can't. I don't even have time for a quickie. But I'll make it up to you later." he grinned and pulled her aside, unlocking and opening the door, "Now, off to the dressing room with you. I don't have time for a hot girl who is shaking her ass everywhere. You're fuckin' distracting me. Go read a book."

She went to the dressing room and Jolly went to the tour office.

An hour later, in the dressing room, Jack was standing before a full-length mirror, shirtless. He was trying on a pair of leather pants that had leather strings in place of a zipper. The pants were very low, and even if the leather strings had been tied all the way up, the top line of his pubic hair was still visible. Jarmila was on one side of him and Bella on the other. Bella was holding various pieces of clothing and two pairs of sunglasses.

"I love it. It's my favorite pair of pants on you. I love how it shows your hips. That little line of pubic hair drives me crazy." said Jarmila, running a finger along the line.

"Crazy enough you'd let me go up that tight ass of yours tonight?" asked Jack.

"Don't you have family here tonight?" she asked.

"Yeah, but they're not going to stay up all night."

"I'm sure you'll find a not-so-nice-girl to keep you up all night." she answered.

"Oh, hell no! You are not turning me down. I call for you, bitch you better be naked on all fours on da bed!" Jack exclaimed, "Bella, let me see those sunglasses. Da ones with da gold. Those. What do you think, Jarmila?"

"Nah."

"What about these?" he put on the other pair Bella handed him.

"I think you should go without sunglasses tonight." Jarmila responded.

Jolly suddenly appeared in the mirror, over Jack's shoulder.

"You *are not* wearing those pants onstage tonight." Jolly emphasized.

"I most certainly *am* wearing these pants onstage tonight. Jarmila, what do you think about a shirt? No shirt? What about a vest. A leather vest?"

"A leather vest? Is there a Judas Priest look-a-like contest going on tonight?" Jolly jested.

"Shut da fuck up, Jolly." said Jack, "Don't you have some tourey managery shit to do?"

"I've been doing it. That's why your family are pleasantly sitting in a nice room eating excellent food, waiting to take their very nice seats so they can watch your very nice concert."

"Jolly," asked Jarmila, "am I still in time out?"

"Time out?" enquired Jack, "What did you do? Spill your Enfamil? You wouldn't have this problem, Jolly, if you beat her ass on a regular basis. I beat her ass and she loves it. Doncha love it, Jarmila? She screams with pleasure and begs for more."

"You are such a vile human being." said Jolly, going in the direction of the door, "I just…can't."

"What's up fuckin' *Milwaukee*!" screamed Jack to the packed house. Lenehan opened with "Room for Hysteria" from their first album. The band was known for not keeping the same opening songs on the set list. They liked to switch things around.

The crowd went savage when Jack sang:

"There's no room at all to fall

There's no room at allllll

To fall

Hysteria, hysteria

When you did your last eight ball

And your momma hid the Stadol

There's no room at all to fall".

Jolly watched from the side of the stage. He tried to shield his eyes from the reflection of the stage lights, to see if he could spot Jarmila in V.I.P. box seats. But he couldn't see her from his location.

Into the second set, Lenehan was lava. They were consuming everything in their path.

"Wanna stop a second and say hello and loves ya to all da family and friends who came here to this great city of Milwaukee from different places to be a part of our show." started Jack, "Gonna start with Benny Mann our drummer's cousins, came all da way in from San Antonio, Texas to see da show. Where they at? There they are. Shine a light on 'em. Everybody give 'em a big Wisconsin welcome!"

The crowd complied with total madness, screaming, shouting, clapping.

"Gotta give a shout out to Alice," continued Jack, "standing right here in front of da stage. Shine a light on Alice, pretty Alice. She gonna kick my ass for calling her out, but I'll hide behind Benny. She likes Benny. Alice and her friends follow us to a lot of different cities. It's because of people like her, and people like you, that we're up here living our dreams. You're da backbone of this band. Y'all buy our albums, download shit like crazy, buy our merchandise. You're da reason we have three singles in da top ten and an album at #1 on da charts. You're da reason we got *two* double platinum albums. We wouldn't be here singing our fuckin' balls off if it wasn't for spectacular fans like you!"

The audience went berserk. Jack knew how to work a crowd, thought Jolly, who had moved behind the stage and over to the side of the venue Jarmila was on. He went up the stairs to the V.I.P seating.

"What do you think, Miss Malone?" he asked Jarmila.

"I think this band is ready for stadiums!" she smiled.

"Gonna give a big hello to our guitarist Chandler Riley's family." said Jack, "It's like one big Riley family reunion out there. Don't think I can catch y'all with da spotlight, so just stand up and scream a lot so I know where you're at."

Lots of screaming and yelling and whooping from the Riley clan.

"Wanna give a big thank you to Chandler's mom and dad. Mr. and Mrs. Riley put up with all our shit for years. They let us use their garage for rehearsals. Fed us, chastised us, tolerated our late nights, and early morning fridge raids. They are like a second mom and dad to everyone in this band. Without your support, we'd still be in your garage, raiding your fridge at 6:00am. Shine a light on 'em. They over there in da V.I.P. seats."

It was complete chaos now, with the Riley clan joining the audience in cheering.

"Wanna say hello to one special lady. She sitting up in da V.I.P. seats too. She is our bass player Johnny Dunne's mom. We call her Ma Dunne. Ma Dunne came from Poland when she was a teenager to help out her family. Lost her husband when Johnny was young. Worked three jobs so Johnny could have music lessons. When we went to her place, she always had food, and you better eat, if you were hungry or not. Ma Dunne is a driving force behind this band. If we were down or disappointed or wanted to give it all up, Ma Dunne would sit us down and say 'You very talented boys. Do not waste da talent God gave you'. And I know she got an ear to some special higher power cause here we are together, 9 years later and we still haven't killed each other."

The crowd roared with laughter. Chandler added "Yet. Shine a light on Ma Dunne and give her some Wisconsin love!"

If this has been the Bastille, the audience would have stormed it already.

"Can't forget our special girl. We all met Jarmila Malone when we were kids. We've been best friends ever since. She's been our solid, our sister, our saint. She has gone through much personal sacrifice by always putting Lenehan first. Big, big shout out to our special girl. She in V.I.P. Shine a light on Jarmila. She's going to kick my ass for shining a light on her, but I'll hide behind Johnny. Johnny's like a brother to her."

The audience became insane with noise.

"One more shout out to my mom and my grandpa. They came all da way from da Humboldt Park neighborhood of Chicago to support me. My mom put up with my wild child alter ego, but she believed in my dreams and helped me to achieve them. I'm up here, mom, because you said I could do it. You believed in me when I needed confidence da most. Want to give a shout to my cousins and their husbands and their kids. It means a lot to me to know I have your support. Lastly, I want to give a big thank you to my grandpa. He's up there in V.I.P. with my mom and cousins. Shine a light on them. Tomorrow is my mom's birthday. Everybody say Happy Birthday to my mom!"

The crowd responded by singing "Happy Birthday". Jack pointed his microphone to the audience.

"How many y'all got a grandpa?" asked Jack, to the wild shouts of the crowd, "My grandpa named Jack. I got lucky to get his name. He's 97 years old and jogs every morning. Swear to God, he can out run me any day. He used to be a famous jazz piano player on da local Chicago circuit. Story is, he was 13 years old and had to help support his parents' family. He went to this local jazz club and pretended to play piano so they'd hire him. And they hired him! He taught me piano, said it would keep me off da streets and out of trouble. Now I'm a rock star and I just get in trouble backstage." he smiled and laughed a little, and the audience ate it up, "My Grandpa Jack, he said all those musicians and dancers in da jazz clubs would get up to some behavior that was SCANDALOUS!"

Then Jack went into their hit, "Scandalous", and the noise was so deafening you could barely hear the band.

"Jesus, that was one crazy ass show." Benny commented, later in the dressing room.

"If Milwaukee is like this, imagine what Chicago is going to be like." commented Chandler.

"Shit, I hope New York is this good." said Jack.

"New York is a tough market to crack." said Scot.

Jolly, reading an industry paper, handed it to Scot, pointed out something on the paper. Scot took the paper.

"Holy living hell," said Scot, "your first album just re-entered the charts at #8 and "Penny" went to #5. Everything else is holding steady."

"*Two* double platinum albums on the charts bitches. *We have arrived.*" said Chandler.

"It's like living the dream," said Johnny, "but it's scary."

"How?" asked Jack.

"We'll always have to do better than anything we released before. It's a lot of pressure." answered Johnny.

Back in Jolly's hotel room, the Lenehan boys busy either going out to party with family, visiting at the hotel or partying with fans, Jolly knew he'd probably have an actual night off with no emergencies. The family kept the boys busy. Maybe shows with lots of family members weren't bad after all, thought Jolly.

Jarmila came out of the bathroom wearing a mid-drift light blue tank top and a flouncy dark blue skirt with ruffles on the bottom half of the skirt. It barely covered anything. Jolly was sitting at the desk looking at financials. She sidled up to him and massaged his shoulders.

"Whatcha doing?" she asked.

"Looking at financials." he said, looking at her entire body.

"Are they interesting?"

"Not as interesting as that outfit you have on. Planning on wearing that tomorrow?"

"No silly, this is lingerie. Strictly for Jolly eyes only."

He turned the chair facing outward.

"Come here." he said to Jarmila.

She moved so that she was standing in between his legs.

"I love you. With all my heart. But we have to discuss these drugs Johnny found in your bag."

"You can kill a mood, Jolly."

"I don't mean to. But we need to get this conversation out of the way before I can concentrate on more important things. Like that fantasy #3 you owe me." he kissed her gently.

"How much are you doing a day, Jar?" he asked

"I haven't done any since *before* you found the one in my purse."

"Truth, Jar? Because you say you don't lie but you've lied to me several times, and that hurts me."

She gave him a sad look.

"I didn't buy that first one you found in my purse before our talk about drugs. I bought it the next day. That's why it was in my purse. It wasn't that I forgot to dump it. I had just bought it."

"Jar." Jolly said, shaking his head, "You are making it difficult for me to make decisions because you are doing shit like this. You're a grown woman, you can do whatever the fuck you want. But I *love you* and I don't want to lose you to drugs. I *never* want to lose you. I should send you back to the guys and have them deal with this. I *can't* physically punish you. I just can't! I can't do that to you. I don't want you to get hurt, but at the same time you're forcing me to make some serious decisions."

"I won't do anymore. I haven't. I didn't do any of the stuff Johnny found in my gym bag. I promise you, Jolly, I love you and won't do anything like this again. Please don't send me back to them. I'm really enjoying this time with you. I'm afraid Jack is going to force me back to him when the family leaves."

"I won't let him. You're with me. Besides you have a bit of a reprieve. The families will still be here for the second Milwaukee show, the 24 Hour Party People will be in NYC, and it's family again at the Chicago shows."

"Then what? Then I go back to Chandler's garage."

"No, then you move into my house."

"I love you!"

"I love you. Promise me no more drugs. Or you and I are going to have a problem."

"I promise."

"I'm going to trust you. Please don't break that trust. Now, move out a little, turn around, put your legs outside of mine."

"I'm going to fall over, Jolly."

"No, you won't, I'll hold on to your waist." he said, grabbing her waist with his hands, "Now, bend over."

She bent over as he requested. It was not a comfortable position, but curiosity got the best of her. He looked at her exposed private parts. He was always so proud of his self-control. This girl destroyed it. He stood her up, and put her on his lap. Her bottom was positioned on one of his thighs, her legs across his lap.

"Now what were we talking about?" asked Jarmila, "Oh. Balls! Specifically, how nice your balls are."

"You have a serious obsession with my balls." Jolly laughed, "You keep with that and they might have to take a restraining order out on you."

"I don't think they'd do that. Your balls have a serious obsession with my tongue."

"Lay across my lap."

"What?"

"Lay across my lap." repeated Jolly.

"But you said you'd never do that to me!"

"I'm not going to hit you. You told me about a fantasy, when we were on the bus. But I didn't do it *exactly* how you wanted it because I didn't want to trigger anything negative. Because of what had just happened between you and the band. So, I improvised. But now, I can do those things you want, exactly as you want them."

She kissed him, long and slow, exploring the inside of his mouth with her tongue. She stood up and positioned herself, face down, across his lap.

"If you get uncomfortable, or start having bad memories, tell me and I'll stop. I want you to enjoy this."

He flipped up the ruffled portion of her skirt and started to massage her bottom. First very lightly and slowly, and then deeper and deeper until she started moving around back and forth. He then put one hand between her legs while still massaging her bottom. He started in circles, and pressed down. Within a few minutes, Jarmila was crying out in pleasure and making small whimpering sounds. She finally became quiet and still. He stood her up and sat her on his lap. She put her head against his chest, and he noticed she was crying.

"Are you okay? Did I hurt you?" asked Jolly, stroking her hair with his hand.

"No. I'm crying because I'm so happy! I really enjoyed that. It was one of the best things to ever happen to me. Thank you, Jolly. I love you so much!"

"I'm going to take a shower, sugar," Jolly said as he helped Jarmila off his lap and stood up, "Want to join me?"

"No."

"One day I'll convince you it's fun." he said, kissing her and going to the shower.

When he got out of the shower, Jarmila was laying in his bed, the covers covering only her feet. She was on the internet on Jolly's phone. When she saw he was out of the shower, she quickly put the phone back on the bedside table.

"I'm sorry I was just looking at YouTube." she said, apologetically.

"It's ok, honey," said Jolly, drying his hair with a towel. He grabbed some clothes out of one of his suitcases and sat down beside her. "You can use my phone anytime you want."

He took the towel off his body and dried himself, then put on blue sleep pants and an W.A.S.P. t-shirt. He took the towels back to the bathroom and hung them up to dry. If there was one thing Jolly detested, it was the smell of moldy towels. He blow-dried his hair and went back to Jarmila.

"The guys don't let me use the internet. It's why I have a flip phone with no internet. They only let me watch some YouTube and educational videos. And movies and tv shows they've downloaded, but only on their phones."

"Jesus Christ on a cracker, Jar, you're a grown woman. I think you can be trusted with the internet."

"The guys don't want me to see negative shit about them."

"I'm getting you a nice internet capable phone tomorrow. If the guys don't like it, too bad. It's a present from me." he went to the opposite side of the bed and got in, "Are your feet cold?"

"Yes." she answered, "I only brought a couple pairs of socks. Mostly I go bare legged or wear fishnets, or some type of stockings."

"I'll buy you socks tomorrow. And a nice pair of slippers."

"Fuzzy slippers?"

"Fuzzy pink slippers. That sound okay?"

"Yes. I love you."

"Come closer to me." Jolly said as he turned on his side.

"How come you got clothes on when you said you don't wear clothes when you are gonna make love?" she asked, turning onto her side to face him.

"Because I'm taking things slow with you. Remember, I told you I want to go slow with you, and follow your lead. I want you to truly understand how sex is a good thing when two people care about each other, and have their best interests at heart. You want a pair of my socks to wear?" he said, running his finger up and down the outside of her thigh.

"Yes."

He started to get out of the bed when Jarmila jumped up and said she'd get them herself. He watched her perky bottom barely covered by the short skirt. She sat down on the bed and put the socks on. Then she got back into bed and turned on her side toward Jolly again.

"Jolly?" she queried.

"Yes, sugar?"

"Can I ask you a sorta weird question?"

She rolled onto her stomach. Jolly put his hand gently on her bottom and stroked up and down from there to the back of her thigh.

"Of course, you can. No question is weird. But I'm telling you, Jimmy Hoffa is not alive and being held captive by aliens at Area 51."

"His bones gotta be somewhere!" she said, playfully pushing his shoulder, "One day the government is going to tell the truth!"

"I'm on pins and needles waiting for the day."

"I got these fantasies, and I think I'm not right in the head for having them. Because they are fantasies that are like what the guys did to me. Except I like what is going on in the fantasies. And I think that's weird, that there's something wrong with me."

"Is Chandler or Jack or Benny included in these fantasies?"

"No. It's always you." she smiled.

"There's nothing wrong with fantasizing about something that might seem similar to something that has happened to you. What the band does to you, it's not sex. It's rape. Rape is not sex. Rape is about control. Especially with Jack. He's very controlling just on an everyday basis. That's why I think you should re-evaluate and re-define your friendships. Because friends don't do shit like that to friends. When you are having fantasies, it's because you want to try those things with someone who would be gentle and kind to you, to see if you would enjoy it."

"If I tell you some of them, you won't laugh at me or think I'm weird?"

"Of course not!"

"I just…I just think sometime I want to try anal sex, but slowly, so it wouldn't hurt so much."

"I think sometimes it hurts no matter what, sugar. Some people like it, and some people don't."

"Do you think sometime we could try it? I don't mean right now. I mean in the future?"

He looked into her cornflower blue eyes. He took his hand off her thigh and moved her hair back. He kissed her lightly on her cheek.

"Sugar. Would you like to try something now? Not the whole thing. I think you are still too traumatized to go for a complete anal sex session. But how about if I try something, and you tell me if you like it or not?"

"Okay, but will it hurt?"

"If it does, I'll stop what I'm doing immediately."

Jolly got out of bed and went to the leather case he kept his comb, brush and various small items in. He took out a small jar of Vaseline that he always used for his chapped lips. Not the greatest choice for what he wanted to do to Jarmila, but better than calling Chandler and asking for more appropriate stuff. He got back into bed. He took the cap off the Vaseline, put some on his finger, put the cap back on the Vaseline and reached over Jarmila to put it on the bedside table. Jarmila looked at the jar sideways, then turned her head to face Jolly.

"You're going to do something to me that involves anal, aren't you?" she asked.

"If it hurts or you don't like it, I'll stop immediately."

"Okay." she sighed, and put her face in the pillow.

"Baby, if you don't want me to do this, I won't. I don't want you to be sad."

"I want you to do it," she said, turning her face to him, "I want someone I can trust, someone I love, and that's you."

He put his finger near her anus. She took a quick breath, in and out.

"You tell me when, sugar."

"Now, Jolly."

He rubbed his finger around, and then slowly put it in her. She gasped and cried out a little. He stopped.

"I'll stop, baby." he said.

"No, keep going."

"Not if it hurts you."

"No, it's okay. It just hurt for a quick second. But not bad. Please keep going."

He kept going, slowly in and out, but no more than the tip of his finger. He had a flashback of his third wife saying he could put his dick up her butt, but just the tip. The flashback made him grin.

"Mmmmm." groaned Jarmila.

She moved her hips up and down to the same rhythm he moved his finger in and out of her. She started softly saying "oh oh oh", so Jolly put his other hand underneath her, between her legs, and started rubbing vigorously. She climaxed immediately. He went to the bathroom and came back with a washcloth. He cleaned the Vaseline from her, and took the washcloth back to the bathroom. Returning, he got back in bed with her. He turned to his side and took her in his arms. She rested her head against his chest.

"That was even better than earlier." she said.

"I'm glad you enjoyed it."

"Can we do it again?"

"Right now?"

"No, I mean can we do it again sometime."

"Absolutely."

Jarmila moved and slid down Jolly's pants. She took him in her mouth. She looked up at him and smiled, because he was already hard. After he came she put her head back on his chest. He put his arms around her.

"You know, Miss Malone, I love you?" he said.

"I love you. Big day?"

"Not too bad. The band is only doing that one song for soundcheck. For Jack's mom because it's her birthday. They're doing a 4 o'clock soundcheck. Everyone, and I mean all the fuckin' families, will be at soundcheck. After Jack sings to his mom, they are all going by chartered bus to some restaurant that has actually closed its doors to the public for this party."

"Wow. That's a lot of people. Must have been difficult for to organize."

"I didn't organize it. It was all done by the time I joined the tour. I think Scot had to arrange everything because of lack of tour manager at the time. Miss Malone, why don't you know about this?"

"Damn, Jolly, you could've answered your own question. *Because Scot organized it.*"

"What a fuckin' bitch. I'll make sure you're included."

"I don't want to go. Jack's momma, she don't really like me. Once, when I was 13 and Jack was 15, he snuck me in his window. He forgot to lock his bedroom door and his momma came into the room in the morning to get his dirty clothes, and she saw me in bed with him. He had his underwear on and I had taken my pants off but had my shirt on. We weren't doing anything. She got real mad. Next day I'm sitting with Johnny and his momma on the stairs of their apartment building, and Jack's momma she comes rolling up and says she has to talk to me. So I say, talk. And she telling me that Jack is going to have a big music career and he's going to go to Northwestern University for some music program and she didn't want him to father any babies

"She sounds like a real winner."

"She's super strict. I don't want to go. Thanks for offering to help me if I did want to go."

"I'm here if you want anything."

She kissed him good night and fell asleep in his arms.

Jarmila woke up with Jolly looking at her.

"How long have you been laying there looking at me?" she asked him.

"Ten minutes." he answered.

"Why didn't you wake me up?"

"I love looking at you sleeping. You're so peaceful."

She kissed him softly.

"What time is it?"

"A little after 8:00am." he answered.

"Shouldn't you be at the venue?"

"Today is Operation Opera Birthday day. That's all on Scot. I don't have to be at the venue until around 10:00am. I have a rare sleep-in day."

"But if I wasn't here, what would you be doing?"

"Going over financials for the 1000th time. Checking up on things for the NYC show. A billion other things to keep my mind occupied. Then I'd go to the hotel breakfast buffet. Then to the venue to yell at various people and threaten to fire everyone at least ten times."

"See that's what I've been trying to tell you. I'm keeping you from doing your job."

"Miss Malone," said Jolly, stroking her arm, "you *are not* keeping me from doing my job. I've actually been more productive since we've been together."

"How so, if you're laying up in bed with me instead of working?"

"I'm more focused so I get more done. I'm calmer, which helps things run smoother. If I'm ready to fire someone, I think of massaging that perfectly round ass of yours, then I'm happy, so I don't fire that person. See? You laying all up in my bed saved somebody's job."

"You're so not funny."

"I'm being real with you! Jar, I would not joke about something like that. I love you. You're my world. I've never been in love before so if I say something stupid or something that irritates you, it's because I've never experienced feelings like this before."

"Never?"

"Never."

"Not even with your wives?"

"Nope. I think I was in love with the idea of being in love. I didn't love any of my wives. But I didn't realize it until I got married."

"Not any girl? Ever?"

"Nope…well…there's this one girl."

"What was her name?"

"Jarmila Malone."

She playfully pushed his arm.

"You're so bad, Jolly." she laughed.

"And you love me anyway."

"I do. I want to stay with you forever."

"You will."

"What is your house like?"

Jolly moved closer to Jarmila and stroked her hair.

"Well," he started, "it doesn't really have a front yard, but it's got a nice backyard. I built a deck so I can bar-b-que and drink a cold one while the sun sets. It's got three bedrooms, all upstairs. There's two bedrooms facing the back and one in front. That's my bedroom, it's the master bedroom. There's a bathroom in there. That's my bathroom. When you move in, you get the bathroom in the upstairs hallway so you can put all your make-up all over the place and I won't care."

"I'm sorry if I leave my make-up everywhere."

"I don't like the extra added time I have to spend getting your make-up off the bathroom counter so I can brush my teeth. These hotel room bathrooms don't have enough counter space. In my house, you get your own bathroom. You can only be in my bathroom if you're naked with me in the shower."

"I don't think I'll ever go into your bathroom."

"One of these days I'm going to get you in a shower with me." he laughed, "Then there's a closet by the upstairs hallway bathroom that I keep towels and linens and household stuff like that. Then downstairs I have a very nice kitchen, I updated it recently. There's a pantry next to it. Then down the hallway, on one side is my office. It was actually listed as a bedroom/office space because it's small. Next to it is another bathroom, then another closet I put my old photo albums in."

"I want to see them!"

"You will. You'll get to see me when I was younger."

"I like you now. Tell me more about your house."

"Next to the downstairs closet is the piano room. I keep my piano in that room."

"I didn't know you played piano."

"I love playing piano. You know those perfect Chicago nights, when it's like 65 degrees and there's a breeze coming in off the lake? I love to open my windows and play piano. It makes me happy." Jolly smiled and kissed her.

"Can I go in there and watch you play?"

"Absolutely. Opposite the piano room is my front room. I have a TV in there. I mostly watch the news. Back down the hallway, next to the front room, is the dining room. Then there's a coat closet, and then the kitchen again."

"Does it have a basement?"

"Yes. It's where I keep a washer and dryer and a lot of equipment, stuff I've picked up on tours. And extra cases of beer, and soda."

"Pop."

"Pop. Ten years in Chicago and I'm still navigating the terminology."

"Where am I going to sleep?"

"Anywhere you want. Jar, you don't have to have sex with me or think you have to pay me back because you're staying at my house. Consider it your house. I want you to be happy and safe, and I would never ask for anything in return. You can have one of the spare bedrooms if you want."

"What color paint is on the walls?"

"One has grey and the other light blue."

"I'm going to paint one neon pink."

"That would be very pretty. Like you." Jolly said, kissing her deeply, long, "I have to get ready for the day."

"Do you want to have sex before you go?"

"Morning sex." smiled Jolly, "I love morning sex."

"More than any other time of the day?"

"With you I love it anytime of day."

She lay on her back, guided Jolly's hand to between her legs.

"Jar." said Jolly.

"Yes?"

"You're always bare."

"Jack doesn't like women with hair down there. He flies this lady in to wax me. She bleaches Chandler's butthole too."

"I don't think I needed to know that." Jolly laughed.

"You said you wanted to get to know more about the band."

"Sarcasm, duly noted."

"I like when you got on top of me. That was the first time I had that happen. Jack always does it from behind, Chandler wants me sitting up on him, and Benny likes me on the side and facing him."

Jolly thought, any other girl would start talking about past lovers, he'd kick her out of bed so damn fast. But not Jarmila. He knew she needed to talk about things, to get a better understanding of her relationship with the band. To understand how things actually were, in reality, outside her tiny band member world. He could tell her and tell her and tell her, but she needed to see it for herself. He slowly got on top of her. He started kissing her neck, that scent of bergamot and cloves filling him, kissing her stomach, going down further.

"No!" Jarmila shouted.

"Okay." said Jolly, looking up at her. He inched his way to being face to face with her.

"I don't want you doing anything like that down there. I don't want your mouth down there."

"Okay." he said quietly, kissing her. "I didn't mean to upset you."

"It's okay."

She guided Jolly into her. He loved how tight and wet she was. He thought, how could he have guessed, at 56 years old, he'd finally found someone where the sex was so incredible, he'd lose his breath touching her. She squeezed him inside and he wanted to explode right there. He never had a woman do that to him before. He kissed her and continued kissing her until his rhythm got faster. She was making little squeaking noises and then louder, and he came inside her, everything inside him was now completely sated. He rolled on his back.

"You are incredible, Miss Malone." he said, breathless.

"I love you." she responded, taking his hand.

He turned to his side and put his arms around her. She smiled and kissed him.

"Now I have to get ready for work." he said, "You coming with?"

"I was going to sleep a little longer. Can I get there at like 2? Or is that too late?"

"That is fine. Soundcheck's at 4:00pm."

"I'll be there are 2."

"I'll send a car for you."

Jolly got out of bed, kissed her, and went to shower.

Things at the venue were pretty quiet considering the massive amounts of things that were going to go on. Jolly checked with production, but Ryan wasn't in yet. He was going to have to beg some more comp tickets for tonight's show. He went to the dressing room, checked on a couple things, and then went to the tour office. His assistants Chandra and Kirk were there. Keith was not in yet. One of the perks of being a senior assistant, he could come in later than the others. Jolly set up his equipment and sat down.

"Kirk, I've emailed you some items I need you to buy. Use my account. Make sure they are put in a big pink gift bag with a big pink bow. Please get them to the production office by 1:00pm. Reserve a car to pick up Jarmila at the hotel by 1:30pm." Jolly said.

Kirk left the office to run the errands.

He texted Ryan: I'm leaving a package in your office. Jarmila, the band's friend, will pick it up around 2-ish. I need comp tickets again, same number as last night, no add-ons. I know, I owe you. I got season tickets to the Cubs. Anytime you want to go, let me know and I got you.

He texted Jarmila: I didn't want to call and wake you, sugar. But when you get to the venue, go to the production office first. There's a package there for you. Kirk is arranging a car to pick you up at 1:30pm.

"Chandra, go ask Levi about the seating arrangement for this afternoon's soundcheck. I want to make sure we have enough people to escort guests to the right seating. And go to the box office or production and get a seating chart. The one emailed to me is not accurate."

Levi was head of venue security. He had worked with Jolly before, and they were good friends. Scot came into the office with Shera and Camille.

"Where were you all morning?" asked Scot, "Hotel buffet breakfast run late?"

"I slept in."

"Lazy motherfucker. I should be more like you: *We got a show to run motherfuckers!*" Scot laughed, imitating Jolly ranting.

"You're almost as funny as the inaccurate seating chart you sent me." Jolly handed Scot the tablet.

"Oh shit. I think that's the seating chart to the Vic Theater."

"Getting a little ahead of yourself, Scot?"

"What can I say, I'm quick on the draw."

"That's what your ex-wife said."

"I'm not going to tell you the things your ex-wives said." Scot laughed, "Where's your side show?"

"Jarmila is still at the hotel. But don't worry Scot, she'll be here soon enough to annoy you AF. Oh, and a super thank you for not including her in tonight's birthday dinner." Jolly said sarcastically.

"Must have been an oversite on my part."

"I'm not sure if you know this, being that you've only managed this band for what, two years, but Jar is their best friend. They like to include her in everything they do."

"I'll make sure she's included."

"She doesn't want to go."

"So, you shit your pants over nothing?" asked Scot, derisively.

"You could be a more decent human being to her. That's all I'm asking." Jolly responded.

4:00pm with families and friends assembled in seating, the band took the stage. Jack looked up into the V.I.P seating where his mom was sitting.

"I always wanted to be a musician." he started, "I was totally into this band called Blind Melon. Sadly, their lead singer, Shannon Hoon, died of an overdose in 1995, so I never got to meet him. But I'd jam to those records. Their song "Change" was da reason Lenehan was formed. My mom, she is a huge supporter of me. Did everything she could to develop my musical talents. She made sure I had voice lessons, guitar lessons, flute lessons. My dad died when I was young, and my mom, she kept things running. Today is my mom's birthday. She's not going to let me tell you how old she is! She's a huge fan of da musical "Les Miserables". Her favorite song is "I Dreamed A Dream". To prove to her those voice lessons weren't a waste of time and money, I'm dedicating this song to you, Mom. I love you! Happy Birthday!"

From the time Jack started the song until its end, he held the audience of family and friends completely captive. His mom had to be handed a Kleenex.

Band, family and friends off to the birthday dinner, Jolly decided a break would be nice. Roadies were doing soundcheck. No need for him to sit in the balcony and see what surprise songs Lenehan would play for soundcheck. He made himself comfortable on the loading dock, dangled his legs and shoes over the edge. Almost immediately Scot sat on his right and Everett to his left. Everett began rolling a joint.

"Shouldn't you be working?" Jolly asked Everett.

"It's my contractually agreed upon toking hour." smiled Everett, sealing the paper and lighting the joint. He inhaled and handed it to Jolly.

"Hey Everett." said Scot.

"What up Scottie, my man." responded Everett.

Jolly inhaled, handed the joint to Scot.

"Did you know Jarmila has a new iPhone, and cute little fuzzy pink slippers?" asked Scot, inhaling, then reaching over and handing the joint back to Everett.

"No, *really*?" said Everett in fake astonishment, inhaling and handing the joint to Jolly, "I wonder where she got those from? She must be a very good girl to Jack."

"Are you kidding me?" said Scot, taking the joint from Jolly, "The band doesn't let her have access to the internet unless they are there to supervise. You know they don't want her to see anything negative about them."

"Hmmm. Who gave her such nice gifts?" asked Everett as Scot reached over again and handed him the joint, "Hey Scottie."

"What up Everett?" asked Scot.

"Did you know there's an unwritten rule on the road that crew doesn't mess with the band's girls. Unless, of course, you're offered one." said Everett, handing the joint to Jolly.

"I think I've heard that rule!" exclaimed Scot, taking the joint from Jolly, "Have you ever taken a band's girl for yourself?"

"Not unless she was offered to me." responded Everett, taking the joint from Scot, tapping out the roach and putting it behind the laminate pass hung around his neck.

"Okay," said Jolly, "you all done being on my jock? The girl's 22-years-old. She's old enough to handle the internet. And Jack makes her wear those high heels all the time. Her feet could use a break. And since you're so inclined to give me shit about giving a few gifts to a lonely girl everyone seems to ignore, I also bought her two packages of pink socks in different designs. Because the poor girl had only two pairs of socks."

"Crossing lines, Jolly, not very good." advised Scot.

"Jack's gonna lose his shit." said Everett, "He sees her with that iPhone, he's gonna turn her over his knee and whoop her ass."

Jolly looked at Everett.

"How many people know what this band is doing to her?" asked Jolly.

"Fuck me!" exclaimed Everett, "How long you been on the road, Jolly? C'mon now, you know tours are like small towns. Everybody knows everything everybody else is doing. Besides, she wears such short skirts, you can see the bruising and marks."

"But the band thinks I'm the only other person outside of them who knows about this. And I happened upon it by coincidence." said Jolly.

"What the band thinks, we just leave it at that." Scot said.

"Yet nobody says anything about this? This girl is being beaten until she can barely walk, and you all ignore it." Jolly said.

"Fuck," said Everett, lighting a cigarette and offering one to both Jolly and Scot, "have you seen my salary?"

"As a matter of fact," said Jolly, lighting the cigarette and handing a lighter to Scot "I oversee the financials. So yes, I know what your salary is."

"I make more on this tour than I would on a bigger tour." said Everett, "My crew makes more money on this tour than they would on another tour of the same size. You should see what they're offering us for Lenehan's next tour. No one wants to lose their jobs."

"So, you keep quiet because you like your BMW in your driveway." Jolly said.

"Actually, I own a Lexus." responded Everett.

"Where is the annoying AF anyway?" asked Scot.

"Probably picking Jolly's pubes out of her teeth." Everett responded.

Jolly looked at Everett and shook his head.

"She's my friend. We're only friends. Poor girl is lonely, has nobody to talk to. She doesn't bother me." Jolly said.

"C'mon Jolly," said Scot, "you think we believe that horse shit? She's been in your room like a week now."

"That's because the 24 Hour Party People were around and Jar doesn't think of an orgy as a spectator sport. I couldn't put her in Johnny's room because he had those headaches. He needed to rest, not stay up with Jar all night watching movies and crying about his mom. Now we've got the band's families. Am I supposed to put her in Chandler's room so when his super religious Irish Catholic mother knocks on the door, and he's too passed out on alcohol and drugs to answer the door, and Jar answers it, what should I tell her? 'Oh, yeah, Mrs. Riley, that girl you've known for years, your son's been fucking her, still, even though he's married. But don't worry, he does it in the garage. Did I also forget to mention he sucks cocks?'" Jolly said caustically.

"Jolly," said Scot, "do you know where my bunk is on the bus? It's right next to the back lounge. Where you and Jarmila go. And, oh my God, I am so *lucky* I get to hear her moaning 'Jolly, oh Jolly, that's so good, thank you thank you thank you'."

"It must have been a dream, Scot, because it never happened." Jolly said, tossing his cigarette, "Now you all can go back to Junior High. I have work to do."

Jolly passed Ryan in the backstage hallway.

"Just the person I'm looking for!" Jolly exclaimed.

"Done." said Ryan, "I'm a Brewers fan, but I'll take you up on your offer."

"Should make a Brewers fan happy to see the Cubs lose." laughed Jolly, going to the dressing room.

Crew and staff were in and out of the dressing room, replenishing the rider for the night, doing various tasks. Jarmila was not there, but a big pink bag with a big pink bow was sitting on a side table. She'd gotten her present.

Jolly went to wardrobe. Chandra and Bella were there.

"Scot has a problem with the band guest list. Jack added two more people, but there's no comp tickets left." Chandra said.

"Not my problem. I'll talk to Scot." Jolly said, "Have you seen Jarmila?"

"She said she was going to get something to eat." responded Bella.

On his way to crew hospitality, Jolly texted Scot.

Jolly: I had to suck Ryan's balls to pull extra comps. Your boy wants to invite some girls he wants to fuck, you can get the comps.

Scot: He's inviting the chef and the chef's wife.

Jolly: Still not my problem. That is why it is a band guest list which clearly falls under the duties of the band manager.

Scot: You handle box office.

Jolly: I cannot get more comp tickets. Try texting Jesus Christ. I hear he multiplies loaves and fishes, see if he can multiply you some comps.

Scot: You are such a dick.

Jarmila was sitting in crew hospitality with her feet in fuzzy pink slippers up on the table, Dum Dum in her mouth. She had on dark green tights and bright red cut-off jean shorts, and a black Lenehan shirt from the current tour. She was looking at the iPhone. When she saw Jolly, she jumped up, hugged him.

"I love it!" she exclaimed, "Thank you!"

"I'm glad, sugar. Get that thing out of your mouth." he said, grabbing the Dum Dum from her mouth and tossing it in the nearest trash can.

"I have an Instagram account now! And Chandra showed me how to take selfies. Can I take a picture of us?"

"Absolutely." said Jolly, smiling for the picture, "Have you eaten today?"

"No."

"Come on over here and get some food." he said, standing by the food buffet.

"I'm not very hungry."

"Miss Malone, you are going to eat." Jolly said sternly, "I'm having a shitty day and I need you to bring me some sunshine. Pick something to eat. I'll make a plate for you."

She moved with him down the table, picking this or that. She wanted only broccoli, but Jolly talked her into chicken breast, potatoes, cantaloupe. She said next to him, looking at her iPhone. She didn't touch the food. Jolly put his fork down and took the phone away.

"Hey!" she exclaimed.

"No phones at dinner." Jolly responded. "Jar, I love you."

"I love you."

"Tell me something about yourself that I don't know."

"Umm…hmm…I have always wanted to go on the swan boats at Humboldt Park."

"Okay."

"What about you? Tell me something about yourself that I don't know."

"When I was a kid, I was a horrendously bad child. My brother and sister were the good kids. I gave my parents enough trouble for a dozen kids!" Jolly laughed.

"Did you get hit a lot?"

"My parents didn't believe in that. They believed if you hit a child, the child grows up and thinks violence is a solution."

"What did they do when you were bad?"

"They took things away from me. Grounded me. I still would leave the house by going out my window! I gave my folks a hard time. But they still loved me and supported my career decision."

"You were lucky."

"I count my blessings, sugar. Miss Malone, I need to talk to you." said Jolly.

"Okay."

"Don't give me those sad eyes. I need your sunshine tonight."

"Okay." she said, kissing him long and slow.

"Scot and Everett, and apparently everyone but the band, know we're in a relationship. Not what kind of relationship, but they know we're together."

"Bad? Good? Should we tell the band?"

"What do you think we should do, sugar?"

"I think we should wait until we get back to Chicago. I don't want to put anyone in a bad mood that might fuck up their performances. But do you think we can hold off that long from telling them? I think they already suspect something is going on."

"Let's play it out. If they directly ask, we'll tell them. We have no obligation to tell anyone."

"I think we'll have to tell them when we get to Chicago because I'm moving in with you."

"I have a solution for that. They're just getting home. They'll want to relax. You can move in with your "manager"."

"I love you." she kissed him deeply.

"I have to get back to work. Are you following me, not exactly assistant assistant?"

"Yes!"

"Okay, I will let you. But you have to dance for me naked in those pair of shoes you were wearing. And you have to tell me another fantasy. We have tomorrow off. Then on to NYC. Then we're going home. Are you excited?"

"Kinda."

Jolly and Jarmila walked out of crew hospitality and went toward the dressing room. The band was still not back from the birthday dinner.

"Why only kinda, Miss Malone?" asked Jolly.

"I've never stayed in one place before since I was a kid. What if the band gets mad and doesn't want to be friends with me anymore?"

"Miss Malone. These guys, they are not going to end their friendships with you. Jack might get pissy, but he'll get over it. If your heart hurts, I'll hold you until it heals."

If there was anything to top the first night in Milwaukee, it was the second night. Lenehan was slaying it onstage. Once again, Jack did introductions, the audience sang "Happy Birthday" to his mom. The boys were better behaved because their families were around. The band not only played songs from their first two albums, but threw in some from a couple demos they had done before they made a deal with their record label. One song, in particular, was a favorite among the long-time fans. It was called "She Coulda" and some of the lyrics went like this:

"When the boys are lined around the block

 And things get outta hand

 Baby pick up all the pieces

 And come and see the band."

Outside, you could hear the roar from the crowd a long way.

In the dressing room after the show, the band was utterly exhausted. The next day was arranged so they could have a day off to say goodbye to their families. For Benny, it would be particularly tough. He probably wouldn't see his cousins again for months. Not until the next tour, when there was a show scheduled for San Antonio. The good news, Alice was moving to Chicago to be with him.

Jack was sitting on the couch with his legs up on chair. He had a towel over his face. Chandler was next to him, his legs dangling over the back of the couch, his head over the edge of the seat cushion, looking at social media on his phone. Johnny was in the shower, and Benny was shooting up before plans to party with his cousins. Scot was settling the show. Jarmila and Alice were in wardrobe, talking fashion with Bella. Jolly sat down next to Jack.

"What up, mouthy cretinous tour manager?" derisively said Jack, taking the towel off his face, "Looking for advice for engagement rings for Jarmila? Don't waste your time. She'd never marry your moronic ass."

"Such *big* words, Jack!" exclaimed Jolly, "You've been reading Websters Dictionary!"

"Fuck off." said Jack, vehemently.

Chandler swung his legs over the couch and sat upright.

"Jarmila is marrying Jolly?" he asked

"I'm not even dating her." responded Jolly.

"But you're fucking her." declared Benny, sitting in a chair next to the couch.

"No, I'm not." Jolly said.

"Everybody knows you're fucking her." said Jack, "You think we don't got ears to hear? Da crew yaks and yaks and yaks."

"She don't kiss you like you're her friend." said Chandler, "She kisses you like you got yourself some sumthin' sumthin'."

"He give her some shit we don't give her, now she's all Ahhhhhhmm in loooove." sneered Jack.

"Got that tongue going up her pussy, all up and down, up and down." Chandler laughed.

"She tastes pretty good, Jolly?" asked Jack, coarsely.

"More importantly," started Chandler, "how do we taste?"

Jack, Chandler and Benny roared with laughter.

"What's so funny?" asked Johnny as he returned to the dressing room from the shower.

"Nothing." replied Jack.

"Well," said Jolly, "now that you've all had your 5th grade humor for the night, you might want to read this." He handed Jack a paper.

"Holy shit!" exclaimed Jack, sitting up straight, ""Penny" is at #4."

"Damn!" exclaimed Benny.

"Bitch, we gonna have all the top spots 1,2,3," said Chandler, "We have arrived!"

"Arrival and departure, because the label is talking European tour next spring." said Jolly.

"Well shit, Jolly," said Jack, "You better make sure your passport ain't expired."

"I didn't know you loved me so much Jack, to take me on a European tour." Jolly laughed.

"Are ya kidding me?" asked Jack, "You're da best tour manager in da business. We ain't gonna let no other band near you."

Later on in Jolly's hotel room, he was sitting at the table with his laptop in front of him, working. Jarmila came out of the shower. He looked at her and wondered if he should tell her what the band said to him about he and Jarmila's relationship, then decided against it. It would upset her and she'd probably want to talk with the guys, which could lead to problems. Especially with Jack, who's moods changed like gusts of wind.

Jarmila was wearing his tan robe and the black Manolo heels he liked her in. She stepped between his legs.

"I'm working, baby." said Jolly.

She dropped the robe. She was completely naked.

"You wanted me to dance naked in heels for you." she said, "Here I am."

"I'm working, baby." Jolly responded, "I have a couple more emails to send out and then you'll have my full attention."

Jarmila responded by turning around and bending slightly forward.

"Jar," said Jolly, taking her by the waist and turning her around, "I'm working. I'll be with you shortly. Go sit down."

She sat in a chair by the window. She was facing his side. She got up, retrieved her purse. Rummaging around in it, she took out two chocolate licorice sticks. She put her purse on the ground. Lifting one leg over the chair arm, she bit a small piece off one of the licorice sticks, and chewed slowly. Jolly turned to look at her. He grabbed the robe from the floor and handed it to her.

"I'm working. Stop distracting me." he said, motioning with his hand for her to give him the candy.

She handed the licorice to him. He took the full piece and gave her back the half-eaten piece.

"You're letting me have candy?" she asked, incredulous.

"Once in a while. If you eat healthy, I'll let you have a treat." he replied, taking a bite of the licorice, "Besides, chocolate licorice is my favorite candy."

"Do you know what my favorite candy is?"

"Let me guess…hmmmm…Dum Dums?"

"No!" she laughed her musical laugh, "I eat those because they're around all the time. Benny loves them. My favorite candy is green apple Laffy Taffy."

"Do you have a passport?" he asked.

"No. Why?"

"The label is talking sending the boys on a European tour next spring."

"Oh my God! I'm so happy for them! Do they know?"

"Yes, I told them after the show. Jack asked me to go along as tour manager."

"This is the best news *ever*!" she cried out with joy.

"Finish your licorice and let me finish my emails."

She put on the robe, picked up her purse, and went to the bed. Grabbing a magazine she had put on the shelf under the bedside table, she got under the covers and started reading. Ten minutes later, Jolly sat on the bed beside her.

"Aren't you getting in?" she asked.

"I'm going to take a shower first." he responded.

"Jolly," she whispered, "is there something wrong? You seem, I don't know how to say it. You seem off. Like not yourself."

"I'm fine, sugar. Just a lot on my mind."

He leaned down to kiss her. She gave him his robe back and he headed for the shower.

Next to her in bed, clad in light blue sleep pants and a M.O.D. t-shirt, he positioned the pillows so he was sitting up beside her.

"What are you reading?" he asked her.

"A bridal magazine Bella was done reading."

"I heard she was getting married."

"Yeah, but not for a while. She wants a big wedding, and she said those take time to plan. Look at these rings, aren't they beautiful?" she handed the magazine to Jolly, pointing to a picture of rings.

"They're very pretty rings."

"I'm never getting married. But if I did, I'd just want a simple band for an engagement ring in palladium with inlaid chocolate diamonds. And a wedding ring with just a simple palladium band. I'd want to have a wedding dress just like my great-grandma Jarmila had. Did I tell you she was 14 years old when she got married?"

"You did. I'm sorry I never found time when you could tell me all about her. I promise when we get home, I'll make time."

"It's okay. I know you're busy. It's the same way with the band. They get tired of me telling stories about her."

"I won't get tired of your stories. I want to know about your family." he said, kissing her and handing her back the magazine, "Why do you say you'll never get married?"

"Nobody would marry me. Johnny is waiting for a Polish or Irish virgin, Benny will probably marry Alice, Chandler is already married. And seriously, would *you* want to be married to Jack? The bruises would never heal."

"They're not the only four people in the world as marriage choices."

"Yeah, but I'm ugly. Nobody would want me for a wife."

"Miss Malone!" exclaimed Jolly, "Don't say that about yourself. You are the most beautiful woman in the world."

"My grandmother said I was ugly. She said I looked just like her mother, who was my great-grandma Jarmila, who was supposedly ugly. Well, they called her "plain". Do you want to see a picture of her? I've got only one. It's of her and her husband on their wedding day. He was her father's first cousin, so I'm not so sure how she was related to him. He was older than her, like in his 40's. But I know his last name was Bisnik, like hers, so she didn't have to change it."

"I would love to see the picture." said Jolly.

Jarmila grabbed her purse from the floor. Getting back into bed, she adjusted it on her lap and opened it. She took out a large plastic sandwich bag which contained a sepia-tinted photo. She took the photo out and handed it to Jolly. The photo was of a young girl next to an older man. He had on a suit and she had on a mid-ankle white laced dress, pointed shoes, and a lace headband with a veil in the back. In her hand she held a bouquet of peonies. The young girl looked remarkedly like Jarmila.

"Isn't that wedding dress gorgeous?" she asked Jolly.

"It's very pretty." said Jolly.

"I want to be married in a gown like that. With those pointed tiny heeled shoes. In white. Everything in white. The lace! I love the lace."

"What year was this?" asked Jolly, turning over the photo, where there was faded handwriting, "1916". "You'd probably have to have a replica of the gown like that made."

"You don't think I could find one on the internet?"

"You might be able to. I don't know the quality it would be, since it would be over 100 years old. You're so skinny I don't know if you'd find one in your size." said Jolly, handing her the photo.

"I could have it altered." Jarmila responded, putting the photo back in the sandwich bag and her purse on the floor.

"You could. You would look very pretty in it. You look very much like your great-grandma. She was very pretty."

Jarmila snuggled close to Jolly. He held her in his arms and stroked her hair.

"You make me feel like a princess." she said.

"You are my princess." Jolly said. "Jar, do you really love me?"

"Yes."

"I mean, really, really, truly love me?"

"Yes!" she exclaimed, looking into his eyes, "You don't think I love you?"

"Forgive me, sugar. I overthink things. I've never had this feeling, this true love. I can't understand how I got so lucky to have you by my side. Then I start overthinking things. I think, you're surrounded by young guys, you're young, beautiful, why would you want to be with someone like me?"

"Because you're amazing, sexy, good-looking, smart, I could go on all night," said Jarmila, "but I would like to make love to you instead of talking. Oh! I was supposed to dance naked for you!"

"That's okay," Jolly replied, "I'm happy you wore those heels for me. Would you do me a favor?"

"Yes."

"Will you stand up with those heels on? I want to just look at you."

She stood up. Jolly sat up on the edge of the bed and looked at her, up and down, turning her in a circle.

"Yup," he said, "you're making my head spin."

She took her heels off and she and Jolly went back to bed. He held her in his arms, kissing the top of her head.

"I'd stay in bed with you all day if I could." she responded.

"That would be Heaven for me," he said, "but I want you to get out more. You're on tour, see the things different cities have to offer."

"I'd rather stay in the room reading. I'm on *Wuthering Heights* now."

"Would you at least go to dinner with me? We leave at 8:00pm for NYC, but we could make it an early dinner."

"Yes, I'd like that. But I want a steak dinner." she said, snuggling tighter against him, "You can kiss my inner thighs and that's it."

"That came out of nowhere."

"Just don't put your lips anywhere else down there."

"I promise."

Jolly started kissing her on the check, moved to her lips, breasts, stomach. He lifted one of her thighs and kissed the inner portion. He lifted her other thigh and kissed it up and down. He gently put two fingers in her vagina, and explored the rest of her. Then he moved up and started kissing her stomach, her breasts, her mouth.

"I liked that." she said.

"You're beautiful down there. You're beautiful everywhere."

"Are some vaginas ugly?"

"Well, some aren't quite as pretty as others."

She kissed him and he entered her. He wanted to stay there for the rest of his life. He wanted happiness forever, and here it was, lying underneath him, with blonde hair and cornflower blue eyes.

They woke to Jack screaming in the hotel hallway.

"I guess it's going to be one of those days." remarked Jolly as he got out of bed and put on some jeans.

"Why we gotta leave at 8 o'clock tonight? I thought today was our day off!!" Jack raged.

"It's a long drive to NYC." explained Scot, "It was decided it would be better to leave tonight and give you some rest when we get to NYC, rather than taking a chance we'd barely get there and you'd have to go right onstage."

"This is supposed to be my motherfuckin' day off! I'm fuckin' resting!" Jack screamed.

"We're not leaving until 8:00pm." Jolly explained, "Rest until then."

"Fuck you all and fuck this tour!" Jack screamed, walking back to his hotel room and kicking the door.

Week four, New York City-Chicago

Everyone assembled in the back lounge of the bus, Jolly gave a run down for New York City.

"I think we'll be arriving no later than 10:00am tomorrow. I have nothing scheduled for you until the afternoon. There'll be a podcast interview at 3:00pm, and a contest winner meet and greet at 4:30pm. You're free to roam after that. April 3rd I've put aside time in the afternoon for the five of you to have your private birthday party for Jack. The cake has been ordered, as well as the ingredients Jarmila says she needs to make rum punch. I've alerted all staff and crew to leave you, as Jack requested, "da fuck alone" during this time. Soundcheck at the usual time, 5:00pm. This place is the biggest venue you have ever played here. It's sold out, which should give you an indication of your rise to stardom. I'm of the understanding you have only played clubs in NYC?"

"Only small clubs." replied Jack.

"You're breaking into the NYC market," said Jolly, "not an easy thing to do. A great indicator of how well you are doing."

Scot, Benny, Chandler and Johnny went to the front of the bus. Jolly, Jarmila and Jack stayed in the back lounge. Jack put his feet up and sprawled out on the seat. Chandler re-appeared with a stack of folded shirts, placing them on the table. He continued standing, pulling the first shirt from the pile, a bright green long sleeved t-shirt.

"I'm trying to decide on which shirt to wear to the afternoon meet and greet. What do you think of this one?" he asked.

"Like da leprechaun needs to be put back in his cage." Jack said with disdain, "Why don't you have Bella pick you something from wardrobe?"

"Because I don't want to look too rockstarish." Chandler replied.

"You *are* a fuckin' *rock star*." Jack replied.

"I wasn't asking your opinion anyway. I was asking Jarmila." said Chandler, "Jarmila, what do you think of this one?"

He pulled out a shirt and unfolded it. It was black with an American flag on front.

"Like you're going to a fuckin' Fourth Of July picnic." Jack ridiculed.

"My poppa used to have a shirt like that." said Jarmila.

"Your father was a bad man." said Chandler, pulling out another shirt.

"Don't say that about my poppa! He raised me after my momma abandoned me!" cried Jarmila.

"Your grandma raised you, and she did a piss poor job of it." Chandler retorted.

"Your father was an alcoholic pedophile who raped little girls" Jack added.

"That's not true!" exclaimed Jarmila.

"It is true. How do you think you were conceived?" asked Jack.

Jarmila ran from the back lounge. Jolly, watching the entire exchange, closed his laptop.

"What was that all about?" he asked.

"Jarmila's father was a pedophile. He never got arrested or went to jail. Family had connections with da police superintendent. Probably paid him off and paid off da victims' families so he wouldn't get arrested." explained Jack, "Got an eleven-year-old girl pregnant. She miscarried. Got a fourteen-year-old girl pregnant. She gave birth to Jarmila da day after she turned 15. My mom got this info about Jarmila's dad from someone she knew, a couple years ago. Jarmila's father was 25 years old when he got Jarmila's mom pregnant. Fuckin' child rapist."

"Do you think he molested Jar?" asked Jolly.

"Who da fuck knows." answered Jack, "She's never said anything to any of us. She used to tell this story about how every morning when he got home from a drinkin' spree, she'd sit on his lap and he'd sing "Molly Malone" to her. She said he always called her "Molly" cause he said "Jarmila" was too heavy a burden of a name for a child to carry."

Jolly put his laptop in its bag and went to the front of the bus.

Jarmila was in Jolly's bunk. Jolly laid down on his side to face her.

"You okay?" he asked.

"Yeah." She answered, but there were tears in her eyes.

He wiped away the tears that started falling.

"Don't mind those guys. They say lots of stupid shit without thinking. You loved your father and that's all that matters. Keep those memories close to your heart and his spirit will always be with you. Fuck what anyone else says." he said, as he drew her into his arms.

New York City was a city that never slept. It offered the band plenty to do the day before the show. With the exception of Johnny, the 24 Hour Party People kept the band busy. The day of the show it was Jack's 24th birthday. Lenehan and Jarmila gathered in Jack's suite early in the afternoon. It had been a tradition since the boys were 17, to have a small private party with only them and Jarmila.

Jarmila had ordered a cake from a local bakery. Keith had brought by all the necessary ingredients for rum punch, and a cooler full of ice, and told them if they needed anything else, please call him. Jack looked at everything and his mood was uplifted. Here he was with the most important people in his world celebrating the most important day of his life. He didn't want to do that with anyone else.

Jarmila made the punch, a recipe she had found on a handwritten piece of paper between the pages of her grandmother's cookbook. It was a recipe from her great-grandmother, Jarmila Bisnick. Every year it was certain to get the guys intoxicated. The birthday cake was white icing with green piping, Jack's favorite colors. Vanilla inside with strawberries. His favorite. Favorite people, favorite cake, favorite old recipe drink, he couldn't be happier than he was at that moment in time.

Jack looked at the presents piled on the table in the living room part of his hotel suite. All presents had been wrapped in green wrapping with white ribbons. He first opened the gift Chandler gave him. It was a Tudor Black Bay Fifty-Eight 18k watch. Jack was so delighted. He loved high end designer watches and had a collection he switched according to what he was doing or where he was going.

"Dude. Dude!" he exclaimed to Chandler, "Thank you so much!"

Next, he opened up Benny's present to him. It was a Serpenti Forever Leather bracelet.

"Dude!" Jack exclaimed, putting on the bracelet, "This is going to look so cool onstage. Thank you!"

He moved on to the gift Johnny got him. It was a Balenciaga Men's Macro-Logo wool scarf, in black.

"Dude!" Jack exclaimed, "Now nobody can say I'm not taking care of my throat. Now I can keep it warm. Thank you!"

Then it was on to Jarmila's gift to him. He opened it slowly and smiled at her. It was a Shure ADX2FD/K8B wireless handheld microphone. Jack looked at it as if Heaven had rained down all the bounty it held.

"Jarmila! This is like da best mic out there. I only dreamed of owning one, after I became a worldwide legend!" he laughed, "I can't believe you got me one. You are da best, Jarmila. You are my special girl. Come over here and give me a kiss."

She sat next to him on the couch and he pulled her on his lap and kissed her, long and deep. Johnny cut pieces of the cake while Chandler poured some rum punch into glasses from a large punch bowl. Jack had ordered it from concierge. Can't have rum punch without a punch bowl.

With Jarmila still seated on his lap, he fed her a couple pieces of cake. Putting the plate on the table, he let her have a few sips of his drink.

"Only fair, you made it, you should get a sip." Johnny said, kissing her again, deeply, tongue exploring her mouth.

A few glasses more of rum punch and the guys broke out the Macallan M Single Malt Scotch Whiskey, a gift from Jolly. Benny brought out the cocaine, high end stuff, a gift from Scot. Everett had given them a 2006 bottle of Moet & Chandon Dom Perignon Rose. He felt so loved and appreciated at that time, his mood remained elated. He loved being a rock star. He was born to it.

Jack whispered into Jarmila's ear, and they went hand in hand to the bedroom side of the suite. Jack started kissing her passionately.

"You see I wore da favorite pants you like so much on me, da leather ones with da line of pubic hair."

"I love those."

"I want to give you a present." he said.

"But it's your birthday, Jack. I'm the one that's supposed to give you a present." Jarmila replied.

"You gave me da best present ever. Now get on all fours on da bed."

"But Jack, it hurts so much. I know it's your birthday, but it really hurts when you have sex with me like that."

"I'm not going to do you like that. I have a surprise for you. Now get up on da bed on all fours."

She took off her green Manolo heels and got on all fours on the bed, facing the headboard. Jack took off his pants. He wasn't wearing a shirt. He positioned himself behind her, pushing up her black dress and removing her black lace panties. She started crying.

"Why are you crying?" he asked her, "I'm not going to hurt you."

Jack rubbed his penis around her bottom, then stuck it by her vagina and rubbed around. Finally, he plunged right in. She made a gasping sound, but not out of pain, out of surprise. He had never taken her vaginally before. After a few minutes he turned her on her back, and continued thrusting up and down. He got next to her ear.

"Do you like it?" he asked.

"Very, very much." replied Jarmila.

She moved to his rhythm. He ejaculated with loud grunts, and laid on top of her for a few seconds. Then he rolled off of her, sat on the side of the bed, and lit a cigarette. Jarmila laid there as if stunned.

"Am I better than Chandler or Benny?" he asked.

"Well," she began, "Chandler is only into himself and getting his needs met. It's like he's the only one in the room. He'll feed me lines about how I'm the best yada yada yada. Benny…he's doped up a lot. Sometimes I just lay face to face with him. He's kind and gentle, though, when he can have sex. Definitely, you are better."

"And Jolly?"

"What about Jolly?"

"Jarmila, everyone knows you're fuckin' him. I know I've been super busy. If you want to keep your plaything for da tour, you go right ahead. But when the tour is over, you go back to da band."

"Do you remember when we first started having these private parties for us five?" asked Jarmila, changing the subject in the hopes of keeping Jack in his good mood.

"Yeah, me and da guys and you. You were 15. We were 17. Well, Benny and Chandler were turning 17, and da next day was Johnny's birthday. Benny's mom was gone for da weekend cause of a friend's funeral. Benny didn't want to go to a funeral. His mom said he could stay home as long as he was responsible and no wild parties. I remember getting drunk as fuck on that rum punch you made. Benny had all da ingredients in da house except da liquor. Chandler got his Uncle Warley to get us some cause we were too young to buy any."

"I bought a cake from Roeser's bakery. It had red icing and it had a guitar, and a drum and drumstick fondant figures."

"I remember. Roeser's got da best damn cakes of anywhere."

"You didn't like the cake I got you today?"

"I fuckin' *loved* it. Just nothing beats Roeser's."

"Now you're a rock star, we can have one flown in from Roeser's for your next birthday!" exclaimed Jarmila.

He put out his cigarette and leaned down to kiss her.

"Do you love me, Jarmila?" he asked.

"Of course, I love you.'

"More than Chandler? Or Benny? Or Johnny?"

"I love you all the same. Maybe Johnny on a little deeper level. He's like a big bro and everything to my heart."

"What about Jolly?"

"Why do you keep bringing him up? He's only the tour manager."

"Jarmila, you shouldn't lie to me on my birthday." admonished Jack, getting on top of her again.

He kissed her, wrapped his arms around her shoulders, laid on his back.

"Give me head." he commanded.

She complied by moving down the bed and putting him in her mouth. She sucked and licked until he was hard. The he grabbed her by the shoulders and laid her on her back. Once again, he rubbed his penis around her vagina, then thrust in and kept up a momentum. When he was done, he laid next to her.

"You're going to be late for soundcheck if you don't get dressed and out of here soon." she said.

"Fuck soundcheck. I'll go naked. I'll go naked with a hard on. You can suck me off on stage."

"Benny can nod off on heroin, and y'all can make it a true sex, drugs and rock-in-roll show."

"Yeah!" exclaimed Jack

"I was joking." responded Jarmila

Everett walked into the tour office. It was empty except for Jolly.

"Where's everybody?" asked Everett.

"Scot's out to lunch, Shera had to get Benny another wrist brace. I'm not sure what happened to the first one. Everyone else is either at lunch or running errands."

Jarmila bounded into the room. Everett handed Jolly some papers.

"Elias Weiss is Benny's new handler. Here's his papers." Everett said, handing the papers to Jolly, "I emailed you a copy of his ID."

"Local guy?" Jolly asked.

"Yes." Everett answered.

"Competent?" asked Jolly

"Yes. Worked as a door bouncer for Lenehan at a few club gigs. Seems trustworthy."

"I wish Alice would have come with us to NYC. Much easier to handle Benny."

"Alice is packing all her stuff to move to Benny's, so she stayed in Milwuakee." chimed in Jarmila.

"I've heard." responded Jolly.

"I know how Benny lost his wrist brace." added Jarmila.

"I'm almost afraid to ask." said Jolly.

"Lanita was giving him head, and he had his tongue in Larita's vagina, and somehow in between that he lost his wrist brace." she answered.

"No," said Everett, "you're wrong, "Larita was giving him head and Lanita was on his face."

"Everett, go back to fuckin' work. Jarmila, who are these people?" Jolly asked.

"They're twins. They are part of the 24 Hour Party People." she answered, as Everett left the office.

She moved next to Jolly. She tried to kiss him but he pulled away.

"You don't want to kiss me?" she asked Jolly.

"You smell like Jack's cologne."

"I was just at a party for his birthday. He hugged me because he was so excited by his present."

"Must have been a twenty-minute hug. Now go wash your mouth out with some anti-septic mouthwash."

"I brushed my teeth before I came here! I don't have bad breath!"

"I am not kissing you when you just had Jack's dick in your mouth. And don't deny it didn't happen."

She turned around and slammed the door on her way out. Scot walked in a few seconds later.

"What's up the annoying AF's ass?" he asked Jolly.

"Jack. Literally." Jolly answered.

"Consensually."

"Apparently. Hey, can you hold things down for a couple hours? I got business to take care of."

"Sure."

"I'll be back by soundcheck."

"I got you covered." said Scot.

If there was one man in NYC who knew his diamonds, it was Ari Feldman. Jack had used his services for rings for his first two wives. This time, he wanted a special ring. Sitting in Ari's private showroom, he saw Ari had a beautiful display of diamonds and diamond rings.

"I brought you all size four bands. It wasn't easy to find the diamonds you had requested. I think I am close enough to fulfill your request. My brother makes all these rings, so I assure you they are good quality." said Ari.

"That's why I do business with you and only you when I'm shopping for jewelry."

Jolly carefully went over the rings. All were exquisite. But one caught his eye. It was a simple band with chocolate diamonds, 1-1/2 carat in vanilla gold. It may not be as inlaid as Jarmila wanted, or the metal she wanted, but he knew she'd fall in love with it.

"I'll take that one." he told Ari as he pointed to his choice., "now I need a simple wedding band with no diamonds."

"For yourself?"

"No. But maybe I should get a ring too. You know, I've been married three times and never wore a ring?" he laughed, "Do you have any men's wedding bands with you?"

"For you, I think ahead. I've brought a few that complement the rings you requested."

First, Jolly picked out a wedding band for Jarmila. He decided on a simple tapering band in the same vanilla gold as the engagement ring. Then he looked over the men's rings. He put a few on. He chose a platinum band surrounded by black with a gold inlay design.

"I'll take these three." he decided. He took out his Amex card.

Ari swiped it and gave it back to him. He put the rings in black boxes, put those in a velvet bag.

"Congratulations on your upcoming engagement and marriage." said Ari.

"Thank you." Jolly said, and went back to the hotel to put his gifts in the safe.

Once back at the venue, the soundcheck had already started. Jolly, impressed by the venue, sat in the lower balcony. Jarmila sat two seats away from him.

"I don't have time to talk to you now." said Jolly, "I'll talk to you on the way to Chicago."

"But you always talk to me when you work!" she cried.

"Remember before I came on tour? And you read books in your downtime? Great fuckin' idea. Bye."

Jarmila stomped off, arms crossed, face enveloped in a pout.

Jack took the stage like a cyclone. Despite their constant partying with their "unofficial" fan club, all manner of drugs and alcohol in their system, they owned that stage. First song up was a raucous song from their second album. Called "Three Times", it was never released as a single, although the band preferred it would be. Lenehan insisted there were rap songs with much more grimy lyrics. Scot told them when they moved to rap, they could have those types of lyrics. Lenehan fans, though not prudes, weren't going to accept a song with those lyrics. Granted, Lenehan lyrics weren't anywhere near g-rated clean, but they weren't that obscene. Lenehan played it live, anyway. After that song, he went into "Countess" from their first album.

"What's up NYC!!!!!!!" he screamed.

Then Jack had a pizza delivered to the stage. He asked the delivery man to stay a minute. He took a slice and handed the box to Johnny who took a slice and handed the pizza box to Benny, who also took a slice and handed the pizza box to Chandler. Chandler took a slice and handed the box to a person in the first row of the audience. The audience went fanatical.

Jack took a bite of the slice of pizza and put the rest on the drum riser. He walked in the direction of the pizza delivery guy, and put his arm around him.

"This is Lou D'Angeli, Jr.." started Jack, taking his arm off of Lou, "He and his father run D'Angeli's Pizza in Brooklyn. Best pizza ever. Don't tell my Chicago fans, they won't let me back in da city!" The crowd whooped and cheered, "Story is, Lou's great-grandfather, Dominic D'Angeli, emigrated from Italy in 1917 to seek da American Dream. He opened up a little pizza joint in Brooklyn. At da same time, in 1917, our guitarist Chandler Riley's great-grandfather, Fintan Riley emigrated from County Louth in Ireland, was also looking for da American dream. Dominic and Fintan became close friends. There's a picture of them on da wall of da pizza joint. They look like old time gangsters! Story goes, Fintan convinced Dominic to let him run a numbers game outta da back room and he'd give him a cut of da bank. Dominic agreed. So why they were serving up pizza up front, they were serving a gambling racket in back. People in da neighborhood started noticing Dominic wearing flashy jewelry and expensive clothes. But this was a mind-your-own-business time, so people believed that da pizza business had been very good to Dominic D'Angeli."

The crowd continued the noise.

"I want to thank you, Lou, for delivering da best pizza in NYC." Jack said, "How late you open?"

"Until 4:00am." answered Lou. He shook Jack's hand and exited the stage.

"Y'all heard him. Now after da show head on down to D'Angeli's pizza in Brooklyn and get yourself a slice of da best pizza in NYC. Don't forget to take a selfie by da wall where da picture of Dominic and Fintan hangs. Hashtag numbersracket. Post it to all your social media sites so my notifications can go off da wall."

Jack then went into a song called "Stories", from their second demo. The crowd ate it up.

"We're going to put that on our third album," said Chandler, smiling, "but don't tell our label."

The audience became cacophonous. After a few more songs the band took a break before the second set. In the dressing room, Jack sat next to Jarmila and held her hand.

"You not only cracked the NYC market. You obliterated it like Godzilla." she commented

"You are da backbone of this band, Jarmila. We couldn't have done all this if you had not been in our lives. You kept us going, no matter what. We all got good advice from our parents. But you gave us da emotional fortification we needed to go on." he kissed her, his tongue in her mouth, whispering to her to find a quiet, dark place she could give him head.

Jolly, who had just bought rings that would symbolize he and Jarmila's eternal love, watched the exchange between Jack and Jarmila from the couch.

The second set was more high-spirited. It was like if the band was possessed. They dove into their songs as if it were the last time they would sing them. Jack stopped after three songs.

"What's up NYC!!!!!" he shouted.

"Wanna say, thank you to our bass player Johnny Dunne!" he shouted.

Johnny played a few notes on his bass guitar. Then Jack introduced Benny, who did a quick drum solo. Next, he introduced Chandler, who played some notes on his guitar.

"Chandler got a wife right here in da audience. She don't come to many shows. She came tonight because it's my birthday."

The audience became rowdy. A few were singing "Happy Birthday:"

"Thank you," said Jack, "thank you. Chandler's wife, she named Marie, shine a light up in V.I.P. for her. She requested a song tonight. It's a sad song we don't usual sing live. When Chandler was first dating Marie, she had a brother, Antonio. Used to be a hard-core gangbanger slinging dope on da corner. Then he saw a 9-year-old girl gunned down in da streets on her way to school. Happens a lot in Chicago. Antonio quit da gang, raised money for a youth center. Kids could go there after school and in da summer, do homework, play basketball and other games, form groups to help other kids. I used to go to da poetry slams just to see what talented young artists we have in Chicago. Da youth group kids cleaned up vacant lots, painted murals, made sandwiches for da homeless, held free community dinners. Did all kinds of things to improve da neighborhood and stay off da streets. All that was Antonio. Only 23-years-old, that was his vision, his goal. And he did it through perseverance and love and a boundless determination to keep Chicago youth safe. Good man Antonio. Heart of gold. Then one day he was out in front of his house talking to an elderly neighbor when he was gunned down. Chandler wrote these lyrics to commemorate Antonio and I wrote da music. I dedicate this to Antonio and other victims of street violence, in every city, and to those loved ones left behind. This is called, "House on Humboldt".

Jack sat at the piano and played the intro. The audience became quiet. By the end of the song, there were tears among both audience and band members.

"While your mayor is dreaming

And your politicians scheming

Our children bleed out in the streets."

There was a moment of silence than clapping and whistling. Jack went straight into "Rulers of Chance", from the second album. Then "Buried Madness", also from the second album.

"Shine a light on these girls up front." said Johnny, "They came as a group of 3. They never seen Lenehan live before. I met them outside da backstage door, standing in da chilly weather. I said, 'Come inside girls and I'll warm you up'. But there's 8 of them so I think I got to divide four and four, four right after da show and four later."

The young women laughed along with the audience.

"Or maybe Johnny can take one." continued Jack, "He ain't got no girlfriend. He's too shy. Maybe one of you girls help him get over his shyness."

Johnny, nearly hiding behind an amp, wondered if any of those girls were virgins.

"Now I got to take some time to bring out a special lady who is da reason we continue to play our balls off. I saw her hiding on da side of da stage, let me see if I can get her out here." Jack said as he went to the side of the stage and returned with Jarmila. She was dressed in a pink strapless gown, with the red Louboutin heels that were her favorite. Her face blushed brighter than the Louboutins. She didn't like to be called out for anything.

"This woman, Jarmila Malone," continued Jack, "she been with us since da beginning. We met her when we were little kids. All us in da band, we're close in age. We were born same year, same month, we on lockdown as friends. Had to unlock our lockdown to let this incredible person in. Loyal as fuck this girl is. Encouraged us to form a band. Insisted we'd be rock stars someday. Never missed a rehearsal or recording or gig. Yelled at us if we got outta hand. Stood between us, this skinny girl, if we got into any confrontation. Jarmila Malone, me and da band, we want to thank you for all you have done for us. I know we don't always show it, but we appreciate everything you have done for us. You are our solid, our sister, our saint. You are da true backbone of this band. You never gave up on us and celebrated every victory, and was sad with us when things got bad. But you always had that buoyant attitude that lifted us up again and never let us wallow in sorrow. It's because of you, I had today da best birthday party. Your rum punch fucked me up. Fucked us all up. Jarmila got her great-grandma's recipe for rum punch. Tastes like juice, kicks your ass with that liquor. This girl here not only got me fucked up on rum punch, but gave me da greatest birthday present I ever got, this microphone I've got right in my hand. Without you, Jarmila Malone, we wouldn't laugh at your conspiracy theories and your jokes and join in your boundless infectious energy. We don't say we love you enough. But I want you to know, despite da insanity that is happening around us, you are always on our minds and always in our hearts."

Jack gave her a long and lasting kiss. He hugged her tight, and the rest of the band came over to do the same. She cried, tears of joy, as she left the stage.

"This next song, "The Only Cost", I dedicate to my special girl, Jarmila." said Jack.

Jack stood silent at the mic for a few minutes. Jarmila was in happy tears on one side of the stage. Jack had dedicated Lenehan's #1 chart topping song to her. Jolly was on the other side of the stage, trying to organize his thoughts.

Jack started singing. The audience sang right along.

"Somewhere in the shadows

Of the coldness of the dawn,

As the day passes on

And you're still all alone,

You give away, you give away

When memories fade

Into the silence,

Just remember, I loved you

I loved you.

When the heartache that you have

Disappears with the emotions,

You've long since discarded

You've long enshrouded,

Thoughts of death surround you.

When all hope is lost

And despair the only cost,

Just remember, I loved you

I loved you."

Chandler's guitar solo kicked in. Then Jack continued the end of the song.

"When all hope is lost

And despair the only cost,

Just remember, I loved you

I loved you."

The crowd went rabid.

"NYC!" Jack shouted, "Because of you motherfuckers that song is #1 on da charts! Our second album is #1 on da charts, and we got two other songs in da top ten on da charts, and our first album re-entered the charts, because of you! And because of you dedicated fans who come to our concerts and buy our stuff and download and buy our material, support us in any way you do, we are playing this beautiful venue tonight. This is our first time outtta da clubs in NYC and into da big leagues, and I know all you motherfuckers out there are going to make sure next time we play New York City, we'll be in an even bigger venue. And it's all because of *you*! We sincerely thank you for all you have done for showing Lenehan some NYC love!"

Jack then went into the story of his grandfather, Jack, and the jazz clubs of the 1930's, as an intro to "Scandalous." Then they played "Penny", then ended the show with a song called "Home", from their first album.

Three encores later and the band was in the dressing room, but only to relax a bit and take showers. Then it was off to party with the 24 Hour Party People the last time on this tour. They wanted to celebrate Jack's birthday in their own special way. They found a private club that was notorious for being one of the wildest clubs in New York City.

"Be back at the bus by 7:00am." Scot told the band. "Bus leaves at 7:00am for home."

7:30am on April 4th, 2019, the tour bus left New York City and headed Lenehan home to Chicago. The band members were all in their bunks, either passed out from liquor and drugs or still high and drunk from liquor and drugs. Quiet, shy, Johnny Dunne promised Jack he would go along on their 24 Hour Party People club field trip. He promised to have one drink to salute Jack's 24th birthday. He said that he had already had two glasses of rum punch, and didn't want to overdue his alcohol intake. Johnny Dunne was not an imbiber of alcohol. 2 hours and 8 various alcoholic drinks later, Johnny lost his senses and his virginity to some girl named Virgen. His first horrendous hangover was waiting in the wings.

Scot was asleep in his bunk. Jolly was in the back lounge working on the Chicago shows. He had caught a few hours of sleep while the band was away partying. As a general rule, Jolly slept little. He was naturally wired to sleep little and work much. Jarmila did not go with Jack's entourage, and instead stayed in the bus reading *The Great Gatsby*. She entered the back lounge with the book. Jolly looked up at her and looked back at his computer screen.

"Busy?" she asked him.

"Huh."

"Can I stay back here and read? It's more comfortable than the bunk. And I don't want to be alone up front."

"Yup."

"You're a man of little words tonight."

"Yup."

She opened the book but couldn't concentrate and kept reading the same paragraph over and over. She knew something was upsetting Jolly.

"Are you mad at me?" she asked him, "You haven't talked to me most of the night. It seems you're avoiding me. Did I do something to upset you?"

He took out his cell phone, pulled up the text screen, and handed it to her. It was a text from Jack to Jolly.

Jack: I fucked Jarmila twice in da pussy. Damn, I should have done that sooner, cause that was some wet, tight pussy there. Also, she gave me head. She gives excellent head. Did she tell you I taught her how to give head, when she was a teenager? Took a few lessons, but she got it right. What I'm trying to say here is, she's been da band's for years, and she will always be ours. You got a couple more days to play with her. Then she comes back to us.

Jarmila started crying.

"You don't love me, Jar, do you?" asked Jolly, "It's all a lie, all a game to you. Did you have fun playing with my heart?"

"I didn't play with your heart!" she exclaimed, "I love you!"

"Why did you throw it in my face by coming up to me smelling like him?"

"I wasn't thinking right! It was Jack's birthday and he got me in the bedroom. I told him I didn't want to do it because it hurt so much. But he said he wasn't going to do it to me that way. He did it in my vagina. He's never done it that way before. I got caught up in the moment! I'm so stupid! I don't know why I let him do that!"

Tears fell abundantly down her face and fell onto the front of her dress. She wiped her nose with her hand. Jolly put his laptop away and moved closer to her.

"I explained to you I don't want a relationship where I am constantly wondering who my lover is fucking. You asked me what to do if any of the guys want sex from you. I told you I'd handle the situation. Instead, you seemed to have your own way of handling a situation like that."

"It was Jack's birthday!"

"So, every birthday you're going to fuck one of them?"

"No! It's never going to happen again. I'm with you and you only. I'm going to tell them the truth about us! I want to be yours forever. I don't want to go back to changing places every day and being available 24/7 if they want sex. I'm tired of living that way. You are my love and I want to live with you forever!"

"It's tough to believe, Jar. Jack's all over you, hugging you, kissing you, dedicating Lenehan's #1 hit to you, going on this big speech about how important you are to him and the band."

"But I am important to the band. At least I was. I don't have a purpose to them anymore. They've achieved what I wanted for them. For what they wanted for themselves. I'm no longer useful."

"Jar, I love you with all my heart. I never make people choose one or the other when it involves relationships. But you are going to have to choose, sex with the band or a relationship with me. You can't have both. I can't have both. I don't mind if you stay friends with them. It would be cruel for me to take that away. You've been friends a long time. But you have to stop having sex with them if you want us to be together. My heart is sore."

She moved closer to him, put her head on his chest. He stroked her blond hair. Reaching over to a shelf behind him, he grabbed the Kleenex box and put it next to him. He took a couple Kleenex out and put his hand under her chin, lifting her face.

"Now listen, sugar," he said, wiping her face, "you've got to make a decision. It's got to be now. I don't want to hurt like this anymore. I feel disappointed in myself getting entangled in a relationship when I said I'd never do this again. This is love, Jar. I *love* you. I've never felt this way, I know it's real, true love. But I can't have it a one-way love. If you don't love me, there is no love at all between us."

She snuggled closer to him.

"I've made my decision. I love you and want to spend the rest of my life with you. I'll tell the guys when they all wake up."

"Baby, I think you should wait. For one thing, they're all going to have dreadful hangovers and be in bitchy moods. They will not take this news well. Probably not even if they were sober. But our best time to tell them would be when they are a little less hungover. Let's wait until after the Chicago shows. They're playing a historic place for the first time. I want them at their best. We'll tell them at the after tour party. I arranged the party to be right there at the Vic, after the second show. We don't have to be out of there until 8:00am. That gives the chance for the whole crew and staff to party. The band says after they chill out for a bit, they're going to play some cover tunes. I ordered a cake. Some liquor too. A little. Don't want drunk roadies trying to load out."

"Then can I move into your house?"

"You can move into my house as soon as we get back. We should be hitting Chicago Friday morning. Do you have a lot of stuff at the guys' houses?"

"I have some clothes in Chandler's garage. Mostly I carry everything I own with me."

"An easy move-in."

"Are you still mad at me?" she said, and kissed him.

He held her in his arms and kissed her.

"You know I never stay angry with you for long."

He held her as he heard her soft rhythmic sleep breathing. But his heart was torn. His emotions a mess. Did he get everything wrong? When he first met her, she was having sex with the band. But was it truly forced, or did she consent? Or did she think she was consenting because she felt she had to do what the band told her to do? He had settled on believing it was the latter, that her innocence, naivety, and isolation had caused her to act in ways that weren't normal. She was undereducated, taking all her ideas from what the band told her. He wanted to think that was true. But then why fuck Jack? After she knew she was in an intimate relationship with him, and not the band? It didn't make sense. But maybe she didn't understand how to tell the whole story. Jack was secretive and controlling. He could be forceful to the point of violent.

Jolly wanted to marry Jarmila and spend the rest of his life being happy. But sometimes he jumped into relationships too fast. He believed this was love at first sight. From the time he first saw her cornflower blue eyes, he was in love, even if he didn't admit it to himself. Jarmila was his soulmate. Time didn't matter. Age difference didn't matter. While sitting in the back lounge, waiting on the bus to leave for Chicago, he ordered a wedding gown. It was from the same year Jarmila's great-grandmother was married, and very close to the same style. It would probably have to be altered, but the pictures looked it to be in very good condition considering its age. There wasn't a headband veil, but he found a seamstress who said she could make it in a few days. The shoes he ordered from Italy. He could not find any from 1916. But the shoemaker promised he could make the exact same style, and would put a rush order on it.

He knew exactly what he wanted, and he wasn't going to let bullshit from a 24-year-old entitled spoiled lead singer get in the way. He'd plan the wedding for Jarmila's birthday. Her birthday was in June, and fell on the first day of tour rehearsals for Lenehan. He'd plan it all out with the guys. They could rehearse, and then he would surprise Jarmila with the gown and veil and shoes, and then go by a judge he prearranged to marry them. Jolly had it all figured out. Except the marriage license. He had to figure out how to get Jarmila to fill it out without tipping off what her birthday surprise would be. He'd ask the band. They could probably get her to fill out and sign anything, no questions asked.

This could all be his good planning he honed over years of being a tour manager, or it could all be a pipe dream. But he was hoping it would happen and he could finally share his life with a soulmate. He fell asleep, Jarmila still in his arms, dreaming of waking up to the most beautiful woman in the world. His Jarmila.

At 3:00pm, Jolly was up front in his usual seat, Jarmila next to him. Jack was laying down with his feet on Jarmila's lap, and ice pack on his head.

"How much longer!" Jack groaned, "We'd been there by now if we had a plane!"

"Give me 10 million in album sales and you'll get your own private jet." said Jolly.

Jack starting play kicking Jarmila's side.

"Get me a coke, Jarmila." he said, "Or some coke, or something for this fuckin' migraine."

"Restraint would have prevented you from a migraine." said Scot, sitting in his usual seat behind the driver.

"Fuck restraint," said Jack, "I'm a fuckin' rock star."

"With a fuckin' rock star migraine." responded Scot.

"Here," said Chandler, walking from the back of the bus, handing Jack a Coca-Cola and sitting across from him, "quit your fucking whining. It's annoying."

"We're stopping soon to switch drivers and get something to eat." said Scot, "Maybe you'll feel better with some food in your stomach."

"Fuck that shit." Jack retorted, "Benny gonna be passed out so bad, when we get to Chicago, they probably gonna have to load his ass in a car home and carry him into his house. And all Johnny can do is puke. They gonna have to follow him with a bucket."

"You mean Saint No Longer A Virgin Johnny." Chandler laughed.

"Canonized by a woman named Virgen!" Jack laughed, sitting up, "Mouthy, inane tour manager, have you got any of that Extra Strength Tylenol I could have a few?"

"If you weren't my employer, I'd have a few words to say to you. But I'm trying not to lower my standards." Jolly said.

"I don't need no speeches," said Jack, "I need some Tylenol."

Jolly instructed Chandler on where to find the Extra Strength Tylenol, in his tour bag on the top bunk above his bunk. Chandler took two tablets and gave them to Jack, then sat down. Jack took them immediately.

"How long is it before we fuckin' get home?" Jack asked.

"We should be in Chicago by 8:00pm or so. Maybe 9:00pm, since we're stopping, and we have to consider traffic." said Scot.

"Shit, da first thing I'm gonna do is crash in my bed. I am worn da fuck out." said Jack.

"You're not going to say hi to your folks?" asked Chandler.

"Hell no. I'll call them and tell them I'm home. I'm going to see them again da next day anyway, at da show." answered Jack.

"I'm going to hug my wife, and then call my folks to let them know I made it home safely. Then spend the rest of the time with Marie. Gonna hold her tight in my arms all night straight through to morning." said Chandler.

"You just fuckin' saw her in NYC." sneered Jack.

"That doesn't mean I don't miss her from me being months on the road. I want to hold her and be with her." Chandler answered.

"If her name was Thomas, you'd hold her a lot tighter." laughed Jack.

"*You're such a fuckin' homophobe!*" screamed Chandler.

"I am not a homophobe." said Jack, "In my opinion, you should admit you're gay."

"It doesn't matter what label you want to put on me, Jack." said Chandler, "I love my wife. I like to be with women. Okay, I like men better, but that doesn't give you the right to belittle me!"

"Hey," said Jolly, "before this turns into one of those orange throwing fights, can we change the subject? Like, Jar, I really like your shirt. Is it new?"

Jarmila was wearing a white shirt with a New Yok logo, dark blue jeans and red Reeboks. Pink socks peeked above the shoes.

"Yes." she answered.

"I like it." said Chandler, "Where'd you get it?"

"In fuckin' Portland!" yelled Jack, "Where ya think she got it?"

"I meant what store did she get it from." Chandler yelled back.

"Bella gave it to me. She's reorganizing the wardrobe." answered Jarmila.

"I can't wait to stop and get a hearty meal. And have a few moments of peace." Jolly said.

Jolly had never seen Jarmila in full length jeans. Only capris. And that was only once. His thoughts turned to how sexy she looked, how he'd like to pull down those jeans and rub her butt and take her from behind.

"What color panties are you wearing?" he whispered in her ear.

"Red silk, with a lace border." she answered.

"Mmmm." Jolly responded.

They stopped at a diner/gas station to switch drivers, and have a meal. Jarmila asked Jolly if they could sit together, just the two of them. He responded that would be great. Benny and Johnny were still passed out. Scot sat at a table with Les, Chandler and Jack.

"What's going on, Miss Malone?" asked Jolly.

"I wanted time to ourselves. Is that okay? Like, the back of the bus is not really alone time for us. I like the hotel rooms. I like being only you and me."

"I do too. But it is difficult on tour. I've got a lot of people I'm responsible for. Very soon we'll be home and we'll have more alone time together."

The waitress came over and they ordered two coffees. Jolly ordered steak and eggs.

"I am starving." said Jolly, "What do you want, Miss Malone?"

"Nothing, just coffee. I'm not hungry."

"She'll have a turkey club with extra bacon. And thick cut fries if you have them." Jolly told the waitress.

The waitress went to put the order in.

"I'm not hungry." said Jarmila.

"Miss Malone, I think you are upset and when you are upset, you don't eat." responded Jolly, "Want to talk about what's upsetting you?"

"Myself. I'm upsetting me. I'm so stupid. I don't deserve you. I fuck up our relationship all the time and I put you through hell."

"Where did this come from? Sure, I was angry about the whole Jack birthday fucking. But I don't stay angry with you for long. I have to consider what you've been through with them. Those are not normal relationships. I'm willing to overlook shit, and very happy to help guide you to a normal relationship and sex life. I want to be with you, forever. You are my soulmate. Not every relationship is perfect. Ours has a lot of baggage, from both sides. But if we work together and work things out, we'll be fine. I'm 34 years older than you, Jar. Sometimes that hits me hard. I can't understand what you see in me. I'm old enough to be your father! So, sometimes, Jar, my love, you might have to remind me why you think I'm worthy enough to be by your side."

"Because I got lucky to have a man like you." Jarmila responded.

Jolly smiled and leaned over to kiss her. The waitress brought the food.

"Now, Miss Malone," started Jolly, "You are going to eat at least half of that. Then, when we're done and we return to the bus, you and I are going to go to the back and you are going to pull down those jeans and let me see those panties."

"You're so horny." smiled Jarmila, taking a bite into the sandwich.

"That I am, Jar, that I am. But only around you."

When everyone was back in the bus, it took off for the last leg of the journey to Chicago. Benny was still passed out, but his handler Elias assured Scot that Benny was still breathing. He had a few sips of water earlier, and passed out again. Alice was picking him up when they got to the drop off point in Chicago. Marie would pick up Chandler. Jack insisted on taking a limo to his house, and said he would drop Johnny off on the way.

"I don't care what all of you do when we get to Chicago. Just make sure you're at the venue the next day at 5:00pm for soundcheck." said Jolly to Chandler and Jack.

"They should change your nickname to "Soundcheck"." joked Jack, "I'm going to sleep. Wake me when this slow ass bus gets to Chicago."

Jolly took Jarmila's hand and went to the back lounge. He told her to stand between his knees.

"I love it when you do that." he told her, "Now lower those jeans. I want to see those panties."

Jarmila lowered her jeans to her knees. Jolly put his hands on her bottom, stroked it, rubbed his hands on the panties.

"Will you give me head?" he asked

She sat next to him. "I have a question."

Jolly knew it would be a sexual question. Jarmila had many sexual questions lately. It seemed she was finally coming into her own, sailing rivers she was unfamiliar with, but willing to board the boat.

"Yes, sugar." said Jolly.

"Do you think a guy knows when he loses his virginity? Like if he's really drunk and it happens? Would he know it happened?"

"You're worried about Johnny, aren't you?"

"I don't know how he'll take the news. He's kinda religious. He wanted to wait until he was married."

"From what I've heard, the drunken state he was in he probably won't remember. But you know how Jack and Chandler are. They'll tell him everything. Listen, if he gets too upset, I'll talk to him. I'll tell him it's better if a guy has some experience before he gets married. That way he can be gentle and know what to do when he finally marries a virgin. That myth has been going around forever. He can go to confession and be a new man and all the stuff that's Catholic doctrine. He'll be fine." he took her in his arms, "Don't worry, Jar. Your brother is going to be ok. Now will you give me head?"

"Can I ask you another question?"

Jolly really wanted head, but knew patience was always the word of the day with Jarmila.

"Yes." he answered, sighing.

"Did you ever spank a girl?"

"Jesus, Jar, you come up with the oddest questions at the most unusual times."

"I think you've told me that before. But there's a lot I don't know about you. I don't even know when your birthday is!'

"February 6th."

"I missed it! I'm going to do something for you to make up for not knowing you then!"

"Like, give me head right now?"

"Did you ever spank a girl?"

"That and a lot more."

"Did she like it? Did you like it?"

"We both liked it because we both agreed on it. Every time an opportunity like that came up with any woman, we both agreed on it."

"Jack has a closet full of whips and belts and straps and all kinds of stuff. Sometimes he uses that stuff on women he brings to his house. Chandler likes to be spanked and tied up and stuff like that. But only by men."

Jolly was beginning to regret telling Jarmila he'd like to get to know more about the band.

"Did Jack ever use any of that stuff on you?"

"No. But after I get a punishment, he almost always goes up my butt. He says it's part of the punishment. But he does that when I'm not being punished, too."

"Jar, look at me." Jolly lifted her chin so she was looking him in the eyes, "That will *never* happen to you again. I won't let it. I promise to always keep you safe."

"Does it hurt, being spanked for sex?"

"I imagine it hurts. But some people like that, they find it pleasurable. It arouses them."

"Did you ever get spanked like that, for sex?"

"No, I wouldn't like that. If you want answers to those kind of questions, I suggest you ask Chandler."

"I was just wondering. I want to try some things that the guys did to me, but with someone who is doing it in a loving way. I want to see if I'd enjoy it."

Jolly thought at this point Jarmila's attention span had taken a vacation and he wasn't getting any head.

"I don't want to ever hurt you, Jar. But I also am willing to try anything you ask me to do to you. But *only* if you're certain. I understand you're trying to figure things out, and I'll help you through it. But I never want to do anything that hurts you."

"I guess I'm just curious. You said how sex is different and better when you're doing things with someone who wants you to be happy."

"It is. And even better when you love someone. I'm trying to walk you through it slowly. You've been traumatized for so long." Jolly said, stroking her jeans with his hand, "I like those jeans. I usually only see you in dresses and skirts."

"Bella ordered them for me when she ordered some of the guys' new stage clothes. I like them. Keeps my legs warm."

"I'm taking you shopping, Jar, when we get back to Chicago. You can buy any clothes you want."

A knock at the door. Jolly wasn't going to get any head. But he knew he had to be patient and not rush into anything, although Jarmila made him feel 26 years old again. Jarmila pulled up her pants and Jolly opened the door. It was Jack.

"Hi," said Jack, "am I interrupting anything?"

"No," responded Jolly, "we were just talking."

"Ummmhummmm." said Jack, sitting next to Jarmila.

"Couldn't sleep?" asked Jolly.

"Got a lot of things on my mind." Jack replied.

"Anything I can help you with to ease your mind?" asked Jolly.

"Can a band have da top three singles on Billboard at once?" asked Jack.

"Waiting on "Penny" to move up, huh?" asked Jolly, "Yes. Ariana Grande did. Drake had three singles debut in the top three on Billboard. The Beatles had three in the top spots too. Justin Bieber had singles in the three top spots on the European charts. I can see "Penny" moving up to #3. Lenehan could have all top three spots."

"How are we on the European charts?" Jack asked.

"#2 and #3." answered Jolly.

"The Only Cost" at #2 and "Scandalous" at #3?" Jack asked.

"The other way around." responded Jolly, ""Penny is on there also, but dropped from #11 to #14."

"Shit." sighed Jack.

"You'll have your downfalls with your successes. Rock and Roll is a fluctuating bitch." Jolly said, "I think once you play live in Europe, you'll do much better. Sometimes people like to see a band live before they buy albums or singles. It's okay to have doubts. Especially since things are going so fast for Lenehan right now." Jolly explained.

"I honestly wasn't ready for this. I know we're a fuckin' excellent band, but there's so much competition. I feel like I'm in a whirlwind." said Jack.

"That's a good description of what is going on with Lenehan right now." said Jolly.

"You're quiet." said Jack, moving closer to Jarmila.

"Don't have anything to say I guess." she said.

Jack took out a Dum Dum, unwrapped it and put it in his mouth.

"What flavor is that?" asked Jarmila.

"Cream Soda." said Jack, putting it in her mouth.

"Absolutely fucking not!" exclaimed Jolly, taking the lollipop out of Jarmila's mouth and handing it back to Jack, "Stop fucking sharing those things."

Jack responded by putting the Dum Dum back in Jarmila's mouth.

"I swear, Jack," started Jolly, "if you weren't my employer, I'd lose my religion right now. Two more gigs with you fools, and I'm fucking *free*."

"Nah. You'll get a break from us. But I heard you signed on for da next tour. *Officially*." Jack said, taking the lollipop back from Jarmila.

"You're officially signed on? You signed the contracts and everything? I'm so happy!" exclaimed Jarmila, kissing Jolly on the lips.

"I think I had a brain glitch for a moment when I signed that shit." laughed Jolly.

"Where's my kiss? Don't you love me anymore?" asked Jack, taking the lollipop out of his mouth.

"I love you very much." she said, kissing him on the lips.

Jolly looked on and shook his head.

Chicago.

The tour bus pulled into the Chicago city limits at 9:45am. Alice, with her car, and Marie with Chandler's car, were waiting at the drop off spot. Jack and Johnny got into a white limo. Suitcases and packages were loaded into the limo and various cars. The instruments and equipment, except for Johnny's favorite bass and Chandler's Lucille, would be dropped off later at their houses or the rehearsal space. Johnny and Chandler could not be separated from their favorite instruments. Scot's friend had brought Scot's car, and he gave his friend a lift back to Scot's condo in Belmont Harbor. Alice and Benny took Elias to his home and Marie and Chandler took Les to his home. Jolly and Jarmila were standing in the parking lot as the bus took off.

"It's bittersweet when that bus leaves after the tour is over." said Jarmila.

"Yes, it is." answered Jolly.

"Hey," said Jack, opening the limo door, "y'all can ride with us."

Jolly looked at Jarmila, who nodded her head yes. They entered the limo.

"Jolly, you live in Noble Square?" asked Jack.

"Yes." answered Jolly, "About two blocks from Lenehan's rehearsal space. And two blocks in the opposite direction from your recording studio."

"I'm going with him." said Jarmila to Jack.

"Whatta I care? I'm going home to sleep." he answered, "You know who you belong to. I don't have to remind you you're da band's."

Jarmila started to shout out something, but Jolly put two fingers against her lips and mouthed "shhhhhh." He thought it wasn't worth the fight.

"Are you okay Johnny?" asked Jarmila.

"Yeah." he said quietly, "I am disappointed in myself. What's my ma going to say?"

"Why tell her?" asked Jack, "You're a grown man. She got no business in your private life. You don't have a neon sign hanging over your head blinking "NOT A VIRGIN ANYMORE"."

"I should have never had that shot of tequila." Johnny said, "It made me forget my morals."

"Or maybe it was da shot of Jagermeister that made you forget your morals. Or da Bacardi, or da Kilian Paris vodka, or da Remy Martin, or da Bushmills, or da Pappy Van Winkle, or da Bombay Sapphire." replied Jack.

"Jesus, Johnny," exclaimed Jolly, "did you drink up the whole bar?"

"Don't forget the rum punch you had at Jack's birthday party that afternoon." Jarmila added.

"I feel like the bus dragged me underneath it from New York City to Chicago." said Johnny.

"Don't puke in da limo." said Jack.

"I ain't got nothing left to puke." Johnny said.

Jolly and Jarmila were first to get dropped off. The limo driver placed all the luggage and cases on the sidewalk. Jarmila kissed Jack and Johnny and she exited the vehicle. Jolly said he would see them again soon and followed Jarmila. Jarmila held her make-up case and an over-the-shoulder purse. Jolly held his briefcase and had his tour bag and laptop bag slung over his shoulder. They stood a few minutes in front of Jolly's house.

"It's really pretty." said Jarmila.

"Wait until you see the inside." said Jolly.

Jolly gathered up some suitcases and went to the front door. He unlocked it for Jarmila, then went to retrieve the rest of the luggage. She sat at the piano bench in the piano room. Jolly stood behind her and kissed her neck.

"I'm taking everything upstairs. You have a couple options. You can stay in my bedroom and put your stuff there, or you can stay in one of the guest rooms." Jolly said.

"Can I see the bedrooms first?" she asked.

"Of course! Then I'll give you a tour of the house."

They went upstairs. Jarmila looked at Jolly's room first. It was large, dark blue paint, with a queen-sized bed, engraved wood headboard, finished wood floors. The windows looked out onto the front street. It had a dresser on one wall, and a huge walk-in closet.

"Don't worry, I won't go look at your sacred bathroom." she laughed.

"You can look at it, you just can't use it." he smiled.

"Nice closet." She said as she went to the walk-in closet.

"If you want to stay in my room, I'll build a shoe cabinet just for your shoes."

"I have a whole suitcase full of shoes."

"That's why I'm building you a shoe cabinet. You can put all your shoes in compartments. Maybe you can have Chandler come over and arrange them by color, style, and price."

Jarmila playfully slapped his shoulder. She then went to the first guest bedroom. It had a full-size bed and a white dresser. The closet was of regular size, with two shelves on the top in back. The second guest bedroom was much the same, only slightly smaller. There was a full-size bed, a desk and chair, a small maple dresser with a mirror, and a similar size closet like the other guest bedroom, only it lacked shelves. Both bedrooms looked onto the back yard.

"The back yard is pretty. You have a garage? I don't remember you telling me you had a garage. Or that you drive anywhere. I thought you called a car service if you wanted to go somewhere."

"Sometimes I drive. But have you seen parking in Chicago? Especially downtown. Now Miss Malone, in that garage are two very special things in my life that I worked my ass off for. One is the car I occasionally drive if I'm going someplace that has reasonable and available parking. That's my 2016 BMW M4 GTS. The other I occasionally drive if the weather is beautiful or I'm going to a car show. It's my 1938 Rolls Royce Wraith."

"I need to get a driver's license!" exclaimed Jarmila, "What color are they?"

"Black. And you'll never drive either of them."

"Jolly! I can't drive your cars or use your bathroom. What next, I can't lick your balls?"

"Oh, sugar, you can always lick my balls." he said, putting his arm around her waist and drawing her closer, "So which bedroom do you want?"

"Yours. I want to share a bed with you like we did on tour. It makes me happy."

"Awesome. Let me get your luggage from the hallway and put it in my room. Then I'll give you a tour of the house."

They started down the hallway to Jolly's bedroom. Jolly stopped at the hallway bathroom.

"Where is your make-up case?" he asked.

"Right here." she answered, lifting the rectangular case from the floor.

"It's going in *this* bathroom." stated Jolly.

After putting the luggage in Jolly's bedroom, he gave Jarmila a tour of the house. She fell in love with it, and that made him happy. He loved it when they shared the same joy over things.

"The fridge and freezer are stocked, so is the pantry. My housekeeper shopped before she left for vacation yesterday. There's extra cases of bottled water, soda…I mean pop…in the basement. And beer. Occasionally you can have a beer. And a cigarette. And a joint. But no going overboard and no other drugs. Understood?" said Jolly, as he and Jarmila stood in the kitchen.

"Understood." she answered, opening up the fridge and cabinets.

"There's also a washer and dryer in the basement. Do you want to see the basement?"

"Are there snacks down there? Like chips? Because there's none in the cabinets or pantry."

"Miss Malone. You do not need chips. There's plenty of healthy snacks. Fresh fruits and vegetables, cheese, all kinds of good, healthy stuff. Don't forget I'll be grilling a lot." Jolly said, opening the backyard door, "Come out here and see the deck I built."

"You built that yourself? It's very nice. I bet it's relaxing to sit out here."

"It is." He said, putting his arms around her and kissing her deeply, "I love you, Jarmila."

"I love you, Jolly. I'm kinda freaking out a little."

"Why?"

"I'm not used to having a place I can call home. Can we go upstairs to your bedroom?"

"*Our* bedroom. It's our bedroom now. If you want to paint it neon pink, I won't mind at all."

"I like the dark blue it is now."

They went to their bedroom. They laid on the bed above the covers.

"I don't feel like unpacking." said Jolly, "Technically we're still on tour with two more dates, even if they are in Chicago. I think I can justify living out of my suitcase until the tour is officially over. You can have the dresser in the walk-in closet. I'll move my stuff to the dresser in here. I'll clear a side of the closet for you to hang your dresses and skirts. I promise you as soon as these Chicago gigs are done, I'll build you a shoe cabinet."

"I feel like I'm crowding you out."

"I've been married three times. I know how to share space."

"I think it's going to take me awhile to unpack. I'm used to always living out of a suitcase because I rotated between the guys."

"I won't rush you, Jar. I know it's an entirely different scenario for you now. You'll get used to it."

"I don't cook. And I don't clean."

"I will teach your lazy ass to cook. I have a cleaning crew that comes by once a week. But if you use a glass, or utensils, or plates, or cups, when you're done, you will wash them and dry them and put them back where you got them from. Do not leave dirty dishes in the sink."

"Why don't you have a dishwasher?"

"I had one, and had it taken out. I like washing dishes by hand. I know they're clean then. Unless my housekeeper is here. Then she does stuff like that. And my laundry. She also cooks meals for me if I'm too busy to cook or grill."

"When does she get back?"

"She has a month's vacation. Her son and daughter-in-law had another baby, so she went to Florida to see her new grandson. That will give us time to be alone together and get to know each other much better."

"Do you think she'll like me? Do you think she'll cook meals for both of us? Or only you because you're busy?"

"I'm sure she'll cook for the both of us." Jolly laughed, "She'll see how skinny you are and insist you eat more. I pay her to do certain things in this house. I don't expect, and neither will she, for you to do those things because you live here now. I've talked to her a few times about you. She will like you very much."

"Did you other wives live here?"

"Only the last two. Don't worry, I got a new mattress several weeks before I went out on tour. I wanted to buy a nice comfy mattress for retirement. Then look what happened. Scot asks me out on tour, and I fall in love with the most beautiful woman in the world."

"Oh yeah? What's her name?" joked Jarmila, turning to her side to face Jolly.

"I have corners in this house, Jar."

"I hate it when you put me in a corner. I hate standing still!"

"I know. That's why I stand you in a corner."

"But I still have that fantasy where you stand me in a corner and you're standing naked behind me. I saw this video where this woman was facing a wall and a man was having sex with her from behind."

"Am I going to have to put parental controls on your phone to keep you from watching porn?" Jolly laughed.

"I was only checking out different sexual positions. There has to be more than a few."

"I'm joking, Jar. I don't care what you watch on your phone. It's *your* phone. There's more than a few different sexual positions. There's a lot of different positions."

"Can you teach me some?"

"Only if you are comfortable with them. If you don't like something, then tell me and I'll stop."

"Okay." she said, getting off the bed.

She took off her clothes and dropped them in a laundry hamper in the walk-in closet. Completely naked, she stood in front of the bed.

"Shouldn't we take a shower before we go to bed?" she asked.

"Look at you, sugar. You steal my heart the first day I meet you and you steal my bathroom the first day in my house." he laughed and took her hand, and went to shower with her.

At 6:30am the next morning, Jolly was seated at his kitchen table drinking his second cup of coffee. He had already made and ate his breakfast; waffles, sausage patties and hash browns. This was going to be a big show. It was also his favorite venue. He decided he'd get there early on a full stomach.

Jarmila came into the kitchen in a black t-shirt that had the word "Humboldt" in green lettering on the front, with a Puerto Rican flag on the back. She was wearing green capri jeans and white Converse All-Stars. In her hand she was holding a brush, comb and hair ties.

"Can you braid my hair for me?" she asked Jolly, "Just down the back?"

"Sure," he answered, "Move closer to me and turn around. I've never seen these clothes on you before. I like that shirt. Where did you get it?"

"At Bandera a Bandera. It's a festival in Humboldt Park. It goes on Division Street from Western to California avenues. It's usually held in late August or early September. Lots of entertainment, food, music, vendors."

"I think I've heard of that." said Jolly, "Isn't that the one with the big parade and carnival and music artists that's held in the park?"

"No, that's the Puerto Rican Days Festival. That festival is held in June. It's much bigger."

"We'll be here in June." said Jolly, putting a hair tie on the end of her braid. "We should go."

"I'd like that. I sometimes miss it because the band's usually on tour all summer. Anyway, I had these clothes with me, but Jack doesn't want me to wear anything but dresses and skirts. He gets upset if I wear pants. But I figure, I'm back in Chicago, so I might as well represent the West Side."

"Why are you up so early? Do you want some coffee? Something to eat?"

"I want to know if I can go with you."

"Sure. But it's probably going to be a long boring day for you."

"I'll take an extra book, just in case. If I get tired, I can take a nap in the dressing room. Is it okay if I go with you? I'm not going to be in the way?"

"Of course you can go. You won't be in the way. I'm going to be super busy. There's a lot of family and friends coming to this show."

"Did you have to fight Scot for extra hospitality rooms?"

"Not this time. There's plenty rooms we can use."

Jarmila went to the coffee maker and poured herself a cup. She opened the fridge and took out the half and half, pouring some into her coffee.

"Jolly, can you do me a favor?" she asked him, putting her coffee on the kitchen table next to Jolly's.

"Yes I can, my love."

"Can you get some of that Cremora powdered creamer? I like it better."

"I will put that on the shopping list. But you'll probably have to wait a few days, as I'm stuck at The Vic for the next two days. You should have breakfast."

"Are you driving to The Vic?"

"Hell no. The parking in that neighborhood is nearly non-existent. What parking they have I'd have to sell a kidney to pay for, because of how long I'll be there. If you can find parking in Chicago, it's expensive. Now I have some questions for you that you may be able to answer. How is the band getting to The Vic? Do they drive themselves? Carpool? I've received no information. I'm guessing Scot handles it. And who is Sofia Panchak and why is she listed on the guest list as "dog handler"? And why is she listed as All Access Band?"

"The band goes in a limo together. Johnny takes his dogs, Capone and Gotti. He brings them to all Chicago shows. Sofia is their handler for when he's onstage. Capone and Gotti have their own All Access All Areas Band laminates attached to their collars."

"Johnny must really love his dogs."

"Oh, they're like his babies. They were scheduled to be euthanized at the city animal shelter. Every Christmas Day he goes to the city animal shelter with a truckload of donations. One Christmas day he loaded in the donations and walked out with two pit bulls. They're nice dogs. Johnny's momma is super attached to them, too. Can we stop and get a bagel and cream cheese on the way? Some place that has veggie cream cheese and onion bagels?"

"Yes. I'll order the car service in about 15 minutes. Make sure you have everything you need for the day."

She took a sip of her coffee and put her arms around Jolly. She gave him a long kiss. He kissed her back, hugging her tight to him.

"Tomorrow we have to tell them." said Jarmila.

"I know. But let's wait until after the show, okay? These next two days are super big deals for them. I don't want anything to kill their momentum, and I know you feel the same way." Jolly said.

"I definitely don't want anything to be a distraction. But I am still a little apprehensive."

"I know, sugar. But I'm right here by your side."

He hugged and kissed her again. Then gathered his plate and utensils and the coffee cups, and washed and dried them, putting them back in their places. He gathered all his equipment he would need for the day, and called for the car service.

Jarmila was sitting on the edge of the front of the stage reading *Catcher In The Rye*. Jolly sat beside her and kissed her on the lips. She put the book down.

"Everett is going to ask you to move soon because they'll be setting up this side." said Jolly.

"I know. He already told me he'd let me know when I needed to move." said Jarmila.

Jolly put an arm around her.

"You see those windows up there?" he said, pointing to a space underneath the balcony.

"Yeah." replied Jarmila, looking at the spot Jolly was pointing.

"That was the office of a very important man. His name was Big Bob. He worked for a major production company in Chicago, the very same one for this show. He also was one of the owners of The Vic. He had a reputation for scaring his staff because he'd yell a lot. He was a mentor and inspiration to me. I don't think I'd be a tour manager if he hadn't seen it in me. I came through here on several tours. He'd always remember my name and where I was from. When my mom was first diagnosed with cancer, Big Bob would ask 'Bill, how are you? How's your mom?'."

"He called you Bill?'

"Yes. I didn't get the nickname "Jolly" until I became a tour manager."

"You've never been here as a tour manager, have you?"

"Nope. After I became a tour manager, I was never on a tour that came through this venue."

"So, this is your first time here as a tour manager. No wonder these are special gigs for you."

"Yes, they are. One time, I was in the hospitality room. Back then they called it the Green Room. Some places do. I had just gotten my food when Big Bob walked in. He was yelling at staff. When he saw me, he came over and asked how I was doing, how my mom was doing. Then he asked me, 'Bill, what do you plan to do with your life?'. I said I wanted to be a tour manager. And he said, 'Bill, you are tour manager material.' That meant so much for me to hear it from someone who knew the music business like Big Bob did. If Big Bob saw it in me, then I knew I could go for it. Sadly, I never saw him again. He never got to see me come through here as tour manager."

"What happened to him?"

"He passed on. Heart attack. Sometimes, after he passed, when I would come through here on a tour, I could swear I'd hear his voice on the stairs, asking 'Bill, how are you?'. I'd like to think he's in his office up there, looking down, nodding his head with his thumb up, proud of me that I met my goal."

"I'm sure his spirit is up there, doing that. I'm sure he's proud of your accomplishments."

"You say the most spectacular things. I needed to hear that. I miss him very much, and being here is bittersweet." said Jolly, "I love you so much, Miss Malone. You help heal my heart."

At noon time, Jolly, Scot, Keith, Shera and Chandra were in the tour office. Jarmila came in with a plate of food. She put it next to Jolly.

"I brought you lunch. I figured you'd be so busy you'd forget to eat." she told Jolly.

"That's so sweet of you, sugar." Jolly replied, kissing her on the lips, "Have you had lunch, baby?"

"I had some steamed broccoli. And a salad." she said.

"Hey," said Scot, "where's my plate of food?"

"In the hospitality room. You pick up an empty plate, fill it with food, and there's your plate of food." answered Jarmila.

'Ohs' and 'damns' went around the room.

"Shots. Fired." said Jolly, laughing.

At 2:00pm, Jolly and Chandra were the only people in the tour office. Everyone else was running errands. Johnny showed up in the doorway. A large blue and white dog ran up to Jolly and jumped on him. Jolly started petting the dog. Johnny pulled the leash back.

"Sorry," he said to Jolly, "he's as excited as I am to be here."

"That's okay," said Jolly, "I like dogs.'

Jolly continued to pet the blue and white dog while Johnny let go of the leash and entered the room. Behind him was Sofia the dog handler, holding a leash that was attached to a large brown and white dog. When Johnny sat down, the brown and white dog sat in a chair next to him, and Sofia sat next to the dog.

"This is Sofia.Panchak. She takes care of my dogs when I'm on stage." said Johnny.

"Pleased to meet you." said Jolly, "This is my assistant Chandra. Which dog is Capone and which is Gotti?"

"Capone is the one you're petting." said Johnny, "Gotti is the one sitting next to me."

"Beautiful dogs. I love the color of Capone." Jolly said, still petting the dog, "I was surprised to hear you were getting to the venue early. I didn't think I'd see the band until right before soundcheck."

"Jack and Chandler are so tipped on cocaine, Jack's jumping over chairs. He called me from the limo, while he was in front of my house. I called Sofia and asked if she could show up here earlier than planned, because Jack already had the limo at my house. I get in the limo and Jack and Chandler are talking so fast I could barely understand what they were discussing. Benny was nodding off. Alice won't be here until closer to showtime. You know Benny; he has to have either his Alice or his heroin. Then Jack gets this idea to stop at a White Castle and order 100 hamburgers. But he and Chandler don't eat them because they're so hyped they don't have appetites. Jack tells the limo driver to pull over where there's this homeless encampment, under an overpass. Then he and Chandler get out of the limo and start handing out hamburgers to the homeless."

"Jesus, I feel like I'm in for quite a show tonight, *offstage*." said Jolly.

Jolly, Johnny and Sofia were in a deep discussion about dogs while he was arranging the guest list with Chandra. Jolly loved to multi-task. Gable, lead sound engineer, appeared at the door.

"There's a problem with Jarmila and Scot. It's intense. They're in front of the soundboard. Everett is standing between them." Gable said.

"Fuck." sighed Jolly, exiting the office.

He walked up the stairs to the front of stage area. In front of the soundboard was a raised platform with five tables with three to four chairs each. This was one of the sections of V.I.P. seating. Jarmila and Scot were standing on the platform screaming at each other, Everett between them. Jolly walked up to them.

"*You can both stop screaming now*!" he screamed, "*Because I can scream the loudest*! What's the problem?"

"This one," said Scot, pointing to Jarmila "is a stupid bitch."

"Can I go back to work now?" asked Everett.

"Go. I've got it handled." Jolly answered Everett.

"Scot, I'm not Dr. Phil, I can't change people's personalities. If you think Jarmila is a stupid bitch, you have every right to your opinion. But that doesn't tell me what the problem is that has you two at each other's throats."

"He's been at me since he got hired. Two years I've had to put up with this dick. I was here before you and I'll be here long after you're gone, Scot." said Jarmila, glaring at him.

"Wouldn't bet on that, bitch." Scot sneered.

"I want that table." said Jarmila, pointing at a table behind Scot, "But this asshole say I can't have it. He says it's logi...logis..."

"Logistically." Jolly said, "Look at my face, Jar. Lo-gis-ti-cal-ly. Logistically"

"Lo...gistic...ally." Jarmila pronounced slowly, "This asshole says it's logistically impossible for me to have that table tonight. I don't know what logistically is, but my status is ALL ACCESS ALL AREAS BAND and Jack says I can sit anywhere I want, and I want to *sit there*!"

"You are such an uneducated bitch." said Scot. "Logistically means that if I switch your seat in V.I.P. box to a seat at this table, what am I supposed to do with the other two people at this table since there are *zero* seats available because this show is *sold out* and we have a large guest list which means there are *no complimentary tickets available*."

Jolly was watching the argument like a tennis match, his head going from side to side.

"I don't know. I'm not the person in charge of seating. And I'm not sitting with strangers." Jarmila said.

Then a flurry of long blonde hair and leather came flying up to the platform. Jack.

"Why da *fuck* can't she sit there?" screamed Jack. Jarmila had texted him complaining she couldn't get the seat she wanted for the show.

"Because," explained Scot, "she has a seat reserved for her in the V.I.P. box. Just one seat. Because she has one ass to put it in. There are three people who this table has been reserved for in this V.I.P. section. So, If I switch one of these people with her V.I.P seat, where am I going to put the other two people? Jarmila said she won't share a table with strangers, and I'm sure no one wants to share a table with her stupid bitch ass."

"Why aren't you saying anything?" asked Jack to Jolly.

"I'm waiting for the TKO so I can pick someone off the floor." Jolly answered.

"Well, *fuckin' genius*," said Jack to Scot, "why don't you move Ma Dunne and Johnny's Aunt Freida and Jarmila to that table, then move da people who this table was reserved for to da V.I.P. box section. Ma Dunne and Freida like Jarmila a lot. They'll find it a pleasure sitting with her."

"There!" exclaimed Jolly, throwing his hands in the air, "Problem solved."

Scot made a huffing sound and walked away.

"You okay, my special girl?" Jack asked Jarmila, kissing her on the lips.

"Yeah. Thank you." Jarmila said.

"Always. Always my special girl. Come with me to da dressing room." said Jack.

Jarmila started to make her way down the platform to go with Jack. Jolly grabbed her arm.

"You and I are going to have a serious conversation when we get home tonight." he told her as he let go of her arm.

Jack and Jarmila went to the dressing room. Benny was reading a drum magazine. Johnny was petting his dogs. Sofia had gone to lunch. Chandler was sitting on the floor snorting cocaine off a coffee table. Jack sat down on a couch.

"Sit on my lap, pretty girl." he said to Jarmila, "Tell me something about yourself."

"Tell you something about myself?" she asked, surprised, as she sat on his lap, "You've known me since we were kids."

"Well, it seems me and da guys don't know you as well as we think we do. Or maybe you don't know us as well as you think you do. Cause we know for a fact, you been snorting coke behind our backs. And you bought pills from some girl with da 24 Hour Party People." Jack said, putting his hand on Jarmila's outer thigh.

"But I'm not doing that shit no more. I promised Jolly I wouldn't do drugs like that anymore, and I've kept my promise."

"Jolly, Jolly, Jolly. Good for you you're Jolly's responsibility. Or your ass would be black and blue. All these years you broke promises to us and broke rules. But you keep your promise to some old man you met a few weeks ago who just wants some young woman pussy. What's up with that?" Jack said, pinching Jarmila's thigh.

"Ouch!" she yelled, pushing his hand away.

"Tell us more about this Jolly. It's just us here now. No reason to keep any secrets from us. We're your best friends, remember? You do remember right? We were the ones keeping you safe and feeding you and clothing you and giving you shelter. Remember us? Or did you lose da memory of us somewhere between Jolly's dick and his balls?" Jack said.

Jarmila stood up and sat in a chair near Benny. Benny looked up from his magazine. Chandler stopped snorting coke to look at Jack, while Johnny sat with a stunned expression.

"Y'all pushed me onto him anyway. Y'all the ones who signed that contract and made him manage me. I didn't ask for that." Jarmila cried.

"I didn't ask that he put his dick up your ass." said Chandler.

"He's never been there! He's not like you guys!" she cried out.

"Oh," said Jack, "so he *has* been someplace. You think we're stupid. You don't think we hear and see things? Music tours got da most gossipy bitches on da planet. But it don't take much gossip or imagination to see you two with your tongues down each other's throats every chance you get."

"Why do you care? Y'all too busy with your careers and being rock stars to notice I'm still breathing!" she exclaimed.

Benny reached out and held her hand.

"It's not that Jarmila," he said, "we still notice you're here. Our feelings for you haven't changed. I know our schedules are crazy. We don't have a lot of free time. That doesn't change how our hearts feel toward you. You're the best friend we got. You're the backbone of this band, and I'm not just saying that because everyone in the band is always saying it. I'm saying it because it's true. We don't want anything to happen to you. We don't want anyone to take advantage of you. If you and Jolly got a thing going, and you're happy, good for both of you! Chandler already said he'd be maid of honor at your wedding. He's even got the pink high heels already bought."

"I'm going to debut them on Instagram today." said Chandler.

"You can't be *maid* of honor," said Jarmila, laughing, "because you're married. You'd have to be *matron* of honor. Yeah, Jolly and I are in a relationship. But not engaged or anything like that. We were going to tell you after the second show, so nobody would be so angry at the news it would mess up their performance. We weren't planning on keeping it a secret forever."

"Fuck me," said Jack, "nothing could affect my performance here. The whole place could fall down around me and my dead body would get up to sing. We've been waiting for a headlining gig here for-fuckin'-ever"

"Do you love him?" Johnny asked.

"Very much." she replied.

"Does he love you?" asked Benny

"He says very much. He says I'm his soulmate, and the first time he's truly been in love." she said.

Jack got up from the couch and stood in front of Jarmila with his arms extended.

"Come here, my special girl." he said, "Let me hold you in my arms. I don't get as much of a chance to do that lately."

Jarmila stood up and Jack hugged her tightly.

"I can't say I'm not going to miss your tight little ass," he said, "that would be a lie. I am going to miss you being asleep by my side every few days or so. I'm going to miss your scent of bergamot and cloves, and that shampoo you use, that smells like blackberries and lemonade. But just because you're Jolly's girl now don't give you da right to stay away from us. You are still a huge part of our lives. I better see or hear from you *every day.* And your tight little sweet round ass better still be at our gigs and on tour with us. Jolly's our permanent tour manager now. You have no excuse not to be with da band."

"I'll still be at every gig and every rehearsal and every studio session. That will never change." she said.

"Good." said Jack, sitting on the couch, "Now get that motherfucker Jolly in here. I have a few words to say to him."

Jolly heard his name mentioned as he was passing the dressing room. He went in.

"You rang?" he said.

"Jolly!" exclaimed Jack, "Look, Johnny, your future brother-in-law is here."

"Someone put PCP in your cocaine, Jack. You are clearly hallucinating." Jolly said.

"They know, Jolly," said Jarmila, "they already know. And I confirmed it. I didn't want to keep the secret any longer."

"You weren't exactly discreet about it." said Chandler, "Crew saw you with Jolly on the side of the stage in Milwaukee with his hand up your dress. What was he doing, looking for your backstage pass?"

"He was doing some kinda backstage pass," said Jack, "backstage, passing those fingers up her tight little butthole."

"We need to talk to you." said Johnny.

"I think that's a good idea." said Jarmila.

"No, Jarmila," said Jack, "you go find something to do. Go read a book. Go annoy Scot. Go away. No eavesdropping. We need to talk to Jolly alone."

Jarmila gave Jolly a scared look. But he kissed her on the cheek and whispered in her ear that it would be ok to leave the room. He told her she could sit in the tour office and he'd be along shortly. Then Jolly prepared to face what he thought he had at least one more day to deal with. Being a tour manager gave him the experience to face the unexpected. But would he be able to face this pack of rabid wolves?

Jarmila went to the loading dock. Diet coke and *The Bell Jar* in hand, she sat on an equipment case. She saw Everett going in and out of the semis, frantically, as if he had misplaced something important and couldn't find it. He saw her and went to her.

"Hey," he said, "have you seen Lucille? I swear she was on stage with the rest of the guitars ready for set up. But Easy says it's not there. I'm going to lose my job if that guitar is lost."

"It's in the dressing room, with Johnny's bass. I was just there. Chandler probably saw it onstage and took it to the dressing room. You know that's his baby. Like Johnny's Fender."

"Damn. He could have said something about taking it to the dressing room. I was losing my mind." said Everett, rolling up marijuana.

"You know how it is. They all live in their own little worlds sometimes, and don't think about other people."

"I'm astonished you're not in the dressing room with them." he said, offering her the joint.

"They're having a discussion with Jolly. No girls allowed." she said, shaking her hand no to the offer of the joint.

"Ahhhh. Anything, *not band related*?"

"You act like you already know."

"I think even the parking attendants know. *Everyone* fuckin' knows. Y'all were lip locked practically his first day of the tour."

"No we weren't!"

"Okay, maybe it was the second day. But for two people trying to hide their relationship, you two get a grade of D-."

"I think it was more of an F. Hey, can I get a cigarette?"

"You're not supposed to be smoking."

"And you're not supposed to be talking or hanging out with me, per Lenehan rules that no crew can fraternize with me. But here you are, hanging out and talking to me."

"I just want to make sure I get an invite to the wedding." he laughed, handing her a cigarette and lighting it for her.

"I'm only living in his house. We're not engaged. We're kind of at that stage before engagement and after dating."

"Fucking. That part of the relationship is called fucking."

"You're so ignorant! No it's not!" Jarmila exclaimed, playfully pushing his shoulder, "He says he's in love with me. He says it's true love, that he's my soulmate."

"This man has been married three times, and I've never seen him act this way with *any* woman. It's like he's in some teenage dimension."

"How long have you known him? I think he told me a long time."

"Fifteen years. I was on his first tour out when he started being tour manager. He threatened to fire me five times,"

"Only five times?"

"Slow day." Everett laughed with Jarmila, "But I owe that man. Big time. He's the one who recommended me as a road manager to the management company. That's what I wanted to be. I was a guitar roadie before then."

"Do you remember when you first met me?"

"Do I? Girl, I'll never forget that day. You know it's been four years? Four years I've been in this madness." he said, putting out the joint and putting the roach in the back of his laminate pass, "We were in Omaha. Oh shit, the band was so mad they were opening the tour in Omaha. Their first record had just been released; this was their first headlining gig at venues of that size. But they were *so pissed*. I had signed on to that tour because the management suggested it. A band headlining venues of that size for the first time could use an experienced road manager."

"Who was tour manager then?"

"I don't remember his name. Lenehan had gone through tour managers so fast I couldn't pick them out of a police line-up if I had to. There was talk of not having a tour manager, of having me take on those duties, because it wasn't a really big tour. I'm like, no way. These guys are certifiable. There's no way I could handle both jobs."

"I remember." said Jarmila, "I had just turned 18. They wanted to open in LA, but they started the tour in Omaha. It was a really nice place, but Jack and Chandler were already storming before we even got there. I don't remember the tour manager's name either. I wasn't supposed to talk to any crew. But I remember the band manager was that guy Phillipe, the French guy. The label fired the guy who had been their band manager since their club days. His name was Tarique. Tarique wasn't a very good band manager."

"So, it's after the show," said Everett, "and I'm in the hallway supervising load out, and I hear screaming from down the hallway. I'm talking like airline decibel screaming. I go to check it out and it's Jack screaming at this blonde-haired girl. You. But I hadn't met you yet. I'm like, what the fuck? I thought you must be his girlfriend or wife. It sounded like one of those kind of fights. Then he stops yelling at you and starts kissing you. I'm like thinking, yup, they're a couple."

"I remember. He was yelling at me because he smelled alcohol on my breath, and he didn't like me drinking."

"The next night we were in Pierre, South Dakota. It was before the show. I went to the dressing room to discuss an issue with one of Johnny's bass guitars. Chandler was naked sitting on the couch. You were kneeling in front of him giving him head! In front of the rest of the band, and crew and staff going in and out of the dressing room. I'm thinking 'ooohhhhhhkay'. I've seen freaky shit on tour, but I assumed you were Jack's girlfriend. I was thinking, that Jack is mighty generous, sharing his girlfriend like that. Then that night, after the show, it was a stay-over. Benny called me and asked to meet him at the front desk. He had lost his hotel key card and all his identification was locked in the room. I go to the front desk to verify his identity so they would give him a new key card. Tour or band managers usually keep the extras from check-in, because band members often lose their hotel keys. I don't know why he couldn't get ahold of the tour or the band manager. Anyway, I see you next to Benny, and he's holding your hand. Benny gets his new key and we're in the elevator going to the same floor, and he's all over you, hand up your skirt, lips on lockdown. When we get to the floor we're staying on, his room is just a couple doors down from the elevator. He takes you in his room! Then I'm thinking, okay, she's the band's groupie. Not just any groupie, but more of a permanent clutch."

"When did you find out differently?"

"A few days later when Johnny and I were discussing meeting a Fender guitar rep in St. Louis and buying him this specific Fender he wanted." Everett said, lighting a cigarette, "I asked who you were. He told me the entire complicated order of things. Like some telenovela. The relationships, the rotation. Wacky shit, and like I said before, I have seen some *wacky shit*."

"I guess I didn't see it as wacky because it's the way it had been for years. Those boys they took good care of me. I'd be dead if it wasn't for them. They saved me from the streets. But now, they're off in a different direction. I was always supportive of everything they did. I always had their back, always was there for them. I told them, someday they're going to be big rock stars. All of them told me when that happens, it's because I believed in them, that they could get there. Now they're there, and they don't need me anymore."

"I don't think that's the case. They still need you. But in a different way. You'll find your purpose again."

"Thank you." she said as she slid off the equipment case, giving Everett a big hug, "You're a good friend."

She finished the hug and kissed him on the cheek. Then she went inside.

While Jarmila was on the loading dock talking to Everett, Sofia had returned to the dressing room from lunch. Johnny asked her to wait in hospitality, as the band was in a meeting. She suggested she take the dogs for a walk, and Johnny agreed that was a good idea. He'd text her when the meeting was over.

"I'll call the label Monday morning," said Jolly as the door closed, "and tell them I rescind my contract and resign."

"If you break her heart," said Johnny, "I'll kill you."

"Damn!" exclaimed Chandler, "Johnny traded his virginity for some balls!"

"I'm fucking serious Chandler." Johnny said, "That's my little sister, she's my world."

"If you fuckin' try to resign," said Jack, "I'll chain you to a radiator in my house until da next tour starts."

"That wouldn't be bad, Jolly," said Chandler, snorting another line off the coffee table, "You'd probably be chained next to a hot naked chick. That's how Jack plays in Jack's House."

"I expected the worst when Jarmila and I were going to tell you about us." Jolly said, sitting down on the couch, "I expected meltdowns and threats."

Chandler offered Jolly a line. Although he usually didn't do more than smoke a blunt when working, in this circumstance, cocaine seemed the right option. He snorted a line and went for a second.

"You crossed a borderline." said Jack, "You know crew is supposed to keep hands off of da bands' girls."

"I can't explain what happened." Jolly said, "The first time I saw her, sitting on the table in a hotel guest laundry room, it was instantaneous. When our eyes met, it was love at first sight for me, and I don't even believe in love at first sight! Then there's the age difference. I've been married three times before. I kept trying to doubt it all away, but thoughts of her…it was like my heart melting."

"I didn't know you had a heart." Jack joked, snorting a line of cocaine from the coffee table.

"Now I know why you requested in your rider a mirror topped coffee table in the dressing room." said Jolly, "I know I crossed the boundary. I can't stay away from Jarmila. She's the love of my life. I know it sounds ridiculous from a man my age. But I'm truly in love for the first time in my life. I feel alive again."

"We questioned your motives." said Jack, "Still do, kinda. You are 34 years older than her. I know your type. You go after those young girls. Then tire of them and move on. We don't want that to happen to Jarmila. She's fragile, and I know she wouldn't recover from that."

"Can I show you all something? It's in my briefcase. I'll be right back." said Jolly, exiting the dressing room.

He came back a few minutes later with his black briefcase. Here he kept a secret, even from Jarmila, since New York City. He opened the briefcase and took out a large black velvet bag. From there he removed three boxes.

"In NYC, I bought these for her." he said, opening two of the boxes.

"Damn, "said Jack, "obviously we pay you too much salary."

"This one is the engagement ring. It's hand crafted. It's similar to something she told me about the engagement and wedding rings she'd like to have if she ever got married." Jolly explained, "This one is her wedding ring. She wanted something simple."

"What's in the third box?" asked Johnny.

"It's my wedding ring." Jolly answered, opening the box.

"She agreed to marry you?" asked Chandler.

"I haven't asked her yet. I planned on asking her after the second show. I thought first we'd have to deal with four angry best friends. I'm not sure what changed your attitudes toward Jarmila having independence and a relationship outside your own little group. But I am deeply grateful."

"Da four of us talked about da situation. Jarmila is a grown woman," said Jack, "she has da right to happiness. We want her to be happy. But we also want to make sure she's safe. You have our blessings, but know if your break her heart we'll come at you making "The Texas Chainsaw Massacre" look like a Disney film."

"I have ideas in mind about when I want to marry her. I want to surprise it on her. These are probably crazy ideas, but hear me out, because I need your help."

"Jarmila don't want no big wedding." Jack said, "She's said that a bunch of times over da years. She said if she ever got married it would just be da groom, her and us, da judge and nobody else."

"That works perfectly. Here's my idea. Your first tour rehearsal date is June 1st. That's Jarmila's birthday."

"Yeah," said Johnny, "but we planned on taking her drinking after rehearsal. Our plans are: our private party in the afternoon, rehearsal and then out for Jarmila's birthday. We were going to make it a short rehearsal so we could go celebrate."

"You still can. Here's my plan. I won't be insulted if you think it's insane. But let me tell you what I've done. And what I plan to do." Jolly said, "Jar showed me a pic of her great-grandmother, who she is named after."

"Oh shit," said Jack, "here we go with da great-grandma stories again."

"I've heard only bits and pieces." said Jolly, "But she seems to be an important figure in Jar's life. She has this pic of her great-grandmother on her wedding day. I think the girl was like 14-years-old. It was dated 1916. Jar wanted a gown like that, if she ever got married. And the headband veil, and pointy white shoes. I did research and found a similar gown from 1916, so I ordered it. It looks small, I think it will fit. I couldn't find the headband veil, so I had a seamstress here in Chicago make one. I still need to pick that up when it's done. I couldn't find the shoes, so I ordered them from Italy. They won't be here until the end of May. I put a rush order on them."

"So…" started Jack, downing 2 two-milligram Xanax with some Don Julio tequila, "what do you want from us?"

"Did you just pop two Xanax and wash it down with tequila?" asked Jolly.

"2 two-milligram Xanax to be exact." Jack replied.

"You have a show in a few hours." Jolly commented.

"Da Xanax is to help even out da coke. I don't want to be twirling around da stage like some deranged ballerina."

"That pretty much describes all your performances." laughed Jolly.

"Go on and tell us your plans." said Benny, "I've got to bump soon."

"I was thinking, what if I marry her the day after her birthday? She talks about how the Formal Flower Garden in Humboldt Park is her favorite place. We could marry there. I know a judge who'd marry us. We could make it a four o'clock wedding. Maybe you'll all be over your hangovers by then. The day before, on her birthday, I'll show up at rehearsal at 7:30pm. I'll give her a gift and it will be the wedding dress, veil and shoes. You will all be there, and I know she'd want it that way. Then you all can take her out to party for her birthday." Jolly explained.

"Well, brainless, mouthy, tour manager who will be Johnny's brother-in-law, and in some weird way related to the rest of us, I like your plan. With one revision: you go out with us to celebrate her birthday. It could be a bachelor/bachelorette party, too." said Jack.

"No, Jack," said Jolly, "I don't want to break up your five-person pack. I don't want to alter your relationships with her, or your traditions. I'll see her after you take her out drinking. Jar and I will have the rest of our lives together. I don't want things to change between you. You've been friends for so long, you are why her heart beats. I think of what she's told me, how you saved her from the streets, not caring if you got caught by your parents. You sheltered her, you fed and clothed her. When you guys were young teens and working minimum wage jobs, you gave her your money if she needed it, although that often left you broke. You're the reason I can hug her at night. You're the reason I am happy, and in love for the first time. You're the reason she's here for me to marry. Because if you hadn't taken care of her, she'd probably just be a statistic, and I'd have never met my one-and-only. I only ask one thing of you. Please leave your private parts away from her. I'm not a jealous person. But I would like to keep sexual intimacy with Jar for myself."

"You're killing me." said Chandler, "No more head? Have you gotten head from her? It's like my brain hits the ceiling."

"Yes, Chandler, I understand." said Jolly, "I am asking all of you to please not have any type of sex with her anymore."

They agreed.

"I think it's a reasonable request." said Johnny, who wasn't involved in the request, "Chandler, Jack and Benny have plenty options, especially on the road."

"I'm faithful to Alice!" exclaimed Benny

"When she's around." laughed Jack.

"Are we good then? Everyone okay with this?" asked Jolly.

All four members of Lenehan stood up and shook his hand. Jack gave him a hug.

"Welcome to da family, Jolly." Jack said.

Jarmila popped her head around the doorway of the tour office. Jolly was finalizing guest lists with Chandra, Scot and Everett.

"Hiya." she said, Dum Dum in her mouth.

"That lollipop better be an illusion." said Jolly.

"Yeah," said Jarmila, "Criss Angel is making it appear like I have a lollipop in my mouth."

"Get in here and give me that." Jolly motioned with his hand, and took the Dum Dum out of her mouth, throwing it away, "Next fuckin' tour I'm banning those things."

"You can't." said Scot, "Benny insists they be in all riders."

"Great. I'll be a tour manager to a band with no teeth." Jolly laughed.

"Y'all seem remarkably calm for a show this big." commented Jarmila.

"Everything seems to be working out just fine." said Jolly, "Crew guest list in already, which must be a sign of the pending appearance of the Four Horseman, because I have never gotten a guest list so early from Everett."

"Fuck you." joked Everett.

"Family will be here a half hour before doors open so we can get them all settled in so they can watch their little deranged sociopathic spawn perform. Hospitality rooms are almost set up. We don't have many contest winners to deal with. There's a few people who know people who know people who are on the list. The groupie list is so big I should have given them their own hospitality room. They're spawning like sea monkeys."

"It's Chicago, Lenehan's hometown. You're gonna see an increase in groupies." said Scot, "You should put them in the dressing room after the show. That's where they'll end up anyway."

"I wouldn't think so with the families being here." said Jolly.

"It's their hometown." said Scot, "The families go back home after the show. No worry that Chandler's mom will catch him licking a dude's balls in a hotel room. His parents live in the suburbs and they're driving back after the show. They'll be here for tomorrow night's show, too. They don't want to stay in the city when it only takes them about 30 minutes to get home."

"I think it's interesting how the band gives a guest list with the word "SPECIAL" written across it to indicate that it's a list for groupies." said Chandra.

"Think of the ones they don't know about yet, the new ones who just discovered the band. They'll eventually be on that list someday." Scot said.

"Spawning like sea monkeys." Jolly repeated.

"I gotta get out front." Everett said, "Stage is almost set up. Opening band is local and supposed to be very good."

"Jesus, I hope so." said Jolly, taking out his phone from his pocket as it gave him a notification, "Chandler is on Instagram showing off a pair of pink high heels, a pair of pink booty shorts that are way too small for him, and a white leather vest."

Everyone in the room got out their phones.

"Those are my shorts!" exclaimed Jarmila.

"I don't want to imagine how he fit into a pair of your shorts." Jolly said.

"Tuck n' roll," said Scot, "tuck n' roll."

"I've seen Chandler naked." said Jolly, "That's a lot of tuck n' roll. Jar, sugar, I think you're going to need a new pair of pink booty shorts."

"I'm going out front." said Jarmila, "See you at dinner, Jolly?"

"Yes, my love." Jolly said, kissing her. "I'll be out front soon."

Scot went to the dressing room. Jolly sent Chandra to the box office with the guest lists. Kirk and Keith entered the office and he sent them to check on all the items in the hospitality rooms. Jolly didn't like mistakes, or missing items, especially when it involved the band's family. Everything had to be prefect for them. He then went to the dressing room to talk to Scot. He sent Arne, the CEO of the production company running the shows, a nice text thanking him for the extra comp tickets. Then he went to the dressing room. Lenehan had filled Scot in on the details of the surprise engagement and wedding.

"Fucking her, yes." said Scot, "Marrying her? You just fucking met her."

"Remember my third wife, the stripper in East Saint Louis, who after her shift we flew to Las Vegas and got married?" asked Jolly, "Sometimes I do things impulsively."

"Rarely," said Scot, "very rarely have I ever seen you do anything impulsively. You're a man with a plan for everything."

"This time I'm truly in love. This is it Scot. Jarmila is the one." Jolly said.

"Jarmila is the one for a lot of things, mainly the one who provides the band with their sexual proclivities." answered Scot.

"Not anymore." Jack said, "We promised Jolly we'd stay away from his girl."

"We wouldn't be here discussing this if he had stayed away from your girl." retorted Scot.

"Love," said Chandler, "he's in love. Who can deny love? I never deny love. I reciprocate love to all those who love me."

"Which I heard was half of Memphis." Scot laughed.

"Scot," said Jolly, "I know you're upset about the situation. I know you don't like Jarmila. But she's my soulmate. After all this time, I've found my true love. You and I have been friends for 20 years. Don't you want me to have that happiness? The band put away their negative emotions and are happy for us. Can't you be happy for me?"

"But Jolly," said Scot, "Jarmila? She's a stupid, uneducated bitch who acts like a kid. What can you possibly see in her? She's fucked the entire band you work for."

"Not me!" exclaimed Johnny.

"Okay," said Scot, "with the exception of Johnny."

"I love her. I'm not asking you to love her, too. I'm not asking that you like her. I'm asking that you respect her because she will be my wife. I would also like you to be my best man. Did the band tell you the details for the wedding? I want it kept secret from Jarmila. I want to surprise her."

"Yes, they told me your plans." said Scot, "I'll check if the time you decided on is available at the Formal Gardens on that day, and if it is, I'll book it. I'll handle the park permits and all the shit you need. How many people do you expect?"

"I didn't even think of that." said Jolly.

"Seems you haven't thought of much since you first met her except getting in between her legs." Scot said, crudely.

"That wasn't very cool, Scot." reprimanded Johnny.

"Jarmila don't want a big wedding." said Jack.

"Just family." stated Scot.

"Yes," said Jolly, "the usual suspects. And probably Johnny's mom, right Johnny?"

"Yeah," said Johnny, "and my Aunt Frieda and Uncle Bern."

"Make sure you add Marie," said Chandler, "and Everett and his wife, L'Auvergne, and their two kids."

"And Alice." added Benny.

"Who's going to be maid of honor? Marie, Alice or L'Auvergne, or all?" asked Scot.

"I am! I'm matron of honor!" exclaimed Chandler, "I have the perfect pink dress picked out. I already have the shoes."

"Your wife is going to be there and you're going to wear a dress and heels?" inquired Scot.

"She's already seen him on Instagram in heels and booty shorts!" laughed Jack.

"Is there anything else you need me to do for your wedding?" asked Scot.

"Yes." said Jolly, "You could smile at the wedding. Thank you for being the good friend you have always been to me, and not trying to talk me out of this."

"I think it would be a waste of my time." said Scot, "May you have all the happiness you've always wanted."

"Chandler," said Jolly, "I need you to find a bouquet of peonies. Her great-grandmother had one in the picture. I want her to have one like it. That's a matron of honor duty.'

"No problem." said Chandler, "We got the marriage license thing figured out too. See, L'Auvergne is a court advocate for people who need help getting through the court system. She's going to tell the clerk that Jarmila does not understand how to fill out forms. She'll fill out the forms for her, and have her sign it. The court clerk probably won't ask questions cause L'Auvergne is there, and she's well known. Jarmila will sign anything we tell her to, no questions asked."

"Now that we have all the wedding plans sorted out for the wedding of the century, it's time for soundcheck." Scot said.

Jolly found Jarmila sitting at a table on the V.I.P. platform.

"Staking out your territory?" asked Jolly, sitting next to her.

"Ain't nobody taking my seat." she answered.

"You and I are going to have a serious conversation about your behavior."

"I can sit where I want!"

"I'm not having this conversation with you now. I'm in a good mood and want to stay there."

Lenehan took the stage for soundcheck. Jack stepped up to the microphone.

"Hey Jarmila," said Jack, "this is for you."

The band started playing "Before The Next Teardrop Falls" by Freddy Fender.

"If he brings you happiness

Then I wish you all the best

It's your happiness that matters most of all

But if he ever breaks your heart

If the teardrops ever start

I'll be there before the next teardrop falls."

"Oh, they're fuckin' hilarious." said Jolly.

"They're protective of me. They always will be. You'll have to put up with them."

"I do already. Are you hungry?" Jolly asked Jarmila.

"I am."

"Things are going good, so far, tonight. Let's skip soundcheck and go to dinner."

The two walked downstairs hand in hand, not hiding anything anymore. On the way downstairs they ran into Les going upstairs.

"Band and crew families arrive one half hour before doors open. We'll have security for them. Get handlers up front for that. Chandra is going to be in box office so there's no mistakes." Jolly said, "There's been a change in V.I.P. seating. I don't know if you've been informed. Johnny's mom, aunt and Jarmila are being moved from V.I.P. box to the platform, the table has a placard with their names. Please make sure they are seated there. The original reserves are going into V.I.P. box instead."

"Scot informed me." said Les, "I'll have Elias there to make sure there's no mix-ups."

Jolly and Jarmila proceeded to the crew hospitality room. It was crowded. They took a seat at the first table. It had been the position they had been in the first time they ate together, in Little Rock, almost four weeks prior.

"This is like almost the same seating arrangement like when you were trying to teach me to eat with chopsticks!" exclaimed Jarmila.

"It is!" exclaimed Jolly, looking around, "Without the Flamin' Hot Cheetos."

Jolly went to the buffet. Jarmila followed.

"What are you going to eat, Miss Malone?" he asked.

"Really," she whispered into his ear, "I'd like you in my mouth."

"You're a bad girl, Miss Malone." Jolly whispered in her ear, "Getting me all horny before the show."

"Oooo! Steamed broccoli!" she exclaimed, piling it on her plate, "And potatoes. With gravy!"

"And a piece of chicken!" Jolly laughed, as he put the piece of chicken on her plate.

Plates full, they sat next to each other. Jolly returned to the table for chopsticks.

"Chopsticks." he smiled, "Let's try this again. Without a serious beating included."

Jarmila smiled and let Jolly hold her hand until she got the gist of handling chopsticks.

"Were they hard on you?" she asked.

"Surprisingly, no. They wanted to make sure my intentions were honorable toward you. They wanted to make sure I didn't break your heart. Because if I broke your heart, Johnny said he would kill me, and Jack said he'd come at me like "The Texas Chainsaw Massacre". I'm hoping their calm demeanor wasn't just because someone put tranquilizers in their cocaine. They said the four of them had talked about the situation and decided if you were happy, they would not stand in the way of your happiness. They said you're a grown woman and deserve to be happy."

"I am happy. But in a way I'm sad too. They are my best friends. I feel like I'm closing a chapter in my life, like I'm closing them out. They don't need me anymore, and that makes me sad."

"They still need you!" exclaimed Jolly, "Why don't you think they still need you?"

"They're going places. They're soaring to new heights. I'm stuck down here."

"They are going up and up and up. But so are you! They need you in a different way than they did before. You'll figure it out and you'll fall right into their same rhythm. Don't be sad, Jar. They will *always* be your best friends, and you will always be their heart." Jolly said, kissing her.

"Yeah. I guess. I feel useless toward them now. I'm not running back and forth bringing them things like drinks and towels and clothes and stuff. I sit there and do nothing."

"You don't do that stuff anymore because they have the money now to hire people to do that. You get to sit back and bask in their rock stardom. But no sex with them. They promised me, they won't have sex with you again. *Any* type of sex. Sexual intimacy is between us only now."

"I'm kinda glad. I didn't like it anyway with them. I thought if I didn't do that stuff, they wouldn't be my friends. But you said they'd still be my friends, and you were right. But I'll miss laying in Chandler's arms, falling asleep to his vanilla scent. I'll miss falling asleep facing Benny with his thigh over my thigh. Those things I'll miss. The nice parts of sex."

"I hope you like it with me."

"I *love* it with you! That's making love. Totally different. I read it online."

Jolly laughed and hugged her close.

"I love you, Miss Malone." he said, "Now, the show must go on.

As Jolly went upstairs, Jarmila went down the hallway to the main dressing room. Jack was in front of a full-length mirror checking out a pair of leather pants that had strings crisscrossed in the back. Benny was nodded off in an arm chair. Johnny was seated on a chair by the food buffet, his headphones on, playing his bass. Sofia was on a couch on the far wall, Johnny's dogs next to her. Chandler was looking at his phone, half sitting up, his feet and legs up on the couch, his back to the armrest. He still had on his high heels, Jarmila's pink booty shorts, and the white leather vest. Jarmila went to Johnny first.

"How's your headaches?" she asked, after tapping on his arm to get his attention.

He put his headphones around his neck and gave her a hug and kiss.

"Much better. Not as many migraines. I think the medication helps." he answered.

"Good. I love you." she said.

"I love you too, little sister." he responded.

"Jarmila, come over here and give me your opinion of these pants." requested Jack.

"I like the strings in the back," she said, "but they need to be tighter. See this line by your hip area? It would accentuate it more if the pants were tighter."

Jack twisted around to see his back in the mirror, and then straightened again.

"Where da fuck is Bella? Why can't wardrobe be closer?" Jack complained.

"It's only across the hallway, Jack." said Jarmila.

Jack opened the dressing room door and started shouting for Bella repeatedly.

"Jack, I'll tighten the strings for you." said Jarmila, "You don't have to go shouting for Bella."

"It's not your job! It's fuckin' *Bella's* job! Where are my shirts? There should be some racks of my stage clothing in here and it's *not fuckin' in here*. Where da fuck is Scottie? It's almost showtime. Where da fuck is everybody?" ranted Jack, slamming the dressing room door and returning to the mirror.

"Jack," said Jarmila, soothingly, "let me tighten the strings, okay? I used to help with your clothing all the time. It's like I'm useless now."

"It's not that you're useless," said Jack, "it's that I *pay* people to do certain jobs and they are *not doing them* to my satisfaction."

Bella entered the dressing room while Jarmila was tightening the strings on the back of Jack's pants.

"I'm bringing the clothing racks in now." said Bella.

"I gotta show to do so why are you so fuckin' late with my clothes?" screamed Jack at Bella.

"Jack," said Jarmila, "The doors don't open for another half hour. Security is just now bringing in the families. There's no need to yell at Bella. She's not late with the clothes. She's actually about an hour earlier than she normally brings stuff in."

"Thank you, Jarmila." said Bella, as her assistants brought in the clothing racks.

Jack and Chandler were the only two who wore stage clothes. Johnny was happy wearing whatever he wore on any given day on stage, and Benny loved thrift store clothes, and various band t-shirts. That was if he hadn't chosen to be completely naked at his drum set. Bella and her assistants left the room as Jack looked over the racks.

"Fuckin' nothing. What da fuck am I going to wear? Where da fuck is Scottie? I haven't seen him for like 20 minutes. I don't pay that motherfucker to disappear. I pay him to manage my band."

"Wear the Cubs jersey." suggested Jarmila, "It looks nice with those pants and pays respects to the Cubs fans. You're not that far from Wrigley Field over here."

"I can always count on you, my special girl," Jack said as he kissed her on the lips, "to always make me look good on stage."

"What are you going to wear, Chandler?" Jarmila asked.

"What I'm wearing now." he answered.

"Put a white cowboy hat on and you can look like a college football team's cheerleader reject." sneered Jack.

"At least I don't look like W. Axl Rose bought up Ernie Banks estate sale." countered Chandler.

"Fuck you motherfucker!" yelled Jack, going toward Chandler aggressively.

"Guys, guys!" cried Jarmila, "Please don't fight. There's no one in here to stop you if you fight. Please, I don't like it when you fight. It makes me sad. Y'all like brothers, you shouldn't fight. Jack, don't you want to visit with your momma? I saw her coming in the building as I was passing by. She's probably already been seated. You should go say hi to her."

"I just fuckin' saw her for brunch. Her bitch sister was there, my Aunt Aileen. Hate that stupid bitch. My grandpa says she's da biggest bitch east of da Mississippi. Makes me wonder how big da bitches are west of da Mississippi. Cause my Aunt Aileen one *huge* bitch. My mom wanted to show her how successful I've become. That fuckin' bitch Aileen lives in Winnetka in some ugly ass house her and her "successful" doctor husband built. Well bitch, I got a boulevard house across from the most beautiful park in fuckin' Chicago, and I got 'bout a million more in da bank than your "successful" doctor husband does. And da bitch made me pay da check. If her husband so "successful", why didn't she pay da check?"

"Is she here tonight?" asked Jarmila.

"Thank God no, cause I swear I'd leave da building if she was." replied Jack. "Fucked up my day. I had an excellent night before with Janet…Janice…Janey…I don't remember her name. Kept me afloat *all night long*."

"I binge watched *This Is Us*" with Marie." said Chandler.

"Awww," scoffed Jack, "When you were done did you have door locked lights out missionary position sex?"

"I'm going to fuck you up!" screamed Chandler, going toward Jack.

"No!" cried Jarmila, putting her hands on Chandler's chest, "No fighting! You've been waiting your whole careers to headline The Vic. Don't start the night out by fighting. Have you been doing cocaine all day?"

"I started when Jack picked me up at noon." said Chandler.

"I started right after brunch." answered Jack, "But it's okay, don't worry, I popped a few Xanax in between. I only drank about half of a bottle of Don Julio. Couple more blunts and a side of mescaline, I'll be good to go."

"Good to go straight to the morgue." said Scot as he entered the room.

"Where da fuck were you?" screamed Jack, "I pay you to manage my band, not disappear."

"I had a meeting with my staff." Scot answered.

"Then do that on your own fuckin' time." Jack said.

"It was about the band, so I'll *do it on your fucking time.*" responded Scot, going over to Benny.

Scot shook Benny a few times, slapped his face a few times.

"Benny," he said, "wake up. Wake up Benny. C'mon, up, up."

"Wha....?" slurred Benny, waking up from his heroin sleep.

"Alice is here." said Scot, "She's in the family hospitality room talking to one of Chandler's sisters."

"Which one?" asked Chandler.

"I don't know," replied Scot, "Your siblings all look the same. Like the family from House Lannister. All tall, blonde hair, blue eyes."

"Probably Orla." said Chandler, "She's pregnant again and always hungry."

"Fuck me, didn't she just get married?" asked Jack.

"Four years ago. Third kid." answered Chandler.

"I gotta go see Alice." slurred Benny, leaving the dressing room.

Scot sat next to Johnny's dogs and began a casual discussion with Sofia. Jack returned to the couch he had been sitting on while Chandler cut more lines of cocaine on the coffee table, snorted a couple lines, then sat on the other end of the couch.

"Sit on my lap, pretty girl." Jack said to Jarmila.

She sat in between his legs instead of on his lap, with her feet on the coffee table. He stroked her outer thighs.

"I'm going to miss your tight ass so much." he said.

"There'll be other tight asses. Probably a whole lot lined up around the block. You're a rock star now. You can have all the tight ass you want. You could fuck Chandler up the ass if you couldn't find anyone else." replied Jarmila.

"You're lucky you're Jolly's girl." replied Jack, "Or-"

"-my ass would be black and blue." Jarmila finished, "I know, Jack, I know."

"You do have a tight ass." commented Chandler, "Who's gonna give us head like you do? Maybe you could teach some of the groupies your techniques!"

"No, Chandler." she replied.

"It's not fair some old guy gets the benefits of having you by his side." said Chandler.

"He's fuckin' old enough to be her father." said Jack.

"Do you call him "Daddy"?" laughed Chandler.

"Leave her alone." said Johnny, switching places with Scot, "She's in love. Let her be happy without all your sarcasm."

"Are you going to give me and Jolly shit for the rest of our lives?" asked Jarmila.

"You'll probably live longer, so you'll be getting da shit longer than he does." laughed Jack.

"You need to get married, Jack. And have some kids. You're 24 now. You should find a nice girl like Marie or Alice." Jarmila said.

"Hell da fuck no!" roared Jack, "I'm not getting stuck being monogamous like fuckin' Chandler. Making a vow to his wife to never have sex with anyone but her when he's in town. Fuck that shit. I ain't gonna be tied down to *no one*."

"Except me." said Jarmila, "Chandler used to have sex with me. He told her that before he married her, that he was having sex with me before he met her and he'd continue to have sex with me after they got married. That was the only way he'd marry her. She agreed. She just asks that I not do it anymore in their marriage bed. She didn't like catching me with Chandler having sex there."

"Yeah, except before he married her, he forgot to tell her about all the cock he sucked." Jack jeered.

"Those were insignificant. Jarmila is my special girl." said Chandler, stretching to kiss her, "Besides, Marie knows now that sometimes I like men. She packs me with lots of condoms. She loves me and puts up with me, and that's why I love her."

"We should go on one of those afternoon talk shows." joked Jack, "I love my wife and she loves me but when I'm out of town I get butt fucked by every hot guy I run into. When I'm in town I fuck my special girl…who is not my wife."

"None of you are doing any fucking or sucking with Jarmila anymore." said Scot, "You all agreed to leave her and Jolly their intimacy."

"Bad decision." said Chandler, "Ain't nobody give head like you, Jarmila. Jolly is one lucky man."

"You ain't getting no more head when you're in town!" laughed Jack, "Jarmila was like Custer's Last Stand. You is dead on da field, my brother, dead on da field. Until you tour again."

"August can't get here soon enough." commented Chandler.

Lenehan took the stage to the explosion of a sold-out audience. Chicago's home town boys were back. They opened with "Rockwell Street", a song from their first album, a ripping flurry of guitar and bass, mixed with Jack's searing vocals and Benny pummeling the drums. The song was about a section of Rockwell Street in Chicago, that was known for drugs, alcohol, and fast cars. It was a Chicago crowd favorite, and one Lenehan made sure to always open with in Chicago. Then they went into "Countess".

"Sweet Home Chicago!" Jack screamed after the song, "It is so good to be home! What up ChiTown!"

The audience hooted, yelled, screamed. It was a cacophony of excitement. Lenehan then went into a few of their pre-label demo songs, which the fans devoured. There was a large group of old fans in the crowd, but a larger group of new fans.

"Some of those we're going to put on our third album," teased Jack, "but we won't tell which ones. In fact, we haven't told our label yet."

Laughter and shouting from the audience. Lenehan played two more songs from their second album, and three more from their first. In between the songs from their second album, Jack thanked the audience and his fans for making Lenehan double platinum artists. He went into his usual speech about how they owed it to all of them who made them rock stars. After Jack told the audience they would be back for the second set after a short break, the band went to the dressing room. Exhausted, Jack lay on the couch nearest the door. Jarmila sat down near him and put his feet on her lap. He always went on stage barefoot.

"Massage my legs." he asked Jarmila.

She started massaging his legs starting at his upper thighs. Jolly walked in. Scot walked in right behind. Jolly saw Jarmila massaging Jack's thighs and gave her a hurtful look.

"You guys are on fuckin' fire." said Scot.

"Imma gonna tell ya all something. After this show, I'm going home and not waking up until soundcheck tomorrow. I'm fuckin' wiped da fuck out." said Jack.

"Are you feeling okay?" asked Jolly, "You cut the first set short."

"Benny's wrist is bothering him." said Johnny.

"I'll be okay" said Benny, "I'll put the wrist brace back on. I just need to rest it a few minutes."

"Jack's been up doing cocaine and a bunch of other stuff since before noon." said Jarmila, "He'll be fine once he gets a full sleep."

"Yeah, I got kept up all last night. Janet…Janice…Julie…I don't remember her name. Then my mom wants me to go to brunch with my bitch aunt so my mom can try and one-up her sister by showing her how successful I am. I'm like fuck it, I ain't going back to bed. I'll hoover up a blizzard and go pick up da guys and head to da venue." said Jack, "Geneva! That was her name! Geneva!"

"Geneva starts with a "G", not a "J". Jolly pointed out.

"I didn't see her ID!" exclaimed Jack, "Maybe she spells it with a "J"."

After a half hour break the boys were back onstage shredding it. Jack started out with a solo on the grand piano. Then he segued into one more second album tune and a couple more first album tunes.

"Now we gotta special treat just for Chicago!" exclaimed Jack. "We wrote a song on da road, just for you, Chicago! First time we've played it live!"

The song was called "City Of Stockyards" and was a medium tempo song about Chicago and its past. The crowd went ape-shit. Jack then told the tale of his jazz playing grandfather, as an intro to "Scandalous". Lenehan then played a few more second album songs, and had drum, bass and guitar solos. Then Jack introduced the band by introducing their families in the audience. When the spotlight was put on Jarmila's table to introduce Johnny's mom and aunt, Jack paused.

"Keep that spotlight over there." he said, "There's a girl over there I want to introduce. That is Lenehan's special girl, Jarmila. She been with us from da beginning. She never misses a gig, or rehearsal, or time in da studio. She's been through da worst of times with us and da best of times. She's our solid, our sister, our saint. She's never wavered in her friendship to us even when we were da biggest dickheads ever. Y'all give a big Chicago welcome home to our Chicago girl!"

The crowd became intense. Jack had them in the palm of his hand. One more song from the first album and Lenehan closed their set with their number #1 single, "The Only Cost". The audience sang the entire song with him.

In the dressing room, Jack insisted he could only do two encores. Lenehan usually did three.

"Can't do it. I'll fuckin' pass da fuck out." he complained.

"You're 24 now, Jack," said Jolly, "getting up there in years. Can't act 20 anymore, old age creeping up on you. But don't worry. I *totally* understand."

"Fuck off mouthy birdbrained tour manager!" shouted Jack, "I'm doing three fuckin' encores. When I'm done, I'm gonna fuck a hot chick up da ass while you're on your phone ordering a refill of Viagra!"

Three encores later, a short rest in the dressing room, and Lenehan was ready for the rest of the night. They went to the family hospitality room first, hanging out with their families and then saying their goodbyes. Johnny, his dogs, his mom, his aunt and Sofia went in a limo home. Johnny didn't want anything to do with after show antics. At the last minute. Benny and Alice asked if they could get a lift in the limo and get dropped off at home. Johnny, of course, said sure. They had to take Sofia home too, so Johnny said if Benny and Alice didn't mind the extra time for the trip, they were more than welcome to hitch a ride.

Jack, having gotten his second wind, went with Chandler into the guest hospitality room. After picking out some pretty women, Chandler spotted a pretty man. This gave him a dilemma. Marie had gone home. She knew he was going to party after the show, and she had faith he would keep his vow. But, he thought, it wouldn't hurt to take a beautiful man into the dressing room and just talk.

Jarmila sat watching the action in the dressing room. Jack, going between three women on one couch, Chandler on the farthest couch kissing a beautiful man with deep set hazel eyes and long brown hair. Scot was in the armchair Benny had previously been sitting in, scrolling through his tablet.

"You guys can't stay here much longer," said Scot, "the venue has to close for the night."

"I'm waiting for Jolly. He's settling the show." said Jarmila.

"I know. You can stay until he's done. Shouldn't be long now. Do you want to stay here or go to the tour office to wait?" asked Scot.

"I'll stay here if it's okay. I told him I'd wait for him here." she answered.

"That's fine" he said, "The rest of you, to the limo. Time to go home."

"I'm going to Jack's." said Chandler, giving a kiss to his pretty boy.

"Whatever." sighed Scot, "My lips are sealed."

Fifteen minutes after Scot, Jack, Chandler, and their entourage left, Jolly walked into the dressing room. He had all his equipment with him, and sat in a chair next to Jarmila. He looked very tired.

"Busy, long night." he said, "But not nearly as bad as Milwaukee had been. No serious equipment problems, no begging to sacrifice any babies for extra comp tickets. The production guy, Arne, who is responsible for Lenehan being at this venue, is very awesome. I enjoy dealing with him. I wish he was at every venue. Are you ready to go home?"

"In a limo?"

"No. I called a car service. You've been hanging around rock stars too much." he laughed.

"All my life." she smiled.

When they got home, Jolly went straight to his office to put away his briefcase, laptop, tablet, blue tooth and a cache of papers that were in a brown folder. Jarmila went straight upstairs, pulled out clothes from the suitcases still on the floor of their bedroom, and went to the bathroom in the upstairs hallway. Jolly had gone to the kitchen to get a quick snack and a tumbler of Remy Martin XO. When he went upstairs to their bedroom, he did not see Jarmila. He assumed she was in the shower in the upstairs hallway bathroom. He checked there, and she was not there, but wet bath towels were hung up on the shower stall door. He saw the "Humboldt" shirt sticking out of the bathroom hamper. He went to the larger of the guest rooms and found Jarmila under the covers.

"Why are you in this bedroom?" he said, sitting down on her side.

"I know you're mad at me about the V.I.P seating thing, so I know you don't want me next to you." she replied.

"Bunch of bullshit. I want you by my side always. I never want us to go to bed angry with each other. I'm going to take a shower. Join me in our bed, okay?"

Jolly went to shower. When he came out of his bathroom into their bedroom, Jarmila was not there. She was still in the guest bedroom. She was awake, lying under the covers, on her side, facing the wall. He got in next to her and snuggled up to her sideways, putting his arms around her.

"You know I never stay angry with you long." Jolly said, "Your behavior was unacceptable. I want to give you everything. But sometimes the answer is no."

"But Jack said…"

"Jack said, Jack said. Jack says a lot of things. But even for him, the answer is sometimes no. Running to him when you can't get what you want is old, pre-Jolly behavior. That is not acceptable anymore. You're my girl. You have a situation or a problem, you come to me with it, not cry to the band about it. You understand?"

"Yes," she said, rolling over to face Jolly, "I understand. Sometimes I feel incomplete when shit like this happens."

"How so?"

"I feel like I should get punished. Like I'm not completely forgiven until I've been punished."

"The band conditioned you that way, sugar. That's not right. But acting in that entitled manner wasn't acceptable either. I know your best friends are Billboard charting rock stars, but you don't need to be acting in an unacceptable manner. They do that enough." Jolly sighed.

"Chandler went to Jack's with a guy. A very hot guy."

"Jesus, I hope that doesn't end in divorce for him and Marie if she finds out. Lenehan are due to spend their time off touring by writing and laying down some tracks for the third album. It would suck if Chandler's indiscretion fucked that up.""

"Jack says drama makes good lyrics."

"True."

"Besides, she won't divorce him. They've had shit like this before, where he broke a promise or a vow. She denies sex with him for a couple weeks. And trust me, he doesn't care. He considers it a reprieve."

"That is so sad to have a relationship like that. In my opinion, Marie is Chandler's beard."

"What do you mean by Chandler's beard?" Jarmila asked.

"It's a phrase people use to say a gay man got married to a woman to hide the fact from certain people who would disapprove or disown him if they knew he was gay."

"He's on social media all the time. Dancing naked to songs, or wearing a tutu or my booty shorts like he did on the recent Instagram. Wouldn't you think they'd suspect something?"

"I've always had this theory that people know deep in their hearts that a family member is gay, but they keep denying it to themselves because of religion, or upbringing, etc. I think Chandler's family wants to believe he does it for publicity for the band. I don't think they approve. They probably put up with it because he's become so successful. Besides, men wear all types of clothing and run around naked and it doesn't mean they are gay. Do you think he's gay?"

"I've seen him with women." said Jarmila

"Those women may not be women in a private parts sort of way. Do you know what I mean?"

"That they weren't assigned female at birth. That they're transgendered? Or living female?"

"Yes."

"Like Helga."

"Exactly like Helga."

"I think if he wasn't married to Marie, he'd be with Helga. He liked her a lot. She's moving to New York City. She's very nice. Gender shouldn't matter, or sexual preference. All people should be respected no matter what society has labeled them. They should be able to live however they want to live, whatever they know their true self is. Whatever their truth is."

"You have a good heart, Miss Malone."

Jarmila started stroking Jolly's penis.

"You're not mad at me anymore?" she asked.

"No. But no more bratty behavior. You're a grown woman. With a boyfriend." Jolly smiled

"I've never had a boyfriend before." she kissed him deeply.

He held her closer. She put her thigh over his and guided his penis into her. Slowly they got into the same rhythmic thrusting, until both came, first her, then him. He laid one of his hands on her bottom, and the other one on her arm. They fell asleep in that position.

At 8:00am, Jolly's phone alarm went off. He quietly got out of the guest bed and went to his bedroom. He got dressed and brushed his hair, his teeth, flossed. Going to the kitchen he filled the coffee maker and pushed the on button. Going to his cabinets he searched for a pan and a baking tray. He put the pan on the stove and the tray on the counter, turned the oven on. Getting out a coffee cup, he filled it with coffee and opened his fridge for the half and half. He put the half and half on the kitchen table with a jar of sugar and the coffee cup. He then opened the fridge again and retrieved bacon, eggs, and refrigerated biscuit dough. He felt too lazy this morning to make home-made biscuits. As he was putting the biscuits on the tray, he saw Jarmila in the kitchen doorway.

"Did I wake you, sugar?" he asked.

"No. I smelled coffee."

"Do you want a cup?" he said, as he put the biscuits in the oven, He turned the stovetop on and put the bacon in the pan. Nothing better than eggs fried in bacon grease, he thought.

"I'll get it myself." she said.

"Do you want bacon? Eggs? Biscuits?" he asked as he took two eggs out of the carton, replacing the carton and bacon package in the fridge.

"Just a biscuit. I'm not hungry."

"That's because you're too skinny," he said, placing silverware and plates on the table, then grabbing Jarmila by the waist and kissing her neck, "I'm going to fatten you up!"

He took the bacon out of the pan, putting it on a rack, and cracked the eggs. He decided he wanted scrambled this morning. He took the biscuits out and put one on a plate for Jarmila.

"Do you have any honey?"

"Yes." he said, looking through various cabinets, walking into the pantry and returning with a jar of honey.

"Thank you." said Jarmila, as Jolly took his plate, filled it and sat next to her.

"You don't have to leave this early with me. You can stay home and get some rest. It was a long day yesterday!" Jolly said, "You could come by at lunch."

"No. I don't want to be alone. I'll take a couple of books to read. I wasn't in the way, was I?"

"With the exception of the seating meltdown, you were fine. I enjoy having my sunshine near me." he kissed her.

"I need to discuss something with you."

"Fire away, sugar."

"April 27th is Chandler and Benny's birthdays. Did you know they were born hours apart in the same hospital? It was like they were always meant to be friends. Anyway, we're having our private party at Chandler's. We were going to have it at Jack's, but Marie left Chandler to go to her sister's. Now Chandler says he has the whole house to himself."

"I'm getting the impression she's not taking a vacation to her sister's."

"No. I don't know long she'll be gone. Chandler didn't say. There was some kinda problem after the show last night. Chandler group texted everybody at 6:00am but I didn't hear my phone. I saw the text when I woke up. When he and Jack were leaving The Vic there were all these people taking pictures and calling their names. You know, Chandler is conceited. Jack too. These people were taking all these pictures, and Chandler had his arm around this guy, then he kisses this guy. Then it gets posted and somebody calls his wife right away and tells her to look at social media. She does, and then tells Chandler she's going to her sister's."

"Chandler must have been coked up to group text at 6:00am."

"Probably. He was at Jack's. Chandler starts talking about plans for he and Benny's party. Jack texts that he's busy tying up a girl so whatever plans they have he agrees with. We'll have our traditional party at Chandlers with rum punch, and two cakes, one for Chander and one for Benny. Can you run me by Roeser's Bakery that morning to pick up the cakes and drop me at Chandler's?"

"I sure can."

"You can stay and celebrate with us."

"Is Alice going?"

"No," said Jarmila, "Benny says she said it's a tradition, that only me and the band have our little party, and it should stay that way."

"She's correct. I'm not going to break tradition between you and the band either. But I would like you to save me some of that rum punch. I hear it's powerful but tastes like juice."

"I'll make a batch just for you! Anyway, here's what I have to talk to you about. The band is going out clubbing after the party. They asked me to join them. Can I go?"

"You're a grown woman. You don't need permission from me. I am surprised they're taking you clubbing. Where's the Lenehan "No alcohol for Jarmila" rule?"

"They said I'm your responsibility now, so I can drink if I want to." said Jarmila.

"Great. Pass me off the drunk girl." Jolly laughed, "What about Johnny's birthday? Isn't his the next day?"

"Yeah. We're going to his momma's. She makes him a birthday cake. It is from a recipe she brought from Poland. It is super delicious. She likes my great-grandmother's rum punch, too. Then we'll go to this local bar Johnny likes and he'll have a couple beers and go home. Jack, Chandler and Benny are going out clubbing again, and they asked me along. Can I go?"

"Of course. Like I said, you're a grown woman, you can go where you like."

"Why don't you go with us?"

"Is Alice going?"

"No. Benny says she said it's back luck to break a tradition. She also told Benny she doesn't not want to spend an evening with drunk egocentric rock stars. I don't think she meant Benny when she told him that."

"I'm sure she didn't either. She probably meant Jack and Chandler. I'm not going either. I don't want to break tradition. And I spend enough time with their egocentric rock star asses. You go, have a good time." Jolly said, gathering up the plates and silverware and putting them in the sink.

After he washed and dried them, and put the items back in their places in the cabinets, he asked Jarmila if she wanted another cup of coffee. She declined. He turned the coffee maker off. He took her cup and his and washed and dried them, putting them back in the cabinet. He them put the remaining biscuits in a Tupperware container and put that in the fridge. He tackled the pans next, washing and drying them and putting them away. Lastly, he cleaned the coffee maker and returned it to the counter.

"I should help." said Jarmila.

"You will. I'm letting you adjust to being in this house first. I know it's your first time since you were a child that you had a permanent place to stay. This will always be your home, Jar."

She stood up and went to the kitchen counter and hugged him. He leaned down and kissed her.

"Quickie before we have to leave?" he asked her.

"Yes!" she exclaimed, "Can we do it in here?"

"In the kitchen?"

"Yes! I saw it online. Have you ever done it in the kitchen?"

"I have. And many other places too."

"Like where?"

"In the dining room, on the piano bench, in the bathroom. Pretty much all over my house. I've fucked outside too."

"Oooh! We could try that!"

"Not today. Today I have a show."

"I meant someday."

"You're becoming a healthy horny 22-year-old. Much better than the scared little rabbit I first met."

"You brought that out of me, and I am so grateful for you." she said, bending over the kitchen table.

She was wearing a maroon button-down shirt, a straight, white pencil skirt and Jimmy Choo Leather Burgundy Pumps. Jolly unzipped his pants and got behind her. He pushed her skirt up.

"No panties?" he inquired.

"I'm going to put on a pair of burgundy fishnets before we leave."

"And some panties."

"It's no fun having a boyfriend." she turned her head to look at him, "I have to wear more clothes."

He laughed and took out his penis. He rubbed it against her causing her to make small squeaking noises. He plunged himself into her and thrusts his hips back and forth until they both came. He was zipping up his pants when he got a notification on his phone.

"Holy shit." he said, picking up his phone from the kitchen counter.

"What's wrong?" Jarmila asked, concerned, standing next to him.

"Look." he turned the phone screen to her.

Lenehan had gone triple platinum on their second album. The single "Penny" had taken the #3 spot on the charts, and their second album stayed at #1. Their first album, which had re-entered the charts, was at #7. Lenehan had a double platinum album and a triple platinum album on the charts, and the three top spots on the singles chart.

"I knew they would get there someday." said Jarmila.

"They've said you've always believed in them, but don't tell them yet. Let me and Scot break the news. Now, go upstairs and put some panties on. I'm getting my office stuff together and calling the car service."

Even at 10:30am, the venue was buzzing with road crew, venue staff and venue crew, vendors, production company people and a few security guards. Jolly and Jarmila made their way downstairs to the tour office. Kirk and Keith were there, along with Scot, Camille and Shera.

"Where's Chandra?" asked Jolly.

"Lenehan ran out of Don Julio last night. Jack had a meltdown." explained Keith, "Chandra went to the liquor store to make sure there will be plenty tonight."

"Scot, "said Jolly, "why are my people always running around getting stuff for Lenehan. You're their manager, that's *your* responsibility"

"Because my people are busy running around getting shit for the band!" protested Scot.

"If you can't do your job, Scot," said Jolly, "and you always seem to pass it on to me, then hire some more assistants or get a co-manager. I'm the tour manager; I run the tour. You're the band manager, you're the warden at the asylum."

"No band, no tour. No tour, no tour manager." retorted Scot.

"I should have stayed in fuckin' retirement." mumbled Jolly, handing assignment lists to Keith and Kirk.

He texted Chandra:

Jolly: When you return, start working on assembling the guest list. There's going to be some changes.

Chandra: Okay. Getting liquor now, will be back in 20.

When Jolly walked into the dressing room at 3:00pm, he was surprised to see all four band members there. He had understood they wouldn't be at the venue until closer to soundcheck. Sofia and Jarmila were there also. Johnny in his usual spot practicing his bass by the food buffet; Benny nodded off in an armchair; Sofia and Jarmila on the far couch with Johnny's dogs; Chandler, this time in a seat, snorting cocaine off the coffee table; and Jack near the couch, on his knees in front of a small auburn haired, pale skinned girl, her skirt and knees up and Jack's tongue in her vagina.

"Jack, really?" said Jolly, sitting down on the other end of the couch.

"I'm done." Jack casually said as he put the girl's skirt down and sat on the couch.

"I brought the big pack of Dum Dums you requested. Against my better judgement." Jolly stated, putting the package on the coffee table, "Scot is on his way in here. We have to talk to the band. Your friend has to leave the dressing room, Jack."

Jack told the girl to wait in the hospitality room. Jarmila sat on Jack's lap. She and Jack each took a Dum Dum.

"What flavor is that?" Chandler asked Jack.

"Fruit Punch." answered Jack, handing the lollipop to Chandler.

"What flavor is that, Jarmila?" asked Jack.

"Root Beer. Here you want it. I don't like this flavor very much." she said, putting the lollipop in Jack's mouth.

"Okay. Okay, okay," said Jolly, standing up, "let me explain this in the easiest way you will understand. You see, Chandler, before Jack put that lollipop in your mouth, he had it in his mouth, his tongue all over it, right after he had his tongue up some girl's pussy. Now it's in your mouth, with your tongue all over it. You see where I'm going with this?"

"Damn, Jack, that girl mighty tasty." said Chandler, taking the lollipop out of his mouth, "You got to hook me up with that sumthin' sumthin'."

"It's Teague." answered Jack.

"You mean that auburn haired girl who was just here?" asked Chandler, "The one with the Lenehan tattoos on both butt cheeks?"

"Yeah. Great targets for da cane to come down." Jack said.

"I never caned a woman." said Chandler.

"Shit, dude, you *do not* know what you're missing out on." Jack explained, "They squirm, and cry, and beg, and you can fuck them senseless. Then they want to know when they can come over next. Total fuckin' heaven. And Teague likes it up da ass. And she likes dildoes, she'll do anything you ask her. You could get whatever you want from her."

"I don't want to tread on your territory." said Chandler.

"Fuck me!" exclaimed Jack, "That was last hour's project. You can have her. I got a few lined up for tonight. Last gig of da tour. We gonna party all day and night right through next week."

"But doesn't it hurt to be caned?" asked Jarmila, looking up at Jack, "It hurt when you used the belt on me, and when you paddled me. It always hurts when you spank me."

"But pain for sexual pleasure is different." said Chandler, "It's...euphoric."

"Jack, has anybody done to you what you do to the women you're with?" Jarmila asked.

"Hell no!" exclaimed Jack. "I'm strictly da "S" in "S & M"."

"Do you want us to try a little out on you?" asked Chandler, sitting on the other side of Jack.

"*No!*" emphasized Jolly, "You all made an agreement with me. No sex with Jarmila anymore."

"I think that's a definite "no"." said Jarmila.

"But think about this, Jolly." started Chandler, "We could just lightly cane her and then use a dildo on her. Perfect! None of our body parts are touching her, so we're not actually having sex with her!"

"*No!*" exclaimed Jolly.

"You're no fun, Jolly." said Chandler.

"That's my reputation. No fun. Scot's going to be here in a minute. Sofia, do you mind waiting in hospitality?" asked Jolly.

"I'll take the dogs for a walk." she responded, "Please tell Johnny to text me when it's okay to return to the dressing room."

After calling out "Johnny" three times, Chandler threw an empty water bottle at him, hitting Johnny in the face.

"Hey, what the fuck?" yelled Johnny, taking off his headphones.

"While you were busy being anti-social," said Chandler, "zombies have taken over the universe and only our music can soothe them, so we have to play 24/7."

"Fuck off." responded Johnny.

"As soon as Scot gets here, we're having a band meeting." explained Jolly, "When we're done, Johnny, Sofia wants you to text her. She's walking the dogs."

"Why all these impromptu band meetings?" asked Jack, "We have a band meeting every show day. Why these "emergency" meetings?"

"Because you're superstars." Jolly said, sardonically, "Welcome to adulthood."

"Fuck you." replied Jack.

Scot walked in and sat in a chair by the couch. Johnny woke up Benny, and then moved his chair closer to where everyone else was sitting.

"Jar, sugar, go to the tour office and read a book. Or catch up with Sofia on the dog walk." Jolly said to Jarmila.

"Why can't I stay. I can stay for band meetings." she pouted.

"You're leaving the dressing room because I said *leave the fucking dressing room*." said Jolly, rudely.

"No point in getting stupid with me!" exclaimed Jarmila, "I'm going to go see what Everett is doing."

"Yes, go pester him. He'll love that." said Scot, derisively.

"Fuck off, Scot!" cried Jarmila, as she slammed the dressing room door.

"And you wanna marry that thing." commented Scot to Jolly.

"I'm going to marry her." replied Jolly, "But first I have to ask her to marry me. She doesn't want any man-on-his-knee romantic proposal. I want to ask you all a favor."

"Get to it already," hastened Jack, "I got a soundcheck to do."

"You've remembered soundcheck without being reminded!", exclaimed Jolly, "Mic...drop! I suspect by the next tour you'll enter your toddler phase and learn the simple words in an itinerary."

"For a man who wants a favor from us, you're stepping on cracking ice. Cause I got da final say in this band." replied Jack.

"I'm sorry for the sarcasm." Jolly apologized, "My sarcasm often gets in the way of my sincerity. I want to ask you if I can propose to Jarmila onstage tonight."

"Too cool!" shouted Johnny.

"That would be awesome, and sweet." said Benny.

"I think it's tenderhearted." added Chandler.

"I think I'm going to vomit." said Scot.

"I'll be joining you." said Jack, "Is that it? Can I relax before soundcheck now?"

"Actually, I have another favor to ask. It's a big favor." said Jolly, "I know you don't play cover tunes during your shows. I want to ask if you'll change the rule this one night. I'm asking you to play "Changes" by Blind Melon. The song has special meaning to her, because it has special meaning to the band. I'm asking if you could dedicate it to her from me. I'm going to take her from V.I.P. section to the side of the stage during the song, and when it's finished, I'm going to take her out of stage and propose to her. The Vic Theater means a lot to me personally. I've told her the backstory of how and why it is important to me. I think it would be special to propose to her in my favorite venue. I'd really appreciate this."

Everyone thought it was a great idea, except Scot and Jack.

"It's up to Lenehan." said Scot, "In my opinion, any idea you have involving Jarmila involves a large percentage of your dick. You're not thinking with your brain. But whatever the band agrees with, you'll hear no dissent from me."

"I'm supposed to cut a song from da setlist so you can do your thing?" asked Jack, "You can propose anywhere."

"This is his first time as a tour manager at this venue." said Scot, "This venue has a lot of sentimental meaning to him. Let him have his moment, Jack."

"Valium kick in, Scottie? Two seconds ago, you didn't seem all that happy about this idea." said Jack.

"I think, why not let them be happy? Why block their way? Jarmila has done *a lot* for Lenehan. She's done a lot for you individually. Let's give her one big surprise, the surprise of a lifetime. I may not like her personally, but I see what she has done for Lenehan. She's annoying AF, but she's Jolly's annoying AF. Give them this moment."

"Okay," agreed Jack, "but only during da second set. We'll pick a demo song to cut."

"Thank you, Jack." said Jolly, "You're helping to make my life complete."

"Whatever," replied Jack, snorting a line off the table.

Jolly found Jarmila in the tour office. She was talking to Chandra.

"Want to go to dinner?" he asks Jarmila

"Do we have time before soundcheck?'

"Yes."

"Okay."

The couple went down the hall to the crew hospitality room. Jarmila followed Jolly in the buffet line. He made sure she picked out more than just carrots. They sat at one of the first long tables.

"I like carrots." said Jarmila.

"I do too," answered Jolly, "but you cannot exist off of carrots and steamed broccoli alone."

"I don't like ham."

"Ok. Do you like pork chops?"

"Yeah."

"Trade me the ham for the pork chops." Jolly said, as he took the ham from Jarmila's plate and put it on his, trading the pork chops on his plate.

"When are you going to tell the guys about going triple platinum?"

"After soundcheck. It won't be quite as many people to celebrate because of the time we're doing it, but we're surprising them with cakes. There's going to be a big end-of-tour party anyway. The crew and staff that miss the first announcement can celebrate then. We're having cake then too."

"Lots of cake."

"Lots to celebrate! Why do you sound so down, Miss Malone?" Jolly asked.

"I don't know. I think I'm going to miss touring. I also won't see the guys too much after tonight. They'll be busy writing music and lyrics for their third album. I won't see them a lot until tour rehearsals."

"Before you met me, what did you do when they were busy writing lyrics and music?"

"Sat while they were writing, and read a lot. Now I am with you. It's a big change for me."

"I know, sugar. I'll try to make it as interesting as possible for you. But listen, there are times when I have to be out of town. Sometimes you can go with me, and sometimes not. Will you be okay staying at one of the guys houses then, or do you mind staying at my house alone? Ms. Fraiser, the housekeeper, she's asked for an extension to her vacation, so she won't be back until the end of June. He daughter-in-law became very sick after having the baby, and she needs the extra help. I thought if you can't go with me, maybe you could stay at Benny and Alice's? Or Johnny's? I feel safer if you're there."

"Why can't I always go with you?"

"Because I'm going to Europe to check out some venues. We have to get you a passport for the tour. I'm not comfortable leaving you alone in Europe while I go check out venues and go to meetings. You can't go with me to those things. That's business. I'd rather you stay home."

"But I want to go on the European tour!" Jarmila cried.

"You will! When the actual tour happens, you *will* be there. You know the band wouldn't go without their best friend."

Music could be heard coming from upstairs.

"Time for soundcheck, my love." said Jolly, as he emptied the plates into the trash can and held Jarmila's hand, going up the stairs.

Soundcheck over, the Lenehan boys were back in the dressing room. Johnny, eyes closed, was sitting in a chair with his feet up on a chair in front of him. Gotti was at his feet. Sofia was on the far couch. Alice and Benny sat next to her, Benny's head on Alice's shoulder. Chandler and Jack were sitting near each other on the couch closest to the door. Jack was petting Capone.

The dressing room door opened and together walked in Jolly, Scot, Jarmila, and Everett. Jolly and Everett were each holding a rectangular sized cake.

"Johnny," shouted Chandler, "wake up. I think something has happened."

Johnny immediately opened his eyes and took his feet off the chair. Benny lifted his head from Alice's shoulder.

Jolly and Everett put the cakes on the coffee table. One had white and green icing and had the words "Congratulations On Your Triple Platinum Album" written on it. It was a vanilla cake with strawberries inside. Jack's favorite. The other cake, a carrot cake with white cream cheese frosting, had the words "Congratulations On Holding The #1, #2, and #3 Spots On The Charts" written on it. On the sides of that cake were written "The Only Cost", "Scandalous", and "Penny." All the band gathered around the coffee table, their eyes wide like kids seeing a surprise for the first time.

"We *fuckin'* did it!" shouted Jack.

"We have arrived, bitches!" shouted Chandler, "We have *arrived*!"

Their last night of their tour, Lenehan took the stage like an F5 tornado. The started the night off with the song they always started off with in Chicago, "Rockwell Street". They then when into a raucous "She Coulda" and then "Suffer The Children".

"What up Chicago!" Jack shouted, "Sweet home Chicago. Good to be back in our hometown, seeing a lot of familiar hometown faces and new ones! It's a dream for Lenehan to headline The Vic Theater. It has always been our desire. I used to pass by this place and say to myself, 'One day I'm gonna headline a sold out show there.' Well, we headlined *two* sold out shows here, in a row. This is da last show of this tour, and I can't think of a better place to celebrate it then in my hometown with Chicago fans, friends, and family. Our next tour starts in August, where we start da tour by headlining *two* shows at The Aragon Ballroom, and y'all motherfuckers better be there and sell them out too! Cause we got some news a few hours ago. Our second album has gone triple platinum and is still at #1 on da charts, our first album is going back up da charts, and we have da #1, #2, and #3 spots on da top 10 singles chart. "The Only Cost", "Scandalous", and "Penny" are monopolizing da first three spots. It's all because of you motherfuckers, buying our music and our merchandise, selling out our shows, always supporting us as da *best fans out there* cause nobody got fans like Chicago! Lenehan owes all this to you motherfuckers! We're up here playing our balls off because you made all of this happen, and we're gonna give you da best show you have ever been to. We're gonna give you a show that thirty years from now you'll be saying 'Damn, that Lenehan show at The Vic Theater in 2019 was *da best show I have ever seen*."

The crowd went ballistic. Lenehan went directly into "Shame On You", a song from the second album they rarely played. Then they played "Countess" and segued into two pre-label demos back-to-back. Jack then did introductions, something he would do in the first set, or the second set depending on what the band decided beforehand. But tonight was a special night.

"Chandler Riley on guitar!" yelled Jack, "Lots of Riley clan here tonight, including his parents and relatives. Let's give a big ole Chicago welcome to da Riley clan!"

Whoops and hollers followed with some stomping feet.

"Johnny Dunne on bass guitar!" shouted Jack, "His mom, who we call Ma Dunne, and his Aunt Frieda here to support Lenehan. Ma Dunne worked three jobs so Johnny could achieve his dream of standing on this very stage as a rock star! Give a big ole Chicago welcome to Ma Dunne and Aunt Frieda."

The crowd responded with shouts and roars.

"Benny Mann picking up da drums. His Alice right here in front with her friends. They follow us to most gigs to support Benny and da band. Shine a spotlight on pretty Alice. She's probably gonna kick my ass later for pointing her out, but I'll hide behind Benny. She likes Benny. Show some Chicago love to Alice and her friends!"

The crowd picked up more, made more noise, shouts and shrieks. Jack's intros made them feel like they were an integral part of the band. They were. The band realized how important fans were and treated them as such.

"Can't forget to introduce my mom. When I was young, my dad died, and my mom kept things together. She made sure I had voice lessons and flute lessons and violin lessons. Despite my crazy mercurial personality, she supported me and helped me stay da course to achieve my goal in music. I gave her more of a hard time then actually told her I appreciated her, but I hope she knows how much I love and appreciate her now. Once in a while she'll call me up and say, 'Jack Michael Connelly'-you know you're in trouble when your mom calls you by your full name-'Jack Michael, I saw you dancing naked on TikTok.'." So I says, 'That's pretty cool mom that you got a TikTok account.'."

Laughter and shouts from the audience.

"Can't forget Lenehan's special girl. She out there in da V.I.P. section in the center. Shine a spotlight on her, though she gonna kick my ass later for doing that." Jack introduced Jarmila, "This is Jarmila Malone. She's Lenehan's special girl. Been with us from da first note we played. Never missed a rehearsal or a gig or a recording session. Most loyal fan and friend we have. She's our solid, or sister, our saint. She's da backbone of this band. Been with us through our ups and downs, and her buoyant attitude lifted our spirits and kept us going on many occasions. I can't count da number of times she said 'Y'all gonna be rock stars!'. She was right. We couldn't have gone this far without the support of our special girl, who wouldn't let us quit no matter how tough shit got. We love you, Jarmila, and don't you ever forget that!"

The audience went into a frenzy. Jack then told the story of his Grandfather Jack and the Chicago jazz clubs of the 1930's, as the intro to "Scandalous."

Lenehan took a half hour break between sets. Jack sat in an armchair with his feet on an end table he had pulled out of its place for the very purpose of relaxing his legs. Chandler opted for the loaded cocaine mirror table. Johnny joined Sofia and Alice on the far couch with his dogs. Benny opted for the floor where he could bump up his heroin easier. Jolly, Jarmila and Scot all sat in individual seats.

"Why everybody so quiet?" asked Jarmila.

"We've all decided to join da monks and take a vow of silence." scoffed Jack.

"Chandler would like that. It's all men." said Jarmila.

"If Chandler joined da monks there'd be a three hour wait outside da confessional every day." Jack retorted.

"We're all exhausted, Jarmila," said Johnny, "Benny's wrist kinda hurts him and I'm getting one of those headaches."

"Benny," said Jolly, "let's get you to medical and get them to tape up the wrist, then put the wrist brace over it. That might help ease the pain."

"Morphine would ease the pain." answered Benny.

"With everything else you've taken tonight," said Jolly, "morphine would be your trip to a coffin. I think we need to make a decision. Cancel the encores, and cancel playing for the tour after-party."

"No fuckin' way!" shouted Benny, "I don't care if my arm falls off, I'm not cancelling anything. When my mom died, after the wake I fuckin' played a gig because I knew she'd want me to."

"I'll be fine", said Johnny, "I'll take another one of my meds."

"Okay," said Jolly, "your decision. What do you think, Scot?"

"If they have the passion to play, let 'em play." he answered.

Jolly, Alice and Benny went to medical. Chandler snorted a few lines and ate a few pieces of left-over cake. Jack moved his legs down and Jarmila sat on his lap.

"Are you okay?" she asked him.

"Ever since we have met, way back then, you have always known when something is bothering me." Jack answered, "I'm a little off about you and Jolly. I'm going to miss you."

"I'm not moving to a yurt in Mongolia," she said, "I'll only be about 5 minutes from your house."

"It feels like you're moving to a yurt in Mongolia. I'm used to having you around, especially when I need you."

"I will always be around when you need me. You are you are my best friend, my priority. I'll never desert or abandon you or our friendship. I understand, though. I'd feel the same way if you had a steady girl move in with you."

"By da time that happens, you'll have grandchildren!" Jack laughed, putting his hand on her outer thigh, "Nice outfit. I'm surprised Jolly let you out of da house with it."

"He made me put on panties."

"Next, he'll make you dress like one of those fundamentalist Christian women. Long skirt and long sleeves."

"I don't think he'll make me dress that severely." Jarmila laughed, kissing Jack on the lips.

Jolly returned with Benny and Alice.

"I think that will help ease the pain a little." Jolly said, "At least to get you through the night."

"After tonight," said Benny, "I got plenty time off to heal."

Returning onstage, excitement took over again and the boys transformed into spinning vortexes gathering everyone into their center. They started the set with "Penny". The reaction was unfathomable, a caterwauling of positive emotions. "Penny" was more of a hit than the label thought it would be, and the boys of Lenehan smiled. They believed in their music. Their entire life force gathered in the notes they played. From there they played a couple of songs from their first album, then segued into "City Of Stockyards."

After that, Jack sat at his baby grand piano and became very quiet. The audience caught his vibe and became quiet also.

"We don't play cover songs during live shows. Not since our very early club days, when we didn't have enough of our own material to play." he began, "It's one of those hard and permanent Lenehan band rules. We don't owe anyone an explanation. We don't play cover tunes during live shows, no explanation needed. Recently, we got a new tour manager. His name is Jolly. His personality is far from jolly. That's how he got his nickname, as a joke about how a terror he is to staff and crew. He made this tour what it is, smooth, successful, professional. Although we give him an incredibly tough time, he looks past our insanity and continues to make this tour da greatest we've ever had. He asked me a favor tonight, and after all he has done for us, I couldn't say no. He asked us to play "Changes" by Blind Melon. It was the first song we ever played as a group, so it has special meaning to us. He's asked us to dedicate it to our special girl who I introduced you to earlier, Jarmila Malone. This song goes out in dedication from Jolly to Jarmila."

Lenehan then went into "Changes" and the crowd was no longer silent. The rumble from the crowd seemed to shake the very walls of The Vic Theater. When the song was ended, Jack came out into the center.

"Wait," he said, "I've got some champagne."

Jack went to the drum riser and poured a glass of champagne into a champagne flute. He took a sip and put it back on the drum riser. Benny came down from the drum riser. He joined the rest of the band in filling champagne flutes and joining Jack in the middle of the stage.

During the middle of the song, Jolly had taken Jarmila from the V.I.P. section to the side of the stage. The look on her face was complete confusion.

"Today was an epic day for our tour manager, Jolly," said Jack, as Jolly appeared onstage, "This was his first tour at this venue as tour manager. He'd been through this venue plenty of times on tour, but never as tour manager. The Vic Theater is his favorite venue. Let's give Jolly a big Chicago celebratory toast on his big night. But wait, let's get Jarmila out here too, she's as much a part of this as we are."

Jack went to the side of the stage to bring Jarmila, but she tried to pull back. He kept encouraging her, pulling her out to the middle of the stage. She finally went along. Jolly took out a small jewelry box and Jack placed the microphone near Jolly.

"Jarmila Agata Malone," Jolly started, opening the box, taking the engagement ring out and placing it on her ring finger, you are my everything. I am complete because of you. You are the strongest woman I know. Your love and patience are boundless. My love for you is endless. You are my heart and soul, my soul mate. Will you marry me?"

The noise from the crowd was so loud it seemed the roof would collapse. Lots of "Say yes" was interspersed with the cheering and clapping.

"Yes." said Jarmila, in tears, hugging and kissing Jolly.

Chandler handed them both champagne flutes and Lenehan toasted the newly engaged couple.

After Jolly and Jarmila left the stage, Lenehan played one more first album song, then played three second album songs. They ended with "The Only Cost", which become a crowd pleaser to end the show. The audience sang along.

After the show, in the dressing room, was another cake. This one was lemon cake with red icing with the words "Congratulations On Your Engagement Jolly and Jarmila". Nor Jolly or Jarmila expected a cake to celebrate their engagement. Jarmila hugged and kissed Jolly.

"Hey's where my hug and kiss?" asked Jack, "I'm da one came up with da idea."

Jarmila hugged and kissed Jack and Jolly gave him a hug.

"Thank you so much for everything." Jolly said to Jack, "Thank all of you for all you have done for me to be with the woman of my heart."

Everyone hugged Jolly and hugged and kissed Jarmila.

"I'm happy you have found your one." said Johnny, hugging her, "My little sister."

After having slices of engagement cake, the band went back onstage for three encores.

"Shit," said Jack as he walked up the stage stairs, "I'm having a sugar rush from all this cake. I could do an entire 'nother show."

"Good," said Chandler, "because we committed to play the tour after-party too."

Three encores later and the band was drained. Benny was favoring his wrist but claimed he'd be fine to play the after-party. Chandler and Jack helped get their second wind by snorting long lines of cocaine. Johnny lay on the far couch, his dogs near him on the floor. Jarmila sat with his head in her lap, massaging his temples. Sofia sat nearby with Alice. Following a brief rest, Lenehan went to say goodbye to their families and friends. Johnny sent his mom, his Aunt Freida, Sofia and his dogs, home in a limo. The rest of the families left in the transportation they arrived in. Chandler and Jack went to the other hospitality room to greet fans and pick out the evening's "entertainment". Jack selected three groupies and a fangirl. and Chandler couldn't decide between a transgender male or another man, so he invited both to the after-tour party upstairs.

The main floor was filled with crew and staff. Scot, Jarmila and Jolly were there too. Scot and Jolly's assistants had set everything up. They had brought the cake in and set it on one of the several tables. The cake, a large rectangular affair, had the words written in big letters, "THANKS!!!!!!!!". Half chocolate and half vanilla, the icing was also half chocolate and half vanilla.

As the band took the stage, Jolly walked up to the mic. He jokingly thought that if anyone on this tour developed diabetes from all this cake tonight, he wasn't going to take the blame.

"When I joined this tour four weeks ago," started Jolly, "I expected the worst. A lot of bad information was out there about a promising band going down the shithole because of major problems on their tour. I was hesitant to think I would do any good. I want to thank all of you here tonight who put in the hard work to help Lenehan become one of the most successful touring bands on the current circuit. One person can't make a tour successful; it takes a team. You are the best team I could have wished for. Even if I threatened to fire most of you at least a dozen times a week."

"A day!" shouted Everett

"Okay," continued Jolly, "I admit sometimes I threatened to fire people several times a day. I want you to know that it's my personality and not anything against you personally. Each and every one of you put 110% into this tour and I couldn't have asked for a better crew. And you're stuck with me. Because I signed on to the next Lenehan tour. I also plan on being on the European tour next spring. I'll consider myself a lucky man if Lenehan makes me their permanent tour manager, because I cannot think of a better band to be working for. Thank you all for sharing in my engagement proposal to my intended, Jarmila. It was a very special moment made more special by all of you being here for it. I want to especially thank Lenehan for breaking their "no cover songs during live shows" rule and dedicating and playing Blind Melon's "Change" to Jarmila from me. The song has special meaning for us. Now I'm going to turn you over to the band. Thank you!"

"We are a little crazy, aren't we, Jolly?" asked Jack, holding the mic to Jolly.

"You are certifiably insane." answered Jolly, "But it made the tour wildly interesting."

Jolly exited the stage and went to Jarmila, who was cutting slices of cake. There were tables of pop, liquor, mixers and various snacks and food. Jolly had arranged with the production company to hold off load out scheduled time with the promise they'd be out by 8:00am.

"I want to thank, first, my band," said Jack, "cause if it wasn't for them, none of us would be here. I want to especially thank my manager, Scottie, tour manager Jolly, and road manager Everett for running a smooth tour. You guys worked your asses off for us. A special thanks to Bella in wardrobe who probably wanted to punch me at least once a day. I know I drove her and her staff crazy with my indecisions. You made us look good on stage, and we can't thank you enough. Thank you to da staff and assistants who made sure we had what we needed, and wanted. Big special thanks to Les and his security team. We felt we could be ourselves and know you'd keep us safe. Even from ourselves at times."

Big laughter and shouts from the attendees.

"A big super special thanks to our crew." continued Jack, "What words can I say? You kept it running on few hours of sleep and lots of stress. A big thank you for putting this all together every gig and making sure we could go out there on stage and give our best performances ever. Gotta thank da caterers in every city. Want to thank all da venue staff and vendors and venue security wherever we played. You're not here to hear my thanks, but guaranteed someone will upload this whole speech to social media. It won't be as interesting as naked TikTok dancing! We'd like to show our appreciation to everyone here by giving you a small performance of cover tunes that we don't play live. But some of you might have heard these songs at sound check. Also, big thank you to Jolly for putting this after-party together. There's liquor, pop, snacks, food, and cake. Celebrate! You belong to a band with a *triple platinum album*!"

People went up to the tables and filled plates and glasses. Jolly went up to Jarmila, who was sitting in the V.I.P. section she had sat at during the show, and sat next to her. He brought her an amaretto sour alcoholic drink as she had requested. Lenehan started playing various cover tunes from different artists, ranging from Queen, to Dio, to Guns N' Roses. They threw in some Chicago blues and Benny did a solid rendition of a song by Lil Peep x Lil Tracy called "Your Favorite Dress". Everette walked up to where Jarmila and Jolly were sitting. He had a pop in his hand.

"Teetotaling tonight, Everett?" asked Jolly.

"Wish I could get drunk as fuck," said Everett, "but I still have to load out and deliver equipment."

"Where's it all going?" asked Jolly, not being informed of where the equipment was stored off tour.

"Thankfully nothing is rented. Everything except Johnny's Fender and Chandler's Lucille goes to our storage units or the band's rehearsal space." Everett answered. "By the time I get home, my daughters will be in school and my wife at work. I can sleep undisturbed for several hours."

"You're glad you're home, though, aren't you?" asked Jarmila.

"Absolutely. I love the road, but after a few months I'm ready for home." Everett answered, excusing himself to go talk to one of his crew.

"Walk with me, Jar." requested Jolly.

She stood with him and took his hand, and walked part way down the stairs that led to the downstairs area. They stopped half way and sat.

"I wanted to be alone with you away from all the chaos upstairs." Jolly said, kissing her.

"I feel like I'm in a dream." she said, kissing him.

"Do you like your ring?"

"I *love* it!"

"I know it's not exactly what you had described."

"But it's mine and so it's unique! It's so beautiful."

"I had it hand crafted for you, in New York City."

"I love it so much. It's so pretty! You totally freaked me out with the proposal. I had no idea you were going to do that. Thank you so much for dedicating "Change" to me. It meant a lot to me. You mean a lot to me. I am in Heaven right now. I feel like I'm floating!" she hugged and kissed him.

"I'm glad you said 'yes'. You have made my heart so happy. I am so blessed to be with my one and only." he hugged her tight and kissed her again, "Do you want to go home? *Our* home?"

"Really? I can call it *our home*?"

"Yes."

"On one condition."

"Anything."

"You make me one more of these amaretto sours, to go."

"Anything for you, my sugar."

Suddenly both Jolly and Jarmila looked up the stairs.

"Did you hear what I heard?" asked Jolly.

"I think so. I swear I heard a man say, "I'm proud of you, Bill". I bet it was Big Bob."

"Sure sounded like him." said Jolly, smiling.

Jolly stood up and went back up the stairs, returning with the drink Jarmila requested. Then he called a car service and they went to their home.

Sweet Home Chicago

Jolly and Jarmila's new life together wasn't the idyllic life Jolly had imagined it to be. Love can give you strange illusions. He hadn't lived with a woman in a bit, and that took adjusting to. He liked to keep the same hours for working, even if sometimes that was working in the yard or on the house; Jarmila was used to having an erratic lifestyle. Jolly took the time to teach her to cook. She resisted and he insisted. She retained a portion of the brat he had first met. He knew he shouldn't want her to suddenly change overnight as soon as they were engaged. But he was set in his ways, and she was a breezy changeling. Ironically, he did not want her to abandon her effervescent personality. He was attracted to her boundless joy and her musical laugh. He didn't want to remodel her. He only wanted compromise. Jarmila did not understand the give-and-take of relationships; she only understood to give the band whatever they wanted. Finally, out of Lenehan's tight grip on her, she became at times an arduous fledgling who pouted when she didn't get her way.

The love Jolly had for her vanquished the annoyance he felt at her irksome ways. He took into consideration the life she had before he was blessed to call her fiancee. Time, he thought, would smooth out the small bumps in their relationship. In the meantime, their days were filled with in-bed late morning talks and occasional sessions of morning making love. During the day, when he was done working on the next tour or the European tour, he'd take her to Shedd Aquarium, or Lincoln Park Zoo, or her favorite, Garfield Park Conservatory. He wanted her to get out and make new friends and explore the city that had so much to offer.

At night she would cuddle next to him and he would hold her in his arms.

"When do you think we should get married?" she'd ask Jolly.

Jolly didn't want to spoil the surprise he and the band had planned.

"Do you want a big wedding or a small wedding?" he asked.

"I don't want a big wedding. Just the band and their families and some of the crew and staff and their families, like Everett, Bella, your assistants. I guess you can invite Scot."

"He'd be my best man." laughed Jolly.

"Then I guess he's invited!" she laughed.

"We should get married in June. It's a marrying month! And your birthday month."

"I'd like that." she said, kissing him deeply on the lips and getting on top of him.

She made love to him like no other. It was Heaven for him every time.

"Are you happy with our sex life?" he asked, after she rolled off of him, lighting and handing him a joint.

"Yes!" she answered, "You make love to me and it's like I'm not one person, but one person with another person within my soul. Does that make sense?"

"Absolutely." He said, kissing her, gathering her into his arms and falling asleep with her.

April went by quickly, or so it seemed to Jarmila. She didn't see much of the Lenehan guys as they were writing lyrics and music for the third album, and spent most of their time in quiet solitude. They laid down some tracks in the studio, and she was right there to support them.

"Sit on my lap, pretty girl." Jack said, during a break, "Tell me about your life with Jolly. You never say much on da phone. Is everything okay, my special girl?"

"Everything is okay." she answered, "I'm getting used to a permanent home. Jolly has some rules I need to get used to, certain ways of doing things. But I'm happy. Very happy!"

"Does he treat you right?" Jack asked.

"He's very good to me. I love him."

"Good, cause if not, we'd all go over there and kick his ass." Jack said, as Jarmila kissed him on the lips.

"Your new music sounds good so far."

"Wait til we get it all together. This will be da best album we've recorded. I wrote a song about you. All about you." said Jack.

"I can't wait to hear it!"

"You will. Besides da band, you will be da first person to hear it. Not even da label will hear it before you!"

She kissed him on the lips again. She hopped off his lap and said she had to go home.

"I'll take you." offered Johnny.

"It's only two blocks away." she protested, "I can walk."

"Not at 2 in the morning." said Chandler, "At least let me walk you over there if you don't want to go in the car."

"I enjoy walking." she responded.

"I enjoy walking with you." said Chandler.

She agreed to walk with Chandler. Saying goodbye to Johnny, Jack and Benny, she headed out into the chilly Chicago April air. In a few minutes they were in front of her and Jolly's house.

"Nice house." Chandler said.

"You should see the inside. Come on inside." she responded.

"No, I wouldn't want to disturb y'all this late."

"Jolly won't mind. He's probably up looking at potential financials for Europe anyhow. It's been keeping him up late into the night,

She put the key in the lock and pushed open the door. She turned the light on in the hallway and Jolly came out of his office. He walked toward her and gave her a big hug and kiss.

"Hey, Chandler." Jolly said, shaking Chandler's hand, "Good to see you."

"Sorry for the intrusion. Jarmila insisted I see the inside of the house." Chandler sai

"No intrusion at all." assured Jolly, "How's the album coming along?"

"Well, we've played with a couple tracks, laying them down to hear the sound. I think we'll be done by the deadline." said Chandler.

"Let me make you something to drink. C'mon in the kitchen." said Jolly, and Jarmila and Chandler followed him.

Chandler and Jarmila sat at the kitchen table.

"What do you prefer? I have beer, both domestic and imported, high quality liquor. I have some excellent Irish Whiskey I just bought and haven't opened yet. It's a 20-year-old Middleton Very Rare Dair Ghaelach I've been wanting to open. Would you like that?" Jolly asked.

"Very much!" exclaimed Chandler.

Jolly poured the whiskey into two tumblers and added a few drops of water to each.

"That's how my grandfather used to do it." said Chandler.

"Brings out the flavor." said Jolly, "Jar, do you want an amaretto sour?"

She shook her head yes. After making her a drink, he asked if they'd all like to go in the living room where it was more comfortable. Chandler sat on an armchair and Jolly and Jarmila sat on the couch. They talked about music, touring, families, new series that were good, movies, and general subjects. Then Chandler said he needed to return to the studio.

"Late night, early mornings, that bitch has me on lock." he said, "It's like being married!"

Saturday, April 27th, 2019

Jolly was in the kitchen, cleaning up from dinner. He had made his mom's recipe for meatloaf. Jarmila said she had never had meatloaf taste so good. Jolly told her his mom was an excellent cook, but often they had a housemaid who did most of the cooking.

Jarmila took a shower. She returned to the kitchen, where Jolly was seated at the kitchen table scrolling through his phone and enjoying a glass of Hennessey XO. A thought crossed his mind that he would have to slow down on the expensive liquor and concentrate on a two-person household. However, Jarmila was not expensive. She ate little, no matter how he coaxed her. He took her shopping for clothes but she wasn't interested in very many. He remembered there was a particular shop in Los Angeles that had clothing more her style. He had planned to talk to her about a honeymoon in Los Angeles after they were married, and she could meet his family. He could take her shopping there.

While Jolly sat at the kitchen table, enjoying his drink, Jarmila spun around. She was wearing a short, Magic Purple Iridescent Sequin Backless Mini Dress by Lulus, white fishnets and white Louboutins.

"What do you think?" she asked Jolly.

"I think you are beautiful. I think you are the most beautiful woman in the world. Come over here."

She moved next to him and he asked her to bend over while he moved his chair behind her. Underneath her dress she was wearing a purple lace garter belt. The garters attached to the tops of the fishnet stockings. She wasn't wearing panties. He used his hands to spread her bottom cheeks out. Then he used one hand to play around with her vagina, in and out with two and three fingers.

"I'm never going to make it to this party if you keep doing that." said Jarmila, "I'll want to spend the rest of the evening in bed with you."

"That wouldn't be so bad, would it?" he asked.

"It would be very good. But I never miss a Lenehan birthday party. I love you so much, but I don't want to miss this party. I'll make it up to you when I get home."

"Promise?"

"Promise."

"Anything I want?"

"Within limits. I'm not having no threesome."

"Go put on panties. And have fun."

"You're ruining my style, Jolly."

"Unless you run around showing people that you're not wearing panties, not wearing panties is not a style."

She went upstairs to fulfill Jolly's panty request, and went back to the kitchen, bending over to show him she was wearing purple panties.

"Okay, go, have fun. Who's taking you to Chandler's?"

"Johnny is picking me up. But after that, we're using a limo. No drinking and driving have always been a band rule."

"That's an excellent rule. What are your plans tonight?"

"First Chandler's for rum punch and cake. Then the Smart Bar. Then the G-Man Tavern."

"I remember when that was called the Ginger Man Tavern."

"Then Jack knows this private bar in East Village and they'll let him in so they'll let us all in. Then home. I'm not sure what time. Don't wait up for me, okay? I'll be fine."

"You're not 15 years old, so I won't wait up for you. But please be careful."

"Thank you for letting me go out." she said, sitting on his lap, "A lot of men wouldn't let their fiancee go off partying with other men."

"These guys are like brothers to you," said Jolly, kissing her, "I trust them, and most certainly trust you."

She hopped off his lap, grabbed her black over the shoulder purse, and headed toward the front door. Jolly watched her perky little ass as the door closed, and he knew he'd have to take a cold shower.

All five friends gathered in Chandler's front room, Jarmila was in the kitchen making the rum punch. When done, she called for Johnny and Benny to carry in the punch bowl, ladle and glasses. They put everything by the cakes, on the coffee table. One cake was a three-layer round cake with the words "Happy 24th Birthday Chandler" written in blue icing on top. The frosting was chocolate, as was the cake. The filling was caramel. The other cake was also a three-layer round German chocolate cake, with the words "Happy 24th Birthday Benny" written across it in white icing.

Rum punch was served. Chandler gave his birthday speech and a toast was given by everyone else. Benny gave his birthday speech and another toast was given all around. Jarmila cut the cakes while Johnny poured more glasses of rum punch. They sat around talking about the previous tour, their childhoods, and crazy things that happened in their life. Chandler told a story about how he and Jack got into trouble with Jack's mom.

"We were like, 14 or something. Jack and I were smoking up a bong in his bedroom. We'd been doing it for most of the day. And dropping acid, popping pills Jack stole from his aunt. Haldol, Thorazine. His aunt, she on all kind of crazy pills." said Chandler.

"And she still a bitch!" exclaimed Jack.

"I like got all itchy, so I took off all my clothes. I mean, *everything*. I'm sitting on Jack's floor butt naked, pop a pill, smoke, pop another pill, drop some acid. I was so *wasted*. Jack he go and steal some gin from his grandpa's liquor cabinet. We sit there, drinking it up. Jack gets this idea we should turn the stereo up all the way, and open the windows. Mind you, it's winter and the temps are like in the 30's. Jack passes out on the floor. I'm still popping pills and smoking, and here comes Jack's mom, all mad because the music is too loud and she trying to take a nap. She sees Jack all passed out on the floor with pill bottles and weed and a bong all around him. I'm holding the gin bottle. She grabbed my hair, it was long even then. She grabs my hair and grabs a belt and starts beating me, *hard*. I'm like 'Damn!' so she beats me harder for cussing. Jack wakes up and he tries to get out of the room, and she lets go of me and grabs Jack's hair. He's got long hair, too. She starts beating him as hard as she was beating me and I jumped out the window, stark fucking naked, running down the alley. It's fucking 30 degrees and I'm naked running home. I think I got frostbite on my dick." Chandler said, as everyone was laughing, "When Jack's mom gets done thrashing Jack, she calls my mom. I get home and my dad takes me into my bedroom and gives me a beating! Didn't even give me a chance to put my clothes on. I think I had welts on my ass for weeks!"

Laughter all around. More stories were told of the days of starting out as a band, and how far they've come. Stories of nights with crazy groupies and fanatics and days of hangovers that felt like death sitting next to you. Stories of the feeling of being up on stage, thousands of people cheering you on, making you feel like king of the universe.

Jarmila felt left out. There were no stories of her doing crazy things with the band. They used to go to the museums and parks and Navy Pier. They used to go to the festivals and skate and bike parks. But no more. Now Lenehan's days were filled with writing, recording, interviews, videos, tour rehearsals and tours. There was no more room for Jarmila. They said it often enough of how much they loved her. Friends forever. Lenehan's backbone. She knew these sentiments were sincere through most of their friendship. But things had changed for the band; those words were just words for something to say. She was no longer an integral part of the band. They had succeeded where she knew they would succeed. They didn't need her anymore. She was obsolete.

After the cake and rum punch, Lenehan and Jarmila made their way to the Smart Bar. Already tipsy from the rum punch, the guys were ready to see how long they could celebrate Chandler and Benny's birthdays before passing out on the floor. It was easy to get into the Smart Bar. Practically everyone who worked there or music industry people who partied there knew Lenehan. Home town boys made good. Lots of free drinks and shots came their way. Jack convinced Jarmila to have a drink.

"Amaretto Sour?" he asked

"Yeah!" she answered.

But before she could finish her Amaretto Sour, Johnny walked up to her and gave her a big kiss on the cheek.

"You'll be at my party tomorrow? 5:00pm." asked Johnny.

"I will never miss your birthday party! But, are you leaving now? We still got the G-Man tavern to conquer, and this exclusive club Jack's taking us too."

"No. After the last time I stayed for a party, I got wrecked. I don't want to do that again.. I'm going home. You have fun. Don't let them talk you into drinking too much." Johnny hugged her and went to say goodbye to the rest of the band.

Jarmila watched Johnny, her brother Johnny, walk out the door and she knew she would miss him the most.

At the G-man Tavern, Lenehan were treated like rock stars. The band made sure to offer a round to anyone in the tavern. Free drinks and shots flowed their way also.

"What do you want to drink?" asked Benny to Jarmila, as he headed to the bar.

"Alice had a drink called a Fuzzy Navel at the tour party. Do they taste good?"

"Peach Schnapps and orange juice." answered Benny, "Alice likes them."

"I'll try that."

Jack had bought and entire bottle of Clase Azul and placed it on the table they were seated at. This would be the shot bottle. Jack poured five into shot glasses; one each.

"I can't drink tequila." Jarmila said.

"Who says?" asked Jack, "Your Pseudo Daddy"?"

"That wasn't nice, Jack." said Chandler.

"Do a shot for Chandler." Jack demanded, "It's his birthday. Get some Don Julio over here, do a shot of that for Benny's birthday. A couple of shots won't hurt you."

"You used to punish me for drinking." Jarmila said to Jack.

"Times change," said Jack, "You're a grown woman now, engaged to Methuselah."

"He's not that old." said Jarmila, taking the shot glass of Clase Azul from Jack.

Benny returned from the bar with a Fuzzy Navel for Jarmila and a bottle of Don Julio.

"See?" Jack said, "We're so connected we know what each other wants. I didn't have to tell Benny to get Don Julio. He just knew to bring a bottle over. Psychic, I'm telling ya."

The owner of the tavern brought over more shot glasses, tumblers, and a bottle of Laphroaig 30 Year Single Malt Scotch Whiskey.

"Happy birthday. Where's Johnny?" the owner asked.

"He doesn't really like to party hard." answered Jarmila

"If you need anything, just ask. And congratulations on your triple platinum status. I hear you're hogging the singles charts too." said the owner.

"We have arrived!" exclaimed Chandler, as the owner left the table.

Lenehan and Jarmila took shots together first of the Clase Azul, then the Don Julio. Jack poured the whiskey into the tumblers and handed one to Jarmila.

"Now drink it slow. It's sippin' whiskey." he told her.

After half of the liquor had been consumed, the band decided to continue the party at the private club in East Village. They thanked the owner, told him whoever wanted the rest of the liquor could have it, and bought one more round for the house. They then got in the limo and headed to East Village.

Jarmila, a bit more than tipsy, started thinking about her great-grandma Jarmila Bisnik. Back in her day, East Village was called East Ukrainian Village. Jarmila wished she could have lived in her great-grandma's time. Emotional ties seemed deeper.

They arrived at the private club. There was a huge line outside, but Jack walked up to the bouncer and Lenehan and Jarmila were immediately let in. The owner greeted them at the door, introduced them to the three attendants who would make sure they had whatever they wanted. He escorted them to their own private V.I.P. room. The birthday presents Jack had requested be put there were on a large table filled with food and high-quality alcohol and mixers. The attendants asked each band member what they wanted to drink, and if there wasn't something on the table they wanted, they would get it for them.

"I want a Fuzzy Navel!" exclaimed Jarmila.

The guys ordered various mixed drinks and shots of various alcohol. Benny decided snorting heroin would be better than shooting up. It was his birthday present to himself. Chandler and Jack snorted cocaine and dropped Xanax and Mollies. Blunts were being passed back and forth but Jarmila declined. Whenever they wanted something, all they had to do was push a button on the back wall, and the attendants would arrive.

"Do you know it's after midnight?" asked Jarmila.

"No, I didn't. Time has no meaning to me right now. Why? Does Methuselah think you'll lose your glass slippers after midnight if you're not home by then?" Jack jeered.

"Jolly is not old, so stop calling him that." Jarmila said, "It's after midnight which means it's now Johnny's birthday!"

"I'll drink a shot to that!" exclaimed Chandler.

"Jarmila, you need to drink a shot to that too!" exclaimed Jack.

She reluctantly agreed and Jack poured five shot glasses of Patron Silver. They saluted Johnny and did the shot in unison. Women started joining their party. Benny took on two brunettes and Jack invited three blondes to sit next to him. Chandler had gone to the restroom. On his way back he brought a tall blonde, blue-eyed male that could have easily been mistaken for Chandler's twin. Liquor, weed, and pills were passed around. Jack brought out more cocaine and mescaline.

"It's Chandler and Benny's birthdays," he announced to the guests, "make sure you give them a happy, happy birthday."

"Can we open the presents?" asked Jarmila.

The guys had almost forgot.

"Yes!" exclaimed Benny, "Let's open presents!"

Jarmila gave Chandler his present first. It was a Bulova brown leather brushed gold double wrap bracelet. He kissed her deeply on the lips, thanking her and immediately putting it on. Jack gave him a Mene 24K guitar pick. Chandler said he had no words but 'Thank you'. The gift was stunning. Benny gave him a necklace with a replica of Chandler's favorite guitar, Lucille. On the back was engraved "We have arrived, bitches!"

"Benny," Chandler said, hugging him, "I don't know what to say. Thank you."

"This is from Johnny." said Jarmila, handing Chandler a gift bag.

Chandler removed the tissue paper. Underneath was a Calleen Cordero Nisha Guitar Strap. It was something Chandler had mentioned that he would like to have, especially for the upcoming tour. It was just like kind-hearted Johnny to remember.

Next it was Benny's turn to receive gifts. Jarmila gave him the first one. It was a set of Promark 12-pair Japenese White Oak Drumsticks. He kissed Jarmila and gave her a big hug before thanking her. Chandler gave his present next. It was a TAMA Iron Cobra 200 Series Double Bass drum pedal.

"OMG, Chandler, these are the best!" exclaimed Benny, hugging Chandler, "Thank you so much!"

Jack gave his present next. It was a Cartier-Santos De Cartier Bracelet in gold. Jack thought Benny would really like the chain look. Benny hugged Jack and thanked him. He put it on immediately and showed it to their guests. Jarmila handed him the last present, from Johnny. It was a collection of vintage rock shirts. Led Zeppelin, Deep Purple, Queen, Motorhead, about two dozen different kinds. Benny loved vintage rock shirts. He had a whole closet full of vintage rock shirts. He couldn't wait to add to his collection. He texted Johnny and thanked him for the gift. He added that he couldn't have a better brother.

"Can I go home?" asked Jarmila to Jack, "I don't feel well."

"You're not used to all that alcohol. I'll walk you to da limo." Jack said.

"But how will you guys get home?" she asked

"Da limo will come back for us. Text me when you get home." Jack said.

Jack walked Jarmila down the stairs and out to the limo. The limo driver opened the door for her. Jack leaned in to kiss her.

"I'll see you at Johnny's." Jack said, and closed the door, watched the limo pull away, and went back inside to party.

Jolly had fallen asleep on the couch in the front room, while watching television. He realized it seemed he was waiting up for Jarmila. Self-consciously he probably was. He woke when he heard someone at the front door. It sounded as if someone was trying to break in, struggling with the door. He went to the front door and found Jarmila struggling with the key. He opened the door and she fell into his arms.

"Hiya, Jolly!" Jarmila slurred, "Whatcha doing?"

"Holding a drunk girl at 3 in the morning." Jolly responded.

"You love me?" she said.

"I do. Did you have fun?"

"I did! I had cake and rum punch and an Amaretto Sour, and a Fuzzy Navel, and food called pate that tasted kinda like raw liver, and I had some shots! I'm not sure what kind they were but I know it was some type of alcohol. I had a few of those. To honor the birthdays. Whatcha do while I was gone?"

"Worked and watched TV. Fell asleep." Jolly kissed her, lead her upstairs to their bedroom, "Let's get these clothes off you, drunk girl, and get you comfortable in bed."

"Oh, I love being comfortable in bed with you!" she exclaimed as Jolly helped her lay down on the bed., "Whoops! I made you a promise, and I don't go back on my promise."

After Jolly got her out of her clothes and into the covers, he sat next to her.

"What was that, my love?"

"That you could do anything you wanted to me when I got home." she slurred, then pulled the covers over her face, spreading her knees in the air, which exposed her lower half.

"What did you think I wanted to do to you?" asked Jolly

"You said you always wanted to put your tongue in my vagina! I made a promise to you that you could do anything you wanted to me, to make up for me going to the party instead of staying with you."

"I was joking, sugar," he said as he pulled the covers off her face and covered her body.

"You don't want your tongue in my vagina? You don't love me?"

"Of course, I love you. That has nothing to do with my tongue going anywhere on your body. Remember, we have to agree on sexual acts or we don't do them. You said you didn't want that particular sexual act."

"But I made a promise to you!" she cried, "I don't go back on my promises. You said you liked it."

"I do like it very much. But I want you to like it too, sugar. You're not in your full faculties to make any consenting decisions right now. I promise you, when you are completely sober, we'll revisit this conversation. Now, go to sleep. You have another party to go to in a few hours."

Jolly kissed her, took off his clothes, and crawled in bed next to her. He pulled her close and fell asleep with her in his arms.

At 8:00am Jolly was in the kitchen cooking a breakfast of pancakes and sausage links. He squeezed oranges for fresh orange juice, and put the glass of orange juice and a cup of coffee next to the breakfast plate. He started to sit down when he heard retching from the first-floor hallway bathroom. He left his breakfast and went the bathroom. Jarmila was vomiting in the toilet. It didn't faze Jolly; he'd been around rock musicians who suffered the effects of a night of too much hard partying. Holding back long hair was an expertise.

"Oh Jolly," whimpered Jarmila, "I am so sick."

"I know. Cake, pate and liquor can do you in for a day."

"I have to get ready for Johnny's party."

"It's not for hours, my love. You have plenty of time to get ready."

Jolly helped her stand and flushed the toilet. He ran the hot water in the sink and took a washcloth, running it under the warm water. Gently he wiped her face.

"I was going to the have some breakfast, I thought it would make me feel better." Jarmila said. "But the smell is off and I got sick. Something in that kitchen smells horrible."

"I don't know what it could be, darling." Jolly said, "I clean very well. I made pancakes and I know the sausages aren't off."

Jarmila went to get herself a cup of coffee.

"Ewww!" Jarmila exclaimed, "That coffee smells horrible!"

"It's the same coffee I always get, sugar. I'll dump it and make some tea."

He put the water on to boil and made her spearmint tea to settle her stomach. He would have given her a shot of alcohol, but he didn't think that would work for her. She'd probably get a second hangover from it.

"Jack texted me and said they'll pick you up in a limo at 4:45pm to take you to Johnny's. He also raged about why you didn't text him like you promised when you got home last night."

"I forgot. Your sexiness distracts me."

"Don't blame your inebriated state of forgetfulness on me." Jolly laughed, as she drank the tea, "Go back to bed for a few more hours."

"Can you wake me up at 2:30pm so I have time to get ready?"

"Absolutely." he said.

He walked her up the stairs and into their bedroom. He lifted the covers for her as she got in to the bed. He leaned down and kissed her.

"I will wake you at 2:30, baby." He said, and then left the room.

At 4:30pm, Lenehan showed up in a limo, and parked outside Jolly's. Jack and Chandler were standing outside the limo, smoking cigarettes. Jarmila walked down the outside stairs wearing a simple black dress with a sweetheart neckline, light tan pantyhose and black Louboutin Apostrophy Leather Pointed red-soled pumps.

"What da fuck, Jar." Jack said, "You going to a funeral?"

"I'm dressing in a decent manner for Johnny's momma. Do you want me to change?" asked Jarmila.

"No. Go to Johnny's party looking like you going to a funeral. I don't give a fuck."

"Why you gotta be so mean to me?" she asked Jack, as the limo driver opened the door.

She slid in next to Benny, and Jack and Chandler followed.

"I'm not mean to you," said Jack, "I'm being honest."

At Johnny's, they had cake Johnny's mom made from an old Polish recipe, and Jarmila's rum punch. Johnny's mom said she was going to her sister Frieda's for dinner.

"I'm going to miss you, Ma Dunne." said Jarmila, giving her a big hug.

"I only go for a few hours. I be back soon." said Johnny's mom, confused at Jarmila's statement.

Johnny's mom gathered her purse and walked out the front door. Jarmila cut the cake and Chandler poured rum punch. Johnny's mom had made a beautiful Polish Honey cake, with the words written across it "Happy 24th Birthday Moj Syn", which meant "my son" in Polish.

"This cake is almost too pretty to cut!" exclaimed Jarmila, "I'm going to save your momma and Aunt Frieda a couple slices, and some rum punch."

The guys and Jarmila gathered in the living room. It was one of those parlors found in old houses. Johnny had rehabbed it to the specifications it had been when it was first built, as well as he could. He researched house plans and blueprints and pictures. He wanted it to be as original as possible. A two-story greystone, built in 1890, it was one of those beautiful one-family homes built around the time when Humboldt Park was settled by wealthy Norwegians. He filled it with antique furniture, updating only the kitchen and bathrooms. When he moved his mom in, he told her to close her eyes before he opened the door. When he opened the door, she opened her eyes and praised God for blessing her with such a beautiful son and a beautiful house.

Cake and rum finished, presents opened, crazy stories of the rise of the life of a rock star, and everyone was ready to go to Johnny's favorite local bar. A blue-collar working man's bar, Johnny liked it because it was quiet. There were also people there who knew his dad, and he loved to hear stories of him. He was so young when his dad died, he didn't remember him. The stories the bar patrons told made him feel closer to a great man he never got to know. He also liked the bar because it was within walking distance of his house, and they served beer on tap in pints.

The boys and Jarmila sat at a table. Benny and Chandler went to get drinks, and brought them back to the table.

"I didn't know if you wanted a Fuzzy Navel or an Amaretto Sour, so I got you both" said Benny to Jarmila.

"We're turning you into a two-fisted drinker!" laughed Jack.

Chandler got up again and came back with five shot glasses.

"Patron Silver." he stated, and they all did a shot.

Johnny was perfectly happy with his pint of Guinness. Chandler had a glass of Midleton whiskey, Jack was sipping on Jameson whiskey. Benny had a Whiskey Sour. Jarmila was happy with both her drinks. She'd take a sip of the Fuzzy Navel, then a sip of the Amaretto Sour. Chandler got up again and brought back five more shots.

"What's that?" asked Jarmila.

"Jagermeister." answered Chandler, "taste kind of like black licorice."

They took the shots together.

"Blahhhh," said Jarmila, "that's strong. Benny, can you get me another Fuzzy Navel and Amaretto sour."

"Damn, Jarmila," said Johnny, "we're turning you into an alcoholic."

Chandler went back to the bar and ordered another Fuzzy Navel and another Amaretto Sour. He delivered those to Jarmila, then went to get five more shots. One was different, and he set it before Jarmila.

"What's this?" she asked.

"Kahlua." Chandler answered, "It's sweet. I think you'll like it better."

They slammed down the shots, and Jarmila quickly finished her cocktails. Benny went to the bar to get Johnny another pint of Guinness,

"I never thought I'd say this to you," said Jack, "but Jarmila, you better slow down on da alcohol. We've got two more bars to conquer."

The band decided they would head closer to their homes, and go to The Empty Bottle, before heading to the same private club in East Village they were at the night before. Then all hell broke loose.

Johnny was enjoying his second pint of Guinness when two women walked up to where he was sitting. One was a blonde and the other had brunette hair with streaks of blonde throughout it. The blonde leaned down and kissed Johnny on the lips.

"We heard it was your birthday. Happy Birthday." the blonde whispered in his ear.

"I'm Kyn and this is Faith." said the girl with the streaked hair, "Want to sit with us? We could make your birthday very special."

Before Johnny could say 'yes' or 'no', Jarmila grabbed the blonde by the hair and smashed one of the empty cocktail glasses over the woman's head. Then she kicked and punched the women with the streaked hair. They tried to fight back, but Jarmila was like a wild badger. She didn't want these women near her brother.

"He's my brother, stay the fuck away from him!" Jarmila screamed.

Glasses were being thrown and screaming and punching proceeded, with some hair pulling and kicking. Jack was the first to try to pull the women apart, but a guy spun him around and hit him in the jaw. Jack fought back. Chandler joined Jack's fight and was quickly attacked by two other men. Benny kicked one of the guys fighting Chandler and the guy slammed Benny's head into the bar. Johnny grabbed that guy and slammed him into a wall, throwing a punch.

Alice picked up Benny from the jail, paying his bail. Scot picked up Chandler, Jack and Johnny. Johnny was the only one of the band that did not have to pay bail. Because he had no prior criminal record, he was released on his own recognizance. Last picked up was Jarmila. Because she also had no prior criminal record, she too was released on her own recognizance. When Jolly entered the police station, disappointment and anger showed on his face. Jarmila knew she was in trouble.

"I'm sorry." she said, while Jolly was driving home.

"I don't want to talk now. I am very angry and I need to concentrate on driving." Jolly responded.

Parking in his garage, Jolly exited the car but Jarmila sat there.

"Get the fuck out of the car and get in the house." Jolly ordered.

She held her over the shoulder purse with both hands, gripping it tightly in fear. Once again, Jolly ordered her out of the car and into the house. She slowly exited the car and slowly followed Jolly into the house. She sat at the kitchen table, still gripping her purse.

"Is there something in your purse you're trying to hide?" asked Jolly, "You're holding it like you don't want someone to see something. Did the police go through your purse?"

"No. They handcuffed me in front and handed my purse back to me without even opening it."

"What are you hiding, Jarmila?" Jolly said, sitting next to her, grabbing her purse, dumping the contents.

In it were the usual contents, make-up, perfume, etc. And a large baggie of cocaine. He grabbed it and shoved it near her face.

"This." said Jolly.

"It's Jack's. You can ask him! He was wearing really tight jeans and he couldn't get it in his pockets."

"I'm going to ask Jack if that is true. As soon as he gets out of the hospital."

"He's in the hospital?" cried Jarmila.

"He and Chandler and Benny. Scot took them after their bail was posted. Alice was concerned about Benny, so Scot promised he'd take him to the ER with Chandler and Jack. Jack and Chandler are beaten up. Benny has a concussion from his head being slammed into the bar. Johnny is okay, he didn't get any injuries because the cops arrived before he got more than one punch in. By the way, he is *not happy* with you."

"I'm sorry. Can I go see Jack, Chandler and Benny?"

"No. You can stay here until I calm down. You can stay in this house until I decide what I should do with you."

"You're breaking up with me?"

"No." Jolly said, lifting up her chin, "You've got a black eye and a cut lip. Do you want to go to the hospital?"

"No. I'm okay. Why can't I see the guys?"

"They are getting medical help. They don't need you worrying them. Scot called and said Jack told you to stop drinking. When alcoholic Jack Connelly tells a person to stop drinking, doomsday is approaching. You need to stop this behavior, Jar. I know you're young, but you're a grown woman, an *engaged* young woman. Behavior like this is unacceptable. Why would you strike a woman on the head with a cocktail glass?"

"She was trying to get Johnny to sit with her and her friend."

"He's a good-looking grown man. Women are going to try and hook up with him."

"He wants a Polish or Irish Catholic virgin. He doesn't want to mess up and have sex again. He doesn't want to ruin himself. He wants to stay pure before he gets married."

"Sugar, that train done left the station. He lost his virginity on tour."

"I know."

"Then why attempt to be his purity guard? Did he ask you?"

"No. But he's my brother, I was trying to protect him."

"You had too much to drink and you were acting the fool."

Jolly's phone rang. It was Scot telling him the doctors patched up Jack and Chandler and they were going home, but Benny was staying the night for observation of a concussion. Johnny them called and asked if he could come by and talk to Jarmila in person. Or if that wasn't convenient, he could send a car for her. He had drunk a couple beers and did not drive when he had drunk alcohol. Jolly said he could come by the house and he would send a car for him. Johnny thanked him and hung up.

"Johnny's coming by." said Jolly, "Go to the front room."

"I want to go to bed. I'm tired. And sore." Jarmila answered.

"Go to the front room."

"You think you can order me around because we're engaged."

"Absolutely not! I'm "ordering" you around because you're acting like a child. A child who always wants her way. Like when I first met you." he said, sitting in an arm chair in the living room.

She sat on the couch, as far as she could sit from Jolly.

"I would never break up with you because of a bar fight." Jolly said, "I've been in bar fights. That doesn't mean your behavior is acceptable."

"They were the ones kept bringing me drinks!"

"You could have said 'no'. Or stop requesting them. Johnny said you kept requesting drinks."

"Johnny is such a righteous mama's boy." Jarmila sneered.

"He went to jail for you."

"He got released on his own recognizance, like I did."

"You still have to go to court. You still assaulted two women. You could face jail time."

"I don't want to go to jail!" she started crying.

"Scot's got the lawyers working on it. Jack and Chandler have prior assault arrests, but they were never charged. But the arrests are on their records. A judge might consider that."

"Why are you being so mean to me!"

"I'm not being mean to you," said Jolly, as he stood up to answer the doorbell, "I'm being realistic."

Johnny walked into the front room and sat on the couch. Jolly stood in the doorway.

"Do you want me to stay?" he asked.

"No. I want to talk to my sister in private." answered Johnny.

Jolly went down the hall to his office.

"Why? Jarmila, I only want to know why?" asked Johnny.

"Those bar rats were trying to get you to go with them!"

"Jarmila, I am 24 years old. I'm not a virgin anymore. I still want to marry one, but so what if some pretty girl wants to talk to me? I've got notoriety because the band is doing good. I don't need you to protect me. I'm a grown man. If I want to go with a woman, that's my right. I'm not blaming you for the fight I got into. None of the band is. We know we could have walked away. But, Jarmila, none of this would have happened if you hadn't started that fight."

"She asked you to sit with her! You were going to break our tradition of only the five of us celebrating birthdays!" she cried.

"You didn't give me the chance to say 'no' before you smashed a cocktail glass into her head."

"You're really mad at me."

"You ruined my birthday! My ma is furious with me because I came home with a torn shirt. I had to tell her the whole incident. You know how my ma is. Jarmila, I love. You're my sister. My heart hurts."

"I'm sorry. I wish I could reverse everything and give you a good birthday."

"All I want you to do is let me do what I want to do. Stop hovering over me. You don't hover over the rest of the guys when they hook up."

"You're my brother. They're my best friends."

"It doesn't matter. I'm grown, just like they are."

Johnny walked out of the front room and went out the front door. Jarmila sat crying. Jolly, hearing her from his office, joined her in the front room. He held her tight.

"It'll be okay." he told Jarmila, "Like before, once he calms down your relationship with him will go back to usual."

"What if we all go to jail because of what I did?" she cried.

"Don't worry. The band has really good lawyers. One of them agreed he would handle your case too. Scot says the lawyers are working on seeing if all charges can be dropped."

"Do you think that will happen?"

"It's happened before with Lenehan. Jar, you got to grow up, sugar. The boys aren't boys anymore. They're young men who do what young men do. You can't stand in their way and not expect trouble."

"Jack's going to punish me."

"Jack broke a rib. He can't do anything strenuous. I wouldn't let him anyway. We're an engaged couple. Jack has no say in any issues we have in our life. None of the band does anymore."

"Is Jack going to be all right? What about Chandler? And Benny?"

"Jack will be fine. He's been writing lyrics and music and laying tracks down in the studio. That's not physically strenuous. He'll be healed by the time the next tour starts. Chandler has some cuts and bruises and two black eyes. Benny should be okay in a day or two. He's going to have to rest when he gets home. No drumming for a couple weeks. Concussions can lead to serious issues."

"I fucked it up for the band if Benny can't drum!" Jarmila cried.

"You didn't fuck it up, sugar. Right now, they are mostly writing. Jack and Chandler are laying down some tracks just to see what works. Benny's not doing any drumming for studio segments yet. They're not rehearsing for tour until June. You know these boys expend a lot of energy on tour. They like a little time off. But you owe them an apology. C'mon, let's go to bed."

"You're not going to punish me?"

"Oh, I'm going to punish you. You are no longer allowed to go out partying with the band. You can still have your traditional birthday parties, but *you* will come straight home afterward."

"The last birthday party we celebrate this year is mine! The guys said they are taking me out after rehearsal!"

"You're not going out after rehearsal."

"You're going to ruin my birthday!" Jarmila shouted.

"You ruined Johnny's!" Jolly shouted back.

Jarmila ran up to the bigger guest room, slammed the door and locked it.

Jolly woke at 3:00am to the sounds of vomiting coming from the upstairs hallway bathroom. Jarmila had refused to join him in their bed, so he slept alone. He went to the hallway bathroom and found her kneeling over the toilet, violently vomiting. He held her hair back. When she was finished, he sat her on the edge of the tub and flushed the toilet. He got a washcloth and put it under warm water, and then wiped her face. He sat next to her.

"Do you feel any better, or do you want to stay here just in case?" he asked her.

"I feel better. All I ate yesterday was cake. I don't think it sat well with the liquor."

"I don't think the liquor sat well with the liquor." Jolly joked.

"You know that tea you made me? The spearmint tea? Can I have a cup of that?" she asked.

"Yes. You go to bed and I'll bring it to you. To which ever bed you're going to.'

"Ours. But first I'm going to brush my teeth." she said, laying her head on his shoulder, "What is that smell? Is that a new cologne? It's making me queasy."

"It's the same body wash I always use." he answered, "I think the liquor is affecting your sense of smell, because you had the same complaint about the coffee."

"Probably." Jarmila said, standing up and leaving the bathroom, she went to their bedroom.

Jolly went downstairs to the kitchen and made Jarmila spearmint tea. He brought it up to her. She had propped herself up on pillows.

"I'm sorry I'm so much trouble." she said, taking the tea cup from Jolly, "I don't know why you want to be with me."

"Because I love you," he said, getting into bed, "you're my soulmate. Relationships aren't always sunshine and unicorns. Everyone has issues to work through. Tonight was not all your fault. The boys should know better than to ply you with shots of alcohol. Their bodies are used to it; yours is not. However, seriously Jar, you need to grow up. We're going to be a married couple."

"We should start planning our wedding. Or should we wait? Should we pick a date already? Is it too soon to do that?"

"Have you decided on a big wedding or a small wedding, or something in between?" asked Jolly.

"I don't want a big wedding. Just close friends and family."

"Then we have time to plan. Unless you want to catch the next flight to Las Vegas and get married right away!"

"I have thought of that. But I don't want to leave anyone special in my life out of something this important. Besides, I think I'd throw up all through the plane ride if we went to Las Vegas now." she laughed.

"I would definitely invite my brother and sister and their spouses and kids."

"We should make a list."

"Most definitely."

"Will you hold me until I fall asleep?" she asked, putting the tea cup on the nightstand.

"Absolutely." Jolly said, taking her into his arms and laying her head on his chest. This is Heaven, he thought. Despite the craziness, this is Heaven.

For Jarmila

All charges from the bar fight had been dropped, Money exchanged hands and the bar owner banned Lenehan and Jarmila from his bar. This upset Johnny, as it was the place where he heard stories of his father. It was the only way he really got to know his father. Johnny's mom was a good friend of the bar owner. They were on the same boat that arrived to America. They were from neighboring villages in Poland. She took Johnny with her to the bar to talk to the owner. She did most of the talking, in Polish. Johnny apologized in Polish for his and his companions' behavior. He promised those friends would never come to the bar again. He asked permission if he could continue to come to the bar. There were a lot of people there who knew his father, and it was the only connection he had to his dead father. The bar owner agreed to let Johnny back in. But no wild and crazy friends. Johnny thanked him profusely.

Life for Lenehan consisted of writing music and lyrics, practice new tunes and laying down tracks to see how the music sounded. Jack had written a song for Jarmila, just the lyrics. Chandler and Johnny worked on the music together. Their first tour rehearsal would be June 1, Jarmila's birthday. The start of their next tour would be August 22, two nights at the Aragon Ballroom. This would be the start of doing bigger venues with new equipment. For Lenehan, their childhood dreams of becoming rock stars had come true. The tour would be a short one, ending in December. From December until March, they would work continuously on their third album, with a release before their European tour which would begin at the end of April.

Jarmila didn't see them as often as she liked. She was so used to seeing them all the time, she felt like she was on a detox from them. When they were in the studio she was there. Occasionally they would go to dinner together, but the conversation was all about record sales, ticket sales, upcoming tours, video shoots, interviews. For once, she felt left out, and said little. They would ask her how life with Jolly was, and she'd say it was going well. She was having a fabulous life with Jolly. She loved him with her whole heart and he loved her. But there was an emptiness inside her. She felt the band fading away from her. Her best friends didn't need her anymore. They achieved their dreams and goals and she was no longer in the picture. She started noticing the distancing during the middle of the last tour, before Jolly joined. Sometimes she thought being with Jolly would take away the emptiness she felt about the band. Jolly filled her heart and her life. But he couldn't fill the longing she had for the deep friendships with the band, which was now all but disappeared. She thought perhaps she sacrificed her best friends for a soulmate. No one was forcing her to make a decision between them. The decision was happening on its own. She felt her best friendships with Lenehan was dissolving into nothing.

One of those gorgeous Chicago summer evenings, she sat on the back deck at her and Jolly's house, watching the sunset and drinking a beer. It was the second week of May, when temps in Chicago can be beautiful. They had a supper of grilled hamburgers and slaw Jolly had made. He grilled asparagus, eggplant and corn-on-the cob. Jarmila did not like the eggplant. But she was getting less picky and trying new foods. And new sexual positions. They talked about Jolly's upcoming trips to New York and Europe and LA, that were happening in June and July. Arrangements would be made for her to stay at Johnny's when he was gone to Europe. He assured her again that when the European tour started, she'd be right there.

Jolly opened a bag of marijuana and rolled a joint. Taking a long toke, he offered it to Jarmila.

"Yuk!" cried Jarmila, "That smells like dog shit!"

Jolly opened the bag and took a whiff. Smelled like homegrown marijuana to him. Maybe she was coming down with a cold. Or allergies, and it was affecting her sense of smell. She ran to the downstairs bathroom and threw up. Jolly showed up at the bathroom door.

"I'm okay." she said, "Maybe I'm coming down with a stomach bug."

Jolly helped her to their bedroom. He helped her take off her clothes and lifted the covers for her.

"I'll clean up the grill and join you." Jolly said.

"No hurry. I feel really tired. I'm going to sleep."

Jolly kissed her good night. He cleaned up the grill and kitchen, did some work, watched the news, and joined her in bed. He was worried she was ill. People come down with viruses. She probably caught something. If it continued for more than a day or two, he'd take her in to a doctor.

The vomiting continued throughout the next week. Mostly anything she ate, she vomited. She started losing weight, which wasn't good for a skinny girl like her. Certain scents bothered her, and she would get queasy and vomit. Jolly was getting extremely worried for her. He called his sister.

"Nice to hear from you." his sister said.

"I'm sorry I haven't been a very good brother and haven't been in touch as much. How is everyone?" he apologized.

"Everyone is good. But you need to call our brother. He's been calling you and you don't return his calls. It's okay. We know you were on tour. And now a fiancee! I am so happy for you! I'm hoping this one works out."

"It's true love this time. I finally found my soulmate. We're getting married on June 2."

"I got your details and we're all flying in, including our brother and his family."

"It makes me happy to know you all will be there."

"Something is bothering you, big bro. What is it?"

"I knew you used to be an RN. So instead of internet surfing, I thought I'd go straight to an expert."

"What's going on. You know my answer is, 'Go see a doctor'."

"It's just some random questions." Jolly said. "It's not me, it's Jarmila."

"Okay, go on."

"She's vomiting almost everything she eats. She's losing weight and she's skinny as it is. Scents that never bothered her before, bother her now. They make her queasy, and vomit."

"When was her last period?"

"I don't know. She's private about that."

"Listen, you need to take her to a gynecologist."

"You think she's pregnant?" Jolly asked, apprehension in his voice.

"She could be. But she could also have cancer, or a tumor, or an std. You need to get her to a gynecologist. Were you not using protection?"

"No."

"Bill!!!!!!!"

"We talked about it the first time how reckless we were. I'm in love, she's my soulmate, we never talked about it again."

"I am completely shocked that my big brother, "Mr. Responsible", would do something irresponsible like that."

"I'm shocked at myself."

"Bill, get her to a doctor. Promise me."

"I promise."

"I have to go now and pick up the kids. Call me if you need anything. Love you, goodbye. And call our brother!"

"I will. I love you. Goodbye."

He sat in his office with the phone still in his hand. What if Jarmila did have cancer, or an std, or worse, what if she was pregnant? He didn't want children. She knew that from the very beginning, when they first started talking about things. But if she was pregnant, he couldn't blame only her. It took two people to get a person pregnant.

He did some work, took a shower, blow-dried his hair, put on some black sleep pants and a plain white tee shirt. He laid on his back next to her, staring at the ceiling. Thoughts fogged his head, keeping him from sleep. What if she had cancer? She was too young to die. But there were tons of cancer treatments available. What if it was a tumor? That would require surgery and chemo, so much for her to get through. What if it was an std? Jack never used protection on Jarmila, and Chandler didn't use protection the one time he used anal sex on her as "punishment". A thousand fearful things ran through his mind. The most fearful thought was that she was pregnant. Children were a dealbreaker. Parents should be in a kid's life, and he was gone on the road too much to raise a kid. He's seen people take their kids on the road, but still he felt that you couldn't raise a kid if you didn't give it enough attention. The road was your kid, taking all your attention. How would he get her to a doctor? She was terrified of doctors. He closed his eyes, but sleep did not arrive.

In the morning, Jolly heard retching sounds coming from the upstairs hallway. He got out of bed and went that way. Jarmila was already leaning against the tub.

"It's all green and yellow liquid. Do you think I'm still throwing up liquor?"

"No, Jar." Jolly said, flushing the toilet, "It's bile. Because your stomach is empty. Jar, we need to talk about some serious issues. Are you okay to go downstairs? We could sit in the kitchen and I'll make you spearmint tea."

They went downstairs to the kitchen. Jolly made her a cup of spearmint tea, and made an instant coffee for himself. He sat down next to her and held her hand.

"Jar, I love you. You've been vomiting for over two weeks now. It's no longer a hangover." Jolly said.

"What do you think is wrong?" she asked, concern in her voice.

"I called my sister for advice. She advised I take you to a doctor. I agree. I can't let you go on like this. I don't want to lose you. You're my heart. If yours stopped beating, so would mine. I know you are terrified of doctors, but let me make an appointment to have you examined. I'll stay with you the whole time. Please, Jar, I don't ask much of you. Please do this for me. For us."

"Okay." she said, crying, "Is it going to hurt?"

"I won't lie to you. Some tests probably will hurt a little. But I'll be there with you all the time."

Jolly had a friend in high school when he was growing up in Malibu. She had gone a different path than he had, deciding on becoming an OB/GYN. She chose Chicago because she liked their medical programs. Odette, as he had known her in high school, was now Dr. Odette Guillebeaux, and had an office at one of the best hospitals in Chicago. He had decided to call her cell phone. They kept in touch all these years, even when she was in Chicago and he still in SoCal.

"Bill!'" she exclaimed, "How are you?"

"I'm ok. How are you? Am I interrupting you?" he inquired.

"No, not at all. I'm in my office looking through files."

"I have a favor to ask. It's a private matter."

"Anything you need. Tell me what is going on."

"My fiancee, she's really sick. She can't seem to hold any food down. She's dizzy, a lot, and certain scents make her queasy, and that's never happened before. I'm afraid it's something serious. I talked to my sister in California, she used to be an RN. She said I should get Jarmila to a doctor right away. Jar is fearful of doctors. I thought you'd be the best choice for her, to make her feel less fearful."

"Let me pull up my schedule." she said, "How about 4:00pm on May 24th? It's my last appointment of the day and I'd have time to explain results with you and if she needed further testing. Would that work out for you?"

"Yes, I'll put it on my schedule. Thank you so much Odette. I owe you a bunch."

"You don't owe me anything. What are friends for?"

One the evening of May 23rd, Jarmila walked around the house restless. She tried to watch TV. She tried reading a book. But she could not settle herself. Jolly was in his office working, and she'd stop by several times to say hello. She went to the kitchen and made coffee, putting one for herself on the kitchen table and taking one for Jolly to his office. She went to the back deck with her coffee and sat and cried. Jolly joined her.

"I know you're worried, Jar. Women go to an OB/GYN all the time. Usually once a year for a check- up. It's just a check-up. I'll be with you the whole time. I've known Dr. Odette since high school. She's a very nice person. She'll be gentle and explain things so you won't be afraid. I'll never let anyone hurt your, Jar. But I have to be honest with you. Something is not right with your health, and we've got to find out what it is so we can get you healthy again."

"I'm going to bed."

"It's only 8:00pm, sugar."

"Will you join me? I need you. I really need you."

Jolly washed up the coffee cups and coffee maker and headed to bed to be with Jarmila. She wasn't crying anymore. He held her tightly.

"Jolly?" she asked

"Yes, my love."

"Can we have anal sex now?"

"If you want it."

"Do you want it?"

"I want it only if you do. Anal sex is not a requirement of love."

"I just want to know what it feels like if someone who loves you does it. You said it's different if someone loves and cares for you. You love and care for me. I want to see if it is different from the brutal way Jack did it to me."

"It will be different than the brutal way Jack and Chandler did it to you. It doesn't mean you would like it."

"I just want to get everything out of the way before I go to the doctor tomorrow. I'm scared. What if I'm dying? I want to see how the things the band did to me really are different when it's done in love. I had a fantasy that you found out I didn't have panties on and turned me over your knee and spanked my bare butt. And…I liked it. I think I must be crazy for thinking those things. Normal people don't think those things."

"Oh, sugar, trust me, *normal* people not only think those things, they *do* those things."

"It's a crazy time for me to be talking about this. I feel I'll sleep better if I get one thing I'm curious about out of the way. But would it fuck up my tests tomorrow?"

"I don't know if there's going to be tests tomorrow. She might just diagnose you with some food allergy. Something you're intolerant of. Maybe you're withdrawing from Flamin' Hot Cheetos and Dum Dums."

"You're so not funny."

"But you're smiling." Jolly laughed.

"Anal. It maybe my one and only chance. Why are you still in your street clothes?"

"I haven't taken a shower yet. I wanted to make sure you are okay. I'll take a shower, and while I'm in there, you decide if anal sex is genuinely what you want."

Jolly took a shower, dried himself off, blow-dried his hair. He sat on the edge of the bed, brushing his hair.

"I love it when you're completely naked."

"Same here. But I do love that pink little number you have on tonight."

Jarmila had on a pink camisole and pink lace panties.

"I bought them when we went shopping. I'm trying to buy new things that are only for you to see. I'm glad we're not talking about tomorrow."

"Tomorrow will be quick and over with and we'll get you healthy again. Now, anal, yes or no?"

"Yes."

"Turn on your stomach."

"I don't have to do it on all fours?"

"I think you'll be more comfortable on your stomach."

She rolled onto her stomach. He pulled her panties down. The he took the lube he had brought from the bathroom and put it around and in her anus. He put the lube back on the nightstand and got on top of her back. He kissed her neck and kissed her back.

"Tell me when you are ready, Jar. I'll go slow, and if it hurts, I'll immediately stop."

"Okay, I'm ready." she whispered.

He rubbed his penis around her anus, slowly going in. She made a gasping sound. He stopped.

"I'll stop, baby." he said.

"No, please don't stop. It pinches when it goes in. Please keep going."

Slowly he continued until he was in a constant rhythm. Jarmila moaned and gasped a lot, and at one time cried out. Jolly stopped and apologized.

"No, keep going. I like it. I like it a lot"

Jolly continued until he came. He lay on her for a few minutes, catching his breath.

"Did you like it?" asked Jolly.

"Jolly, we have got to do that again!" she exclaimed, "You were right, it's better when you're doing it with someone who loves you. I love you."

"I love you, Miss Malone. I love how you give me your whole self. I love how you trust me."

"I'm tired. I'm going to sleep, is that okay?"

"I'll sleep right next to you, in my arms." Jolly said, as they both fell asleep.

When the morning of May 24th arrived, Jarmila was a crying mess. Jolly made her tea and dry toast, to get her to eat something. She decided to take a shower, telling Jolly the hot water may calm her down. The ride to the doctor was silent. Jolly took Jarmila in the Wraith, to try and cheer her up.

The hospital complex was large, with offices on the first floor. Jolly held her hand as they looked for Dr. Guillebeaux's office number. Jarmila held his hand tightly as they walked down the corridor to the office. Dr. Guillebeaux was seated at the reception desk. She stood up and went to Jolly to give him a big hug, and shook Jarmila's hand.

"I sent everyone home early, except my lab assistant. From our phone conversation, I sensed this is a very private issue." she told Jolly.

"Thank you." he answered.

She led the couple into an examination room. She instructed Jarmila to sit on the exam table. Jolly held her hand.

"I'm first going to run some basic tests, blood pressure, oxygen level, temperature. If you ever feel uncomfortable, tell me." Dr. Guillebeaux explained to Jarmila.

"Jar," said Jolly, "I'm going to let go of your hand, only so she can run these tests. Then I'll hold it again, okay?"

Jarmila nodded yes. The doctor gave her the tests.

"Your blood pressure is a little low. Is it normally like that?" the doctor asked.

Jarmila shrugged her shoulders.

"She doesn't go to doctors. She's frightened of them." said Jolly.

Jolly took Jarmila's hand again. The doctor explained she was going to send Jarmila down the hallway to the lab. She ordered blood tests and a finger stick to check blood sugar levels. She also needed a urine sample, and asked that Jarmila empty her bladder. Jarmila started to sob. Jolly hugged her.

"It's going to be all right, Jar. I'll be with you the whole time." assured Jolly.

Jolly held her hand the way to the lab. She sat in a chair while the lab assistant took a finger stick. Jarmila cried out. Jolly squeezed her other hand. Then she had a blood test done and cried out again. Tears flowed down her cheeks. Jolly took Kleenex from the lab assistant.

"First time?" asked the lab assistant.

"Yes." answered Jolly.

"It's okay, honey. I need to weigh you, then I only need one more thing from you and we're done here." said the assistant.

She gave Jarmila a plastic jar and told her to urinate in it, directing her to the restroom. Then empty her bladder as best she could, and bring the cup back to the lab. Jolly went with her to the restroom. They then returned to the lab. The lab assistant told her she could return to the exam room and the doctor would be back with them shortly.

They returned to the exam room and Jarmila returned to the table. She sat there crying. Jolly held her hand and tried to calm her down.

"What if it's cancer and I'm going to die like your momma? Why did they take all those tests?" she asked Jolly.

"Sugar, those are standard tests they give to patients." he answered.

"There's something wrong! I know it!" she cried.

Jolly hugged her again. The doctor re-entered the room.

"I have cancer, don't I?" Jarmila cried.

"No. You're pregnant. Your blood sugar is low also. Some of the tests won't be back for a few days, but I'll call you when I get the results. You are very underweight. Your weight is 90 pounds. For your height you should weigh more."

The look on both Jolly and Jarmila's face showed how shocked they were at the news of the pregnancy. It didn't seem they heard anything else the doctor was telling them.

"I would like to do a pelvic exam and a transvaginal exam if I have your permission. I want to make sure everything is ok so far. I am going to prescribe you some prenatal vitamins, plus extra iron if your blood tests show low iron."

"What is a transvaginal exam?" asked Jolly.

"It's like an ultrasound but done inside instead of on the outside. I think at this stage of the pregnancy, I would be able to see more of what is going on and make an in depth diagnose."

Jarmila started crying. Jolly kept telling her it was okay. But inside he was very angry. He was adamant he didn't want children. He was mad at himself. He was mad at Jarmila. They should have been careful. He held his anger in. He loved Jarmila. She needed him now more than ever.

"How far along do you think she is?" asked Jolly.

"About 8 weeks." answered the doctor.

"What does a fetus look like at 8 weeks?" asked Jolly.

The doctor got out a small model of a fetus at 8 weeks. It had a big head but arms and legs and feet and hands.

"Why is the head so big and why are the hands and feet webbed?" sobbed Jarmila, "Is that what my baby is going to look like when it's born? Is something wrong with my baby?"

"No, when your baby is born, he or she will look like a regular baby. This is just what they look like at this stage of development." responded the doctor, taking a sheet out of a drawer, "Take off everything below your waist and lay on your back. I'll return shortly."

Jarmila sat there and cried. She sobbed, her whole body shaking.

"Jarmila, it's going to be okay. I'm still here holding your hand. If it hurts, I'll tell her to stop."

Jolly helped Jarmila out of her jeans and panties, and helped her get on the table again. He put the sheet over her lower half. The doctor returned with a medical machine.

"Now first I'm going to do a pelvic exam. Have you ever had a pelvic exam?" the doctor asked Jarmila.

Jarmila shook her head no.

"Okay, don't be scared. I'll be very gentle. Scoot down a little and put your feet in the stirrups." said the doctor, "This might be a little bit cold, and you'll feel some pressure."

Jarmila did as the doctor asked. Jolly stood by her, and she was squeezing his hand. When the doctor put the speculum in, Jarmila cried out.

"It's okay, sugar," assured Jolly, "it will be over soon."

When that examination was over, the doctor explained why she was going to do the next test. First, she explained there's a hormone in pregnant women, called hCG. Jarmila's was a little high. This could mean twins. But not always. She felt more assured doing a transvaginal ultrasound because at this early in the pregnancy, it was her opinion it could show more. She showed Jolly and Jarmila the wand that would go in Jarmila's vagina, and how it would transmit images onto the computer screen.

Jarmila continued to cry. The doctor put the transvaginal wand in and in a few minutes images could be seen on the screen. Two small separate amniotic sacs could be seen on the screen. Heartbeats could be heard.

"Twins." announced the doctor, "Heartbeats sound good. By my measurements they are definitely 8 weeks gestation. The rest of the tests should be back in two or three days. I'll call you with the results."

"But what is wrong? Why the tests if nothing is wrong? You said the heartbeats sound good." asked Jarmila, through sobs.

"The tests are to check for diabetes, hypoglycemia, Rh factors, iron levels. We want a healthy pregnancy! I'm going to put you on some vitamins, and as soon as the blood tests come in, I'll see if you need iron tablets too. Call me anytime if you have questions or concerns. Here are some pamphlets that have information on fetal development, nutrition, etc. Things that you need to know when pregnant"

The doctor left the room. Jolly helped Jarmila get dressed and they exited the exam room. They said goodbye to the doctor, who noticed they seemed very unhappy for a couple receiving exciting news. She knew pregnancy was not always a happy time for a couple.

Jolly sat in the front seat of the Wraith, still in the parking lot of the hospital. He held the steering wheel with his hands, his forehead against it. Jarmila sat in the front seat, gripping her shoulder bag.

"You knew I didn't want children when we first started talking. I told you one of the conditions for me to marry my wives was that they agreed not to have children. I can't raise a child. Jar. I don't have time. I'm on the road too much. I'm too fuckin' damn old to have a baby now. Definitely too old to raise twins."

"I never made a promise with you not to have children. You could retire again."

"I don't want to fuckin' retire again!" he screamed, raising his head, "I want to stay on the road!"

"We could take the babies with us."

"Jar, the road is no place for babies. I've seen people take their kids on tour. They can't concentrate on anything because they have to take care of their kids."

"I don't want to stay home by myself with the babies. I don't like to be alone. The babies would be there, but I'd still be without adult company."

"I don't want to raise babies in between tours and an occasional visit on tour. I don't want to raise any baby at all. I *never wanted children* and you knew that from the beginning of our relationship."

"I didn't make these babies on my own!" she screamed, "I didn't want children either."

"I know you didn't conceive on your own. What if it's not mine?"

"Oh, here we go with the "It's not mine speech"." sneered Jarmila.

"You were with Chandler."

"He wore a condom and the gestation is off."

"You were with Jack."

"The gestational age is too far along. The baby is yours. Fuckin' accept it."

"Fuckin' accept it? Like you brought a stray dog home?"

"I thought you loved me. I thought you were my soulmate and nothing would break us apart."

"I'm not breaking up with you. I love you. You are my soulmate. We have to consider some options."

"If I'm your soulmate and we'll always be together, then what's the problem?" Jarmila asked.

"*The problem is I don't want any children and you're fuckin' pregnant*!"

Jolly leaned his head against the headrest.

"I'll find a high-quality abortion clinic." he sighed.

"I'm not getting a fuckin' abortion! I'm keeping my babies! Twins, just like in that dream I had that I told you about. Some things are meant to be and this is something that is meant to be. It was almost like being foretold. You can't force me to have an abortion! It's my body, *I* make the decisions for my body!"

"You can't force me to be a dad. I'll be a father in name only. I'll be the fuckin' sperm donor!"

"I don't need shit from you. I'll raise these babies on the streets if I have too!" Jarmila yelled, opening the car door, taking off her engagement ring and throwing it at Jolly.

"Jar, come back. Let's calm down and talk about this rationally." said Jolly, trying to hold her arm from getting out of the car.

She pulled herself away from him and slammed the car door, running down the sidewalk, the over the shoulder purse bouncing against her arm.

Jolly sat in the car for over an hour. He never drove when angry. Especially in his beloved Wraith. His Wraith, his BMW, the road, those were his babies. He didn't need another one. Calming down, he didn't want to go home immediately. He didn't want another confrontation with Jarmila. He wanted an adult conversation with the two of them deciding what would be best in this situation. Weighing pros and cons, making lists about how expensive babies can be, his age. While sitting in the Wraith he was forming a calm adult conversation he could have with her.

But first he went to Everett's house. Everett lived in a converted church/rectory on California Avenue, between Division Street and North Avenue. He lived a few blocks from Jack's boulevard house. You literally could walk from Jack's house turning north onto California Avenue from Division Street and be in front of Everett's house. Jolly rang the bell and Everett answered the door.

"Hello, my friend." Everett greeted.

"I need to talk to you. In private." said Jolly.

"We can talk on the front porch. I'll grab a couple beers and some weed."

Jolly sat on the stoop and put his arms back. Everett soon joined him.

"How's everybody?" Jolly asked.

"They're doing great. Glad that I am home."

Everett had been married 20 years to a beautiful, tall woman from Chicago's southside Englewood neighborhood named L'Auvergne. She worked in the City of Chicago court system, helping people who didn't understand how the court system works, or helping them to fill out forms. They had two children, girls, 16 and 11. The 16-year-old, Imene, was an honor student who loved soccer and won many games and awards. She had her mother's deep brown eyes, the ebony skin of her mother, and her father's blonde hair, but wavier than Everett's. The 11-year-old, Branwen, was also an honor student and loved to talk about insects. She had skin the color of extra-cream-in-coffee, black curly hair, and blue eyes that reminded a person of a sunny sky after a storm. Branwen was Jolly's goddaughter.

"Where is everybody?" asked Jolly.

"Imene is at soccer practice. Branwen is at the library and L'Auvergne is working on a complicated case. Where's Jarmila?"

"That's what I wanted to talk to you about. I need advice."

"Pre-martial spat?"

"Unplanned pregnancy. We had a huge fight. I said cruel things. She took off."

"Whoa. To a guy who absolutely wants no children of his own." said Everett, "What do you plan to do?"

"I don't know," said Jolly, "I really don't know. I'm so conflicted. The responsibility is not hers alone; I should have used protection. I've never been in love like this before, and I wasn't thinking clearly."

Everette rolled a joint, took a toke and handed it to Jolly.

"Now what?"

"I don't know," said Jolly, exhaling, "I was hoping to get some ideas and advice from you. You've been married 20 years. You have experience I don't. I get married and never stay married for long. I want this one to last. Jarmila is my one-and-only, my soulmate. I've never felt this way about a woman before. I don't want to lose her, but I don't want kids either. And she's pregnant with twins."

"Twice the blessings."

"Twice the inconvenience." sighed Jolly, taking a sip of beer.

Branwen bounded up the steps two at a time. She had an armful of books. Putting then on the stairs, she hugged Jolly.

"Uncle Jolly!" she exclaimed, "You're home!"

"I was on the same tour as your dad." he responded, "I am glad to see you again. I missed you. How is my goddaughter doing? How are those grades?"

"I'm making all A's. I'm in honors club, and I'm taking pre-AP courses next year!" she answered.

"I'm very proud of you. I'll make a deal with you. If you keep these grades up, I'll ask your mom and dad if you can come out on tour with us for a week."

"Are you and my dad going on the same tour again?"

"Yes. It starts August 22nd. When does your next school year start? I don't want to interfere with school. Education takes priority."

"It doesn't start until September." she said, giving Jolly another hug, "I love you, Uncle Jolly!"

"Same here, Branwen."

"Branwen," said Everett, "is your homework done?"

"Almost." she answered.

"Go inside and finish your homework," Everett told her, "Ask your mom to bring out the six pack of Bud."

Branwen did as her father asked. L'Auvergne came out to the porch carrying a six pack of Budweiser beer and a jar of cashews

"How are you, Jolly?" she asked him, hugging him.

"I'm good. How are you?"

"Busy! But good. We will be at your wedding. What a nice surprise for Jarmila!"

"Thank you." he said.

"Well, I need to tackle this case. If you need anything, let me know. Stay for supper! I'm making slow roasted brisket with all the trimmings." she offered.

"I'm sorry, I'll have to take a rain check on this one. But I promise soon we'll get together."

"Be sure to bring Jarmila!" she said, walking back into the house.

There was silence between Jolly and Everett.

"I don't know what to do" said Jolly, a tear rolling down his face, "I don't want to lose her."

"Tough situation." said Everett, "but see it this way. You love her. If she had a brain injury, would you still love her? Would you take care of her? Would you still want to be with her?"

"Of course! But having a brain injury and having babies are completely different things."

"Not necessarily." said Everett. "You'd have to take care of a living person either way. Babies are tough. Especially for people who are on the road as much as us. We miss a lot of things real time. Video calls just aren't the same. But all that is overridden by the love you have for your child. Nothing can overshadow that. I miss my kids terribly when I'm on the road. I talk to them and L'Auvergne every day on the phone. Sure, it's not the same as being there. But the love is still there. When you get home, it's like being a newlywed all over again. And you get all joyful over all your kids have accomplished. It's when you realize that for people like us, people with music tours embedded in them, we can still make our kids successful human beings by helping to solve a math problem over a video chat."

Everett popped open two more beer bottles and offered Jolly a cigarette.

"I'm not telling you what you should do" Everett continued, "This is a huge decision. Especially for someone who doesn't want children. Although you're super good with kids. My daughters adore you. You'd make a great dad."

"Or just a good uncle and godfather."

"You have to make a decision, Jolly. If you really love Jarmila, you have to make a decision, for both your sakes. Take some time to make the right decision, and let her have time to think. Don't push her into your decision. I've never seen you care so much for a woman before. However, no matter how much you love and care for someone, there are dealbreakers. Stuff you can't abide by or live with. Take time to honestly think about the pros and cons, and then make a final decision. After you make that final decision, have a plan on how you'll tell Jarmila."

Jolly finished his beer. He stood up and Everett followed.

"Thank you, my friend." Jolly said to Everett, shaking his hand. "You've given me good advice to think about."

Going to the Wraith, Jolly turned around.

"Hey Everett," he said, "can I put my Wraith in your garage and pick it up in the morning? I don't like to drive if I've had any alcohol. I'll call a car service to get home tonight."

"No problem. L'Auvergne will drive you home. She needs a break anyway."

With that the two friends parted ways. Jolly had a lot to think about.

L'Auvergne dropped Jolly off in front of his house. There were no lights on. Jolly thought Jarmila must be asleep. He didn't want to wake her up in case there was an argument. Quietly he entered his house and turned on the downstairs hallway light. In silence he ascended the stairs, turning on a small lamp in an upstairs hallway table. From where he was standing, he saw the bed still made. He turned the bedroom light on and saw the bed empty. He went down the hallway to the guest bedrooms. Both were empty. He checked the upstairs bathroom, but the light was also off. Going downstairs he checked each room. Jarmila was not there. He checked the basement, the back deck, the garage. Jarmila was gone. Jolly went upstairs again and into the walk-in closet. He looked above the clothing rack where she kept her tour bag. It was gone. He opened some of the drawers in her dresser and found a few clothes missing. He looked through the shoe rack he had made her and found her pink Converse High tops missing, as well as a pair of leather low heeled sandals. Jarmila was definitely AWOL.

Jolly knew she hadn't gone to the band. They'd have been over at his house like a thunderbolt, accusing him of breaking her heart. His own heart was broken. He wished he could rewind everything that was said.

Les was surprised to see Jarmila at his door. He welcomed her in.

"I didn't know you knew where I lived." he said.

"I remember you saying you lived by the Riveria, in an old brown building. I looked around until I found an old brown building, and found your name on the mailbox. I hope I'm not bothering you." said Jarmila.

"Not at all. Come on in and have a seat. Can I get you something to eat or drink?"

"No, I'm fine. I have a favor to ask you. I was wondering if I could stay here the weekend. I'll be out by Monday. I don't want Jolly to know where I am."

"Had a little quarrel? I've had those with my wife."

"It was a huge quarrel, but I don't want to explain it. Does your wife mind if I stay?"

"She passed on several years ago. Car crash."

"I'm sorry. I didn't know."

"It's okay. I don't tell a lot of people. I keep things to myself. Anyway, you are more than welcome to stay as long as you like. I always liked you, Jarmila. You were always kind to me. And you always remembered my birthday, which meant a lot to me. I couldn't talk to you a lot because of the Lenehan rule."

"I know. Crew can't "fraternize" with me."

"Despite that, you were always had kind words for me and short conversations. I only have one bedroom. You can sleep in there. I'll sleep on the couch."

"No! I don't want to be a bother like that! I fall asleep on couches in the dressing rooms. I'll be comfortable out here. Thank you. I didn't want to stay in a hotel by myself. I con't like to be alone. Lenehan is real busy writing and recording and I didn't want to bother them." Jarmila said.

"Make yourself at home. But I'm warning you, this is a man's dirty apartment! I'm not the best on cleaning!." he laughed, and got her a pillow and blanket.

They sat on the couch for a while watching old black and white movies. Les said he had to go on to bed because he had a security job in the morning. There was a spare key in a cup in the cupboard if she wanted to go in and out. Jarmila thanked him again and put the pillow and blanket on the couch, falling asleep to the movie "The Man With The Golden Arm."

In the morning, Les woke up to fresh coffee and orange juice, bacon, eggs and toast. His apartment was spotless.

"Did you stay up all night and do this?" he asked.

"No, I woke up early and couldn't go back to sleep. I have a lot on my mind. I'm not big on cleaning or cooking, but I needed to keep myself occupied. I found all this stuff in your fridge so I figured that's what you would want for breakfast."

"Do you mind if I hug you?" he asked, "I want to thank you for your kindness and thinking of me. You do have a good heart. Everyone says you do and they are right."

He embraced her in a bear hug and held her there for a few minutes.

On Monday, 27th, 2019, Jarmila left Les' apartment. He was at a jobsite so she left him a note thanking him for his kindness. She ended the letter that she would miss him. When he read the letter, it made him smile, except the ending which confused him. She could see him anytime she wanted now that the tour had ended. Maybe she meant she'd miss him until she saw him again.

When Jarmila left Les' it was already afternoon, and she went to the studio Lenehan was recording in. It was only two blocks from where she lived with Jolly, and worry tightened her stomach that he might spot her in the neighborhood. She did not want to see or talk to him. She had made up her mind about what she would do with her life, and she wasn't going to let him convince her into any other plans.

Jack was sitting at the sound board, smoking a purple marijuana pipe. He heard the buzzer and looking at the camera, saw it was Jamila and buzzed her in.

"Don't say I can't smoke in here." Jack said, "I had this studio built and I own 75% of it, so I'll smoke it all up if I want."

"I wasn't going to say anything." Jarmila said, putting her tour bag on the ground, "I came by to see how y'all are doing. Where is everyone else?"

"Johnny is down with a migraine," answered Jack, "Benny is…I don't know, off being Benny. We don't need them right now anyway. Chandler is at an intervention with his family and Marie. His family is trying to save his marriage. Chandler and I are just practicing shit and laying it down to see if shit works. We'll have plenty of time between da next tour and da European tour to really get serious and release a third album. Or at least da label hopes so. What are you up to, pretty girl? Come over here and sit on my lap."

Jack put his pipe down and Jarmila sat in his lap. She kissed him on the lips and gave him a slight hug. He put his hands around her waist.

"Jarmila, you got to lay off da beer. I know Methuselah gives you anything you want, but go back to liquor. Beer puts weight in places you don't want it to be. You're getting a beer belly. And Jesus, can't he feed you more? You look like you've lost weight."

She didn't want to tell him she was pregnant, and that's where the belly was coming from. The twins were making her belly bump out sooner than she expected. She didn't want to tell anyone.

"Stop calling him Methuselah. He's not old." she said.

"He's old enough to be your father."

"Age doesn't matter. Can we change the subject? I miss seeing you all as much as I used to."

"Would you like to hear some of da new songs me and Chandler have put down?"

"Yes!" she squealed.

"I wrote a song about you."

"I remember you telling me that."

"Want to hear it? It's just a rough cut with Chandler on guitar and me on vocals."

"Yes!"

"Then give me head and I'll let you hear it."

"You are so mean, Jack. I can't do that, I'm engaged."

"We're alone here, we don't have to tell anyone."

"No."

"I was just kidding. I don't want you to hear da song until it is finished. But I promise you, only da band will hear it before you. Well, and da engineers, and da producer."

She kissed him on the lips.

"I love you, Jack."

"I love you, Jarmila. Now listen to some of this music and tell me what you think of it so far."

She listened to several tunes.

"Those are better than the second album. I like that tune "Winter" best of all. I can't wait to hear the full version. I think it's going to outrun "The Only Cost." Anyway, I have a request for you."

"Shoot."

"I've run out of books to read. Can I borrow some from you instead of going to the public library?"

"Sure! I can run you by my place right now and you can pick some more out."

"No, that's okay. I'm meeting Johnny tomorrow at Cali and Division and he can run me over there. I still have your spare key. I'll make sure the books I borrowed for the tour get back to you in a few days if that's okay."

"Donate them to a school. I'm getting a whole 'nother batch in and need the room."

"How is your rib?"

"Oh, it's much better. Hurts a little once in a while. That shit medication they gave didn't do a damn thing. Morphine takes da pain away."

"What medication did they give you?"

"Norcos. Might have well as given me baby aspirin."

She hopped off his lap and sat in a chair next to him.

"Did I ever tell you about my great-grandma Jarmila Bisnick?" she asked.

"At least a hundred times." Jack sighed, picking up his marijuana pipe and lighting it again.

"I was named after her. She came to America from Bohemia in 1910 when she was 8. It was her 8th birthday. I share the same birthday as her, June 1st. She saw the Statue Of Liberty for the first time on her birthday. Isn't that cool?"

"Mesmerizing." said Jack, holding his chin with his hand.

"She didn't like it here. They settled here in Chicago, in the Polish Triangle neighborhood. Her parents wanted her to fully assimilate to American. They thought she'd have a better chance at a good life. They only spoke English to her. There weren't a lot of people from Bohemia in the area. Mostly Polish and Ukrainian. Kids made fun of her accent. Even her teachers made fun of her and she got held back a couple grades. She hated school. She hated Polish Triangle. She wanted to move to the Pilsen neighborhood. Lots of people from Bohemia had settled there. She had relatives there. But her father wanted to stay where he was. She was very unhappy."

"Fascinating." Jack sighed, "Look Jarmila, I got work I got to do. Why don't you come back tomorrow and tell me more entrancing stories of your great-grandmother?"

"I can't. I'm meeting Johnny tomorrow and then I got things to do."

"Your sweet little ass better be here Saturday for our first tour rehearsal. When you see Johnny tomorrow, tell him I said get his ass down here and start putting down some bass tracks to see how they sound. Fucker don't answer my phone calls or return my texts."

"The medicine he's on makes him sleep real deep. But I'll tell him." she said, standing up and kissing him on the lips while giving him a hug, "I'll miss you."

"I miss you every day I don't see you." he responded.

When she walked out, it was already nighttime.

The next day, Tuesday, May 28th, 2019, Jarmila hopped into the passenger side of Johnny's green 1971 Chevy Vega. He was rolling a joint. He licked the seal on the paper, slid an index finger over the seal, and placed the joint on the dashboard.

"John Michael Dunne!" Jarmila exclaimed, "If your momma found out…"

"Blame Benny. He hooked me up with some good shit he got in Indianapolis." he said, taking the joint from the dashboard, lighting it, and taking a long inhale, "How are you, pretty one? I could call you pretty stranger since I don't see enough of you anymore. You seem thinner."

"I'm tired, but good." she answered, "Do you have that shit for me?"

Yesterday she had called Johnny and asked if he knew where to get something to calm her nerves. He assumed she was nervous about being engaged and living in a permanent place, so he told her he'd get her Xanax to help with her nerves.

"Most certainly do." said Johnny, handing her a small zip lock plastic baggie with long rectangular white pills.

"I thought Xanax was blue? I saw pictures on the internet and they were blue." she said, putting the baggie in her tour bag.

"They come in different colors," said Johnny, "these are two-milligram. Don't take more than one of these at a time. Better to cut them in half. They'll probably make you sleepy."

"Thanks, Johnny. I think these will help me. I read up on them on the internet. Sometimes I feel like the two sides of my brain are spinning in different directions. I feel dizzy and can't focus. Did I ever tell you about my paternal great-grandma Jarmila, the one I'm named after? She came with her parents from Bohemia when she was 8 years old. Their last name was Bisnick. She arrived in America on her 8th birthday. I have the same birthday she does! When I was a kid, I heard my grandmother's sisters talking about her. They said she had a limp. Story was that she fell from a second-floor window in Bohemia when she was two years old. But my grandmother's sisters, they said the true story was that her father was a drunk and threw her from the window."

Johnny started rolling another joint.

"Jarmila, I love you like family. You are like a sister to me, so I mean no disrespect. But talking to you is like opening several books at random pages and reading a page from each one. I can't have a cohesive conversation with you lately. What does your inability to focus have to do with your great-grandma being thrown out a window when she was two?"

"Nothing," she responded, "I was just talking random stuff. Memories keep coming back to me. It's really bothering me, being slammed with all these memories. I remember when my grandmother and her sisters would sit around the kitchen table having coffee. They ignored me. I sat in the corner, on the floor, between the kitchen sink and cabinets, playing with an old dishrag and not missing a word of what they were saying. Those memories really, really bother me. I feel agitated."

"Hopefully the Xanax will help. If not, I can hook you up with a good doctor. The one I got here that takes care of my migraines, he's very good."

"Thanks, Johnny. You're an angel, truly. Like how family should be. You're like the family I always wanted and never had."

"You've always got me, little sister. Do you need a lift somewhere?" Johnny asked, finishing rolling joints and putting them in the center console of the car.

"I'm going by Jack's to get some books. It's only a block and a half from here. I can walk."

"I can drop you off there. I'm going in that direction."

"Okay, cool. By the way, I saw Jack in the studio yesterday. He said to get your ass in the studio and lay down some bass tracks."

"I know. He's been calling and texting like an unrequited lover. I just got over a really bad migraine. I'll call him. I've got to run an errand for my ma, then I'll go over to the studio."

Jarmila gave Johnny a kiss on the cheek and a big hug.

"I love you, big brother, and I'm going to miss you most."

"I'm only going to the studio, Jarmila." he said, perplexed at her statement, "If you need me, call, text or video chat me."

Johnny started the car and drove in the direction of Jack's house.

Jack had a large boulevard house that faced Humboldt Park. It could be considered a four-story house, since the basement level was half above ground. There was also a two-story coach house in the back at the end of the driveway. All that space, yet Jack preferred to live alone.

Jarmila opened the front security gate and went up the concrete stairs. She opened the wide wood front door and entered the front hallway. She wanted to find those Norcos, but wasn't sure where to start. There were five bathrooms in the house. She decided to start in Jack's bedroom bathroom, on the top floor. The bottle was not there. Exiting Jack's bedroom, she caught a glimpse of a bottle on his nightstand by his bed. She went there and picked up the bottle. It was 3/4 full of yellow oval-shaped pills with the word NORCO printed above the number 539 on one side, and scored on the other side. She put the pill bottle in her tour bag. She went down two flights of stairs to Jack's personal library. She picked out four paperback books and put them in her tour bag. She then called Benny and asked if he had some pain reliever for her back. Something that was not heroin. She had slept in the wrong position and her back hurt. He told her he had something that could help, and to meet him at his house in Smith Park at 2:00pm tomorrow.

Jolly had been texting and calling Jarmila since the day she took off after their argument in the doctor's parking lot. He had not heard back from her. Worry and concern kept him awake most nights, and during the day he could not concentrate enough to get much work done. His sink was full of dirty dishes and dirty clothes littered his bedroom floor. His bed went unmade. He couldn't live without Jarmila. He was such a fool, he thought. He overreacted and now probably lost the best thing that had ever happened to him in his life.

He didn't know where she was. He knew she wasn't with the band. He had promised them he'd never break her heart. If she had gone to one of Lenehan, one or all of the Lenehan members would have come to him like bull sharks on methamphetamine. He couldn't imagine her staying in a hotel, because she didn't like to stay alone. Although she was around tons of people on tour, Lenehan's "No Fraternizing With Jarmila" rule meant she did not know a lot of the people on tour. Not anyone well enough she'd be staying with them. Scot certainly wouldn't take her in. But Everett. L'Auvergne would take her in. Would Everett keep a secret from Jolly? Jolly had known Everett for 15 years, and they had been best friends almost as long. He was Godfather to Everett's youngest daughter. Would his best friend lie to him? He opened a desk cabinet and took out an unmarked file. In it were the marriage certificate, the event permit for the Formal Flower Garden, the receipt and information for the reception at The Boathouse across the street from the Formal Flower Garden, a receipt and info from the party planner, and the caterer's receipt. Lenehan was going to be the wedding band.

A sweet thought entered his head when he thought of how the marriage certificate was obtained. Before he planned on obtaining it, Jolly had asked Jarmila if she had a copy of her birth certificate and social security card. He knew she had a state ID, he had seen it in the Lenehan files. He didn't know if she would need any more ID than that, but just in case, he asked her anyway. She said she had that and always carried it with her. Jolly asked Jarmila to wait outside the clerk's office, then he and L'Auvergne went in and got the necessary forms. Clipboard in hand, L'Auvergne was always prepared. Jolly was able to answer most of the questions on the form for Jarmila, and the rest L'Auvergne asked. Then she showed Jarmila where to sign it. Jolly filled out his form and signed it. Then the three of them went into the clerk's office. Jolly and Jarmila handed over their ID's to be copied and Jolly paid the fee. Out in the hallway, Jolly thanked L'Auvergne and she gave both of them a hug. On the way to the car, Jarmila asked if that had something to do with being engaged. Jolly smiled and told her it was a very important part of being engaged. Jarmila didn't ask any more questions. She had such an innocent heart, trusting Jolly completely.

Sitting at his computer, rolling the engagement ring around his fingertip, he took a sip of coffee and pulled up Facebook Messenger. He clicked on Everett's name.

"I have a question to ask you." he typed.

"Ask away." responded Everett a few seconds later.

"You haven't seen or heard from Jarmila in the past few days? Or has L'Auvergne?"

A few minutes went by.

"I haven't heard or seen her. L'Auvergne is at work, but I texted her and she texted that she hasn't seen or heard from her either. But if we do, we will let you know."

"Thank you."

"Don't worry too much, Jolly. She's probably cooling off somewhere."

"Yeah, but where? She won't respond to my calls and texts, and all I'm asking is for her to let me know she's okay. She wouldn't be with the band, that's a certainty."

"If she was, I'd be visiting you in intensive care. Did you try Scottie, see if she's there?"

"I think she'd stay with the Devil before she'd go to Scot's."

"Worth a try."

"Yeah. Thanks. See you soon."

"Yup. See you soon. You got to make good on your raincheck to L'Auvergne."

"I will. Soon as I get this crisis handled."

"Later, dude."

Jolly clicked out of Messenger. He thought, should he ask Scot? He decided he'd wait a couple more days. If Jarmila wasn't home by Thursday, he'd call Scot. When the doorbell rang, he got up to let the cleaning crew in.

Wednesday, May 29th, 2019, Jarmila did not find Benny at his bungalow across from Smith Park. Ringing the bell several times, she decided that he must have forgotten he told he to stop by. Heroin made him forgetful at times. Maybe he and Alice had to go somewhere. As she turned to leave, she saw Benny on a swing in the park. He was slowly swinging back and forth, Dum Dum lollipop in his mouth. He stopped swinging as she sat on the swing next to him, putting her tour bag on the ground.

"What flavor is that?" she asked about the lollipop.

"Pineapple." he answered, handing it to her.

"Did I ever tell you about my great-grandma, Jarmila, the one I'm named after? The one I share a birthday with?"

"I don't recall. Did she like Dum Dums?"

"I don't know. She lived in the early 20th century. I'm not sure if there were Dum Dums then. Anyway, she and her parents came from Bohemia in 1910 and settled in the Polish Triangle neighborhood. She hated it there. My grandmother's sisters used to tell stories about how her parents made her do all the chores in the house. She used to sweep the stairs and the front entryway. The front door had a stained-glass window. When the sun shone through it, triangles of color would look like they were suspended in the air. Story goes, my great-grandma Jarmila would dance in the colors with the broom in her hand and pretend she was Queen of Bohemia. She quit school when she was 12. She had to help her family with income. She didn't mind quitting school. She didn't like it and rarely went."

"I see parallels in her and your life stories." said Benny.

"How so?"

"You rarely attended school and you quit when you were 12."

"Yeah, I can see that. Where's Alice?"

"She volunteers all day at a food pantry and free food diner on Wednesdays."

"That's sweet of her. She's a very nice person."

"I'm going to marry her. I don't know when, but I am."

"I know you'll be very happy."

Benny jumped up from the swing. He reached into the pocket of his tight black jeans and took out a tiny, tan manila envelope, similar to the ones jewelers use for small necklaces and earrings. Jarmila opened it and looked inside, where there was a translucent rectangular object.

"What is it?" she asked.

"It's a fentanyl patch." answered Benny, "It will help with your back pain. It can take up to 24 hours before you feel any effect. But sometimes sooner. Stick it on the skin on your shoulder blade. It's a serious pain killer. Probably knock you out cold. But if it doesn't help, let me know and I'll find something else for you."

She put the envelope in a front pocket of her tour bag and stood up and gave Benny a big kiss on the lips and a big hug.

"Why are you carrying around your tour bag?" asked Benny

"I picked up some books at Jack's. Thank you so much! I love you! I'm going to miss you so much!"

"I love you too. See you Saturday for your birthday and tour rehearsals."

Jarmila smiled and walked east toward Western Avenue.

Every day for Jarmila was a lot like it was when she was 12 and her grandmother and father died. She spent time in the library, rode the city buses and trains, sat in the parks, weather permitting. Every day she went to the Eckhart Park Fieldhouse indoor pool and swam. Then she took a shower and put on fresh clothes. Then she would take the Chicago Avenue 66 bus to the nearest Blue Line "L" station. She'd take the train to a stop where she knew there was a laundromat in a neighborhood where no one would recognize her. She didn't want to answer any inquiries as to why she wasn't doing laundry at home. As far as she was concerned, she no longer had a home. Jolly's was not her home anymore.

She'd wash her dirty clothes and her swimsuit, sit and read while her clothes were in the dryer. Her swimsuit was a one-piece. She didn't like the way she looked in bikinis. On tour, a lot of hotels had indoor pools, and she loved to swim. Now, when she put on her one-piece swimsuit, she could see the tiny baby bump in her waistline.

At night she would ride the buses and trains all night, switching to different routes. Sometimes she would fall asleep and the bus driver or train conductor would wake her up at the end of the line. She would fall asleep sometimes during the day on the buses and trains too, and the same happened, bus drivers and train conductors waking her up to let her know it was the end of the line. She saw her life as the end of the line. Soon. Soon it would be the end of the line for her.

Thursday morning, May 30th, 2019 she called Chandler in the afternoon and asked if she could hang out with him. He said sure, he was in the studio alone and could use the company. When he heard the buzzer, he didn't bother looking at the camera. He buzzed her right in. She was wearing light color blue jeans and a white Lenehan t-shirt from their first album. It was an x-large t-shirt she picked up at Jack's. She wore it to hide her tiny baby bump. Jack may think she had a beer belly. But Chandler had sisters who had kids. He knew what a pregnant belly looked like, even early on in a pregnancy. She didn't want to take any chances he'd figure it out. She put her tour bag on one side of the love seat and sat on the other side. Chandler was at the sound board, in a black and red office swivel chair, which he spun around to face Jarmila.

"What's up, my special girl?" he asked, "You don't spend much time with me anymore. Why? Oh, don't answer that. I know why. It's because you're under Methuselah all the time."

"Stop calling him that. Jack calls him that too. He's not that old."

"He's the same age as my dad. Would you marry my dad?"

"Well, if he wasn't married to your momma and he asked me, I might say yes. Your dad's a hottie."

"I think Jolly has turned you onto obsessions with old men."

"Well, there are worse things he could have turned me onto. Where is everybody? Why aren't they here?"

"It's not 1950. We don't have to all be in the studio together to record. Besides, right now, we're just putting down tracks to see how shit sounds. We won't start the serious recording until after this next tour."

"But when you recorded your last album, you guys were stuck together like caramel popcorn."

"Sophomore record. Second records can be scary as shit. They have to be better than the first album, or it could sink a band. Third album, we're a little more relaxed."

"Do you think your third will be released before your European tour?"

"I think so," answered Chandler, "the label hopes so. We'll do some recording on the road too."

"When will you find the time? Between Henry and Harold? Liam and Logan?"

Chandler swiveled his chair over to Jarmila. He put his hands on her knees.

"Ha ha ha." he said, deadpan.

"Can I sit on your lap?"

"I don't know. Do I have to change my name to Jack?"

"Ha ha ha, very funny. I sit on your lap a lot too."

"No, you don't. Your face is in my lap a lot, but your butt is not. Hop on up, my special girl."

Jarmila sat on his lap and he swiveled the chair all around the room.

"Wheeeeeeee!" he exclaimed as he flew around the room, "I'm going to ask for one of these in the rider, so I can spin around the dressing room. Hey, maybe I'll take it on stage with me and spin around on stage!"

"Stop it, Chandler, you're making me dizzy!" exclaimed Jarmila.

He stopped at the sound board.

"You're losing weight." Chandler said as he slightly squeezed her right arm, "Is Jolly chaining you up in the basement and forgetting to feed you?"

"I think it's just being off tour. On tour there's always food around. Now I'm eating like a regular person, three meals a day." she lied, as she had not eaten that day.

"I ordered some food. Want to share it with me?"

"I don't want to take away any of your food."

"Puh-lease! You're my family, I can share. Besides I ordered a lot of food because I got caught up in this song and haven't eaten yet."

"I am hungry."

"You look like a famine victim at a border crossing."

"Thanks, make me feel uglier than I already do."

"I didn't mean it that way. I'm sorry." Chandler apologized, "You're my beautiful, special girl. I'm just concerned about your weight loss. Because I love you."

"It's okay. I love you." she said, kissing him on the lips.

The door buzzer sounded.

"That's the food." said Chandler, "Get off your lazy ass and go get it."

Jarmila went to the door and collected the food. She put three plastic shopping bags on the table.

"Oh my God Chandler, do you think you're Jesus feeding the 5000?" she laughed.

"I got enough in case I get hungry again later." he said, sitting at the head of the table with Jarmila sitting on the side, "I may be here all night with this creativity I got flowing right now."

Jarmila and Chandler took out the food containers from the bags. Chandler had ordered cheeseburgers, Italian beef sandwiches, tacos, burritos, fish sandwiches, fries, mozzarella sticks, chicken wings, a 3-piece perch dinner.

"Perch!" exclaimed Jarmila, sitting down, "I love perch!"

"Do you want a pop?" Chandler said, going to the fridge.

"Yes, please."

"Diet Coke?"

"Yup. You like Fresca so you can put vodka in it, Benny likes strawberry flavor, Johnny likes grape flavor and Jack likes cherry cola."

"You know us well!" laughed Chandler, returning with the pops and sitting down again.

"I saw Jack here on Monday. He said your family and Marie had a marriage intervention with you. Is everything okay? Is it because of that incident with that guy after the Chicago shows?"

"Yeah. Marie was genuinely upset. I broke a vow to her."

"You're lucky Marie didn't get her family involved."

"Marie tells her family to stay the fuck outta our marriage."

"You should tell your family to stay the fuck outta your marriage. Your marriage is between two people, you and Marie. Nobody else." she said, taking a bite of perch.

"I don't have the balls to do that."

"Grow some. Because if people keep interfering with your marriage, you and Marie will continue to have problems. People marry each other, not the entire family. Work it out between the two of you."

"You're right. But it's not easy." he responded, "Give me a piece of perch."

Jarmila put a piece of perch on the container of chicken wings that Chandler was eating.

"What was the outcome of the "Riley Marriage Intervention?" Jarmila asked.

"They want me to go to gay conversion therapy. But I'm not gay."

Jarmila stopped eating and looked straight in Chandler's eyes.

"Chandler, you're gay." she said.

"I am not gay!" he protested, "I love Marie! She's a woman. Born a female. Marie thinks I'm bi."

"Gay men can love women. Just because you're gay doesn't mean you can't love someone of the opposite gender. But you told me you don't like having sex with her. You told me it's not her that's the problem, it's that you don't like having vaginal sex. You told me you only have sex with her because it's your "marital obligation" and she wants babies. You're gay, Chandler. You like men."

"I want to have babies too! I love my nieces and nephews, especially when they're newborns and you can hold them against your chest. They make these cute squeaky noises."

"Gay men love babies too! Gay men have babies. These are excuses you are telling yourself to convince yourself you're not gay. Stop trying to deny your truth."

"I like having sex with you." he said, biting into a chicken wing.

"You watch basketball games when we were having sex."

"It was March Madness! Besides, even if I was gay, I don't have any obligation to tell anyone."

"Seriously Chandler, real talk. Unless you own your truth that you are gay, you are never going to be completely happy. You're going to have this internal struggle that affects you and Marie's marriage. It affects your life. You don't have any obligation to tell anyone you're gay. That's your business and nobody else's. And don't you dare go to any "gay conversion therapy". That is a bunch of bullshit. But you should admit your truth, to yourself. You owe yourself that. There's nothing wrong being gay. But there are two people in your life that you should admit it to, so you don't have this struggle anymore. You should admit it to yourself. Then you should have an intense conversation with Marie and tell her your truth. She probably already knows. I mean, she does make sure one of your tour suitcases is filled with condoms, dildoes and BDSM stuff."

"That does not make me gay. Straight people own stuff like that too. Jack owns a whole closet full of BDSM items."

"I know. I've seen it."

"Has he ever used anything on you?"

"No. With him it's always, 'Give me head. Now get on all fours on da bed' then he would do anal to me."

"One time when I went over to his house, he had a naked woman chained to a radiator in his hallway outside his bedroom. That man is twisted!" Chandler laughed.

"Back to what I was saying," said Jarmila, "You need to own your truth. You're gay. Nothing wrong with that. I know your family is of the religious type to think all gay people go to hell. Let them think what they want. Your soul ain't none of their business either. You have to accept yourself first. If you don't accept yourself, you'll always be Happy Tour Chandler who gets a buffet of fine-looking men to fuck, then Sad At Home Chandler who goes to check the back gate in his yard."

"I liked your "back gate"."

"Did you like my "back gate" more than my "front gate"?

"Yes."

"You're gay, Chandler. And hey, you were supposed to be punishing me when you went in my "back gate". You weren't supposed to like it."

"Couldn't help but like it. You got such a nice, tight butthole." he said, rubbing his fingers along her arm, "Can I get another round of that nice, tight butthole?"

"No. You promised Jolly no more sex with me."

"This is all Jack's fault. If he hadn't kept firing tour managers, we'd have never gotten Jolly as one. You would have never met him and you and I would still be getting up to all kinds of sumthin' sumthin'."

"I have to go," said Jarmila, closing the empty food container and standing up, throwing the container and the empty pop can in the trash, "Hey, what's that?"

She pointed to two brown cubes sitting on gold foil on a table next to the trash bin.

"That's straight up opium." answered Chandler, "Hard to find and expensive as hell."

"How do you use it?"

"I don't know how other people use it, but I cut a slice off it and smoke it up in a bong."

"What does it do to you?"

"It's like Heaven. It makes me feel like I don't have a care in the world. It really helps with my creativity. I do best creatively when I'm on opium. I heard back in the day people used to commit suicide with it. They'd eat a whole cube, or several cubes. Strong shit. That's why I only use a little at a time."

"I don't have much money on me, but can I buy one of those cubes from you?"

"You're my special girl, you don't have to buy it from me. Take one. But be very careful. Shit is powerful. Want to take my mini-bong?"

"No, I can get one from the gas station. Can I use this foil to wrap it up in?"

"Sure, just put the other one aside."

She took one cube off the foil, putting it aside, and wrapped the other in the gold foil. She then put it in the front zipper compartment of her tour bag. She went over the Chandler, wiped hot sauce from the side of his mouth, and kissed him on the lips.

"Thank you. Thanks for the food, too."

"Take some with you." he said.

"No. I'm full. Thanks anyway. Promise me you will own your truth. Promise me you will have a sincere conversation with Marie. Tell her you still want to be married to her, and you still want babies. But you're gay. Ask her if she can accept that. Promise her you will respect her when you are in Chicago and won't run around with men. Or at least do it discreetly. You're a rock star now, Chandler. *Everything* you do could end up in the media, especially social media. You could sneeze and it could trend on Twitter."

"I promise. I love you. Your advice helps a lot."

"I love you, too. I'm going to miss you." she said, kissing him on the lips again.

"You're so weird. You're going to see me again on Saturday. Tour rehearsals, remember?"

She hugged him and left the studio.

Friday, May 31st, 2019, Jolly spent the day getting ready for the next evening. He had received the shoes from Italy. They were exquisite. An exact replica of the one's Jarmila's great-grandmother had worn at her own wedding in 1916. He had picked up the headband veil which also was an exact replica of the one in the 1916 sepia photo. He packed the wedding dress in a long white box, covered it with pink tissue paper, added the shoes and veil, and wrapped the box in pink wrapping paper. He placed a large pink bow on the top of the box.

He would keep his plans to go to the first tour rehearsal the next evening at the agreed upon time. He had everything planned as to what he would say. First, he would ask for forgiveness. He would get on his knees and beg her to forgive his stupidity. He would promise to never say cruel things to her again. He would tell her he couldn't wait to lay on the grass in their backyard with the sunshine on her big pregnant belly. He looked forward to running his hand up and down her pregnant belly and feeling his twins kick. They would name them William and Jarmila.

He would tell her she could go out drinking for her birthday with Lenehan, like she had planned until he derailed the idea after the fight in the bar at Johnny's party. He was going to tell the boys she was expecting twins, so no alcohol. Non-alcoholic drinks only.

Jolly had discussed with Jarmila a honeymoon in Los Angeles. She could meet his family and he could combine it with a business trip to talk to Lenehan's record label. He realized how selfish that was. It was all about him and business and combining a honeymoon with it. That was not fair to Jarmila. She would not complain. She'd go along with whatever Jolly planned. Thinking about it, he decided they'd go to Los Angeles as planned, then she could pick anywhere she wanted to go for the rest of the honeymoon. She loved going to the casinos with him. Perhaps she'd like to go to Las Vegas. Or Iceland. She was always showing him pictures of Iceland and was interested in any shows about Iceland. Anywhere she wanted to go, he'd take her. As long as they were together, his soul would be healed.

The same day Jolly was getting everything together for Jarmila's birthday surprise, Jarmila was riding the buses and trains around the city. She stopped at the places she used to meet the boys, before they were a band. She went to the pavilion behind Roberto Clemente High School at Division Street and Western Avenue, where the boys used to ride their bikes. It was the place she first met them, when Benny approached her, introduced himself, and asked if she'd like to ride his bike. She went to a bike/skate park in Logan Square the boys also frequented. She went to Garfield Park Conservatory where she and Jack, Chandler, Benny and Johnny used to look for amphibians who had been abandoned there in the ponds and water displays. She went to Humboldt Park, sat at the lagoon and watched people on the water in the swan boats. She walked across the street to the Formal Garden and sat on a concrete bench. She took a book out from her tour bag and read a short time from George R. R. Martin's *A Clash Of Kings*. She put the book back into her tour bag and headed west toward California Avenue.

Jarmila then took public transportation to the Harold Washington Library. There she looked up old city directories for the time her great-grandmother and great-great-grandparents lived in Polish Triangle. She found the address. She took out a notebook from her tour bag and a pen. The paper inside the notebook was pink, and her pen was pink, with black ink. She would have preferred pink ink, but she didn't think it would show up on pink paper. She wrote the address down in the notebook. Jarmila then turned to a blank page and wrote "Dear Jolly". The letter took her sometime to write, because she wanted to make sure she was saying what was in her heart. When she was done with the letter to Jolly, she turned to another blank page in the notebook and wrote "Dear Jack". Finished with that letter, she folded both letters into squares and put them in the front pocket of her jeans. She returned the rest of the items to the tour bag. The library closed early on Friday, so she used the restroom and quietly left the building.

Saturday, June 1st, 2019, Jarmila's 23rd birthday

At 10:00am she called Johnny while sitting on a bench at the Jefferson Park Blue Line Station.

"Hello?" answered Johnny, brain thick with sleep fog.

"Did I wake you?" asked Jarmila.

"Yeah, but it's okay. What's up?"

"I just wanted to say hi."

"Hello." he said, "Is the Xanax working?"

"I haven't had to try it yet, but I will soon."

"Well, let me know if you need something else."

"Can you stay on the phone with me for a little while? I need someone to talk to. Can I tell you a story? Did I ever tell you about my great-grandma Jarmila Bisnick who came to Chicago from Bohemia as a kid? Oh yeah, I told you about her. She was 8 years old when she saw the Statue Of Liberty for the first time. It was her 8th birthday. Today was her birthday. Today is my 23rd birthday. But I know you already know that. I'm just babbling. My grandmother's sisters said her father was a mean drunk. There used to be these metal buckets you put beer in. You'd go to the bar and the bartender would fill it with beer and you'd take it home. Jarmila would be in the front entryway sweeping and her father would throw the bucket at her and tell her to hurry and get more beer. She didn't like being there, in the Polish Triangle neighborhood. She wanted to move to the Pilsen neighborhood and be with her relatives and people she could share her language and culture with. She wanted to belong. I wanted to belong. I know how she felt. When she was 14 years old, she married her father's first cousin. He was her father's age. But she didn't care because she wanted to move to Pilsen and he lived there. She knew she'd never move back to Bohemia. She didn't care about his looks or his age as long as he lived in Pilsen. I have their wedding picture. She married him and moved to Pilsen and had a slew of kids and was very happy living an ordinary life. Can you believe someone being happy being ordinary? Johnny? Johnny? Are you still there?"

Johnny had fallen back asleep, dropping his mobile phone on the floor.

Jarmila took the Jefferson Park Blue Line train to the stop at Ashland/Division/Milwaukee. She walked north on Ashland and found the address to the Bisnick's previous apartment building. She didn't think it would be there. Gentrification was heavy in this neighborhood, and old addresses change. But there it was, the three story greystone her great-great-grandparents once lived in. The building her great-grandmother Jarmila Bisnick hated so much.

The number of the address was etched in the greystone above the arched front doorway. As she approached the front door, she noticed the wooden door with the stained-glass window was there. The door popped open when she stood in front of it. She took this as a sign that she should proceed with her plans. Walking into front entryway, she noticed how the sunshine through the stained-glass window made prisms of color seem to dance in the air, exactly as her grandmother's sisters told. She smelled lemon cleaner and saw the polished dark wood floors and stairwell. She walked up to the first landing and put her tour bag down next to her. She had her bluetooth in her ear, the one Jolly gave her. She had programmed Sia's "Bird Set Free" to play on a continuous loop. The song made her feel brave.

She took out the notes she had written Jolly and Jack and along with a notecard with Johnny's name, his relationship to her, the rehearsal address and rehearsal space phone number, slipped in under her tour bag. Lenehan turned off their cell phones during rehearsal. The rehearsal space phone number was for emergencies. She had stopped at a gas station along the way and gotten a large Icee, cherry and cola flavored. She believed it would be easier to swallow the pills. She put that down on the opposite of where she had put the tour bag. She put her phone and bluetooth in the tour bag, and from the bag she took out all the items she had collected over the week from the band. The bottle of Norcos she took from Jack's; the Xanax Johnny gave her; the opium cube Chandler let her have. The fentanyl patch Benny had given her she had put on in the gas station bathroom a half-hour before. She hoped it worked quicker than he said.

She started with the Norcos. Two at a time, so she wouldn't vomit them up, she swallowed them with big gulps of Icee. She thought she swallowed about 20. When the last two settled in her system, she took all the Xanax at once. Almost choking, she kept talking big gulps of her frozen drink and persuaded herself to not throw up. She waited a few minutes, looking around the area. What a pretty building, she thought. She could imagine her great-grandmother Jarmila sweeping the stairs and front entryway.

Next, she took the opium cube. It was bitter but she chewed and swallowed it. By then she was getting dizzy, woozy. She felt her brain spinning but her body relax, as if she was falling into a deep sleep. She lay down between her tour bag and the empty bottle of Norcos. The Icee fell to the floor. The empty packages that formerly held the rest of the drugs were scattered on the stair below her.

She suddenly sat up. Behind her she could hear the voice of her "poppa", singing the old Irish ballad "Molly Malone". He used to sing it to her when she was little, when he would come home drunk in the morning, smelling of whiskey and cold. She would sit on his lap and tell her he didn't like the name Jarmila. It was too heavy a name for a child to carry. He called her Molly. He would sing the song to her, then her grandmother would bring him coffee that smelled a little like whiskey. He'd drink it, give Jarmila a kiss on the cheek, and leave again. She missed him.

The she heard a tune she had never heard before in a foreign language. It was coming from the front entryway. She turned and saw her great-grandmother Jarmila as a child, holding a broom in her hand, singing and dancing in the prisms of color floating in the air. Jarmila Bisnick the great-grandmother put the broom down and stretched out her arms to her great-granddaughter, Jarmila Malone. Jarmila Malone stood up and descended the stairs. She let Jarmila Bisnick embrace her. She had to leave life for good now. The dead were calling.

Saturday, June 1st, 2019, 6:15pm

Jack was late to tour rehearsal. Jack was always at least an hour late to everything. When he swaggered in at 6:14pm, none of his bandmates wanted to argue about his lateness. They wanted to start off the first night of the tour rehearsal of their first big venue tour with no negativity in the air.

"Where's Jarmila?" asked Jack, looking around the rehearsal space.

Jack saw a pink iced triple layer birthday cake on the table. It had "Happy Birthday Jarmila" written on the top in purple lettering. A pink candle numbered "23" stood up in the center. He knew the inside of the cake was pink, because that's what he had ordered. Birthday gifts wrapped in pink with white bows were piled around the cake. Jack put his present on the table near the others. Next to the gifts and cake was an empty punch bowl, and around that all the ingredients for rum punch. But where was Jarmila? Jarmila never missed a rehearsal, recording or gig. She was Lenehan's first and most loyal fan. She was never late to a Lenehan event.

"I offered to swing by and get her, but she said since she only lived two blocks away, she'd walk." answered Chandler.

Jolly's house was two blocks from the recording studio and two blocks in the opposite direction from the rehearsal space. In fact, Jolly planned on walking to the rehearsal space too, when the time came for Jarmila's birthday surprise.

"I haven't seen her since Monday." said Jack, "She came by da studio and asked if she could go to my house and borrow some books. I think she also "borrowed", without my permission, a bottle of Norcos and one of those special limited edition Lenehan t-shirts from da last tour, that Bella designed for us."

"I saw her on Tuesday," said Johnny, "at the gas station at Division and California. She had called me asking if I had anything to calm her nerves. She said she felt like her brain was spinning. I told her it's just her adjusting to living in permanent place. Having to get used to the new surroundings and living with Jolly as a couple. I gave her ten 2-milligram Xanax. I told her to be careful, that's powerful medicine. Then I dropped her off at Jack's. She also told me she was getting some books. She did call me this morning, saying she wanted to talk. But I fell back to sleep and didn't finish the conversation."

"She *did* borrow some books." Jack said, "She always leaves me a note about which ones she took. But I'm sure she took da Norcos from my bedside table, *and* one of those special shirts Bella made only for Lenehan."

"I saw her Wednesday, in Smith Park." said Benny, "She said she slept wrong and hurt her back. She wanted to know if I had a strong pain reliever that wasn't heroin. I gave her a fentanyl patch and told her to use it carefully because it would probably knock her out."

"I saw her on Thursday, at the studio." said Chandler

"And?" prompted Jack.

"We hung out, ate some food, talked about being gay. Then she saw my opium cubes and wanted to buy one from me. I'm like no way, because she's family. I gave her one."

"Why would she want all those drugs at once?" asked Johnny.

Panic slowly set in.

"Chandler, call Jolly, see if maybe she's still there." Jack said, "Maybe Methuselah is having trouble getting it up for her birthday fuck and making her late. I'll text Everett, see if maybe she is over there. He texted me earlier and said they had a gift for her. I figured we could stop by on da way to da clubs. But maybe Everett or L'Auvergne contacted her too, and she went over there to get da gifts. Johnny, call Les. It's a longshot, but anything is worth a try now. Benny, call Scottie."

"Seriously, Jack?" inquired Benny.

"I know it sounds crazy, but it's worth a try. Maybe he has a soft spot in his heart for people with birthdays." answered Jack.

"We should call Jolly." suggested Johnny.

"Good idea." said Jack., "I'll call him now."

Jolly was sitting nervously at his piano, mindlessly playing any melody his fingers led him to. He had put the big pink wrapped box next to him. His cell phone ringing made his heart skip a beat. Maybe it was Jarmila.

"Jolly, it's Jack. Is Jarmila still over there?"

Jolly's heart dropped to his feet. Jarmila would never miss a Lenehan rehearsal.

"She's supposed to be over there at 6:00pm, correct?" asked Jolly

"Yeah," answered Jack, "but she's not here."

It was apparent to Jolly that the boys didn't know about he and Jarmila's blow-up and how she had taken off, and not come home. Had not been home for over a week.

"I'm coming right over." said Jolly.

Jolly grabbed the pink wrapped box and walked quickly to the rehearsal space. When he arrived, he saw the cake on the table and the gifts and the empty punch bowl with all the ingredients for rum punch stacked beside it. He saw Jack look at a notification on his phone.

"Everett texted back and says she's not been there." Jack said.

"Scot says she hasn't been there either." said Benny.

"Les says he hasn't seen her since last weekend. She left his place Monday." said Johnny.

Jack got a funny look on his face. He was standing in the middle of the room, next to Jolly.

"Why would she spend da weekend at Les' place?" Jack inquired, staring straight at Jolly, "Huh, Jolly? Why would she be at Les' for da weekend? Were you there too? Was there a rat infestation at your house and you needed a place to stay for da weekend? Did you think, 'hey, Jack has a big house where there's plenty of room so instead let's go to Les' one bedroom apartment'? Benny's got a guest room in his house. Johnny does too. In fact, so does Chandler. But instead, you think it's better to stay in Les' small one bedroom? Why is that, Jolly?"

Jack got into Jolly's face and Chandler got in between them.

"There has to be a reasonable explanation," said Chandler, "right, Jolly?"

"We should sit down," sighed Jolly, "there is something I need to explain to all of you."

They sat around the table. Jolly told the tale in its entirety. The pregnancy. The fight. Her taking off and not returning home, gone for a week. Jack picked up the punch bowl and threw it, sending it crashing against a wall.

"I'm gonna kill you motherfucker!" Jack screamed as he lunged across the table at Jolly.

Johnny and Chandler held him back. Jolly moved toward the door, still holding the big pink box. The buzzer rang. Benny looked at the monitor and saw two police officers at the front door.

"It's the cops." said Benny. "Somebody answer the door."

"Hell no!" exclaimed Jack, "We've got enough drugs in here we'll never see da outside of a prison again."

"I'm sure they're not here for a search warrant." Jolly stated, "There would definitely be more than two police officers if they had a search warrant."

"Fuckin' fantastic!" screamed Jack, "You go answer da door, Jolly."

Jolly went out the rehearsal room door and down the long corridor to the front door. Benny continued to watch on the monitor.

"He's letting them in." said Benny.

"Jesus!" emphasized Jack, "Let's invite them to da rehearsal!"

Jolly stepped into the room, followed by two Chicago police officers, one short, one tall.

"They want to talk to Johnny." said Jolly.

Johnny inched forward slightly.

"Are you Johnny Dunne?" asked the tall officer.

"Yes." Johnny replied.

"Is Jarmila Agata Malone your sister?"

"Yes." Johnny quietly replied.

"Is this her ID?" asked the short police officer, showing Johnny Jarmila's ID.

"Yes. That's hers." replied Johnny.

The short police officer handed Johnny the ID and stepped back.

"I'm sorry to inform you that your sister passed away this afternoon." said the tall officer, offering Johnny some papers, "Please contact the Medical Examiner's Office for more information. The phone numbers you'll need and instructions on what steps need to be done next are on these papers."

Several things happened at once: Jolly dropped the pink wrapped box and fell into the nearest chair, Benny vomited and started shaking violently, Chandler and Jack simultaneously said "Wait, what?" and Johnny crumpled to the floor.

Alice gave a lift to Ma Dunne to Norwegian American hospital, where Benny and Johnny had been taken. Marie arrived shortly after with Chandler and Jack, followed by Scot and Everett. The hospital administrator put the group in a private family waiting room. Jolly paced outside the room, occasionally leaning against a wall.

Benny was given IV fluids and medications to stop the convulsions and vomiting. The effect was a deep sleep. In the ambulance on the way to the hospital, Johnny's heart stopped for a few seconds. Defibrillation brought it back to normal rhythm. A nurse came to the waiting room and told Alice and Ma Dunne they could come to the back and be with their loved ones. Marie asked if she could go with Ma Dunne, and the nurse agreed. Marie knew someone would need to sit with the lady who had been like a second mother to the band. Johnny was Ma Dunne's only child, all she believed she had left in the world.

Jack, Chandler, Scot and Everett sat in various chairs and couches. Jack jumped up and started looking all around the TV.

"How do you fuckin' turn this damn thing off!" he yelled.

Everett found the remote and turned the TV off. Jack sat next to Scot and tapped his shoulder with the back of his hand.

"See that motherfucker?" Jack said, pointing to Jolly pacing outside the room, "I'm gonna kill that motherfucker!"

"Jack, you need to calm down." replied Scot, "We don't really know what happened to Jarmila yet. The Medical Examiner has to determine that."

"Don't you fuckin' read anything?" Jack screamed, "Citizen App reports "Possible suicide of female at Ashland/Milwaukee." Which is near where Jarmila's great-grandma used to live. She fuckin' killed herself because that motherfucker got her pregnant and wanted to force her into an abortion."

"Jack, you don't know that's true. For now, that's hyperbole." replied Scot.

"Jolly told us da whole fuckin' story of da fight they had after they found out she was pregnant." Jack said, "How she took off. Where was she all week? Not staying at Jolly's, not at my house or Benny's or Chandler's or Johnny's. She stayed at Les' a few days and then what? Where did she go? When I saw her she didn't seem different. She didn't mention anything about being pregnant or having a fight with Jolly or where she was staying. She's always told da band everything. What changed? What did Jolly do to her to make her not want to tell us what happened? That motherfucker fucked her up and I'm going to fuck him up."

"Jack," said Chandler, "just shut the fuck up. Your screaming doesn't improve anything. Remember she got the drugs from us. You can't blame Jolly for everything. We need to retrieve those papers the cops were handing to Johnny. Maybe there's more info there."

"Where are the papers?" asked Scot.

"At the rehearsal space. Johnny dropped them when he fainted. We were all too much in shock to pick them up off the floor." Chandler replied.

"We'll get them later." Scot said, "Let's wait until we know everything is all right here first."

Jolly couldn't stand to hear Jack's screaming anymore. He decided to go to the cafeteria to get a coffee. On his way out of the cafeteria, coffee in hand, he ran into his friend, Odette, the OB/GYN who confirmed Jarmila's pregnancy.

"Hello Bill!" she said, giving him a slight hug, "How are you? How's Jarmila?"

"I'm okay." he answered, tears starting to form in his eyes.

"What are you doing here?" Odette asked, "Did something happen?"

"Jarmila has died." said Jolly, as the tears started flowing.

"Oh no, Bill! Come here, let's sit over here." she said, leading him to a table between vending machines, sitting down across from him. "Do you feel comfortable telling me what happened?"

"We had an argument, outside your office. I don't want children. My lifestyle is too erratic to raise a child. A parent should be in a child's life and I am on the road too much to fulfill that obligation. Jar knew I didn't want children. I'm not putting all the blame on her. I should have used protection. It was my responsibility, too. I said some cruel things to her. I told her I'd find a good abortion clinic. She said she didn't know if she wanted an abortion. She thought she may keep the babies. I told her that I would have nothing to do as the father. I'd be a sperm donor, that was it."

"Oh, Bill."

"She spent several days collecting various drugs and medications from the guys in the band she's been friends with since childhood. I don't have any other information. Except she's dead. The police gave one of the band members some papers, but they are back at the band's rehearsal space. That's where the police gave us the news. But I don't have any information. The drummer started convulsing and vomiting and the bass player fainted and I called 911." tears fell as Jolly continued, "I don't know where she was found or how she died or anything. The lead singer said Citizen App reported a female committed suicide near Ashland/Milwaukee avenues. That's where her ancestors lived when they first emigrated from Bohemia. What if that's her? *I just want to know what happened.*"

"Bill." said Odette, hugging him and then patting his back, "I am so sorry."

"I was going to marry her. She didn't know it. Today is her 23rd birthday. The band has a tradition that they spend all their birthdays together. I came up with a plan to marry her the next day, at the Formal Gardens in Humboldt Park. She said that was her favorite place. I had all the plans in place. I told the band and some of my friends, and they helped arrange everything. We did it all without telling her. It was going to be a secret birthday surprise. I was going to go to the rehearsal space on her birthday and spring the surprise on her. I already had the rings. I had already asked her to marry me. I had given her an engagement ring. She had told me if she ever got married, she wanted a dress like her great-grandma wore at her wedding in 1916. I found one similar online. She wanted the same outfit, veil, shoes. I had the veil and shoes made for her as I couldn't find that style online. I put the dress and shoes and veil in a box and wrapped it in pink, her favorite color. The band called and asked if Jar was home, and I said no, I thought she was with them. She never misses a Lenehan rehearsal, recording or show and she's never late. In my gut I knew something was wrong. When we had our argument, she threw the engagement ring at me. I was going to beg her forgiveness and return it to her. I'm such a fuckin' idiot!"

"Bill," said Odette, as she stopped patting his back, "we all make mistakes."

"The papers the police gave the bass player are still at the rehearsal space. I want to go get them. But I also don't want to leave unless I know the guys are okay."

"Let me call the ER. Their names?""

"Johnny Dunne and Benny Mann. Thank you." Jolly said, through tears.

Odette made a few phone calls. She put her phone in her white coat, and took Jolly's hand.

"Benny Mann is stable, but heavily sedated. His bloodwork came back positive for heroin, so they are being cautious with what treatment they give him. Johnny Dunne is stable. He's was up and talking, but they have sedated him now. His tests so far have come back good. No heart problem detected. The shock of losing his friend probably sent him into cardiac arrest. As soon as rooms are available, they will move them. Both need to stay at least overnight for observation."

"Thank you so much, Odette. I owe you."

"You do not owe me anything. I remember in school I was so geeky and awkward the girls were mean to me. You were very popular with the girls. You stood up for me on numerous occasions. It helped me get through my studies knowing I wouldn't get bullied."

"You're a nice person. I think those girls were jealous of your intelligence."

"Now, Bill, I have something very difficult to tell you. The preliminary exam by the Medical Examiner shows Jarmila committed suicide. She had traces of opium in her mouth. These things usually take time, the Medical Examiner has to do a full exam. But he says there will be no autopsy. From the police reports from the scene and his preliminary exam, he does not expect foul play, and will probably rule it a suicide. I don't believe you'll have to wait long for the Medical Examiner to release Jarmila's body."

Jolly put his head down on the table, sobbing, his whole body shaking. Odette ran her hand up and down his back.

"What about the babies?" asked Jolly, sitting up straight.

"Bill, the babies died along with Jarmila. The needed her to be able to stay alive."

"Oh God, what have I done?"

"Jolly, I think you need to see the grief counselor. I don't think you should go home like this. I don't think you should be alone right now. Do you have someone you can stay with?"

"Thank you for everything, Odette." Jolly said, as he stood up, "I've got to go. I have things I need to arrange."

Jolly went to the rehearsal space. It smelled like vomit and sweat. He went to the chair and retrieved the box he had left. He picked up the papers Johnny had dropped. Then he went to the table with the cake and sliced off a piece, putting it on a plate. He picked up the folded rum punch recipe, yellowed with age. The band's presents for Jarmila he left behind.

He went to his house and directly to his office. He followed the instructions exactly. He called Odette to see if there was a way for him to speak to the Medical Examiner at this late hour. She said she'd call him, explain the situation, and have him call Jolly back. Within ten minutes the Medical Examiner called him back. He explained he had put a rush order on the examination and it was completed. The examination along with the police reports showed Jarmila Malone had committed suicide on the landing of an apartment building near the Polish Triangle neighborhood. There would be no autopsy as clearly it was a suicide. A toxicology report found hydrocodone/acetaminophen, commonly referred to as Norcos, in her system, including fentanyl, Xanax, and opium residue in her mouth. That led him to believe she had access to edible opium. He ruled her death a suicide. His condolences, she was so young and he disliked seeing young people come through there. Blood test show she was pregnant. He asked Jolly how far along she was, if he'd care to disclose that information.

"She was only about 9 weeks." answered Jolly.

The Medical Examiner explained the next step. Jolly would have to pick a funeral home and the Medical Examiner's office would release the body to the funeral home, along with her personal effects. Jolly thanked the Medical Examiner and hung up. He had to gather his thoughts. He knew Johnny was in no position to plan a funeral. Benny either. Jack was in beast mode, and Chandler was too emotional to make rational decisions. He was Jarmila's fiancee. It fell to him to bury his bride.

Alvarez Funeral home seemed the nicest. There would be a large crowd, mostly music industry people, and they had the room to accommodate large crowds. The funeral director dealt with Jolly personally. They sat in a nice office, the director explaining everything. Jolly knew some things. He had buried his mother and father. Jolly wanted a pink casket with a white rose, even if it had to be special ordered. He wanted pink satin lining. He wanted whatever they had that would make it nice. He wanted chrysanthemums and peonies. The peonies he wanted her to hold. He had brought the birthday package with the wedding dress and veil, and he brought the engagement ring and wedding ring. He wanted her to wear all that. Even the pointed shoes. He didn't care how much it cost. He wanted the best for her. He arranged for the gravestone. He wanted it to read Jarmila Agata Malone Rogers, with her birth and death date. Then Sister, Wife, Mother, Friend in that order. Lenehan was close to her first; honoring them by putting sister first was the right thing to do, Jolly thought. Then he wanted toward the bottom William Bruce Rogers, Infant, and Jarmila Agata Malone Rogers, Infant, with their death dates under their names. He wanted angels carved by their names. He wanted the gravestone in pink granite. Large. Tall. The funeral director assured them they would provide a very memorable funeral and would get and do everything he requested. He gave Jolly Jarmila's personal effects. Jolly then texted Everett what was going on, and Everett informed everyone else.

Jack left the hospital as soon as Benny and Johnny were taken to hospital rooms. He said his goodbyes and headed toward his mansion. He was exhausted both physically from the tour and writing lyrics and laying down tracks. But the emotional pain of losing Jarmila caused his head to explode along with his heart. He lay down on his bed in a fetal position and cried. Through his tears he saw a pink ribbon stuffed into the side cushion of an armchair. He got up and examined it. It was Jarmila's. He knew because once when she was giving him head, he took it from her hair so her hair would fall loose. He took the ribbon and grasped it to his chest, crawling back into bed, resuming a fetal position, and sobbing great shaking sobs that wracked his whole body. He had lost her, forever.

Chandler sat in the family hospital waiting room. He couldn't move. Too grief-stricken, Marie comforted him as best she could. Everett and Scot had left, but L'.Auvergne stayed to help Marie and Chandler.

"I just saw her! I gave her that opium! I killed her!" Chandler cried

"No," said L'Auvergne, "if she hadn't gotten it from you, should would have gotten it from someone else. People who commit suicide are determined. They have a plan and stick to it. It was not your fault. Do not blame yourself."

She rubbed his back to comfort him while Marie hugged him.

Jolly returned to his BMW. He sat in the funeral home parking lot, in the driver's seat and put the big plastic clear bag of Jarmila's personal effects on the passenger seat. The rain came down in great big droplets, hitting the windshield, in rhythm to Jolly's tears. He opened the bag and took out the items one by one. Her tour bag, filled with a few clothes, a pair of sandals, an envelope with important papers like her birth certificate, and her purse. The clothing she wore he put to his nose and took in her scent, bergamot and cloves. It will never fill him again, because he was selfish. Her purse he opened and found the usual, Kleenex, lipsticks, make-up of various sorts, her great-grandmother Jarmila's wedding picture. Her Lenehan band laminate. A diamond necklace she never took off. Jack had given it to her on her 21st birthday. Jolly decided he would give it to the funeral director to put it on her. He didn't know why should would take it off. He didn't know a lot of things he wished he had answers to. Did he treat her too harshly with his rules and demands, with his corrections, with his obstinate nature? Was he trying too hard to change her childlike ways? The grief sometimes overshadowed the guilt, and sometimes the guilt made the grief harder to bear. He should have compromised, kept the babies, raised them and nurtured then and watched them grow. Jarmila's dream came back to him, laying in grass with sunshine and her with a big pregnant belly. He would rub his hands up and down and feel little William and little Jarmila kick. Now it was all gone. He was a fool. A complete fool who had lost the only person he ever loved.

He looked into the bag again and saw two squared pieces of paper. One was marked "Jolly" and the other "Jack". He put the one labeled "Jack" in his pocket and opened the one with his name on it. It read:

Love of my life,

By the time you read this I will be gone. I finally get to meet my great-grandma Jarmila, who I was named after. I went to the place she first lived because that is where my family got their start, where my ancestors started living in Chicago. It is a perfect place to end it.

I know you will be sad. I know your heart will hurt. I want you to hear my story, and take it always with you. The band were falling away from me. They are rock stars now and our relationships shifted. They didn't have time for me anymore. We used to go to amazing places, Garfield Park Conservatory, swimming at the city pools, Shedd Aquarium, Lincoln Park Zoo, The Field Museum. Skate and bike parks or just chilling on Oak Street Beach or North Avenue Beach. We had fun. Now it's all shows and interviews, meet and greets, girls and guys they hook up with, videos and recording and rehearsing. They don't need me anymore. They are what I knew they would become: Rock stars. They are soaring to new heights I am not able to fly to. I was going to kill myself before you came along.

You filled that gap the band left behind. I felt so different with you. Happy. Giddy almost. Like my heart had wings. You taught me what true love is. You guided me through sexual intimacy I had never known. You did things that made me feel good. You were calm and gentle with me when we were together having sex. I never had such a wonderful man in my life. I thank you for that.

But after your anger at me getting pregnant, I decided you didn't need or want me either. I was back to the situation I had with the band. They didn't need me anymore, no matter how much they said they loved me. They were going in a different direction and I felt I wasn't wanted along. Now you didn't want the babies, the babies you had a part in making. I felt all the burden was on me. I knew you didn't want children, but it happened. Your reaction surprised me. I wasn't sure about an abortion. I wanted to make a clear choice. I didn't want to be forced to abort. That is what I felt you were wanting me to do. That made me feel unwanted. It made me feel I was wrong when I thought you had filled the gap the band left behind. Truth is, I was excited hearing I was pregnant. I knew you were not. Your anger made me realize you did not want me or any part of me. These babies are a part of me. Now I have nothing. No one wants me. I am obsolete.

I obtained various forms of drugs from the guys. I lied, said I had back pain, nerves. Benny gave me a fentanyl patch and Johnny gave me Xanax. I stole Jacks Norocs and asked Chandler about those opium cubes he had. I asked him for one and he gave me one. They did not know my plans. I'm going to my great-grandma's first address here in Chicago, near Polish Triangle. I plan to go in the building, find a quiet spot, and leave for good.

I love you, Jolly. I think in Heaven I will still love you. You were my first love. My true love. I was so lucky to have such an incredible man by my side. I say farewell to you, and I hope you will always remember me.

Love, Jarmila

Jolly was now completely devastated. He had a part in Jarmila's suicide. He should have been more rational and talked things through with her, instead of insisting on an abortion. He was so used to ordering people around and having his way, he didn't think correctly about the situation they were in. It could have been worked out, for the best of them. Now, it's all gone. Her smile, her musical laugh, her endless conspiracy theories, her good heart and good soul. Her kindness to others who were unkind to her. It was over. He couldn't take it back. He couldn't bring her back. His heart was broken. He noticed her pink i-Phone her had given her. Her pink converse hi-tops she loved so much. He put everything back in the bag and drove home in the rain. He could barely see through his tears.

Johnny, awake, aware and talking, wanted to know from his mom what had happened. L'Auvergne has stayed by his side with his mom. His mom, too grief stricken to tell through her tears, let L'Auvergne explain. When she was finished, Johnny let out a soul wrenching cry of pain that didn't seem to stop. A nurse rushed in and gave him a sedative. They placed a heart monitor on him for cautionary reasons.

Benny was in and out of consciousness. What he did understand was that Jarmila was dead of an apparent suicide. But he didn't understand why. The hospital had put him on a regime of medicines to counteract the heroin. He would be released in a few days. Alice never left his side.

Late into the night Jolly lay on his bed. Thoughts and grief crowded his heart. This was something he couldn't fix. Notorious for fixing problems, this was something he was at a loss. Jarmila would never be by his side again. Memories flooded him and he shook with sorrow. Her cornflower blue eyes, he'd never see again. The softness of her blonde hair. Her scent of bergamot and cloves, and her hair that smelled like blackberries and lemonade. She was his sunshine. Yet he treated her harshly at times. He wished he could take it all back. Now where would his life go. On, he supposed. On with a forever broken heart.

Jarmila's funeral was scheduled for Saturday, June 8th, 2019. They should have been on their honeymoon, thought Jolly, Los Angeles then Las Vegas or Iceland or wherever Jarmila wanted to go. Jolly wanted to give her the world, Instead, he gave her a pink coffin with a white rose embedded on top. He gave her peonies to hold in her cold dead hands. He gave her a wedding gown similar to the great-grandmother she so lovingly talked about and always wanted to meet. Now she met her. Now she would know all those unanswered questions about her great-grandmother and hear the entire story. Jarmila was in Heaven dancing to Sia and Guns N Roses and Lil Peep, but not dancing in his arms.

The wake was scheduled from 4:00pm to 9:00pm. There would be an hour scheduled at 3:00pm for family viewing. The funeral would be the next day, at noon. Jolly had already bought a plot. It was in Bohemian National Cemetery. He found two plots next to Jarmila's great-grandmother and great-grandfather. He bought both plots. When he died, he wanted to be next to his Jarmila. His life. His soulmate. His heart. A notification on his phone brought him out of his reverie. It was a text from Everett.

Everett: Jolly, don't worry about the wedding arrangements. L'Avergne took care of all that.

Jolly: Thank you, my friend. It is one less burden on my heart. Please ask L'Avergne to save a piece of wedding cake for me. I already took a slice of the birthday cake. I want to put it with Jarmila. She can have it in Heaven.

Everett: No problem, bro. Do you want some company? I'd be glad to come over.

Jolly: No. I prefer to be alone now.

Everett: If you need me, I'll here for you.

Jolly: Thanks, my friend.

Alvarez Funeral Home was a beautiful building. Jolly was glad he chose this one. It had a good reputation and the people running it soothed people's souls. He needed a healed soul. It would take time, but it was a start.

At 3:00pm, on May 8th, 2019, Jolly, Jack, Benny, Chandler, Johnny, Ma Dunne, Alice, Marie, Everett, L'Auvergne and Scot came to say their final goodbyes to Jarmila. Scot wasn't sure if he should be included in the family viewing, but Jolly insisted. Scot had been his best friend for 20 years; his dislike of Jarmila wasn't going to interfere with the friendship he had with Scot. Scot was going to be his best man at the wedding. He was a part of the family.

Everyone but Jolly took a seat in the first row of chairs. Jolly approached the coffin first. Jarmila was dressed in the wedding gown he had ordered for her, and the custom headband veil. He looked down into the coffin and saw the pointed shoes he had ordered from Italy. Her stockings were white. She was holding peonies. Chrysanthemums surrounded the outside of the coffin. He noticed the engagement and wedding rings were on her finger. He wanted her to have that wedding ring. He considered her his wife. The diamond necklace Jack had bought her for her 21st birthday was around her neck. He carried a shopping bag, a pink one with handles. In it he had the two cakes, and the sepia wedding photograph of her great-grandmother Jarmila Bisnick who she was named after. It was immensely important to her to have been named after her great-grandmother. She talked about her all the time, although she never met her. Somehow there was a connection there he had wished he could have connected with also. If only he had more time with Jarmila. If only he hadn't been a fool.

He took out the photograph first and placed it on the inside lid of the coffin. Then he took out the slice of birthday cake and a plate. Taking the birthday cake slice out of the Tupperware container, he placed it on the plate. He then placed it on one side of her. He then took out the slice of wedding cake, and also took it out of its container and placed it on a plate. This he placed on the other side of her. He kissed her lips and told her she could celebrate her birthday and wedding together in Heaven. His tears fell onto her face. He took his wedding ring out of his pocket and put it on his finger. He kissed her on the lips again. Shaking, he sat down in the front row, next to Everett.

Jack was next to go to the coffin. He placed the leather pants, folded up, in the coffin. They were the ones Jarmila like so much. He'd never wear them again. He put her unwrapped birthday gift he got her in the coffin. It was a diamond bracelet that matched the necklace he had given her on her 21st birthday. He stroked her hair and kissed her face, and his heart leapt a little with joy at seeing the necklace he gave her around her neck. He told her Godspeed, and say hi to Shannon Hoon from Blind Melon. His eyes were filled with tears as he sat at the far end of the first row, as far away from Jolly as he could.

Chandler was supposed to be next, but wouldn't move from the chair. Marie comforted him. Benny went next with Alice holding him up. He put in a bag of Dum Dums to commemorate the tours and a bag of Green Apple Laffy Taffy, her favorite candy. Now she could have them forever. He also put in her unwrapped birthday gift. It was a pink Versace La Medusa handbag. She could open it in Heaven. He looked up at the sepia photograph. He kissed her on the cheek and told her at last she would meet her great-grandma.

Chandler finally got the courage to go to the coffin. Marie and Everett held him up. His legs were shaking, it was difficult to keep him upright. In her coffin he put in her favorite pair of red high heels. She'd need those for the endless party in Heaven. He put in the unwrapped birthday gift he had gotten her. It was a Gucci silver and green tiara headband. She had told him on numerous occasions that is what she wanted after seeing it online. He kissed her on the lips and stroked her hands. He noticed the engagement ring and wedding ring. He smiled through the tears. Jarmila would have wanted that more than anything, to be married to Jolly. She had done so much for Chandler, he regretted he hadn't done more for her. He had that serious talk with Marie that Jarmila had advised. That was the last day he saw his special girl. Had a meal with her. Stupidly gave her an opium cube, without going into better detail what she wanted it for. Because of Jarmila's advice, he and Marie were happier than ever. He wished he could share his happiness with her.

Johnny was the last band member to approach the coffin. It took Everett and L'Auvergne to hold up Johnny, and Alice and Marie to hold up Ma Dunne. Both were in deep despair. Johnny considered Jarmila his sister. He had lost a sister. Ma Dunne thought of her like a daughter. The idea that someone young with so much ahead in life would take their own life, perplexed Ma Dunne. She had spent every day at the church since she heard of the suicide. Prayer was her only consolation. Occasionally Johnny joined her. But mostly he lay in bed staring at the ceiling and asking how could a benevolent God take his only sister away from him. He felt God was punishing him for beating her, and disowning her. Even though he asked for her to be his little sister again, and asked forgiveness, it didn't take away the guilt of beating her. She had always been kind to him. Since she was 12, when her father and grandmother died, she shared every holiday dinner at the Dunne's. Now there would be an empty seat. He had the note she had written him on tour. The one that had 'heart of a lion and courage of your convictions'. What had he done to cause her to take her own life? He felt this was his fault. Grief and guilt absorbed him.

At the coffin, Johnny put in the folded paper with the recipe for rum punch. Jolly had given it to him, but Lenehan would never drink it again. He put in the unwrapped birthday gift he bought her. It was two bottles of her favorite perfume, Dior Poison. Ma Dunne put in a piece of Polish Honey cake, one of Jarmila's favorites. She told Jarmila she'd eat good in Heaven. And put on some weight.

Everett and L'Avergne went next. The said a prayer together, for the family to be healed of the bonds now broken. As parents, it was difficult telling their daughters about what had happened. But they knew they were old enough to understand. They had always been honest with their children. Their daughters were supposed to be in the wedding, and now they understood there would be no wedding. The decision to keep them from the viewing was one they tossed back and forth. In the end, the decision was to keep them from the viewing. Seeing their Uncle Jolly in the state he was in would be too much for the girls. Plus, they didn't think it would be a good idea to see their auntie-to-be dead in a coffin. They would bring them to the funeral service at the cemetery the next day. L'Auvergne put in two pink crocheted crosses her daughter had made for Jarmila. They both kissed her on the cheek and sat down.

Scot was last to the coffin. He said a Jewish prayer called "El Malei Rachamin", which specifically prays for the soul of the deceased. He knew Jarmila wasn't Jewish. But he believed Hashem heard all prayers no matter what denomination or religion people followed. He put her Lenehan tour laminates, from the first and second tours, in the coffin. Jolly had returned them to him, but he thought it better if they stayed with Jarmila. He sat down by everyone in the front row.

People started streaming in. Jolly and Johnny were head in the receiving line by the coffin. They shook hands and hugged and heard dozens of sentiments. The line was out the door and around the block. Some people waited in the parking lot. Music industry people, Lenehan parents and relatives, Les and other Lenehan security, venues staff and security, fans. Jolly realized this was mostly for him and the band. No one really knew Jarmila. They didn't know her kindness, they didn't know steamed broccoli was her favorite food. Or that Guns 'N Roses "Estranged" was her favorite song. They didn't know much about her because the band had kept her isolated. These mourners were mourning for Jolly and the Lenehan boys.

After some time, Jack and Chandler took over at the head of the reception line, and Jolly and Johnny sat down. Benny joined Jack and Chandler. Jack's mom and grandfather came up to offer condolences. Next were Chandler's mom and dad. His sisters and brothers and their children followed. There were music industry people next, including the man who produced their first two albums. Some fans were next, then Chandler's cousins and their kids. More music industry people and relatives came up to offer condolences. Jolly and Johnny replaced Benny, Chandler and Jack so they could rest.

The reception line seemed to never thin down, but eventually the last of those in line said their sympathies and final farewells. Johnny sat down but Jolly stood by the coffin. A few more people had come in. Jolly thought, Jarmila would be so happy, she loved sold out shows. This was a sold out funeral. People had to stand along the walls for lack of space. He saw his brother and sister and their kids arrive. They came up to him and both hugged them and cried. His nieces and nephews did the same. Then they took seats reserved for them in the front row.

Jolly started his eulogy. All of Lenehan, and anybody else who would like to, could say a few words.

"Jarmila Agata Malone was the love of my life." said Jolly, "Her laughter was musical. She saw the good in people. She was always willing to help. She loved to read and tried to read a book every two days. She had conspiracies theories that sent us all laughing. But I'd give my life to hear any of those again. The first thing I noticed was her cornflower blue eyes. When our eyes connected, I knew she was my soulmate. I kept denying it until love flooded my heart and I knew she was my one and only. I proposed to her on stage at the Vic Theater. It meant so much to me. Everything was arranged. Then she died on me. Why did you go away, Jar? Why did you leave me?"

His weeping made him unable to go on. Everett guided him to his seat. Jack went to the front of the coffin.

"Nobody else in da band wants to say anything." Jack started, "They are speechless with grief. So, I'll say words for all of us. Jarmila was our best friend and like a little sister to Johnny. She was family. We met her as little kids, and she had been a special part of our lives. When me and Chandler and Johnny and Benny started Lenehan, Jarmila always said we'd be rock stars someday. She was right. But now we won't get to share it with her. I hope in Heaven they got Billboard charts so she can see how we're doing, and know we're doing it for her. We couldn't have done it without her. She was our solid, our sister, our saint. She never missed a gig, rehearsal or studio time. She was our first and most loyal fan and will always be that to us. No one will replace her. No one could replace her. She was a unique, loving person people are lucky to have in their lives. She sacrificed much of her own personal self to make sure Lenehan would rise to the top. She believed in us, and when things didn't go right with the band, she would encourage us to continue with her determination that we would succeed. I don't know what we will do without her. We'll continue with Lenehan. She'd want it that way. But our broken hearts will never heal."

With that last sentence her turned to the coffin. He kissed her lips and cried.

"I'll always love you, my special girl." he wailed.

He sat down in the first row in the same chair he had first chosen, as far away from Jolly as he could get. He still blamed Jolly for Jarmila's death. But he also blamed the band for giving her those drugs. Because Jarmila stole the Norcos from his house, he didn't consider he had any fault in her suicide. Typical Jack, his ego superseded reality.

The repast was held at the Humboldt Park Boat house. The same place a week before, the wedding reception was to be held. That is what Jolly wanted. She was there in spirit, his wife, he felt it in his soul. Just because the wedding never took place, he would consider her his wife. He would consider him her husband. The guilt and grief still smothered him. But he would do his best to honor Jarmila Agata Malone Rogers' life. He could see the swan boats, gathered and tied up for the next day. He imagined Jarmila's spirit would be on one of those boats tomorrow. The crowd that gathered was so large they spilled out on the terrace. There were many tears, but laughter, too. Stories of Jarmila's conspiracy theories drew laughter. A story about how Jarmila got mad at Jack at a city pool. They were young teens then. She went into the men's dressing room and took all his clothes and his shoes and cell phone. Then she hid in a shower stall and while he was taking a shower, she stole his swimsuit and towel. Humboldt Park pool was not that far from Jack's parents' house, but it was embarrassing walking home naked. Chandler told a story about their first tour when he had locked himself out of his hotel room. Jarmila told the front desk that she had no clue who the guy who said he was Chandler Riley and who the guy was who said he was Lenehan's tour manager. She swore she was a big

Lenehan fan and these guys were imposters. It took Everett and Scot to clear up the misinformation. He thought that was okay. He'd find a way to get even with her. She'd occasionally pull pranks, but never wanted anyone to get their feelings hurt. She was a good heart, Chandler told those assembled

After consuming lots of food and lots of alcohol, the crowd dissembled, until it was only Lenehan, Jolly and Everett. Alice had taken Ma Dunne home. L'Auvergne took Marie home. She assured Marie that Everett would drive Chandler in his car home. Marie was concerned Chandler was too upset to drive. Jolly approached Jack.

"You are the last motherfucker I want to talk to." said Jack in a menacing voice, "I don't want to see your face."

"Jack, Jarmila left two notes. One for me and one for you. I'd like you to come over to my house at your convenience so I can give you the note." said Jolly.

"Why didn't you bring it here?"

"I wanted to give you the note in private. They found the notes with her body. None to the rest of the band, only you and I."

"I'll be by your house at 6:00pm tomorrow." said Jack, slinging back a glass of tequila.

The funeral was as sad as funerals are. The four Lenehan boys locked arms as the coffin was lowered. Johnny broke away and tried to crawl into the grave. Jolly grabbed him and held him tightly, as Johnny kept wailing about his sister.

Jolly was playing the Guns N' Roses version of "It's Alright", a Black Sabbath song. The window was open and a breeze from the lake was blowing in. In Chicago, in June, the nights could still be chilly. Just the right temperature to open a window and enjoy the evening air. The doorbell rang and Jolly stopped playing to answer the door. Jack, dour-faced and smoking a cigarette, stood on the front porch.

"Welcome to my home." Jolly said.

"Nice house." Jack said as he stepped inside and went directly to the piano room, "Holy shit, is that a WT Payne piano?"

"Yes."

"My grandpa would go apeshit if he saw that. It's hand painted, you know."

"Yes. I had to have it restored, but it's close to the original. Plays well too."

"I heard as I walked up. I didn't know you played piano." Jack said

"It's a hobby. I'm not very good at it. It relaxes me. Especially on beautiful nights like this. You're welcome to play it. Your grandfather too. He can come by anytime and play it. I'd like to hear him play. I've never had the chance. I hear he is phenomenal."

"Still plays jazz clubs sometimes. Best jazz piano player in Chicago." Jack said, sitting at the piano and playing randomly.

After a few minutes Jack stopped. He looked directly at Jolly.

"Where's da note?" he asked.

"I've got it in my office." replied Jolly, "Hey, would you like to stay and have a drink? Talk? Get all this shit we need to get out? Jarmila wouldn't want any bad blood between us. You know how she was. She didn't want any trouble to fuck up Lenehan's performances."

"True. She didn't like confrontation. Much, anyway."

Jack followed Jolly to the kitchen. Jolly reached into his liquor cabinet.

"I just got this Jameson 18-year-old Triple distilled Irish whiskey. Haven't opened it yet. Or would you prefer tequila? I got some Cazadores." offered Jolly.

"You collect good liquor like I do." Jack said, sitting down at the kitchen table

"Somewhat of a bad hobby. I drink too much of it!"

"I'd like to try da whiskey."

Jolly took out the whiskey bottle, two tumblers, a bottle of water and set everything on the table. He poured Jack a tumbler full and then himself one. He opened the bottle of water and poured a capful of water into the whiskey in his tumbler.

"My grandpa does that," Jack said, "but I don't know why."

"Brings out the aroma and flavor."

Jolly excused himself and went to his office to retrieve the note. He returned to the kitchen with the square folded piece of paper and gave it to Jack. Jack poured himself another whiskey. He opened the note and read it.

It read:

Dear Jack,

By the time you read this, I will be gone. I did not write to Johnny, Chandler or Benny. They will point fingers of blame and come to their own conclusions. They don't need a letter from me to do that. I want to let you know I did not kill myself because of the sexual torture you put me through. I did not like the things you did to me. The spankings and the anal sex hurt. When you asked if I liked anal sex, I only said yes so I wouldn't get you mad. I want you to know when you find out I killed myself, it was not your fault or the band's, or Jolly's or anyone else's. I wanted to kill myself for a while now. I am no longer needed by you guys. I've served my purpose. Lenehan are rock stars. You got to where I knew you would go. You are soaring and I am stuck on the ground. I am going no place. I feel like I am obsolete. You could tell me a million times you love me, but I feel it doesn't mean anything anymore. Remember when we used to go to The Lincoln Park Zoo? And Garfield Park Conservatory? I loved the Field Museum. I even remember going to Shedd Aquarium and how much fun we had. Skate parks and bike parks and running crazy through Humboldt Park, me riding on the handlebars of your bike. Now those adventures have been replaced by video shoots and interviews, studio sessions and rehearsals. Tours and lots of gigs. And so many meet and greets and fans who admire Lenehan and want to meet the band. You are going in a direction I can't follow. I am in the way. I would never stand in the way of your continued success. I want you and Lenehan to be the biggest rock band in the world. I know you will be. You'll do much better if I didn't hang on to you so deeply. I love you. You are my family. You took me in when I had no place to go. You and Chandler, Benny and Johnny saved me from being a statistic. I am pregnant with Jolly's twin babies. I don't know what their gender is yet, but I am deciding they are a boy and a girl. William Bruce and Jarmila Agata. They're going with me to Heaven, because they're still inside me. The three of us will finally meet my great-grandma Jarmila, who I was named after. I know you got bored with my stories of her. But that is where I belong. I always wanted to belong, just like she did when she was a child. Be kind to Jolly. I know you don't have the best relationship with him, but try and make it better. For me.

Love, Jarmila

Jack dropped the note to the floor and began a deep soul encompassing wail. Jolly held him. When his tears were spent and his voice a hoarse whisper, Jack sat upright.

"It was all my fault," he said, "it was all my fault."

"No, it wasn't." Jolly responded, "I know Jarmila would have never blamed you. I won't ask to read the note out of privacy, but if you want to talk about it, I'm here."

"I'm selfish. I should have asked you if you'd like to talk about da note you got from her."

"I'm okay. I can deal with what she said. But I'm here for you if you want to talk about it."

Jack poured another tumbler of whiskey, and topped off Jolly's.

"Somehow, Lenehan made her feel she wasn't wanted anymore. She felt obsolete." Jack cried, "I never wanted her to feel that way. I loved her. But I did things to her I shouldn't have done. I should have been better to her."

"You saved her life by taking her in when she had no place to go. That's a big thing, Jack. We all make mistakes we regret. I should have never demanded she get an abortion. I wasn't thinking. Regrets won't bring her back. All we can do from here on is do the best to honor her life. On the gravestone I ordered the words Sister Wife Mother Friend because I knew you had a relationship with her long before I met her. I put the babies' names on there too."

"What did you name them?"

"William Bruce Rogers and Jarmila Agata Malone Rogers. As far as I am concerned, Jarmila and I were married. I had her name engraved on the tombstone as Jarmila Agata Malone

Rogers. I hope you don't mind. I picked a large pink granite monument." Jolly said, drinking the whiskey in one long swig, then filling it up again.

"I am honored you put sister first. And thankful. That was kind of you. I like da gravestone you picked. I want to see it when they place it. It sounds like something Jarmila would want. She loved anything pink." replied Jack, "In the note she asked that I be kind to you, and you and I form a better relationship. I am a selfish prick who always wants his way. I admit that. But I'll try and make our relationship better."

"I'm a selfish prick who always wants his way. Maybe that's why we clash." Jolly said.

"We should be best friends then. Twin Pricks."

Jack and Jolly laughed.

"I don't like tour managers." Jack commented.

"I kinda figured that out." laughed Jolly.

"But I like you. You know your shit. You turned our tour around. It was a shitstorm before you got on." said Jack, "Truce?"

"Truce." said Jolly, extending his hand and shaking Jack's.

They drank two more tumblers of whiskey, and Jack said he had to go, the studio was one demanding bitch.

"I'm glad you're going over there. Jarmila wouldn't want you to stop on your path."

"It's uncanny how recording takes my mind off of Jarmila and yet still I am reminded of her."

"She'll always be with us in spirit." said Jolly.

Jolly escorted Jack to the front door.

"Come by anytime. Your grandpa is welcome too." Jolly said.

"You're welcome at my house. It's a nice house." said Jack.

"I've passed it by a few times. Spectacular. Boulevard house, right?"

"Yes. Built in da late 1800's, when Humboldt Park was full of wealthy Norwegians." said Jack, shaking Jolly's hand again. "Goodbye, my friend."

Jolly watched Jack as he got into a limo. Jack might be a pretentious twat, thought Jolly, but at least now they were friends.

Johnny fell into a deep depression. Music was his only way out. He practiced his bass guitar more and more, missing meals, missing showers, making his bass the only thing in the world that mattered to him. His beard grew out, which made his mom unhappy. She thought beards made a man look unclean. She cooked his favorite meals and found them left untouched outside his bedroom door. She didn't want to intrude on the rest of the band's grief. Perhaps Jolly could help. He always seemed like a nice man who was well organized. She hesitated contacting him, because she knew he must be in the deepest of grief. Losing the love of your life the day before you were to marry, and losing twin babies as well. He must be overwhelmed. She decided after much consideration to call him. She could offer support if needed, and possibly discuss Johnny.

"Hello, Ma Dunne," said Jolly as he picked up his cell phone.

"I not disturbing you?" she asked.

"No. I'm keeping busy working on financials and things for the next tour."

"I having trouble with Johnny."

That surprised Jolly. Johnny was the least trouble of Lenehan.

"What's going on?" Jolly asked.

"He stay in his bedroom playing his bass guitar. He don't eat, he don't sleep! He don't shave or shower! I do not know what to do, Mr. Rogers. You good with people. Maybe you can have a talk with him."

"I will be glad to. When do you want me to come over?"

"I do not want to disturb your work. Whatever time is best for you. Johnny needs help, Mr. Rogers. I know you can help him. He listen to you."

"Ma Dunne, you can call me Jolly. Or Bill. That is my given name. Jolly is just a nickname. I can come right over."

"Oh Mr. Jolly, thank you so much. God bless you. I say special prayer God bless you."

Jolly hung up the phone. He smiled at the thought that as far as Ma Dunne was concerned, "Mr." proceeded his name. He closed out the work he was doing and shut off his computer. He went to the garage and got in the BMW. Within ten minutes he was in front of Johnny's house. Ma Dunne answered the door with Gotti and Capone. She told the dogs to go sit in the kitchen, and off they went. Johnny had his dogs well trained. She led him upstairs to Johnny's room. She knocked and knocked but he wouldn't answer. Jolly pounded on the door until Johnny finally opened it.

"What?" he screamed, "I told you I don't want to be disturbed!"

When he stopped screaming and realized it was Jolly who had been pounding on the door, he became very quiet.

"You always scream at your mom like that?" asked Jolly.

"I…I…" Johnny stammered, "I'm not in a good place in my heart."

"You'll be a worse place if you keep treating your mom like that. Now apologize to her." Jolly scolded.

"I'm sorry Ma." he said, and gave her a hug.

"I leave you and Mr, Jolly to talk. Would you like something to drink or eat, Mr. Jolly? Perhaps you can get my Johnny to eat and drink."

"Not right now, Ma Dunne. Right now, I'm going to have a chat with Johnny, and then we'll be down after he showers and shaves."

"Good!" she exclaimed, "I cook you some sausage and potatoes with cabbage. Sound good?"

"Sounds delicious. Thank you very much." Jolly replied.

Ma Dunne went downstairs. Jolly pushed his way past Johnny and shut the bedroom door.

"You look like a fur trapper from the 1700's and smell worse. If that's even possible." retorted Jolly.

"Fuck off." responded Johnny.

"I am not going to sit around here and explain why you should not be acting like you are."

"Good. Then leave. I didn't invite you here."

"Johnny, everyone deals with grief on their own terms. It's been two weeks since we buried Jarmila. I know the hurt is still raw. But you can't go on like this. You have other people in your life who love you and you love them. Don't make them suffer. It's okay to grieve. But when it gets this bad, you need help getting through the process."

"Are you Dr Phil now?"

"Johnny, don't be this way. You are always the easiest person to deal with in this band."

"I *fuckin'* lost my sister! Do you want me to be happy about that?"

"No, Johnny. I lost her too. And my two babies with her. There's no happiness in this situation. But we can't let grief stand in the way of what Jar wanted for us all. To continue with our lives. For Lenehan to be the biggest rock band in the world. Grieve, but don't feel guilty in going on. It's what Jar would have wanted. It's what had always made her happy. Imagine her smiling down from Heaven at how you are honoring her life by going on with yours and your continued success."

"I failed her so terribly!" Johnny cried, "I hurt her so bad. I beat her. I physically *beat* her. I talked to a priest and he told me to ask for her forgiveness, and I did. And she accepted it! I'm a horrible person. I chose band loyalty over my sister! I held her down while they beat her so hard she cried and begged. I couldn't take it, I cried too! But when they all looked at me, I just went along with it. I hit her hard because I was angry. I can never take that back. I should have taken her place. I could have withstood the beating. Now I've lost her forever. She killed herself because I didn't protect her. I wasn't a good brother to her."

Jolly put a protective hug around Johnny. Johnny responded by putting his head on Jolly's shoulder and crying.

"Johnny," said Jolly, as Johnny sat straight again, "you were a good brother to her. Still are. Her spirit is still with us all. She'll always and forever be your little sister, just in a different place. She's with the person she always wanted to meet, her great-grandma. Yes, of course none of us wanted her to die. But she had this planned for a long time. Way before I met her. She told me in a letter she wrote me."

"Jack said she wrote him a letter, too. Why didn't she write me a letter? I asked Chandler and Benny and they didn't get any letters either. She didn't love us?"

"She loved all of you. You, she loved a little more deeply than anyone in the band." Jolly said, "I think she didn't write you letters because she felt you didn't need any. I can't explain it. Jack might know. You should ask him. You should *talk* to him. All four of you should talk. Get everything out, even if it's negative. I can be there to referee and ask Scot to be there too. I'll talk to the rest of the band and arrange a time, okay? But today, you need to shower, shave and change your clothes. Then you and I and Ma Dunne are going to have dinner. I know grief took Johnny Dunne away. But now Johnny Dunne needs to eat and sleep and do all those things Johnny Dunne always did. Okay?"

"Okay." said Johnny, as he went to take a shower and shave.

After a shower and shave, Johnny got dressed.

"Let's go downstairs. Ma Dunne has promised a wonderful dinner." Jolly said

Jolly and Johnny went downstairs. Jolly decided he didn't need grief counseling. Counseling Lenahan members seemed to help him through his grief.

Ma Dunne had prepared a feast that could serve 20 people. There was polish sausage and potatoes, cabbage and beans, mushrooms, cucumbers in sour cream, several types of bread, and butter and jam.

"That's a lot of food, Ma Dunne." Jolly said.

"I make extra, so you take home." she answered, "I make sure you eat good food."

"Thank you." Jolly said, kissing her on the cheek and sitting at the table.

"You a good man, Mr. Jolly." she said, "Look at Johnny. He look like my Johnny again."

"You don't mind if I steal him away in a couple days?" Jolly asked, "He really needs to get back to tour rehearsals."

"I don't mind at all, Mr. Jolly. My Johnny, he has lots of talent. God has blessed him with talent. God has blessed me with a wonderful son." she responded.

"He's been blessed by having a wonderful mom." Jolly said.

They dug into the food. Jolly had seconds. Ma Dunne tried to push more on him, but he said he had no more room. She sent him home with several packages of leftovers.

After Jolly returned home and put all the packages of leftovers away, he started to think about Benny and Chandler. He hadn't talked to Benny at all since the funeral, and he talked briefly with Chandler on the phone, who was too broken up to talk much. He decided he'd check on them in person. First, he texted Scot.

Jolly: Scot, we need to set up a time soon for the guys to get together and hash things out. I was at Johnny's. He was bad off, but I think I helped a little. I haven't heard from Benny at all. I had brief convo with Chandler over the phone. Jack came over to my house. Jarmila had written him a letter before she died. She wrote me one, too. She didn't write one for anyone else in the band, I'm not sure why. Jack has an attitude that it's not his fault because Jar took his Norcos without his permission or knowledge. Typical Jack, never his fault. Anyway, let's get them together day after tomorrow if that works for you. At the rehearsal space. Less chance of them destroying studio equipment.

Scot: Sounds great. 6:00pm work? Let's pull in Everett, he can be a calming presence to them. And back up security if it turns into a physical fight. Which it probably will. Let's call Les in too. I want to keep it insular, but I also want to keep it safe.

Jolly: Sounds good. I'm going to do a group text with the time and place. Mandatory meeting. Right now, I'm going to Benny's to check up on him, then on to Chandler's.

Scot: I'll loop in Everett and Les and let them know what's going on. How's Johnny doing?

Jolly: I got him to shower, shave and change clothes and when I left, he was still sitting at the dinner table with his mom. She sent me home with a ton of food. Do you want me to bring some to the meeting?

Scot: Absolutely. She makes the best Polish food on the planet. See you day after tomorrow.

Jolly: Sure thing. See you soon.

Jolly put his phone in his pocket and went to his garage. He got in his BMW and went to Benny's house.

Benny lived in a small bungalow across from Smith Park. Usually crowded with drug addicts or people doing recreational drugs and drinking. It was silent when Alice opened the door and Jolly stepped into the entryway.

"You know, I've never been in here. But I have heard it's usually brimming with a partying crowd." said Jolly.

"Not while I'm here." Alice stated, as she led Jolly to the front room. "Can I get you something to drink or eat? I'm afraid there's no alcohol in the house. I told Benny I won't allow it. Alcohol and heroin are a dangerous combination."

"No, thank you. I was at Ma Dunne's a little while ago. She made me gain ten pounds over there." Jolly said, "Heroin alone is a danger. You do know he does other drugs too?"

"Slowly I'm getting him to stop those. If he wants to marry me, he'll have to be clean from any drug for at least a year. Well, I compromised and said he could still smoke marijuana. I still do occasionally."

"I'm glad you are going to marry him. From the first moment I met you, I thought what a nice young woman you are."

"With pretty blue eyes."

"Alice Blue Eyes we nicknamed you. Are you coming out on the next tour? Are you going to Europe with us too?

"Yes. I am very excited about both. I applied for my passport. I've never been to Europe and can't wait! I want to show you something." Alice said, as she left the room and went down a hallway.

She came back with a ring box. Jolly's heart skipped a beat.

"This is the engagement ring Benny picked out for me." she said, opening the box and showing Jolly a beautiful oval shaped, 1 carat diamond ring in platinum, "Oh my God…I'm so sorry! That was callous and unthinking of me to show you this. I'm so sorry for your losses. I hope I didn't bring back anguishing memories."

"No, don't worry. All kinds of things remind me of Jar. I can't avoid everything." responded Jolly, "That is a beautiful ring. For beautiful Alice Blue Eyes."

"You are such a flirt, Jolly."

"I guess I am a bit of a flirt." Jolly chuckled.

"It's good to hear you laugh. We need laughter in this house."

"How is Benny doing? I haven't talked to him since the funeral."

"Doing a lot of heroin. But I've convinced him to slow down and stop on most everything else. How are you doing?"

"Trying my best to not lose my mind. I discovered talking to Johnny seemed to help a lot. Actually, talking to Jack helped some, too. Eases the grief talking to someone."

"Benny and I are always here for you if you need us."

"I've made some excellent friends from that tour." Jolly smiled, "Is Benny here?"

"Yes. He's in the garage sorting through old equipment. He's going to donate it to a local Chicago Public School. He says the band is getting new equipment for the next tour, so he wants to give something back to the community. He believes Jarmila would want it that way. She had a giving heart like that. Let me call Benny and tell him you're here. He'll be glad to see you."

Alice punched in Benny's number on her cell phone, and when he answered she told him Jolly was visiting. Benny said he'd be right there.

"Jolly!" exclaimed Benny as he walked into the room, hugging him, "I'm glad to see you!"

"I'm glad to see you. How are you?"

"I'm okay." he said, sitting down, with a far-away look in his eyes.

"I've been checking in with everyone, seeing how you all are holding up."

"I really miss her. I think of her all day long, every day. I second guess myself. I could have been kinder to her. Maybe she'd still be with us then."

"Her suicide had nothing to do with how you treated her." Jolly responded, "She had always told me how sweet and gentle you were to her."

"I don't understand why she didn't write me, Johnny and Chandler goodbye letters. We all loved her. I was certain she all loved us."

"She did love all of you. She wanted Lenehan to be rock stars. When you achieved that, she felt she had no purpose anymore. All those times you had before you became famous were replaced with things rock stars have to do. She felt you had no more time for her. She felt she was in the way."

"She wasn't in the way!" cried Benny, "She was our strength. Honestly, we couldn't have gotten as far as we have if it wasn't for her being our backbone. What are we going to do now?"

"You'll honor her life by continuing to keep going. Write, rehearse, record, go on that stage, for her. Imagine her in Heaven looking down and being so proud of how far you're going."

"It's tough."

"I know it is. But you have to go on with your life. If Jarmila could come down from Heaven and say one thing to you, what do you think it would be?"

Benny thought for a few minutes.

"She'd say, 'Get up on that stage and do it, Benny. You and Lenehan will play stadiums someday." he replied.

"Then that's what you need to do. Get up on that stage and trade rock stardom for superstardom."

"But how *are you* doing?" Benny asked Jolly.

"I'm managing as best I can. Keeping busy. I really want to break down, but I know Jar wouldn't want me to. She'd want me to go on and be the best tour manager to Lenehan, the best band in the world."

"I can hear her saying something like that! She had that upbeat attitude."

"I'm going over to Chandler's now. I want to check in with him."

"He's doing better with Marie. Jarmila gave him some advice, the last time she saw him. They seem a happier married couple now. But Marie told Alice that he cries himself to sleep every night because her misses Jarmila deeply."

"I'll see if I can bring him some type of comfort."

"What about you? You lost so much, you probably could use some comfort, too." commented Benny.

"Strangely, talking to you guys brings me comfort. She was very close to you. I feel I'm beginning to understand her more through talking to you. That brings me solace. Day after tomorrow is a mandatory band and manager meeting at the rehearsal space." Jolly said as he stood up.

"I got the text." Benny said, "I'll be there."

Benny and Alice stood up and each gave Jolly a hug.

"If you need *anything*," said Alice, "do not hesitate to call or come by."

"Thank you." Jolly replied, as he walked out the door.

Next was Chandler's. Jolly had spoken briefly on the phone with him, but the conversation was cut short by Chandler's grief. He parked his BMW on Thomas Street, a few houses west of Chandler's. He walked up the stone steps and rang the doorbell. Marie answered.

"Jolly!" she exclaimed, "It is so good to see you! Come in!"

She opened the door completely and Jolly entered the foyer.

"How are you?" she said, hugging him, leading him to the kitchen, "Can I get you something to drink? Eat?"

"No, thank you. I was at Ma Dunne's a few hours ago and she made a super spread of food."

"Ma Dunne always makes enough food to feed a battalion. Did you know she gives away the leftovers to a homeless shelter?"

"I didn't know that. But charity seems to run in the family. I heard Johnny goes every Christmas to the city animal shelter and drops off a truckload of donations."

"How are things going with you?"

"I'm holding on."

"If you need anything, don't hesitate to ask."

"Thank you. Is Chandler around?"

"Oh yes, he's in the garage, writing some new music. I'll call him in."

"No, it's okay. I'll go to him. I'd like to see how the writing is coming along."

Jolly kissed her on the cheek and went through the back door to the garage. Chandler had set up the garage as a mini recording studio. He was seated in his favorite chair, right next to a blue painted table. On the table was an opium cube, a half full bottle of Cava de Oro Extra Anejo tequila, and empty glasses next to a half full one.

"I hope you're not mixing that opium with that tequila." commented Jolly as he entered the garage.

"Jolly!" shouted Chandler, "Pull up a seat. I got some great tequila here."

"Looks like *very* good tequila." said Jolly.

"Grab a glass and pour yourself some." responded Chandler, "And no, I'm not mixing it with the opium. That's for later so I can sleep and not have nightmares."

"Lots of nightmares, Chandler?" asked Jolly, pouring a glass and sitting down.

"Every time I close my eyes. I was the last one who saw her alive. I gave her a damn opium cube. I didn't even ask her why. I fuckin' killed my best friend."

"That's not what killed her. It was not your fault. She took a large combination of dangerous drugs. *That's* what killed her. You cannot blame yourself. None of Lenehan can. She felt she wasn't needed anymore. All her life she wanted to belong, and with you guys she finally found a place to belong. But with your rise to stardom came a shift in your relationship with her. The time she spent with you before you became famous was not there anymore. It had been replaced by things required for the band and the band's success. You didn't do anything to make her think she wasn't needed. That was the idea she formed in her mind long before I was hired."

"But I don't understand! I loved her! Things did get hectic when our albums and singles starting hitting the charts. But if she had told me she felt left out, I'd have dropped everything for her!" Chandler cried, standing up Lucille on the side of the table next to him, "She saved my marriage. She saved me! The last talk we had she came by the studio. We had a meal together. She convinced me I needed to own my truth. I'm gay. She gave me the best advice. To own my truth and not to give a rat's ass what my family thinks. She told me to have a sincere conversation with Marie. I did, and our marriage has never been better. Marie accepted me as I am. She always has, but now she knows that I own who I really am. We came to terms that makes our marriage awesome. And we're going to have babies someday, hopefully soon. Lots of babies!"

"I suggest you put the drugs and liquor in a place where your future kids can't get to them."

"Shit Jolly, that was super insensitive of me." Chandler said, "I'm so sorry. You lost your love and your babies. I don't know what to say to console you. Like, there's no words for that type of loss."

"It's okay. I know you didn't mean it in a hurtful way. I'm delighted you and Marie have worked things out. She's an outstanding woman. Especially, to put up with your insanity. Anyway, I wanted to check up on you and make sure you're doing okay. It's a tough time for all of us. But you know, Jar would have wanted Lenehan to continue on this shooting star path you're on. It's a good way to honor her life. There's a mandatory band and manager meeting at the rehearsal space the day after tomorrow at 6:00pm. Les will be there too. Because we know how volatile Jack can be."

"He's always been that way. Even when he was a kid. Used to get into all kinds of fights. His mom is fierce. She'd whoop his ass practically every day. Didn't seem to have any effect on him. But he's still like a brother to me. He's still my best friend. Even when we're trading punches and screaming at each other, he's always been there for me. We're all hurting, intensely, from the loss of Jarmila. But I think he'd be the last to admit how much he's really mourning."

"He's Jack Connelly, greatest singer ever, he'll never admit there's anything perceived as weakness about him." declared Jolly, "I need to go home. See if I can get some sleep. Thanks for the tequila. Great stuff. You should request that on the next tour's rider."

"I will!" exclaimed Chandler, "Jolly, if you need to talk, I'm here for you. You have to talk about her death, too. I can see how you and Jarmila got along so well. You've got a virtuous heart just like she did. Always making sure everyone was okay. Always putting her own feelings aside for the good of others."

"Thank you." Jolly answered.

He stood up and put the empty glass on the table. Chandler stood and hugged him.

"You're family, Jolly. I am honored for that."

Jolly and Jar were dancing in the Humboldt Park Boathouse Pavilion to Ed Sheeran's song "Perfect". Jolly had picked it for their first dance as a married couple. Lenehan was the wedding band. Jolly was wearing a black morning coat, a white shirt, light pink vest, and grey trousers that matched a grey tie. Jar was dressed in the 1916 wedding gown, the handcrafted wedding headband, the pointy white shoes Jolly had specially made to match her great-grandmother's wedding shoes, and the diamond necklace Jack gave her for her 21st birthday. On her wrist was the diamond bracelet Jack gave her for her 23rd birthday. On her ring finger was her engagement ring and wedding band Jolly had bought in New York City. He wore his wedding band. They were dancing alone with all the guests surrounding them. When the song came to certain lyrics, Jolly bent to Jar's ear and sang them.

"Well, I found a woman, stronger than anyone I know

She shares my dreams, I hope that someday I share her home

I found a love, to carry more than just my secrets

To carry love, to carry children of our own

We are still kids, but we're so in love

Fighting against all odds

I know we'll be alright this time

Darling, just hold my hand

Be my girl, I'll be your man

I see my future in your eyes

Baby, I'm dancing in the dark, with you between my arms

Barefoot on the grass, listening to our favorite song

When I saw you in that dress, looking so beautiful

I don't deserve this, darling, you look perfect tonight."

    Jolly woke up in a cold sweat. The dreams alternated between two. One was the wedding dance. The other was he and Jarmila laying on the grass in his backyard in the sunshine. She was wearing one of his t-shirts, and he was running his hand up and down her big pregnant belly. The babies kicked and he smiled at Jar's musical laughter. Those two dreams plagued him anytime he tried to sleep. He sat up on the side of his bed and took two Ativan Everett had given him. Everett always had the finest prescription drugs. It was no wonder between the prescriptions and the weed, he was so calm.

    He took his cell phone from the end table and saw it was 5:00am. He'd be up in a couple hours anyway, he thought, trying to stay as busy as possible. Anything to not sit around and mourn. Jar would consider that interfering with his work. She'd say 'Promise me I won't interfere with your work'. He'd always keep that promise to her. But every thought he had was of her.

    He stood up and got dressed in blue jeans and a plain white t-shirt. He turned and looked at Jar's closet. It was dark. He missed her musical laughter as she insisted he help her pick something to wear, and he'd sarcastically tell her that fashion was not his thing, she should go ask Chandler. The things I could have done, he chided himself, the things I regret I can't get back.

    Jolly went into the closet and turned on the light. So many clothes. He had built her a wooden shoe rack that went from floor to ceiling. So many shoes. He opened the dresser drawer and saw all the contents. A memory came to him, of Jar wanting to give some of her clothes to local non-profits. She wanted to give back to the community because Chandler let her take his families used clothes from the charity box in their garage. Jolly remembered Jar saying that's why she had designer clothes: One of Chandler's sister's bought designer clothes and wore them once or twice and put them in the charity box. He thought about the Chicago non-profits she talked about. Her three favorite ones were: Blocks Together, and organization that helps young people with legal issues, job searches, and had youth groups within their organization that helped the community; Humble Hearts, an organization that collects food and other items for the homeless and for pregnant women and women with children; and The Healing Corner, that began as an idea to start up conversations with the young men and women street gang members who hang around corners and sell drugs. It expanded to events with free food, household and hygiene items, gun locks, etc. The organization helps get students school supplies, and helps families in need, while still continuing the mission to talk to Chicago youth about opportunities and resources.

He decided he'd keep a few items. Her shoulder bag, that carried so many of her important things. Her tour bag. The black Louboutins he liked so much. He looked through her dresses and picked a few out that were his favorites. He kept her light blue capri jeans, and her pink Converse High Tops. He'd keep all the lingerie. He decided eventually he'd put them in a storage bin and set them at the bottom of the closet. For now, he'd keep them in the drawers Jar had meticulously put them in. There were a few items of lingerie she had hung up next to the dresses. He took those down and put them in the drawer with the rest of it. He went through her skirts she had hung up. Finding nothing he wanted to keep, he went on to where she hung up her shirts. He had already been to the drawers that held some of her shirts, but had not looked through the ones she kept on hangers. He found a few he liked and put them on the pile of the items he was keeping. He'd split the rest between Blocks Together and Humble Hearts. Blocks Together had yard sales to collect donations to fund their programs. They could get good money with the designer clothes. Humble Hearts always had people in need of clothing. He'd buy some plastic bins and load up everything he didn't want to keep. He felt Jar's spirit right next to him, giving him the go-ahead to give back to the community by giving away her clothes. Jolly would make a monetary donation to The Healing Corner. Taking the "keep" pile out of the closet, he put everything on his bed. He fell asleep next to it.

His cell phone woke him up. He noticed it was twelve noon. Ativan, knocked him right out. He answered the phone. It was Scot.

"How are you, my friend?" Scot asked.

"Not well. Trying to keep it together. Ready for a mental breakdown any time now." Jolly answered.

"Meet me at our spot on The Riverwalk."

"Right now?"

"Yes now. It's my fuckin' lunch hour."

"Give me 45 minutes. I just woke up and need to get ready."

"See you then." Scot said.

Jolly stood up and stretched his back. He had slept in an unusual position, half on the "keep" clothes pile, one leg dangling to the floor. He went to his bathroom and washed his face. Back in the bedroom, he changed his clothes, then sat at the dressing table and brushed his hair. Memories crashed into him; Jar, sitting on his lap while he brushed her hair. Tears trickled down his face. He took two Kleenex and wiped his face. That simple act reminded him of Jar and her seasonal allergies. Would there be a time when he could stop thinking of all the wrongs he had done to her? Would there be a time when he'd stop questioning himself, drowning in "what ifs"? What if he had accepted the pregnancy and been happy that she was happy? Would she still be here? In her letter to him, she said she had been thinking of ending her life for some time. But she also said he was the gap she needed filled that she felt she was losing with the band. Did his reaction to the pregnancy send her over the edge? He was such a fool, losing the one person in his life who made him the happiest man alive.

He sat back down on the edge of his bed. On his cell phone he pulled up The Healing Corner website and clicked "Donations" and donated money in memory of Jarmila Agata Malone

Rogers. He emailed asking them if they could honor Jarmila's memory in some way. He explained Jarmila was his newlywed wife and she and their twins had passed on recently. He wrote that Jarmila often talked about The Healing Corner and the good they do in the community. Jolly left his phone number in case they needed anything else, and not to hesitate to call.

He then went on Amazon and found the page for Chicago Animal Care and Control. That is where Johnny took a truckload of items for the animals every Christmas. It's where Johnny saved Gotti and Capone's lives by adopting them one Christmas. Jolly loved dogs and so did Jarmila. He ordered enough to fill a truck. Then he wrote a note asking that his donations could be in memory of Jarmila Agata Malone Rogers. He explained they were newlyweds and she and their twins had passed on recently. She had loved dogs. He then paid the adoption fee for every adoptable dog and cat there. He might be seeing his retirement account dwindling, but at least it was in dedication of Jar's life.

Jolly clicked back to the home screen on his cell phone and called the car service. No way was he going to try and find parking along Chicago's Riverwalk area. He saw Scot sitting at their usual table at the outdoor seating of their favorite café. He approached and took a seat.

"You're late. I only have a lunch *hour*." scolded Scot.

"Jesus," responded Jolly, "you own your own company now. You could have a lunch week if you wanted to."

"I shouldn't be giving you shit at a time like this. Bad habit."

"I'd think something was wrong with you if you didn't give me shit once in a while." responded Jolly, as he ordered a coffee from the waiter.

"Not ordering lunch?" asked Scot, ordering himself another coffee.

"Not very hungry. And you?"

"Already ate, waiting for your lazy ass to get here." Scot teased, "I wanted to see how you are doing. I had heard you have been helping Lenehan get through their anguish."

"It helps to talk to someone else about Jar's death."

"You should be talking about your sorrow to someone. Talking about how you are dealing with things." Scot suggested, as the waiter brought the coffees, "You're not in a good place to be playing therapist to everyone else."

"Physician, heal thyself."

"Something like that. Do you think you need a professional to talk to?"

"I don't think so. I'm doing what I can to stay sane. I went through Jar's clothes, kept what I wanted. I'm going to split the rest between two local non-profits. I made a donation to another of her favorite local non-profits. I also donated a truckload of supplies Chicago Animal Care and Control needed for their animals. That made me feel better. Jar would have wanted that."

"Still, you should consider talking to a professional. A therapist or grief counselor." Scot recommended, taking a sip of coffee.

"You know I'm not comfortable doing that. I like to solve problems on my own."

"This "problem" has no solution. She's deceased. There's no way to solve that. No way to bring her back. You need to face this. You can't fix this. You can't hold in that despair. I know I was horrible to her. I feel profoundly guilty. There is no excuse as to how I treated her. I feel genuinely remorseful. But I can't live in regret. All I can say is I am very sorry for the way I treated her. Please forgive me."

"What was that prayer you said over her in the casket?"

"A Jewish prayer for the dead."

"That was forgiveness. I don't blame you for anything. I'm not angry with you. 20 years, our friendship has been through many trying times. This may be the most trying time since the loss of my parents. I actually feel ashamed that I am experiencing a deeper grief for Jar than I did for them."

"Jarmila was your soul mate. It's like losing a part of yourself. You shouldn't feel ashamed at that. If I had lost my future bride the day before my wedding, and our twins, most assuredly my body would be found in the Chicago River. You've always been a strong person. You're a bit of an asshole, but remarkably strong. Your strength will help you to a great extent. But if you feel you can't go on, please call me. Let me help you find someone professional who can help you get through this. Promise me this, my friend."

"I promise." Jolly said, "I have to go now. The monument company has almost finished her gravestone. Their usual standard is to wait six months for the ground to settle before placing the gravestone. I want it placed as soon as it's done. I'll take the chance it could fall over or settle wrong. I want that gravestone up before the next tour. I know I won't have closer until it is up. I have to go to LA soon and meet with the label. I tried to reschedule but apparently losing your wife and babies is no excuse to miss a meeting."

"Nothing stands in the way of that label making money. And Lenehan is making them money. Still, I have no idea how we're going to get four grieving band members on a plane to LA so soon after such a profound loss."

"Private plane."

"Jack would be early for once. He's always bitchin' about not having a private plane."

"We'll discuss it with them tomorrow." Jolly said, standing and shaking Scot's hand, "I'll see you tomorrow at the rehearsal space at 6:00 pm."

"Wear your riot gear!" Scot laughed.

"Most definitely!" Jolly retorted.

Jack Connelly made his usual grand entrance late. Nearing 7:00pm, the band was getting restless. It was like entertaining a bunch of toddlers. Everett kept Johnny and Chandler busy with a catalogue of bass and guitar equipment. Les tried to convince Benny to hold off on the heroin until the meeting was order.

"Ya know what I hate?" asked Jack, walking in, sitting on an arm chair and lining up cocaine on a nearby end table.

"Being on time," quipped Jolly, "meet and greets, touring, mandatory band meetings."

"You're a fuckin' mind reader!" exclaimed Jack, snorting two lines.

"Listen," said Scot, "we called you all tonight for a meeting strictly about Jarmila. Let's talk like adults about our feelings, our loss, our grief and whatever we need to do to clear the air and continue on Lenehan's path to tremendous success. It's not selfish. Jarmila would want you to continue on. We have to talk all this out, get back on the same page again. We've got rehearsals for this coming tour. Ticket sales look like we'll be adding dates and selling out shows. Jarmila would have been ecstatic. She loved sold out shows."

"The first show of the tour was always her favorite." said Johnny. "Now she won't be there to enjoy it. It's your fuckin' fault, Jack. You and your stupid rules for her and the beatings. She was an adult. She didn't need to be treated like a child."

"As I recall, you agreed on those rules. I recall we came up with those rules together." coldly said Jack.

"I know what you did to her after you punished her." Johnny accused Jack, "She told me. You forced her into anal sex. She hated it, but did it because she thought she had to, to stay your friend."

"What I did in private with Jarmila was none of your business. You didn't know how to handle her. If it was up to you to take care of her, she'd be dead a long time ago." Jack sneered.

Johnny stood up from where he was sitting at the table and moved toward Jack, who was seated on the couch. Les stood in front of him.

"You fuckin' killed her because of the way you treated her!" Johnny cried.

"You don't know shit, Johnny." said Jack, "you act like you know shit because you think you're her brother. But your motherfuckin' Oedipus Complex ass didn't get a letter from her. I did. She wrote that none of us is at fault. She felt she didn't belong anymore. That we had gone to where she wanted us to be. To be rock stars. She felt obsolete. I think no matter how hard we would have tried to change her mind she still would have felt that way. Things have changed for us. She couldn't deal with that. She felt she was no longer a part of us."

"She would have always been a part of us." Benny said quietly.

"Of course, she would have!" exclaimed Jack, "But she didn't feel that way anymore. We didn't do anything to make her feel that way. It was just the way things are going for Lenehan.

Sold out shows, tons of fans, and all the stuff we gotta do because we're rock stars now. Jarmila couldn't deal with the fame. She didn't think she could share in our fame."

"She's the reason we are where we are." said Chandler, "She was the reason we have that fame."

"She didn't see it that way," said Jack, "she thought she was no a part of what was happening to the band."

"I wish she would have said something. I know I could have convinced her otherwise." Chandler said.

"She did say something." Jolly cut in, "She said something similar about Lenehan not having time anymore for her because now there's so much to do. Shows, interviews, fans, etc. She felt left out. I assured her you were and always would be her best friends. I told her things have changed for sure, but she'd get used to this new rhythm of things."

"She said something to me also." said Everett, "I told her she'd find her purpose within the band again. It would just be a different type of purpose."

"It doesn't matter what she said, or the assurance she was given." said Scot, "She believed she had no reason to live anymore. When people set their mind to suicide, it's difficult to change it. No one is at fault. No matter what you were to say to her, she probably would have killed herself anyway. You need to grieve. It is healthy to grieve. In fact, it's a necessity so that you can go on with your life."

"I should have taken her place at the beating." Johnny said.

"Oh, here we go again about us beating her." Jack said caustically, "Round in circles with you Johnny. You want a beating? Would it make you feel better? Then drop your pants and bend over and I'll gladly beat you. It won't bring Jarmila back."

"You're a sick fuck, Jack." said Chandler, "We're all like brothers, we're family. Why would you say something that stupid?"

"To point out the fact that nothing we do will bring Jarmila back. We can sit here until the next tour saying 'I shoulda did this' or 'I shoulda done that'. But none of that would have prevented her from killing herself. Her mind was made up."

"I just want to know why I didn't get a letter." Benny inquired, "I want to know what she said. She wouldn't leave me out. She must have said something about me, or Johnny, or Chandler. I *know* she loved us. Why did she leave us out?"

"Okay, Benny," said Jack, "although my letter was private, as well as Jack's, I'll share something with you. She said she didn't need to write you or Johnny or Chandler goodbye letters because you'd point fingers of blame and come to your own conclusions. She was right."

"She knew us well," said Chandler, "right down to our favorite flavor of pop. That was something she said the last time I saw her alive. She could name our favorite pop flavors. She knew us better than we know ourselves."

There was a silence in the room, as everyone dwelled on what Chandler had said.

"The best thing Lenehan can do for Jarmila is memorialize her life. Go on and become the biggest band in the world. Write songs like you always do, songs that make people fanatical and pack venues and make you multi-platinum artists." Jolly said, "Slam music charts so there's less room for any other artists. Do what you always do: be the wild and crazy and insane and out-of-control Lenehan boys you've always been. Do it for Jarmila."

"I scrapped the song I was writing about her." Jack said, "I'm writing a new one."

"That's amazing, Jack," said Jolly, "now get back to rehearsing. We have a trip to LA on June 26th for Lenehan to meet with the label. Then on June 29th, we're going to New York City to meet the new people the management team hired."

"I hate flying." complained Jack.

"We're hiring a private plane for both trips." responded Scot.

"Did I mention I love flying?" laughed Jack.

"One more thing," said Jolly, "on a more somber note. The installation of Jar's gravestone will be next week. How does the idea of a memorial at the gravesite sound to you all? Just me and Lenehan? I know it sounds selfish to only include us, but I hope Everett and Scot and Les, that you'll accept that."

"It's totally acceptable." said Les, "You and the boys were the closest to her,"

"We can visit her grave anytime." said Everett, "I would actually like to take L'Auvergne and our kids and make a family picnic of it. I know it will help my daughters understand the whole process of death and how to pay tribute to that person's life. Jarmila would have loved a picnic."

"She certainly would have." agreed Jolly.

"I'll visit another time and say a prayer over her tomb." Scot said, "There is one called Kel Maleh Rachamim which translates to Prayer of Mercy."

"Thank you, Scot," said Jolly, "you're a good friend. Is this Saturday a good day for Lenehan? I don't want to interrupt your rehearsals or any studio time."

"We'd drop anything for Jarmila." Johnny said, gently.

"Then let's make it 2:00pm Saturday." Jolly said, "And Jack, don't fuckin' be late."

On Thursday the gravestone was installed. On Friday, Jolly went to it. He carried with him a bag and Jarmila's iPhone. He had kept it to look at all the pictures she had taken. There was the first one she had taken of them together. He had that printed out, framed, and hung on the wall of his home office.

The gravestone was beautiful; tall, pink granite. The words JARMILA AGATA MALONE ROGERS were printed near the top. Then, beneath that, her birth and death date. SISTER

WIFE MOTHER FRIEND were underneath that. Lyrics from Jarmila's favorite song, "Estranged", by Guns N' Roses were below that.

"I'll never find anyone to replace you

Guess I'll have to make it through, this time-

o this time

Without you."

Beneath the lyrics, on the left-hand side of the gravestone, was the name WILLIAM BRUCE MALONE ROGERS, INFANT. Jolly had to decide whether he wanted just one date, the death date, or put the same date twice, representing birth and death. True, the babies didn't get a chance to be born. Jolly decided on the words "BORN AND DIED JUNE 1ST, 2019. On the right side, the same words and date were underneath JARMILA AGATA MALONE ROGERS, INFANT. Two angels graced the sides of both names.

Jolly sat down and took a styrofoam food container out of a shopping bag and place it on her grave. He chose to play Guns N' Roses "Estranged" on Jarmila's iPhone. He gently placed it on her grave. While the song was playing, he opened the food container. It held a turkey club sandwich with extra bacon and thick cut fries. He put a Diet Coke next to the container. These were her favorite foods, her favorite sandwich and favorite pop.

"Rest easy my one-and-only. My soulmate. I know in Heaven you must have an unlimited supply of Green Apple Laffy Taffy, Dum Dums, Flamin' Hot Cheetos and Vitners Hot Corn Chips. There's probably no kimchi in Heaven. Heaven is filled with all those things you liked so much that I constantly scolded you for. I wish I could take that back. I wish I held you more and scolded you less. You were you, and that included Cheetos dust and sharing Dum Dums with the band. Forgive me for any harsh words I had toward you. I loved you more than life. You were the first time I felt real, true love. I'm sorry I threw that all away. It's true, that saying, 'You never know what you've lost until it's gone'. When you took your last breath, all alone there in a stairwell, my heart went with you. It's still beating, but life for me will never be the same without you."

Tears soaked his face. He wiped his face with his shirt sleeve. He took a section of sandwich and bit into it, returning it to the container. He popped open the Diet Coke and took a sip, placing it back on the grave.

"I hope in Heaven the angels make thick cut fries. I love you so much, my angel. My true angel. Kiss Little William and Little Jarmila for me. Little Jolly and Little Jar. I know that's what we would have nicknamed them. You and I in our backyard, lying on the grass in the sunshine, me stroking your big pregnant belly, the babies kicking my hand. Our little family."

Jolly wiped the tears away again. He closed the styrofoam container and put it back in the bag. He poured out the rest of the Diet Coke next to her grave, and put the empty can in the bag.

"That's how they do it in Chicago, right?" he asked, standing, "They pour a little out in respect for the person who passed on. I love you Ms. Jarmila Malone Rogers. I will love you all my life. When my time is over, I know you'll be waiting at Heaven's Gates for me. I love you."

With that, he walked to his Wraith and went home.

The next day, a Saturday, the Lenehan boys and Jolly visited Jarmila's grave. Jack, Chandler, Johnny and Benny stood next to each other, arms locked, as they had at her funeral. Jolly had a bouquet of peonies and arranged it near the gravestone.

"The monument people and the cemetery owners wanted to wait six months before they'd place the gravestone. They wanted to wait for the ground to settle more." Jolly informed the band, "I said '*Hell no!*'. Then the excuse would be that it's winter, and the granite might crack. I wanted the gravestone installed now. I need closure."

"I'm glad it's up now." Johnny commented, "I can tell her all about rehearsals, the studio, the tours, everything Lenehan does."

"I like the way you had it designed," said Chandler, "it's very pretty."

"It's an honor to have SISTER first." commented Jack, "That's what she was to us. Not just to Johnny, but to all of us."

"The color is called "Autumn Rose". Jolly said, "I thought I made a good selection. But I know Jar would have wanted neon pink. I want to thank you all for letting me make all the arrangements."

"None of us were in any condition to do that kind of stuff." stated Jack, "Our emotions were all over da place. I thank you for handling all that. Especially through your own journey of grief."

The wind picked up. The five of them stood in silence. The Johnny let go of Chandler and Benny's arms.

"I miss her so much! The pain is unendurable!" cried Johnny.

Chandler hugged him tightly, keeping him in his arms until Johnny's weeping subsided.

"I can't tell you everything's going to be okay," said Chandler to Johnny, "because it's not going to be okay. But I won't let you fall."

Wednesday, June 26th, 2019

Jolly was up early packing for the trips to LA and New York. He was happy he had a couple days in LA. It would give him time to visit his brother and sister and his nieces and nephews. He had not seen them since the funeral.

He looked at Jar's closet, mostly empty now since he had given most of the clothes and shoes to local Chicago non-profits. He went to an event held by The Healing Corner where they memorialized Jarmila's life. Meeting people in marginalized neighborhoods and speaking to them about the issues they face, the lack of resources they struggle to live with, made him see a different side of Chicago. Jarmila often talked about the Chicago neighborhoods who struggle with basic necessities of life such as quality healthcare and nutritious food. Even getting to obtain food was a struggle, as many of Chicago's marginalized neighborhoods have food deserts, where there is not a grocery store close enough to shop at. Jarmila was once a homeless, poor kid. She knew struggle. With her giving heart she always wanted to give back. He would talk to the label, management, Scot and Lenehan about doing a charity concert in Chicago once a year to benefit local non-profits.

He received an invitation for a private tour of Chicago Animal Care and Control. It made him sad to see all those animals without homes, stuck in cages. He wished there were a bunch of people like Johnny who'd adopt a homeless animal. Too many shelter animals never make it out alive because of lack of space, and not enough people who are willing to foster or adopt. He decided, after the LA and New York City business trips, he'd come back to this shelter and adopt a dog. He'd take the dog on tour with him for American tours, and pay Johnny's mom to watch the dog when Jolly was on out of the US on tour. He made another donation, and asked to speak with the person involved in the shelter's charity events. He wanted to contribute on a regular basis, in memory of Jarmila.

Jolly finished packing and went to his home office to gather his equipment. He stopped to look at the picture of Jar and him standing next to each other. This was the first picture they took together. She was so happy with that i-Phone Jolly gifted her. She was so joyful even with the little things in life. His broken heart missed her terribly. But he knew she'd want him to go on with life. She'd want him to be the support Lenehan needed to continue to be rock stars. And play stadiums. She truly believed in Lenehan playing sold-out stadiums someday. He completely agreed. He would continue on that path, taking care of her best friends; Johnny with his migraines, who was like a brother to her; Benny and his heroin addiction; and Jack and Chandler, The Bacchanalia Twins, as the media now called them, because of their wild rogueries.

His cell phone rang and he answered it. Jack's voice was full of excitement.

"We're waiting in front of your house! Don't be late, *motherfucker*." Jack laughed.

Jolly carried his suitcases and equipment out the front door. He quietly said goodbye to Jarmila's spirit as he locked the door. The limo driver helped carry some of his things to the limo and put them with everyone else's luggage.

"For once, Jack," said Jolly, sitting in the limo, "I am glad you talked me into something. A limo is a nicer way to get to the airport than a car service."

"Rock stars have to be rock stars. We gotta ride in style. Limos and private jets, yup that's Lenehan's style now." Jack responded.

When they got to the airport and were finally seated in the private jet, the entire band sounded like it was Christmas and they got everything they ever wanted.

"Damn," said Chandler, "I'm going to kick my heels up and be as fabulous as I always am."

"My wish is that you would be a toned down fabulous." Scot said, "Because being in the air with your fabulousness for over four hours may make me look for a parachute."

"I wish Jarmila could be here to see this." said Jack, "She would have really dug it. This plane is super phenomenal. I'd give up everything I have if I could bring her back, for this moment right here. Money doesn't always buy happiness. Sometimes all it brings s misery and sorrow, but in a more comfortable bed."

August 23rd, 2019, Aragon Ballroom, Chicago, Illinois, 8:30pm, one hour and a half until showtime.

Jolly and his new addition, Malone, a female all black mixed breed, large "Chicago Dog" he had adopted, sat in the tour office of the Aragon Ballroom. The dog followed him everywhere. He laughed at the thought that Jarmila's spirit probably put Malone up to that. Scot and all the staff were running errands or doing something for the show. After a busy, hectic day, it was nice to have a few moments of solitude. It was the first day of Lenehan's tour of bigger venues. After this tour they'll record their third album, then be on their way to their first European tour.

He sat at the table in front of his open laptop, holding a bundle of stapled papers. He was reading through the papers when Jack walked into the office.

"What's up?" Jack casually asked Jolly.

"Multi-tasking, as usual." responded Jolly, "What's up with you? Nervous?"

"A little." Jack answered, crossing his arms, "I want to change a song on da setlist."

"Ok. But shouldn't you be talking to the band or Scot about that?"

"I don't want da band to know."

"You want to change a song and keep it a secret from the band?"

"Yes. Until an hour before showtime. Then I'll tell them."

"Ohhkay," said Jolly, "what song do you want to replace?"

"I want to strike out "Rockwell Street" and replace it with another song."

"But you always open with "Rockwell Street" when you play Chicago."

"Not tonight. Tonight, I'm doing something different."

Jack had thought awhile about what he was going to do. He'd change the first song on the first setlist to the song he wrote for Jarmila after she died. He felt he had to do something to right the wrongs he had done to her. He knew the band wouldn't agree to this. Lenehan had decided the song would remain private between the four of them. They would only play it at rehearsals and their birthday parties. They made a pact that no one else would hear the song. It would not be recorded or played at live shows. But Jack knew this was the only way he could right things in his heart. The first show of any tour was always Jarmila's favorite day. He couldn't think of a better day than the first day of their first bigger venues tour to honor her memory. A day that started at Jarmila's favorite venue, The Aragon Ballroom. She would look at pictures of the inside of the venue and say one day Lenehan would play there. And now, here they are.

Jack waited as late as he could to ask Jolly to inform the crew of the setlist change. He didn't want the band to find out from anyone but him. He'd tell them an hour before showtime. Maybe he could change their minds, maybe not. Either way, he was going on that stage and the song he wrote for Jarmila would be the first song he played, with or without the band.

Jolly looked at him as if he had finally cracked.

"What is the name of the song you want to replace "Rockwell Street"? asked Jolly.

"Just cross out "Rockwell Street and replace it with "a different song"." answered Jack.

"Consider it done." said Jolly, getting on his cell phone and texting Everett.

As Jack left the tour office, with only a little over and hour to showtime, Jolly thought, yup, that boy has finally cracked.

Everett stormed into the tour office like he had been informed all the marijuana in the world was now depleted.

"You can't change the set list with just a little over and hour to showtime!" he screamed.

"Shit gets changed all the time." said Jolly, putting down the paperwork he was reading.

"Things are set up a certain way. We can't say 'Well fuck it all, let's change shit around on one of the band's most important nights an hour before showtime!'"

"Everett, you're an excellent road manager. You're used to adapting. This is Jack's request. I think it has something to do with Jarmila." Jolly said, rubbing his eyes, "Change the shit, or you're fired."

"Gee," said Everette, throwing his hands in the air, rolling his eyes and going towards the door, "like I've never heard that before."

Jack stood outside the dressing room door next to Les. Usually a confident person, he was slowly losing his bravado. In Lenehan, he always had the last say. But he knew what he was going to tell the band could annihilate all his self-assurance.

"Les," he said, "kick everyone but da band out of da dressing room. Don't let anyone in except Scottie or Jolly until I tell you otherwise."

"Sure thing, Boss." responded Les.

Les followed Jack into the dressing room. He told everyone who wasn't in Lenehan to leave. Sofia took Johnny's dogs to meet fans. Gotti and Capone had become almost as famous as Lenehan. Les then left the dressing room and stood sentinel outside the door. In the dressing room, Chandler was at the buffet table, filling a plate with food. Benny was in an armchair with his feet hanging over the armrest. Johnny was in the corner on a stool, the side of his face against the wall. His eyes were red and tear streaks stained his face. Johnny thought, this was Jarmila's favorite venue, on her favorite day of any tour, the first day. She told Lenehan someday they would play The Aragon. Now they were playing it and she wasn't here.

"I gotta talk to you guys," said Jack, "it's important."

"So, talk." Chandler responded, continuing to pile his plate with food.

"Put da fuckin' plate down and sit your ass someplace!" Jack yelled at Chandler.

"Okay," said Chandler, putting the plate on a table as he sat down. "Jesus!"

Benny sat up straight. Johnny didn't move.

"I've scrapped "Rockwell Street" from da setlist and have replaced it with another song."

"But we always open with "Rockwell Street" when we play Chicago." Benny declared.

"Not tonight. Tonight, we play "Autumn in Chicago" instead." Jack responded.

"No fuckin' way!" screamed Chandler, "We made a pact. We're never playing that song for anyone but ourselves. We're the only people who will ever hear it. *You* devised that plan. That was *your* idea."

"I know. But I've changed my mind. "Autumn in Chicago will be da first song on da first setlist." said Jack.

"No, it won't." Chandler said with determination in his voice, "We made a *pact*."

"Why, Jack?" asked Benny, "Why this last-minute decision?"

"I thought about it," answered Jack, "and I think this is da best way to honor Jarmila's memory. The first day of any tour was her favorite day. She said we'd play here, after I had told her I used to go by here and say 'I want to play The Aragon someday.' Jesus, we were just a garage band then! But she believed in us. Do you honestly think we'd been playing here, with two sold out shows, if it wasn't for her unwavering belief in us?"

"What difference what song we play first makes?" inquired Johnny, tears pouring down his face, "It won't bring her back."

"If you go through with this, Jack, I'm not going onstage. That is *Lenehan's* private song. It's for us only." Chandler threatened.

"I'm not going onstage either." said Benny.

Johnny remained quietly crying in the corner. Jack took Chandler's plate of food and threw it against the wall.

"I really don't give a flyin' fuck if you go onstage or not!" shouted Jack, "I'll do da whole fuckin' concert by myself if I have to! But "Autumn in Chicago" is going to be da first song tonight. I've already arranged it to piano."

Jack went to the buffet table and grabbed a bottle of Don Julio tequila and a pack of Marlboro Reds, and stomped out the door.

Jack sat on the back stairs leading up to the stage. He was wearing a black tank top and dark blue jeans. Between his bare feet was the bottle of Don Julio tequila, half empty, and in his hand was a cigarette.

"You know they're going to say you can't smoke in here." said Jolly, sitting next to Jack, Malone by his side.

Jack crushed out his cigarette on the stairs and threw it over the railing. He started petting Malone as Jolly handed him a joint.

"If they say you can't smoke in here, it might as well be for something worthwhile." Jolly said, taking the Don Julio tequila and taking a long swig. Returning it to Jack, he took the joint Jack handed him.

"I miss her." Jack said, so quietly Jolly could barely hear him.

"She was a good soul." replied Jolly.

Standing up and turning toward the direction of the stage, Jack took one last toke of the joint, a long drag of the tequila bottle, and handed both to Jolly.

August 23rd, 2019, 10:05pm, showtime, The Aragon Ballroom, Chicago, Illinois

Jack sat at the piano. Lenehan's audience, who usually began cheering as the band would go onstage full of energy, "Rockwell Street" setting the mood for the whole evening, were perplexed and remained quiet. Jack adjusted the microphone.

"I had a friend," he began, "she was my best friend. Some of you Lenehan fans might remember I always introduced her at every show. Her name was Jarmila Malone. Our bass player, Johnny Dunne, thought of her like a sister. Truly, all of Lenehan thought of her like a little sister. We were all family. She was engaged to our tour manager, Jolly. Lenehan gave him a rough time, because we were protective big brothers. We met her when we were kids. When Lenehan was formed she'd say we were going to be rock stars someday. Her unshakeable belief in us helped to navigate tough times. I once told her that every time I passed by The

Aragon, I would tell myself how much I wanted to play there. Now here I am. Sadly, she is not. On June 1st of this year, her 23rd birthday, she took her own life. She felt she had no purpose in life anymore. I want to say to all of you, if you ever feel so hopeless you think death is da only answer, please, please, reach out to someone, anyone. Call anyone. Go somewhere and tell someone you are in need. Stand outside and shout for help. Don't take you own life. You have a purpose out there, even if you don't know what it is yet. Your life is precious. Your life has meaning. Don't destroy da wonderful person you are. Death is not da answer. I wrote this song after she died. Lenehan made a pact that we would never play this song for anyone but ourselves. We would never record it or play it at shows. Only members of Lenehan would hear it. Tonight, in this wonderful venue, in my favorite town, my hometown Chicago, you are going to hear it. It may be da only time it's played in front of an audience. Da first day of any tour was Jarmila's favorite day. This is da first day of our new tour. In Jarmila's memory, I dedicate da song I wrote for her. This song is called "Autumn in Chicago."

Jolly stood on the side of the stage, next to Everett. Tears were brimming in his eyes. Everett put a hand on Jolly's shoulder as Jack started playing the first few notes on the piano and began to sing.

"I miss you when it's Autumn

In Chicago

When I button up my coat

Against the rain

When you think your forever is

Tomorrow

And tomorrow will never be

The same."

The audience started stirring, the noise grew louder. Jack continued singing.

"I miss you when it's Autumn

In Chicago

When the breezy moonlight

Shined across your face

When you think all tomorrows

Are forever

And tomorrow will never be

The same."

The audience became louder, shouting, cheering, yelling, clapping. Some fans were crying. Out of the corner of his eye, Jack saw movement. He then heard Chandler's guitar, Benny's drums, and Johnny on bass, bringing it home.

"I miss you when it's Autumn

In Chicago

When the street lamps shown

Dimly on the porch

We'd open up a cold one,

Pour a little out for a loved

One

And think about the memories

That fade."

Jolly's tears were falling to the ground.

"I miss you when it's Autumn

In Chicago

When the turning leaves remind

Me of your eyes

You flew away so quickly

Into the sorrow

And I flew away too quickly

Into the pain."

The positive energy from the crowd fueled the intensity of the song as Jack finished it.

"Oh I miss you when it's Autumn

In Chicago

I miss the cloudy skies and

Stillborn nights

If only tomorrow was

Forever

And forever held us

In its embrace."

Lenehan ended the song with a few solo notes on the piano. The crowd became fanatical. Jack could feel the audience reactions coming through the stage to the bottom of his bare feet. The very air felt like it held all the energy in the world. The walls felt like they would implode, and the stage would collapse from the audience clamor. He knew then he had made the right decision to play the song. For Jarmila.

Made in the USA
Monee, IL
28 August 2022